"In playing in th
expectations, pers
American Faust fol
singular path." –

~~~~~~~~ REVIEW

"More than just a clever retelling, this captivating novel possesses an abundance of vitality and originality. American Faust has an air of mystique, a compelling aura that will have readers feeling as though they're reading something on the edge of cognizance. A fitting modern homage to timeless classic literature."
–INDIES TODAY

"AMERICAN FAUST Recommended for literary students of the classic story, who will find this modern take an intriguing perspective. Classes who study Faust's dilemmas and choices will want to include American Faust in their debates."
–MIDWEST REVIEW

"Romantic, thoughtful, sometimes bizarre, and rendered in crisp, memorable prose, American Faust offers mysteries that will please readers who prefer some subtlety in depictions of the uncanny, particularly the open-ended climax that invites numerous interpretations and will leave readers who relish the elusive hungry for more."–PUBLISHERS WEEKLY BOOKLIFE REVIEW

READER'S STUDY GUIDE INCLUDED IN BACK

AMERICAN FAUST

A NOVEL

AMERICAN FAUST

A NOVEL

RIP BROWN

IBEX
PRESS

Cover by Nancy Natalia Brown Calderon
Interior/Exterior Designs by Leopard Design Studio

Library of Congress Control Number: 2022930754

ISBN 978-1-957510-00-2 (hc)
ISBN 978-1-957510-01-9 (sc)
ISBN 978-1-957510-02-6 (Eb)

FIRST EDITION
10 9 8 7 6 5 4 3 2 1

https://ibex-press.com

For

Nancy Natalia & Emily Gabriela

**Goethe's opening dedication to *Faust Part I*
(*Translation by E Kaufmann*)**

And I am seized by long forgotten yearning,
For that kingdom of spirits, still and grave;
To flowing song, I see my feelings turning,
As from Aeolian harps, wave upon wave;
A shudder grips me, tear on tear falls burning,
Soft grows my heart, once severe and brave;
What I possess, seems so far away to me,
And what is gone becomes reality.

PROLOGUE IN HEAVEN

Theater curtain opens with the Lord and the Devil standing on the top balcony of an Italian palazzo overseeing a beautiful courtyard. The two are separated by a baroque pillar dividing the balcony in two halves. Both train their gaze upon the audience.

LORD: What name does the evil rogue go by today?

DEVIL: Memphis Topheles, at your service. *(Bows)*.

LORD: And who shall you enlist in your lowest ranks of thievery to set forth and do your soul searching for you?

DEVIL: An American, from the early twentieth century.

LORD: Destined to hell most certainly.

DEVIL: Aye, wretched is he indeed, of too much faith in need.

LORD: Do you always find man of such little worth?

DEVIL: I fear for all men and their wickedness of enterprise.

LORD: Are you sure this one can't be saved?

DEVIL: *(Shakes his head)*. His predisposition was determined by the Universe long ago.

LORD: Give me credit for inventing free will. It has the power to transform what's born evil to good.

DEVIL: Or good to evil.

LORD: So much depends upon the presence of love.

DEVIL: Or its absence. What say we wager a piece of heaven on it? *(The two nod)*. We'll serve it up as a dark tale with a villain, hero and a heroine in need of rescue. I chose the villain, now you the hero.

LORD: My torch bearer shall be an American from the end of that century.

DEVIL: A patriotic joust! Is he counted among the Saints?

LORD: *(Shakes his head)*. Though he rises above the exemplum, I cannot claim what is not yet mine. He is bound to his past and could use some goading.

DEVIL: Happy to oblige. Let the truth of their natures fall where they may.

LORD: The heroine must be up to the task of handling these two. On whose side do you wager she will land?

DEVIL: That will be entirely her choice.

LORD: Memphis Topheles, if you win one of them I'll concede; two I'll hand over the keys to the kingdom. None, and you are banished from earth where mankind shall live happily ever after. Beware your greed does not defeat you, again. *(Exits stage right)*.

DEVIL: I can never trust that ol' gent. Nevertheless, it warms me to think he meets me on equal ground now and then. *(Exits stage left)*.

PART I
BEGINNINGS

JAMES' MISSION

1

HENRY MILLER'S CABIN

Big Sur, California, 2000

The evanescent voice spoke to him in a dream. *James, come back for me, it's time.*

A woman dressed in white appeared at the entrance to a maze. She gazed at James as if she had something to share from her heart. As he stepped forward toward her, a shadow figure stepped behind her. She looked at James, then at the figure, then returned inside. James tried to follow, but his body wouldn't obey. The voice echoed in his brain. *James, come back for me, it's time.*

"James!" Pamela gripped the calf leather arm on the passenger side of the car. "Pay attention or we'll end up in the ravine!" He drove the less-than-visible "S" curves of Pacific Highway One with little caution, his mind lost on other things. They'd just left the roadside lounge where they brunched with her father, a Hollywood producer, and some of his friends. James hid his anxiety behind an executive smile; Pamela kept up the banter while finishing off mimosas. Traffic on the road was sparse.

"There it is!" she pointed through the windshield, "Henry Miller's cabin. Slow down, or you'll miss it."

He pumped the brakes and caught a glimpse of it through the woods. "So, that's what you've been talking about, it's much smaller than you made it out to be." He pulled in front of the property. The fog was thick and full of the ocean.

"Of course, it's tiny compared to Hearst Castle," Pamela said. She clicked the door open and hopped out. "You're gonna love it. Books and art and old photographs of Paris. All my friends will be there." Her short black trench coat covered a black cocktail dress, and her high heels dug into the damp ground.

James stepped over the sludge. He wore a London Fog over a black tuxedo. "We can't stay long, Pamela, we've one more group of investors to meet at Hearst Castle, and then—" he took her hand. "I promise, we'll spend as many weekends as you wish with as many friends as you can fit into a hundred Henry Miller cabins."

They reached a broken gate hitched to a collapsing stone wall. "Henry Miller used to live here," James said. "Sure looks like it must've back then, lost in its rustic rustiness."

"Hurry," Pamela said. "We're late." She passed through the gate, skipping ahead from one slate stone to the next, avoiding puddles from the earlier storm. The distance grew between them as she stepped towards the cabin and he stopped along the winding path. Beneath the protection of a coniferous grove, a collection of sculptured art caught his eye.

The first was an intricately carved totem pole. James ran his fingers over its grainy textured grooves, demon-like animal figures, each grimmer than the next as they rose one on top of another. Next the giant palm of a metal hand which could have belonged to God, so big he could sit in it. Together they reminded him of statuesque objects at an amusement park he'd visited as a boy in New Hampshire, deep in the forest below Mount Washington. Story Land, the place was called.

When he reached the cabin, the thrum of a bass string interlacing with taps on a cowbell resounded in his ears; the opening to Miles Davis' jazz composition, "Someday My Prince Will Come." He waved away wisps of smoke hovering in the air, inhaled the cloud of scents––nicotine, marijuana, clove. "Will someone open a window for god's sake?" Along the walls Henri

Cartier-Bresson photographs hung of writers, dancers and half-naked women in Paris from the early twentieth century; Josephine Baker and Louis Brooks, Gertrude Stein and Alice B Toklas, Henry Miller and Anais Nin; Sartre, Beuvre, Camus, Beckett. Ancient whiskey bottles lined the tops of bookshelves packed with worn editions of classical fiction. He perused through a collection of D.H. Lawrence's *Sons and Lovers*, *Women in Love.* He pulled out *The Trespassers.*

"James!" Pamela called from across the room through a sea of people. He slipped the book back and pressed through the crowd. From the edge of a thick oak desk she waved, in the arm of another man dressed in maroon t-shirt and sweatpants, the word "Stanford" written in school colors down one leg.

"This is Harold," Pamela said, "the friend I told you about, the director of this place."

The man brushed the top of his brow with his thumb. "Actually, I just watch it on the weekends. Call me Harry."

James rubbed his hand after the vice grip shake from the young man, who stood a couple of inches taller than his own six feet. He smelled the pungent odor of stale sweat and alcohol. "Pamela didn't tell me I'd be meeting an old boyfriend," James said.

"We didn't date, James," Pamela said, "I babysat for little Harry. Our families have been friends in the Big Sur for ages." She jostled the man's hair.

"He's not so little anymore," James murmured.

"Ol' Henry lived here himself," Harry said, "right up to his last days." He grabbed a postcard off the desk. "Sat behind this desk in that chair, see?" He handed James the card, tapped the photo with his finger, "Miller in his classic black beret chomping on a fat cigar." He placed a copy of *Tropic of Cancer* in Pamela's hands. "This is the novel that made Miller famous," he said.

Pamela grasped it in both hands. "I remember reading this in school," she said. "It was banned."

"That it was," said a friend of Harry's in moon-shaped glasses, "for writing the word 'cunt' too many times." He stood by the desk with his partner, a woman with one Hebrew letter on a chain around her neck.

"There you go, Harry," the woman with a Hebrew letter said, "pushing a twentieth century classic of male conquest exploiting women for their beauty and sex."

Harry defended the book's theme. "It wasn't about the sex," he said. "D.H. Lawrence wrote *Lady Chatterley's Lover* to break a forbidden barrier, and Miller followed. For them, carnal love was a symbol of unfettered freedom from society's restraints. That's what made it an American masterpiece."

Harry's friend pulled out a dog-eared copy of *Lolita* from his Harris tweed jacket. "If you want to talk about a sexual predator in American fiction," he said, "Vladimir Nabokov has it over Miller hands down. The protagonist is a pedophile."

"Nympholeptic," his partner, the woman said. "Humbert likes little girls, not boys."

"Pamela," Harry said, "which of the two in your opinion is most arrogant in its view toward women?"

Pamela weighed the two novels in each hand. She chose *Lolita* to leaf through. "I saw this movie," she said. "Jeremy Irons played the child molester." She read the first line aloud. "Lolita, light of my life, fire of my loins. My sin, my soul. Lo-lee-ta. Hey." She lowered the book. "What if someone wrote the same story, but with the roles reversed?"

"What do you mean?" Harry's friend asked.

"She means," said the woman with the Hebrew letter, "what if somebody wrote a story about an older woman raping a boy."

James' ears perked up. A heart-felt memory rose within him.

"Something like that, yes," Pamela said.

"Holden Caulfield meets Mrs. Robinson," Harry's friend said.

"Is a young boy physically capable?" Pamela asked.

"Why not?" the man with the moon shaped glasses said. "Priests and coaches prey on them all the time."

James stepped into the fray. "If I wrote that, I'd make it a love story." All shot their gaze at him.

"Aren't you the romantic," Harry said. He filled a shot glass with tequila and handed it out, pouring for all who wanted one. "Go on, we're listening."

"All right." James took a deep breath. "Once upon a time there was a young teenager, who had a crush on a young divorcee. One night while babysitting for her, she returned home late from a date and found him naked in her bed, half asleep. Instead of acting shocked and surprised, she took off her clothes and climbed on top of him. He felt all its pleasure and understood all its meaning and then did it with her again, without shame." James stepped back. "Then the two fell in love."

"The end," Harry's friend said.

Harry slapped his thigh. "Oh, for muse of fire that would ascend the brightest heaven of invention!"

"King Henry V prologue," the woman with the Hebrew letter said, chin up.

"Look," Harry said, "enough. He was just saying for effect."

"Yes, for effect," James said, "because maybe all classic literature lost its romance the day Pound and Eliot published *The Wasteland*."

"Touché." Harry's friend raised his shot glass to James. "You know your modernists well. I see the influences in your own novel, a compelling medieval romance which blurs the lines of time. In the end, love conquers all. When can we expect the sequel?"

"There won't be one," James said.

"Someday there will be." Pamela slipped her feet to the floor and took James' arm. "For now, he's my dot.com genius."

James looked at his watch. "Let's go, Pamela," he said. "We're going to be late."

Pamela dropped his arm. "But we just got here."

"Yes, she just got here," Harry said. He reached inside the cabinet of a chipped mahogany credenza for a bottle of Tennessee bourbon and uncapped it. "Still enjoy the harder spirits, Pamela? Or do you prefer Napa Valley wine?"

As James took her arm to leave, Harry grabbed her other. "Let her decide if she stays," he said. "I can drive her home later."

James pulled on Pamela's arm, while Harry held on just as tight. "Please, you two!" She shook them both off. "Now James darling, I've been going to these dog and pony shows for one week straight, and before we leave Big Sur, I'd like to spend one last evening with my friends and unwind before we return to San Francisco." She held her hand out. "Harry, pour me that shot." He filled hers to the brim.

"Fine," James said, "stay why don't you, and drink with Harry the whole night long."

"Hey," Harry's friend said, "we'll be drinking with her too."

"Don't be angry, James," Pamela said, brushing his cheek with her hand, "you'll do fine without me, I know you will." James' lips tightened. He stared at Harry and nodded in surrender. "Thanks, sweetie," Pamela said. She leaned over and kissed him. He did not kiss her back.

2

THE CHAIRMAN

Hearst Castle, San Simeon

Due to the flooding of Pacific Highway One, the investor event at Hearst Castle was not well attended. This did not bode well for James.

A couple of years earlier, he'd started up a promising new software company when interest in such speculative companies was high. Earlier that year, the stock market plummeted, driving down inflated internet stock values. Investors quickly lost their appetite for high-risk ventures such as his. What made it excruciatingly more difficult was that the event was predominately a west coast affair, sponsored by Silicon Valley, the world in which his father was a well-known venture capitalist. This should have guaranteed James a warm reception, but it was the opposite; investment bankers had been warned by his father to stay away from him. Either James must accept his father's pool of funding and cede control, or his father would make damn well sure no one else gave him any. Investment houses from Hong Kong and London listened to his pitch but politely demurred. It was a futile act, competing with his father in the known world of financial capital. If James were to make it on his own, he must find other means. He begged God to open a door somewhere.

A small hand yanked on his tuxedo, and he looked down. A man no higher than his waist dressed in foul weather gear handed him his card:

Clarence Wigglesworth, Solicitor
World's End Venture Capital

He beckoned James' ear down and whispered. He represented a wealthy individual hell bent on committing hundreds of millions of dollars to enterprises such as his. This investor was extending an invitation to James to attend a private soiree in full swing near the entrance gate to Hearst Castle. He must come now; the investor would not be there much longer.

"James Harris! Is there a Mr. Harris here?" The voice in the crowd spoke out like a bell boy looking for a guest. James raised his hand and caught the attention of a woman who immediately approached him. She was followed by a pack of bankers who salivated like wolves ready to feast on their prey. James looked down at Clarence, but he'd disappeared.

The woman represented an interested party in New York who wanted to meet him. James shook his head; there was no time for wasted talk. She pulled out a check for one hundred thousand dollars. All he had to do was agree to board a flight the next day to New York and meet their investor. James stared at the amount, barely nodding yes before the cumulus cloud of bankers drifted off to take advantage of other desperate entrepreneurs, those suffering from the same dot.com crash as he.

❀ † ❀

Outside sea winds blew in a layer of rain with flashes of lightning followed by thunder. The valets drove up with James' BMW, warning him to wait for the storm's fierceness to settle. He preferred to risk the dangers of the natural elements instead. James coasted down the long treacherous drive and just about reached the gate when a flurry of deer leapt across his hood in the pouring rain. He slammed on the breaks; when he looked to see what was chasing them, he saw red lights flashing in front of a cottage tucked in the woods. Tail fins of vintage 1950s limousines blinked as partygoers in white tuxedos and hooped skirts hopped out, valets holding umbrellas over their heads. This must be the place. He drove in.

There was no one to hold an umbrella over his head. From behind shuttered windows under a covered porch, he heard vibrating strums of an electric bass guitar, drum snares, a piano playing Jerry Lee Lewis' "Great Balls of Fire!" He rang the bell and the cottage door opened, inviting him into a front room, barren except for a few candle-lit lamps on the walls and a stone fireplace. The shriek of song seeped out from below a door, shadows beneath it moving. That's where the party was. He took the door's nob and was about to open when—

"Excuse me!" A man in a powdered wig dressed in eighteenth-century garb sat behind him at an antique desk writing with a quill. "Can't go in there," the man said, dipping his pen in a well of ink. He wrote something in a musty ledger. "Many are invited, but few are chosen. Name?"

"James Harris."

"You came from the Castle?"

James nodded.

The man picked up a phone and pressed a lit red extension button. He murmured into it, then pointed with his quill at a door on the opposite side of the room. "Through there," he said. "The

Chairman will see you now."

James crossed the room and turned the brass doorknob. "Excuse me," he said, turning to the man, "a herd of frightened deer galloped passed me on the way here. Any idea what they were running away from?"

The man peered over the top of his bifocals. "Who do you think God runs away from?"

James stepped into pitch darkness; not even the light from the front hall crossed the threshold. Once inside, the door slammed shut. James stood erect. His heart's blood pounded through his arteries. He extended his arms and groped for a wall switch, when suddenly light burst out from a fireplace in which burning logs were popping sparks. His eyes adjusted to its light as he followed the fire's smoky scented trail.

Along the way he gazed up. Heads of game stuffed as trophies covered every inch of the wall, large and small, columns reaching to the roof beams—half the population of Noah's ark, no species spared except mankind. This was no cottage; it was a hunting lodge. Above the fireplace hung a medieval tapestry whose beauty was dulled only by the passage of time. It depicted a white unicorn held captive, fenced in a wood pen without escape.

Down at the far end of the room, a chandelier with almond shaped bulbs lit up. It hung above a table and chair. On a corner of the table sat an antique phone, its heavy receiver in the shape of an upside-down U set in an upright cradle. Across the tabletop lay an ivory cane with the exquisitely carved contours of a black poodle head as its knob. When he lifted it, out slid a sword from its sheath, refracting the light in colors. He heard glasses clink with cubes of ice.

"I'd put that down if I were you." A man stepped from a wet bar in the shadows. He held a tumbler of bourbon in each hand. "Please, have a seat." Broad chested, he dressed in an expensive grey suit with a black jersey beneath, bald except for a light dusting of coal-colored hair. James gazed up at the towering figure, his head nearly touching the chandelier.

"My people read your business plan," the man said. He handed James a bourbon. "They think your ideas about the internet are prescient, and I want a piece of the action." He sat down behind the desk. "As a controlling partner of course." Sitting, he was taller than most men. He nodded at a high-backed chair for James to sit in.

"Who are you?" James asked.

The man reached over the table with his long arm and handed James his card. "I go by many names, but you may call me Chairman."

Memphis Topheles, Chairman
World's End Venture Capital

James set his glass down on the desk without taking a sip. "I'd be happy to consider your offer," he said, "but I'm not going to give up one share of control to anyone."

"Is that so?" The Chairman tapped the side of his glass on the edge of the desk. "Why do you think you haven't found any backers yet?"

Gripping the arms of the chair, James pushed himself up. He planted his palms firmly on the table and leaned into them with all his weight. "Because my father scares them away, so he alone can control me. How do I know you'd be any different?"

The crackling fire filled the silence between them.

James stood straight up. "I decided long ago, there'd be no more meddling from nervous investors impatient for a return on their money. It'll take years before we turn a profit." He nodded his chin at the Chairman. "Are you willing to wait as long?"

The Chairman stood up, so high above James his eyes were hidden in the dark above the light. James could only see his mouth moving.

"With your father out of the picture, you're sinking in a sea of debt. Everyone knows you don't have enough money to keep your business afloat another week. You've run out of leverage." The Chairman bowed down over the table and met James' eyes. "You need someone to rescue you now."

James took a step back down into his chair. "I'll survive," he said. "If you knew me, you'd know I don't give up easily." He crossed his arms.

The Chairman laughed from his belly. "Oh, but I do, James Harris, I know everything about you."

He walked around the table and sat sideways on its front corner. He crossed one leg over the other and nodded his alligator shoe.

"I know the upper-middle class town in Connecticut where you grew up. It was a comfortable life of privilege, until tragedy struck, when your baby brother drowned in your terrace pool. You tried to save him but were too late. That was the pretext your father used to abandon you and your mother." The Chairman took a cigarette out of a gold case. "The two of you moved to Boston where your mother remarried. Drinking soon ended that relationship. Her habit of excess continued, and despite your efforts to save her, you could not. She didn't want help and neither you nor your aunt could stop her. When it was time to go to college, you left for the west coast to Stanford as soon as you could shed your prep school cap and gown." The Chairman lit up and exhaled a puff of smoke. "In college, you studied poetry and literature." With the hot coal glow of his cigarette, he traced letters of a Latin word in the air. "You envisioned yourself a writer, what profit was there in that? You wrote one fantasy romance novel which received scant attention, and reluctantly entered the work force in corporate America.

"Years passed before your father offered you a job in Silicon Valley. You had a talent for choosing successful startups and made him a lot of money. Then the movie rights to your book sold; you made a small fortune. That's when you met your girlfriend, the daughter of the producer who made millions off your story. With her confidence and support, you founded your own high-tech software company. Your father tried to seize control, but your strong-willed girlfriend helped you stand up to him. Furious, he's been trying ever since to torpedo your efforts before your startup has a chance to stand on its own two legs. So far he's succeeding."

The Chairman returned to his chair and threw his feet up on the desk, snuffing his cigarette out in an ashtray. "Compared to him, could I be so bad?" He slid James a leather folio across the desk. James lifted its cover. Inside lay a certified check for one million dollars. As he lifted it up to examine closer, his hand trembled.

"Your idea is brilliant," the Chairman said, "harness the internet for global control of communication and trade. Imagine people one day doing the bulk of their banking and shopping online, connecting across borders with just the touch of a finger. It could set nation against nation. My plans are to take its technology even further."

James placed the check down. "My vision is to bring the world closer together. I will not be the means to another man's dirty ends." He stood up and walked towards the fire.

"Halt!" The Chairman raised his arm as if he could stop time and James in it. "What if I were willing to invest a billion dollars in your startup with no controlling rights. You remain at the helm. Would that satisfy you?"

"You mean I alone decide its fate?" James turned around and faced the Chairman. "Not you?"

"Precisely." The Chairman stood up holding his cane. "However, before I commit to such a hefty sum, you will need to prove yourself worthy."

"Worthy?"

"Tomorrow, my sources tell me, you're headed to New York to meet an investor. During your trip, drive up to Connecticut to that town of yours and visit the former Revson property."

James knew the place the Chairman spoke of. As a boy he and his friends would wander onto the grounds unseen by the caretaker. In its back garden, they discovered the statue of a goddess on a pedestal in the center of a fountain. They fell in love with her beauty instantly. He'd often imagine returning to see if she were still there.

"There's a woman living there," the Chairman said.

"Impossible." James shook his head. "The place burned to the ground in a lightning storm years ago."

"I assure you it stands in pristine condition. The woman was brought to the estate by a man who fell in love with her and promised her a life of riches and adventure. But he delivered neither. He became possessive and jealous of other men, and eventually banned all visitors from entering the property."

James shook his head. "And she puts up with that."

"She's forbidden from leaving. To this day she has never stepped one foot outside its borders."

James held his hand out as if to help her. "She must feel powerless. How does he control, her?"

"By playing on her fears," the Chairman said. "He says he is doing it for her protection, and she believes him."

"So, this is a rescue mission."

"Of sorts. I need you to walk in there and help this woman gather the courage to stand up to him and leave."

"Why are you choosing me?"

"Because," the Chairman looked down and tapped the floor with his cane three times, "you two once had an intimate encounter with each other."

The face of a woman danced at the edges of James' memory, but he couldn't see her clearly.

"She will trust you," the Chairman said.

"Is this man dangerous?" James asked.

"Harmless, really, not there half the time. But if he is, you must remain on your toes. He can be very persuasive. Your greater challenge will be to convince this woman that this man has no power over her and that it's safe to leave with you."

"I'm intrigued," James walked up to the Chairman and nodded at the cane with an open hand. The older gentleman handed it over as if passing a magical sword. James rubbed its black poodle head examining it as a desirable gem to be had at a price. "And if I do this for you, you'll trust me to run my own company, leaving me in full control?"

The Chairman seized the cane away from him. "If you can handle what you are about to step into, James Harris, you will have proven you are capable of surviving anything the business world might throw at you."

James lifted the check from the table and held it up with two hands to the light. "This is crazy." His heart pounded and he tasted success. "All right. I'll do it. But no matter what happens, whatever the result, I keep this." He waved the million-dollar check in the air as if it were cash on fire.

The Chairman nodded, "I'll have my lawyers draw up the paperwork with this condition added and we'll get this signed before you leave."

"No," James said, stuffing the check in his pocket, "this will remain a secret between us. If I do it, it'll be based on a handshake, nothing more." He extended his hand out to the Chairman. "You have my word I'll do everything possible to help this woman."

"I know you will." The Chairman waved away his hand without shaking it. "You're an honorable man, James Harris, I take you at your word."

A door opened at the back of the room. The deep booming voice of Elvis Presley flowed in. "You look like an Angel, walk like an Angel…"

The Chairman pointed his cane at the door. "They're throwing a party in my honor," he said. "High school geniuses from the 1950s who'll become extraordinarily rich by investing in space technology for me."

He swung his cane and pointed it at James. "Beware," he said, "the property has a way of casting a spell on those who enter her. You could end up trapped if you don't keep your emotions intact." He stepped through the door and shut it behind him.

Through the wall, James heard the Chairman's voice shouting to the young crowd. "Welcome my children, your angel investor is here, come pay me tribute!"

James walked to the fire and stared into its flames. A poem he'd memorized long ago came to his mind.

And I am seized by a long forgotten yearning,
"She's calling."
For that kingdom of spirits, still and grave;
"All these years I've waited to go back and find her."
To flowing song, I see my feelings turning,
"I feel her presence now."
As from Aeolian harps, wave upon wave;
"My heart is fluttering."
A shudder grips me, tear on tear falls burning,
"As much as it makes me shake, I must go."
Soft grows my heart, once severe and brave;
"If I have the courage."
What I possess, seems so far away to me, and what is gone becomes reality.
"I always knew she was real."

James left by the way he came. In the front receiving room, he found a man snoring behind a desk, his feet resting on top. A fluorescent tube on the ceiling flickered, a plugged-in coffee pot's red light blinked. James knocked on the desk. The man woke and dropped his feet to the floor.

"What happened to your powdered wig?" James asked.

The man touched the top of his balding head, adjusted his cap on. "What are you doing here?" the caretaker asked.

"I was going to ask you the same thing."

James drove back out onto Pacific Highway One and did not find one puddle on the road to splash his chrome wheels through. Nor did anything prevent him from peeling around the hairpin turns with abandon. He wondered what to make of it all. Then his cell phone played a familiar ringtone, and his heart sank. He freed one hand from the wheel. His mother was in the hospital, his aunt said, from an overdose of pills and alcohol. He must come home to Boston right away.

3

PAMELA

Pamela's Beach House, Big Sur

Pamela returned from Henry Miller's cabin at midnight when Harry dropped her off at her father's chalet overlooking the sea. When she walked in, James was wearing his tuxedo jacket and sitting on the couch staring at his laptop screen. Pamela hugged him over the back of the couch. She kissed him on the cheek and squeezed his shoulders; they were tense. He set the laptop down on the coffee table and crossed the room.

"You should've been with me tonight, Pamela, not stayed in that cabin listening to literary jabber from Harry." He spied a framed photo of Joe Montana on the wall with Pamela's father. "A man who could probably tackle Kurt Warner while reciting Shakespeare."

Pamela threw her coat and bag over a chair. "So what if his father played for the 49ers, and his mother taught English at Stanford. He takes after them both. Does that make him a threat to you?" She pulled her hair back in a ponytail and knotted it. "He's harmless."

"You left out muscular and Rhodes Scholar. I studied literature." He pulled a book down from a shelf and pointed it at her. "I wrote this novel, see?" He tossed it on the table and it landed with a thud. "Can he claim to have done that? I know how to box too." He took a few jabs in the air.

Pamela sat down on the couch, throwing her stockinged feet up on the coffee table.

"Stop comparing yourself to Harry," she said. "I grew up with men like him my whole life. They think they need to prove something, especially to women. You're a different kind of man, James, don't start acting like them."

"You're right." He sat down next to her. "Sometimes it's hard to turn away when I feel a fight coming on."

She laid her head on his lap. "What's really bothering you, James? You're never jealous like this. What happened at Hearst Castle?"

He played with the strands of her hair. "That's a conversation for later. Right now, there's something else greater on my mind." The insides of his stomach fluttered, his chest muscles tightened. "My aunt called. It's my mother. She's back in the hospital, again." Her condition reverberated in his mind. Recovery, drinking, recovery—relentless.

"I'm sorry to hear that." Pamela sat up from his lap. "You must go to Boston right away."

"Like I have time for this now."

"Bring her to California, James."

"That I know she would resist." He stood up. "And I thought I had nothing but good news to share with you tonight."

He circled the room to the fireplace where the flames seemed to draw him in. On the wall above he imagined seeing the white unicorn tapestry hanging. "I spoke to two investors tonight," he said. He pulled from his coat pocket two checks. "One gave me a hundred thousand dollars. The other a million." He held both up high like two wet socks drying on a clothesline. Smiling, he dabbled them in front of her.

"James, you did it!" She jumped in his arms. "The gang's going to be so relieved. I'm proud of you!"

"Hold on, we're not there yet." He set her down. "If we're going to make it, we need more cash than this." He checked his calendar on his laptop then closed it. "The timing is uncanny. My aunt calls urging me to fly east, and two investors completely unknown to each other ask me to do the same."

"It's fate. Now you must go. What do you know about these investors?"

"Very little. One is represented through a reputable New York banking firm. The other is a venture capitalist who seems to have all the money in the world to give. But in order to guarantee a generous investment, I must do him a favor first."

Pamela's eyebrows raised. "A favor?"

"Handle a sensitive matter for him." James walked into the center of the room and rubbed the back of his neck. "Help out a woman. Who's in trouble."

"Who's in trouble."

He circled the coffee table rubbing his knuckles. "She lives in my old hometown in Connecticut. I may even know her. All I've got to do is check in and make sure she's safe."

"Safe. Safe from what?"

"A very controlling man."

They listened to the crackling of cedar in the fireplace.

"That's quite a condition to include as part of a financial deal, James."

He faced Pamela. "I know how it sounds but I'll be in and out, you'll see."

A strong wind rattled the pine wood walls of the cabin and howled. "As long as she's not in any kind of danger."

Pamela stood up from the couch to right a framed painting which slanted off its hook. "I don't like the sound of this, James. Don't do it."

"I already promised."

"You're not trained for this."

"It's no big deal."

Pamela did not look convinced.

James walked across the room. "For Chrissake! He's committed to investing a billion dollars. He's already given us this million."

"I have a bad feeling about this, James. Give him back

his check."

James held his hips shaking his head. "I can't walk away from this sort of money, not in the financial shape we're in."

"Hang your hopes on the other investor."

"Okay. I'll listen to them first. But I don't know anything about them either or how interested they are, and if nothing of any substance materializes, I'm sticking with this one. He has a serious interest in us and has shown he understands what we're trying to accomplish."

James walked to the oceanside window and gazed up at the night sky.

"You know our young geeky techs are on to something. They're ten years ahead of their time. Someday the world's going to be controlled from the information highway, Pamela, and when it is," he paused, staring at the Milky Way spilling its stars, "we're going to be at the top."

She joined him at the window. "If he asks you to take care of personal business once, he'll never stop. How do you know you can trust him?"

"I don't. But I'm going with my gut on this. We're broke."

"Fine. I'll go with you to make sure there's no trouble with this woman. Let's go to bed." She tugged his hand toward the bedroom, but he didn't budge.

"I need to handle this on my own, Pamela. I'm going to be dealing with memories and events from my past I've tried to forget for a long time." He felt his heart rise.

Pamela took his hand and squeezed it. "I know how painful this is going to be, James. That's why I want to be there, so you don't have to go through this alone."

"Pamela. Please."

She stepped away, removing the pearls James gave her for their first year anniversary from around her neck. "Why do you so insist on doing this yourself? A relationship is built on trust, remember?" Pamela balled the pearl necklace up in her fist, its ends dangling out each side. "I'm going with you."

James shook his head. "I've made up my mind." He held Pamela gently by the arms and looked her straight in the eyes.

"After this is over and the money is in the bank, we'll go east together. We'll celebrate in the city and afterward head to Boston. Then I'll introduce you to my mother." James rubbed the side of his face and exhaled slowly. "When she's in better shape." He stepped towards Pamela to hug her, but she stepped further away.

"Does she even know I exist?" Pamela threw the pearls down, scattering them across the floor. "The past is gone, James. Don't be blind to what you see standing in front of you now. I'm your present."

She grabbed her bag from the chair. "If you keep acting independently like this, I may not be your future."

Pamela disappeared down the hall to the bedroom before he could say another word, slamming the light switch down on her way.

That left James in the dark, and in the dark, he gazed out at the Pacific through fragile rattling glass. He heard tall torrent waves splashing against the surf, unseen except for their curling white crests. He followed Pamela to the bedroom to comfort her if she'd let him. The door was locked. He slept on the couch. The two returned the next day to San Francisco, barely speaking. That same evening James boarded the red eye for New York. Alone.

4

MRS. GODWIN

Investment Bank, New York City

Gilt-edged portraits of the patriarchs of American industry lined the walls of this investment bank as badges of honor; Vanderbilt, Carnegie, Morgan and Rockefeller. In his black Armani suit, James stood on polished tiled floors below slanted tinted windows which faced the Empire State Building. He leaned up against the wall of a vaulted-ceiling hallway feeling nauseous. Sweating, he dashed into the executive restroom on the eighty-sixth floor, leaned over the marble sink with head bowed as if in prayer, and vomited. A toilet flushed; a stall door opened. He looked in the mirror and saw the reflection of a woman with long flowing hair dressed in a light-colored gown. *James, come back for me, it's time.* He turned around to face her, but she'd vanished. His dizziness, he suspected, must have caused him to hallucinate.

The inquisition had been grueling that morning. The once resilient entrepreneur from San Francisco nearly dropped in a faint, stumbling to catch himself on the back of a chair. He'd been excused to freshen up. It was over; he need just return to the boardroom for the exchange of pleasantries, salutations, shaking of hands, look once more into the poker-faced expressions of bankers who—contrary to his fiercely independent nature—he'd been forced to grovel, plead—beg—for funding. It didn't inspire in him any great confidence that they didn't ask a lot of the right questions, and his belief they would invest anything was diminished when the investor who beckoned him east did not appear. They offered to buy his company, keep him in charge, but they would have ultimate control. The herd of them then headed out the conference room chattering away about their next deal. As they did, a woman appeared at the door and they quieted, clearing a way for her to walk in. James stood at the wall-size window gazing south, searching in the distance for the Statue of Liberty when the woman spoke his name.

"James Harris."

He turned around to face a woman dressed in grey and groomed to the teeth. His eyes widened. "Mrs. Godwin." He stepped back, sliding his tie knot up.

"My oh my, what a handsome man you've become." She fanned a manila envelope she carried in front of her face. "Excuse me, I'm as flushed as a virgin attending her first prom."

Mrs. Godwin socialized in the same circle as James' parents at their country club in Connecticut when he was young. She divorced around the same time as James' parents. Later, James and his mother moved to Boston, but Mrs. Godwin continued to live in the town. Heir to a southern tobacco fortune, she returned to finish college (which she gave up to marry), then earned an Ivy League MBA at Columbia. "The parties your parents used to throw," Mrs. Godwin said, "drew us in like moths, soaked us in alcohol."

James rubbed his chin. "Yes, my mother was very good at making sure everyone had a good time."

"Will you be headed to Boston to see her?" she asked. "I'm sure it will make her incredibly happy." She shook her head. "What that woman has been through."

James' expression softened. He nodded with a heavy heart.

Anne placed her envelope on the conference table and clapped her hands. "So how did it go?" she asked. "I see you met with our committee, they're not easy to play these days."

James tugged down on his ponytail at the back of his neck.

"Especially if your business is sinking in this dot-com blood bath."

"What Greenspan calls the age of irrational exuberance." She looked up at a flickering bulb in the ceiling lights. "Where it's hard to distinguish reality from fantasy. How did it go?"

"Not as planned."

"I was given the impression it was quite the opposite," she said.

He grabbed his briefcase to leave. "For buying not investing. They suggested I pack it up and work for them. I promised myself after working for my father," he lifted his briefcase by the handle and pointed it at the city's skyscrapers, "that I'd never work for anyone out there again." He collapsed his arm. "I never met their investor, Anne. Not even learned her name."

Anne held her finger to her lip. "Doesn't mean she's not interested." She handed James the envelope from the table. Inside was a signed investment agreement for ten million dollars. The Chairman's offer was a hundred times that.

"How's that for a welcome surprise?" she asked. "This will give you some breathing room from that controlling father of yours."

"But your bankers said—"

"Forget them," Anne said, "this investor knows what she wants and doesn't need a room full of men to tell her what to do with her hard-earned money. She didn't get to where she is because of them."

"I don't know what to say," he said. "Give her my deepest thanks of gratitude. I will spend her money well."

He opened his briefcase on the table and slipped in the offer when Anne touched his arm.

"James, there is one favor you can do for this investor. Since you're driving to Boston anyway, take the Merritt Parkway and stop by the old town first. She owns the entire acreage of the Revson grounds—you remember that place." James nodded. "She needs someone to do a light inspection before she places it up for sale. When I heard you were coming today, I thought, 'Wow! You're the perfect candidate.'" She looked at him as if they shared a deep secret. "If you don't mind the inconvenience of course."

All roads were leading James to the estate. It was as if the property itself were drawing him back for some special purpose.

"I heard it's been restored to its original state," he said. "People live there now."

"Where did you hear such malarkey?" Anne said. "It's as burned out a shell as it ever was."

James tried to fit the opposing truths together, but they wouldn't make a whole. Soon he would know which was the true reality.

"She was thrilled at the idea when I suggested you," Anne said.

James wanted to tell her he was planning to visit the property all along. Instead he said, "Of course, it's the least I could do."

"Oh, mercy she'll be so pleased."

"But tell her I insist on meeting her when the papers are signed," he said.

"I'm sure that day will come." Anne laced her arm in his and walked him to the elevator. "James, are you leaving straight for Boston now?" He nodded. "Great. We'll have the caretaker of the place waiting for you at the gate in a couple of hours." The elevator door opened, and he stepped in.

"Be careful, James, some do believe that place to be haunted. Please come back safely."

"I'm not a believer in that stuff," he said. "I will return safely."

That afternoon, James drove a grey rented sportster convertible along the Westside highway which leads into the Henry Hudson which turns into the Merritt Parkway when it enters Connecticut, to take him home to his past.

WORTHY'S GAMBLE

5

JUSTINE

New York City, 1880

She was born with the hope of class advantage. Her mother, a beautiful chambermaid in a grand Manhattan Estate, became pregnant by the lord of the manor, then died in childbirth. The lord's wife insisted the baby be cast into the Hudson, or, sparing that, sent to a Lower East Side settlement house. The lord overruled such cruelness and instead decreed she be kept as part of the household, though with no higher rank than a common servant. He named her Justine after her mother.

When Justine turned five, they placed her under the care of the Italian gardener, her mother's husband. He knew she wasn't his and mistreated her. One day the gardener died, mysteriously. They said it was from poisoning, a batch of his own homemade pesticide. Some implicated the child, but how could that be possible? The mistress insisted she be sent to their farm up north, in Connecticut. This time, the lord did not interfere.

From her first day on the farm, Justine was taunted by the other children, and no adult came to her rescue. They didn't have to; she was an engine of vitriol, masterful at lashing out with a sharp tongue and a cutting wit on everyone. She was placed under the charge of a slow-witted boy twice her age and lazy, and she made fun of him to no end. Since he could not fight back with words, he did so with fists, and though the girl always lost, she learned to fight. As Justine grew older, the boy dumped on her the most disagreeable of chores: prepare and carry pigswill; sweep up droppings in the hen houses; clean up afterbirths of cows. She was taught to cut the heads off fowls and slit the throats of sheep. They discovered she was good at it.

One day the two were sent down to a stream to drown a surplus of kittens. The boy tossed the feed sack full of them into the shallows and did little else but watch. The creatures meowed and clawed to escape. Justine told the boy he'd better finish the job, or she would for him, and when he didn't, she lugged the bag deeper into the water and held it below the surface, until it lay still. It sank and washed away while the boy cried. The girl told everyone of the boy's skittishness, and they made fun of him by meowing and calling him Kitty. He retaliated against the girl by throwing her cat against the barn wall so hard that it died. She retaliated by slitting the throat of his Shetland.

After that, the farm manager would have nothing to do with her. The lord, smiling at the ferocity of her revenge, brought her back to the manor in the city. The mistress fought the move, successful only in relegating the girl to scullery duties. The lord agreed but ordered she be given her own private room. Accustomed to her treatment on the farm, the girl found the house servants equally unpleasant, but not because of jealousy; instead they feared her, knowing how close she was to her father's heart.

When Justine turned ten, she was caught with a trove of books which had disappeared from the children's library. The lord asked her why she took them, and she said to read. He asked her who taught her, and she said herself. The lord called for the tutor to teach her daily until she could catch up with the other children at school.

A year later Justine was enrolled. Her teachers recognized her high intelligence and encouraged her inquisitiveness. They gave her ample voice to answer questions. She solved mathematical problems no one else could. Her half-sisters complained of favoritism and their mother tried to remove the girl from the school. Her father responded to that attempted purge by bringing her to live with them in the upper chambers of the estate, henceforth referring to her publicly as his daughter. He bought her a wardrobe commensurate with her new station in life, and she partook of all family gatherings and celebrations. But this did not guarantee the girl was any more esteemed within the family than she was with the farm hands or servants.

Justine grew and matured into a beautiful young woman with Mediterranean curves and shining black hair. With such fine dark features, she stood out in any room. When she reached thirteen, she was sent to Miss Porter's School in Connecticut where her popularity among young men soared. At dancing school, she mastered the waltzes, which placed her in high demand at cotillion balls. The young men fought to fill her dance card while her half-sisters remained half empty. She spent summers in Newport, the Adirondacks, Cape Anne—wherever the young society happened to sway that year. She mastered archery, lawn tennis, horseback riding. For her seventeenth birthday, her father gave her a black stallion, sometimes riding with her on the farm. But mostly she rode alone.

On one of these occasions, a stable hand did not strap on tightly the billets of the horse's girth around its belly. When Justine mounted and trotted away, the horse sucked in its belly and the saddle slid off with her in it. Berating the man, she recognized who he was—the dumb-witted boy who prodded and mistreated her in her girlhood. She told him to check the horse's shoes—the frogs of her horse's back hoof. When he bent over to inspect them, she punched the stallion across its face. The horse jumped and kicked the stable hand so hard against the stable wall, he turned lame and never walked straight again.

There was not one woman within New York's Society of the Four Hundred who did not know who Justine was. The whispers, rumors, and lies circulated by her stepmother did not bother her. In fact, she thrived on them, seeing they made her more appealing to all men. She enjoyed the enmity and jealousy her increased notoriety stirred in all women who, with great ennui, despised her ascendancy into their society world, which they considered as high up from her immigrant roots as heaven is from hell.

With the hooks of their hatred deeply grappled beneath her skin, Justine showed no evidence of pain, even when they slighted and smeared her reputation. When they blackballed her from their parlor soirees and teas, she organized her own, and when the boys stopped attending theirs for hers, they were forced to invite her back, despite their strongest personal objections. For her eighteenth birthday, her father gave Justine a gold and emerald necklace which was famed to have once belonged to Marie Antoinette—before the rabble of the French Revolution sliced off her head. The girl paraded it around on her neck, watching her father's wife turn ember red with hatred.

Justine's downfall began in the spring of her last year at Miss Porter's. The most talked about debutante at Mrs. Astor's Annual that year, she received the obsessive attention of a Princeton man. He was known to be a playboy, not serious about anything but horses, European travel, and gambling. Devilishly handsome, women were more than willing to tolerate his debauchery for nuptials. But he had his eyes on her alone, attracted not only to her wild, carefree spirit and exotic beauty, but also to the wealth of her father who favored her. She ignored the man until, forlorn and miserable, he threatened to propose to a rival debutante; only then did she succumb to his wishes and accept his long-suffering offer of marriage.

Her father cautioned her against this move. He had plans for her to attend college, then join him in the expansion of his business interests. His future empire lay within her grasp, he pleaded. But she was too possessed by such blind revenge towards the women of her society who mocked her, she did not see the advantage of what more she could achieve as a woman with vast amounts of wealth——and brain power—behind it. Instead, she preferred to fulfill her single life's ambition of giving her rivals their long-deserved comeuppance. Drunk in the knowledge of her victory, she gave herself physically to her beloved before the ceremony. She fell pregnant, and then her father died.

Her stepmother removed Justine from the estate and disinherited her. Her betrothed, at the overt insistence of her father's widow, broke off the engagement, claiming unfaithfulness on her part. Justine threatened to abort the child until her ex-fiancé's older brother, a strict Quaker, failing to force his brother to marry Justine, promised to support her and the baby if she raised the child a Protestant. Still in shock from her fall from grace, she agreed. After giving birth to a son, Justine ensconced herself and the baby in a Washington Square apartment paid for by the uncle. She did not even attempt to portray an appearance of gratitude towards her merciful benefactor, instead she lived as recklessly as she pleased. This disappointed the boy's uncle. But he did not wish to see the son suffer for the sins of the mother and agreed to support her until the boy's tenth birthday, at which time she should either have been found righteous and pure, or found someone else to support her. The former he doubted would ever occur; he hoped at least, for the sake of the boy, she would attain the latter.

6

WORTHY

Washington Square Park, New York City, 1908

The Washington Square apartment was furnished in black and white, in shadows and in light. A ten-year-old boy named Worthy lay sprawled out on the floor, sweaty palms pressed cold upon his chin, supported by rounded elbows ground on parquet. He watched his mother lean into her vanity as she prepared for a night out. Carefully she applied her make-up, spending what seemed hours to get it right. When she left, the boy sat in her lace-pillow chair and peered into the same vanity. He stared at his own reflection, just as she did, and made himself up. But he never saw the same happiness he thought she found there in the glittering glass. He only saw a sloppily painted clown.

On Saturday evenings his mother returned home after midnight accompanied by a party of guests who would wake up the boy by their noise. He'd listen for his mother's sweet melodic voice floating above the rest, hear the guttural laughter of men. Then he'd drift back to sleep.

On Sunday mornings, the servant girl's day off, amongst odor of bourbon and stale cigars, the boy glided through the spacious flat's hallways and parlor rooms cleaning up. He'd empty overfilled ashtrays of lipstick-smudged cigarette butts, half-filled glasses of diluted whiskey, silver buckets with melted ice. If he knew she were alone, he'd creep into her room, stroll to her bed where she lay sleeping and, holding her cheeks in his hands, kiss her sticky lips. He'd tiptoe about in the darkened quarters, pick up from the floor her silken undergarments, laced boots, transparent gowns, and quietly fold them away. He tried hard not to tremble or make a sound. He was giddy and clumsy, knowing if he woke her by a sudden slip, she'd yell, order him out, and make sure he closed the door hard behind him.

In the spring of Worthy's tenth year, the late-night parties stopped. His mother glowed, walked about the home humming, kept drapes pulled back to let in sunlight. There was talk of a wedding, and she spoke of the new life about to give birth before her; suits of clothes, summer trips to the shore and mountains, a return to the enjoyment of the leisurely activities she cherished in her youth. Her tummy grew, and the doctor ordered she be secluded in Saranac Lake until her condition improved. The boy was sent to the Jersey Shore with his uncle for the summer, where he would stay until his mother's health was deemed restored. Only then would he be allowed to return.

His uncle took the boy with him like a piece of luggage, out of an acute sense of Christian duty. Not knowing how to offer genuine affection, he gave only of his wealth and never of himself, and a time which could have been filled with some semblance of family life, was instead for the boy a lonely one.

The dog days of summer lapped forward. Aimlessly the boy wandered the wooden boardwalks and overpopulated beaches under the care of indifferent butlers, maids, kitchen assistants— whoever had been saddled to watch him that day. He made no friends—not that others didn't notice him—his black curls and sea green eyes drew, despite his age, stares from all women. Instead, he preferred to roam alone, never making eye contact with anyone, preoccupied as he was with homesick thoughts and feelings. Emotionally distant, it was hard for anyone to engage him, and he began to refuse going outdoors all together, preferring the emptiness of an unattended parlor, the cool dark space below a dining room table, seclusion in his boiling attic bedroom, where he'd stand tip-toe on a chair to peer out a sealed portal window on the slanted ceiling through which he'd view the sprawling world outside. Thinking, dreaming, desiring, only her.

At the end of August, the boy was granted a reprieve in the form of a telegram, calling for his return. Expectations filled the train ride home—had she missed him as much as he her? Had she bought him presents, marbles, toy soldiers? With the money his uncle supplied him with all summer, he filled suitcases full of gifts for her: hard candies, taffy, expensive perfume, French toiletries (he envisioned her fluffing her cheeks, spraying flowery scents upon her olive skin).

When his train arrived at the station, the boy, in knickers, spotted her through his compartment window and waved. His mother was more beautiful than he remembered, dressed in a white lace frock and a black satin dress with white lapels, standing upright with perfect poise and posture; chin held high, black and white bonnet balanced firmly upon her head. An expansive long white goose feather slanted forward across the top of her hat; a black veil drooped below her eyes, revealing a pair of dark red lips. Her long black gloves held down a black silk parasol with a tip as sharp as her black high-heeled boots, all planted pointedly together on the train platform, giving her the appearance of a flamingo at rest. But something was different; the bulge in her stomach was gone—she'd been cured. She looked about the crowded station of travelers as if filled with boredom and bitterness. At one point, she looked directly at the boy, his head bobbing out of the compartment window, arms waving. But she showed no recognition or emotion. Was she angry? Had his train arrived late, was he to blame?

He did not know when she looked at him, she saw the torpid face of a devil––that treacherous, lying, cowardly father of his who scandalized her years ago by referring to her among their circle as a common whore. She'd have sold the boy to the highest bidder if it meant never having to be reminded of that terrible hell, that weapon of betrayal his father had thrust deep inside her. Because of this boy, she was branded the feminine Icarus who soared too high, his fault she was prevented from achieving her most coveted life dream, acceptance and admiration in the high society which despised her.

As the steam sputtering train harrumphed to a halt, the boy leapt from the bottom step in her direction with such elation, he did not see the luggage and tripped, propelling him to the station platform. Dazed, he jumped to his feet and ran to her, no longer hiding the emotions he kept buried inside all summer like a molten bubbling core. With tears, he tried to embrace her, but she held him at bay, pushed him back with her parasol firmly planted between them like a medieval sword. Grow up, she said. Control this public display of affection; she had an image of propriety and respect to maintain. She brushed her dress clean of the wrinkles he left on her and, without taking his hand, turned swiftly around to leave; he followed anxiously in her wake.

That day the boy learned he had gained a brother. His room was turned into a nursery in his absence, his belongings moved to an alcove with a curtain for a door. An Irish nursemaid was installed, one who had no time for play. Employed by his mother's soon to be in-laws, this nurse called him a bastard of a bastard. Later when he asked his mother what that meant, she slapped him and sent him to bed without supper. She then dismissed the nursemaid, who was there under protest anyway.

Over the next few days, the boy hardly saw her. With the wedding imminent, a bustle of activity kept the household stirred. The boy didn't mind; after his mother was married, they'd all be a happy family together. The baby would have its father to give it all the attention it needed, and he would have it all from his mother. So, it was a shock when she began to pack their suitcases and trunks for a long trip. Excited, he asked her where they were going. She said they'd be sailing to Europe, she, the baby, and its father––but not him. He was to be shipped off to a school his uncle chose for him in New Hampshire. And no, she didn't know when they'd return––in two or three years, perhaps. The boy dropped to the floor in tantrum—kicked legs, banged head––but this only made her ignore him more while continuing to pack.

On the day of the wedding, at four in the afternoon, Worthy's mother was frantic. Her husband-to-be was to have picked her up hours ago. She ordered Worthy to watch his baby brother and left in a huff. With the baby asleep, the boy scrunched himself down on hall stairs at the top of the apartment landing where he would wait for her return. All the while he thought how much he hated that little dolphin, or dauphin, as they nicknamed the baby, that tiny creature who stole his mother away from him. Boy-o-boy what he would do to it if he ever got the chance.

7

THE BARON

A mountain cave in the Italian Alps, lit torches along its walls. A soldier in full gear (helmet, pack, rifle) enters from backstage. He creeps forward, eyes vigilant, rifle cocked. To the side, a circular stone silo rises with a man on top in a lab coat, his back to the audience. He hunches over a table of boiling liquids, fumes rising from test tubes, flames jumping. A giant sign of a radioactive symbol hangs upon the wall beside a painting of Johannas Faust by Rembrandt. The man tosses a firecracker to the stage floor where it explodes. The soldier drops to the ground, holding his helmet. A pungent odor of sulfur permeates the air. Dust falls from the ceiling. He spots the man in the silo and rises to his feet. Intermittent sounds of bombs explode.

BARON: What brings you here soldier? This is not a safe place for the living. Even at this altitude, the fight is on to take the higher ground. State your name and rank.

WORTHY: *(Stands at attention and salutes).* Lawrence P. Worthington, sir! But my friends call me Worthy.

BARON: What side of this mountain do you defend, Hapsburg or Roman?

WORTHY: Italian. But I'm American and frankly don't give a damn whose side wins.

The man on the platform removes his lab coat revealing a German uniform of the highest rank.

WORTHY: I should have known this was a trap! Who are you?

BARON: Baron Memphis von Topheles, at your service. Chief of many a throned-power, mightier and more all-knowing than any of the human race. In this war, I am the Great Field Marshal watching my creation unfold by design. I was there at Tripoli and Verdun, the Somme and the Marne, and I will soon visit the Argonne too.

WORTHY: What is all that antiquated equipment behind you? Are you one of those alchemists who labor uselessly to turn lead to gold?

BARON: Something far more desirous to man than gold. I am putting the finishing touches on a weapon against which the invention of mustard gas pales, one that will initiate the final war of annihilation. *(He points up at the sign for Radioactivity).* I call it the atomic bomb. Thus, will the great Armageddon begin which will bring down at last the gates of heaven.

WORTHY: All I know about radiation is with it you can see your bones right through your flesh. *(Holds his hand up to the light to see through).*

BARON: This will do more than illuminate the skeleton of a living thing, my son. It is capable of evaporating bones and flesh to shadows. *(He descends to the stage floor).* You look pale and famished. Why don't you sit down and eat? *(He waves his hand. From the dark appears a lit banquet table with a feast spread abundantly. Worthy takes his gear off and sits. He picks up a fork and knife and is about to eat when—).*

BARON: Halt! Refrain from lifting your utensils just yet. *(The Baron holds up an upside-down crucifix).* To my dear arch enemy, I give thanks you placed me high above the angels, and man, you kept far below. While it was thee who created paradise, it is I who had it lost. Amen.

WORTHY: *(Clicks his tongue).* That was some blessing.

BARON: What are you, a supplicant of some religious order?

WORTHY: Hardly. Eight years of boarding school with a high church Episcopalian for a headmaster. Chapel three times daily from matins to eventide. He believed it would shape us into good Christian soldiers. Instead it inoculated us from belief.

BARON: Are you so sure?

WORTHY: Didn't you hear? God was declared dead years ago. *(Worthy picks out a banana to eat).* Now they say we're descended from apes.

BARON: Yes, I see the resemblance. So, you are an educated boy, well acquainted with science and religion. *(He stands and paces the stage, one arm bent behind his back in Socratic pose).* What do they say on campus these days, about that glorious angel unjustly turned into a venomous serpent?

WORTHY: *(Takes up a roasted pig foot and starts gnawing).* With the reality of this war, I'm certain more believe in that infernal snake than the all-loving creator above. If he's so powerful, why doesn't he stop this senseless bloodshed?

BARON: My thoughts exactly. But you see in this world, God must serve the devil.

WORTHY: The twentieth century is a damn ripe time for the reaping of embittered souls. Here's to the devil's fruitful harvest. *(He raises a wine goblet to a toast then drains its contents. Bombs burst outside, shaking dust on them).*

BARON: How did you stumble upon my cave anyway?

WORTHY: Your Huns chased me. I was the sole survivor, one of a thousand prisoners of war loaded into train cars and shipped across the Rhine when we were bombed by allied forces. I escaped into the Black Forest undetected, until the enemy caught my scent and never stopped hunting me. I suppose this is to be my last supper. What will you do with me after?

BARON: *(Laughs).* Recruit you in the name of Lucifer, of course, the bringer of light to mankind.

WORTHY: Why you really believe you're––of course, you're commanding the army of the damned! If you are that Prince––or some earthly spirit of his––I'm afraid you'll have no undue influence over me.

BARON: Why's that?

WORTHY: You offer nothing I don't already have.

BARON: What about bestowing upon you the three greatest American virtues: courage, knowledge, and love.

WORTHY: *(hand to chin).* Oh, you're the Wizard of Oz!

BARON: A darker version I assure you. First, courage. I could send you home a hero.

WORTHY: *(Stands).* See these medals of valor I've won already? *(Pulls his front shirt out so Baron can see a string of war medals hanging).*

BARON: How many dead soldiers did you steal those from?

WORTHY: *(Sits back down).* Wasn't doing them any good. Next.

BARON: Knowledge.

WORTHY: *(Smiles beamingly).* War time graduate of Princeton. Wasn't going to finish but they graduated all of us doughboys anyway. *(Begins to croon the Princeton fight song: "Deī sub nūmine viget--Under God's Power She—").*

BARON: Please! Those cursed lyrics--save them for the gridiron. What your higher institutions of learning teach doesn't hold a candle to what you could learn from me. *(Looks up at the portrait of Faust hanging on the wall and sighs).* Faust. Now there was a true Renaissance man. A hero and a villain at the same time. A man of his word who rejected redemption right to the end. They don't make recruits like him anymore. *(More bombs shake the cave).*

WORTHY: He served you to no good purpose. How many souls did he bring in but one?

BARON: True. He accumulated all the knowledge of the universe and did nothing with it. Could have ruled mankind. Now if that power were placed in the right hands, someone like you...

WORTHY: No thanks. The only person I need to watch out for is myself. Next.

BARON: Love.

WORTHY: Which kind?

BARON: Lascivious, as one might enjoy with Aphrodite.

WORTHY: Do you think I need your help with that? *(Shows his profile to the audience)*. With these Hollywood looks, I've ruined many a virgin, and others not so chaste.

BARON: Eros then, the passionate joining of the hearts. *(Shoots an imaginary arrow like Cupid)*.

WORTHY: Do I look like an idyll romantic who believes love has anything to do with the union between man and woman? Where does it say Adam loved Eve?

BARON: Brilliant insight! If this war teaches your lost generation anything, it is that love is of no intrinsic value—your poets will never write about it that way again.

WORTHY: What do you have left to offer me?

BARON: What your Wizard of Oz never bestowed upon any of his agrarian heroes. What Americans place higher than God––Mammon. Or as the song goes, "Money, Money, Money."

WORTHY: I'm already awash in that. Guilt-ridden religious uncle. Though he has been rather stingy of late. Disapproves of my sinful lifestyle.

BARON: Man's treasures on earth are temporal, my son. What you need is the eternal coin I produce abundantly from my underworld mine, where giant nuggets of lead are swallowed whole, then painfully pissed out like kidney stones by the lowest of the damned into gold.

WORTHY: Why would I prefer your other-worldly wealth? Instead of strings attached to my uncle, they'd be tied to you. Well, Santa, looks like you've reached the bottom of your bag and have been found wanting.

BARON: Come now, you must believe in something we can trade on, some truth.

WORTHY: I believe in nothing, I seek nothing, and my own desire is to mean nothing. What is Truth anyway? *(Takes and eats a fig whole, while bombs drop at a quicker more furious pace than before—he dives under the table, trembling).*

BARON: Ah, so you do believe in something.

WORTHY: Not even in this scientific age does anyone doubt the reality of Death. Whose side does he work for in the scheme of things?

BARON: Death is the impartial referee who takes no sides.

WORTHY: *(Comes out from under the table, dusts himself off).* I'd gamble my soul if it meant I could keep out of his clutches forever.

BARON: I can't stop your appointment with death, but we can sidestep him for a while.

WORTHY: How so? I won't be seen roaming the ends of the world for eternity like some transparent ghost, I wish to keep this flesh. *(He looks down and cups his crotch).* All of it.

BARON: *(Strokes his chin).* You know your tribe's ancient writings, the tale of Elijah, swept from earth in a chariot before his appointed time?

WORTHY: Yes, where did he end up exactly?

BARON: To original Eden, where time is not measured, and
             death cannot enter. I would do the same for you.

WORTHY: Remain as I am, in the flesh?

BARON: *(He points a finger in the air)*. I am the Grand Forger
             of Life, who shall provide you with a new body,
             new blood.

WORTHY: What do I have to do for all this?

BARON: What comes naturally to you with those Hollywood
             looks of course, seduction of the other sex. Then
             when you are through you deliver them to me.

WORTHY: I get it. Torment their hearts enough and they'll—

BARON: Pass themselves through hell.

WORTHY: I know the drill. How shall we begin?

BARON: We'll start you with the seduction of young
             mothers, those so obsessed with losing their beauty
             they'll abandon their own children to stay young
             and beautiful forever.

WORTHY: *(Looks wistful)*. There are worse sins a mother can
             commit than that.

BARON: But they are already in hell.

             (A barrage of bombs drops, spreading dust).

BARON: Come son, let's end this lingering parlay. Are you
             ready to swear allegiance?

WORTHY: I wonder if I wouldn't fare better if I gave my soul
             to the other team.

BARON: You'd have no power there, my son. With me, you'd have prestige and rank. To quote our dear Milton, "'Tis better to reign in Hell than to serve in Heaven."

Bombs burst above. Cave walls rumble, dropping more dust and pebbles.

WORTHY: Show your good faith first. Send me home from this infernal war, then we'll see.

BARON: Don't be foolish, this is your best chance to make something of nothing. How do you know death is not at hand for you this very minute?

(While they speak, an Austrian soldier appears at the cave entrance and lights go off. In the dark, Baron turns Worthy around to see the other soldier and the lights brighten again. The two spot each other and the Austrian fumbles to cock his rifle while Worthy pulls his pistol from his belt and fires. The other slumps, his heart spurting blood, and he crumples to the ground, dead.)

WORTHY: You set me up!

BARON: I saved your life.

WORTHY: And you better keep doing so. Okay, I'll sign. But before I do, I have a few of my own demands.

BARON: Let's hear them.

WORTHY: I shall keep my worldly kingdoms, before and after death.

BARON: *(Nods).* In my house, there are many rooms.

WORTHY: Where neither you nor death can enter.

BARON: Beelzebub cannot enter where he is not invited.

WORTHY: Revenge upon my mother's and my father's families: famine, pestilence, impoverishment.

BARON: I don't think we need of such biblical proportion but yes, they shall be ruined. *Bombs drop closer. Parts of the cave ceiling falls.* Now hurry and sign this. Before it's too late.

WORTHY: This says I must sign in blood. You certainly live up to your macabre reputation. Won't a handshake do?

BARON: Nothing consolidates power better than pen to paper. I learned that from my lawyers. Now sign–– indulge my own eccentricity if you will.

WORTHY: I'm afraid of the sight of my own blood. *(More bombs drop).*

BARON: *He points at the dead soldier.* Then take his, why don't you, before these bombs assure yours will spill too!

            (Worthy catches a trickle of the other soldier's blood on his knife. Baron hands him a quill, which he carefully dips in the blood and signs his name.)

WORTHY: It is finished. How do I make my way out uncaptured, and un-maimed?

BARON: Not far from here, there is a gypsy camp about to set off south to the Sabine Hills. A young virgin is below, picking mushrooms in the dew of the dawn. She has stepped on a German booby trap. Rescue her and she'll hide you. Her people will take you to Rome, and from there you can go wherever you wish without harm.

WORTHY: Very well. *Fits on his helmet and pack. Clicks his heels and bows.*

BARON: Oh, and Worthy, one last thing. Take care not to fall in love with any of your conquests. Remember they belong to me.

WORTHY: Don't worry. Of love I am incapable.

             (Worthy is about to disappear through the cave exit when he looks at the audience in a moment of doubt. He collects himself and exits. Baron shakes his head, walking up the silo stairs.)

BARON: A little buyer's remorse in all of them. *(He begins to pack up).* Reassuring to know as long as man exists, I have a purpose too. *(Looks up at the radioactive sign).* On second thought, maybe a weapon that can cause complete mass destruction is not in my best interest either. Who will I have to tempt then?

             (Bombs fall in rapid succession and the cave implodes on Baron, who disappears in the mountain of dust. Curtain.)

8

EUGENE LEQUIN

New York City, May 1, 1919

After the Great War ended, an American GI, penniless, shabby and thin on hope drifted the streets of the grand metropolis. His unflattering war record made it difficult for him to find work. To be a soldier in uniform meant to be treated as a hero, but for this doughboy, that glory paid no dividends. He was not proud of his service overseas—he'd spent most of it in prison, incarcerated by the French as a derelict ward due to his association with a blue-blooded American playboy motivated by the opportunities the war afforded him for monetary gain, rather than a chance to contribute to the great cause. Then on May 1, the day of the Red Summer riots, Eugene's life changed for eternity. As a soldier he would surely have been swept along in the riots had it not been for his chance encounter with that old army buddy of his. Dressed to the nines in a white flannel suit, silver shirt and gold tie, that man jostled up the steps of a cellar level speakeasy in suede-tip shoes. Eugene worked there as a valet. The man tossed Eugene two bits.

"Ticket eighty-six, please."

Man, of green eyes, light and glassy. At the edge of the sidewalk, he pulled a cigarette from a gold case which Eugene recognized. He drove the gentleman's car from the lot, a 1919 red Stutz Bearcat coupe, looked up at this dapperly dressed patron through the tilted windshield of the convertible, and said three words: "La Ferte Mace."

When Eugene arrived in France in 1917, he was assigned to a platoon of American volunteers in the Norton-Harjes Ambulatory services. That is when he met the nephew of an important American business magnate, the esprit-de-corps L.P. Worthington, or Worthy as he was nicknamed. This frisky young officer claimed he had joined out of patriotic duty, but Eugene knew it was to avoid being kicked out of his university for failing grades. This handsome privileged dandy showed his acumen by getting excused from driving Fiat ambulances to the front lines. Instead, he persuaded his French military hosts he could be more useful if he stayed in Paris servicing the needs of the Allied officers and enlisted men. With boldness and cunning––and Eugene doing most of the leg work––he set up a gambling parlor and brothel, the French supplying the goods, booze, and women. The enterprise would have continued for the duration of the war, except for one less fruitful pastime of Eugene's partner-in-charge; Worthy, a true ladies' man, had started an affair with a French lieutenant's wife. When the lieutenant discovered the indiscretion, he had Worthy––and Eugene by association––incarcerated in the French concentration camp at Ferte Mace. There they would remain until they could be transferred to more permanent facilities. The American army, in light of the accused crime, stepped aside.

They did not suffer greatly. Worthy knew how to charm, cajole, and entice money from the pockets of wealthy inmates. In a relatively short time, the two had another business, supplying inmates with cigarettes, food, and other accoutrements. But this also did not last. One morning Eugene awoke to find Worthy gone. It was rumored he'd performed the warden some lewd favor or paid a bribe. Eugene waited for news that he too would be sprung, but it never came. Unable, or unwilling, to purchase his freedom at the same price, he was transferred to Precigne, a prison for foreigners accused of petty crimes. There he faded into the gray prison walls indistinguishable from the rest. He was released at the signing of the Armistice a year later.

"Get in, big shot, we're going for a ride," Eugene said to the man.

"Hey Lequin, what ah ya doin?" A stocky, pimply buck in a thin tuxedo stood by him, arms crossed over his chest. "Get outta duh gen'lman's crate, now," he said. Eugene ignored the man and revved the engine of the small coupe. "What is this, Lequin? Get out or I'm givin' you duh bum's rush, duh ya heahs me? I said, now!"

As the man reached to grab him by his shirt collar, the customer spoke up. "It's all right, Gerlach." He scratched his nose and looked down at his shoes. "I know this man from the war. Tell your uncle I mean to borrow him for a few days." He slipped the stocky brute a few bills, then hopped into the passenger side. Eugene took off, barely giving him a chance to settle in. Minutes passed before either said anything.

"This isn't a war, it's a goddamn whorehouse!" Worthy said, laughing. "Ol' Freddy Barnes from the 33rd division. One of our best clients. I miss him and the fellas, don't you? Eugene, what a pleasant surprise, how the hell are you, ol' sport?"

"You left me in there, Worthy."

"I had my chance. You would have done the same."

The two drove from Manhattan over the Queensboro Bridge to Long Island. Worthy turned his collar up and pulled his jacket closed to stay warm from the cold East River wind.

"As fate would have it," Worthy said, "after I escaped that rodent infested hell hole, I became a prisoner of war in Germany. I swear the mouth of hell opens at the center of that damnation. With some fortuitous luck of a powerful benefactor, I escaped to Italy where I rejoined an Allied force. I saved lives in the infantry carrying arms, the whole thing. I was a hero, goddammit. I have medals and commendations to prove it." Worthy continued to tell Eugene he was made a combatant officer and stationed near Lake Como, from where he led his men on dangerous missions. None were ever killed. All thought he had the protection of an angel.

"Your uncle must have been proud of you."

"Filthy self-righteous moralist," Worthy said. He placed sunglasses on and looked at himself in the side mirror.

Eugene kept his eyes on passing traffic. "You don't hate his money."

Worthy was independent of his uncle now. His benefactor in Europe brought him into his own lucrative enterprise, gaining Worthy a large import agency in the pharmaceutical business, several automobiles, a yacht, a biplane and a spacious apartment in Manhattan—all without the aid of his goddam uncle.

As the dusky evening overshadowed the spring's afternoon glow, they stopped in East Egg where they spent the night on the grand estate of an associate of his. Worthy led Eugene around to the back of the property in the light of a full moon. At the end of an unlit dock they stood, watching the twinkling red and white lights from across the Sound.

"You see the coast up there, Eugene, that's Connecticut."

"I know that. So, what about it?"

Worthy spoke of fifty acres of farmland filled with fields, woods, and ponds that were ideal for hunting and fishing. It had been in his mother's family since the 1600's. Sitting abandoned and decrepit, with Prohibition gaining steam, its barn would be ideal for producing bootleg liquor. The farmhouse would be restored and expanded to accommodate dozens of overnight guests. Lavish gardens would be cultivated for strolling, tennis courts and a pool added as leisure activities for the high-end clientele it would attract.

"What sort of place do you plan on making it?" Eugene asked. "As if I must ask…"

Worthy picked up a few stones and skipped them into the low tide, which exuded a rotten smell of decaying plankton. "I'd planned on building it up into a country getaway of such ill repute it would scandalize. I was all set to start it up when my partners, an old roommate from Princeton and his wife, backed out. Now I haven't anyone I can trust to help run the place with me."

His midwestern friend, a famous writer and his exuberant racy bride, had conceived the idea during a late-night stupor of drunken jubilee where they summered at Compo Beach in Connecticut. They quickly lost interest, but whimsically offered the services of their butler, a Japanese man who spoke little English. Worthy was hardly comforted by their token offer and had not yet answered them.

"You know you can't go back to that club having shown your boss up like that, Eugene. This is the perfect opportunity for you. You ran things for me in France, now run the show for me stateside."

Eugene shook his head. "No way, not again."

"Come on sport, I need someone I can trust who I can rely on. That's you. Say yes, for old time's sake."

Eugene hated Worthy. But he was being offered recompense, a job, and a place to call home again. It was consistent for Eugene to do what he had learned since he was young, accept whatever opportunity fate threw at him, and make do. Eugene took the ten-dollar advance Worthy gave him on the spot and headed to the small Connecticut town in the northwest edge of Fairfield County with ephemeral relief.

9

LAST HURRAH

Country Estate Connecticut, July 4, 1930

The two succeeded in converting the colonial farmhouse into a classy, stylish getaway, for a world hungering for the glitter of a lost youth and wishing to forget the pains of war. The jazz age had begun and would rage on for a decade, burning the candle at both ends, until it came to a dazzling halt with the crash of an entire nation.

Blinding Chinese fireworks frizzled alive in sparks among blistering booms in the sky, despite the menacing approach of a thunderstorm moving in from the dark moonless Atlantic. Past midnight, the thirty-two-piece band of the Dreamland Orchestra swung away on the south terrace lawn under a white tarpon tent, which took to the salty breeze like sails. A plethora of red, white, and blue patriotic balloons kicked up in the escalating winds. Eugene, sometimes partner but mostly butler, in his white dress shirt, black tie, and tails, frantically kept the booze flowing and the buffet tables filled with every popular delight of the time: truffle soufflés, glazed roasts of ham and golden turkeys, fancy fruit bowls carved from melons. Ice sculptures shaped like pink swans and green dragons kept the ice cream hard and the hard drinks cold and rock-full in the sultry, humid, evening air.

Out on the terrace, Eugene perused the hoi polloi of affluence, who constantly nudged him on the shoulder for service. One of them was Worthy's rival from prep school days—Sir Thomas, a firm believer in the superiority of the Aryan race. He stopped Eugene short under the great hanging tent demanding his full attention.

"See here, Eugene," he said. "Where's that risky tycoon of yours—I must see him at once."

"Pouring over the accounts, Sir Thomas," Eugene said, standing at attention. "I'm certain of that. It looks like he plays hard, but with him, it's all work."

"Oh sure, I know." Sir Thomas sat down on a bench outside the hedged perimeter of the lawn, his white jacket open to show his red cummerbund, one leg kicked up across the other, arms spread out, resting along the top edge of the bench. "And he's going to convince my wife to lose huge sums of her money in his magical schemes." He looked down the front lawn at woods hidden in darkness. "Speaking of whom, where is that libertine wife of mine?"

"I last saw her headed to her room upstairs, sir. She had a headache and was having trouble walking straight."

"Oh, don't remind me." The guest stood up. "Show me the way and I'll go see to her myself."

"That won't be necessary," Eugene said. He rushed to seat him back down while waving at a flapper girl who, on cue, appeared with a magnum size bottle of the bubbly and sat down next to this favored guest. "You stay right here," Eugene said. "Have more champagne with this, lovely." The woman stood the bottle up on Sir Thomas' lap and batted her eyes at him. She stroked the bottle of champagne up and down. "Don't you worry, I'll find your wife," Eugene said. "I'll carry her over my shoulder and deliver her directly if I have to."

"Very well." The man popped the cork off the champagne, never taking his eyes off the woman. "Take your time."

Eugene made his way through a current of guests flowing onto the dance floor which overlayed the pool. Pushing his way against the crowd to the kitchen quarters, he knew where to find the guest's wife. Careful never to surprise any of his discreet clientele, Eugene stopped in front of a pantry closet and whistled. He tapped a secret coded rap on the door and voices inside quieted.

"An honored guest requests the expeditious presence of his most beloved," Eugene said.

The muffled reply of a man inside the closet answered. "Tell him to go fuck himself," it said. "Tell him his wife is leaving him, and she means it this time." The voice was Worthy's.

A woman's throaty response followed, giggly and fruity. "Yes Eugene, please bid for me ta-ta to Sir Da-Da."

"And tell him he can keep the children too," Worthy shouted.

"Oh darling," said the woman, "don't make me feel guiltier than I already do."

"That was the deal we made, Daisy, remember? No children."

"But Worthy, if you really love me, why don't you stand up to him?"

"Because if you really want your revenge for what he did to our good friend, we're going to stick to our plan and run away so you never have to lay eyes on that cheating cad of a husband again."

"But Worthy!" she protested.

As the two argued in whispers, Eugene went about his business in the spacious kitchen where a crew of cooks, busboys, and waiters stood around furtively in need of direction. "Let's start to lower the temperature at this shindig," Eugene told them. "Bring out the coffee pots and the silver dessert trays."

"All of it, Gene, all at once?"

"Whatever's left––all the pastry pies, chocolate éclairs, the last of the ice cream and sherbet—let's wind down and see the guests to their automobiles or rooms." He stood to the side watching as his second-in-command kept the help coming and going, but mostly he stuck around to keep his eyes on the locked pantry.

Minutes later the door opened, and Worthy skated out with his lover in tow. Eugene blocked their hasty exit.

"I repeat," Eugene announced, with a bow and a swing of his arm to take the lady's hand in escort, "the husband requests the pleasure of his wife's gracious company outside. Now."

Worthy ignored Eugene, pulling the woman by the hand

through the kitchen up the servant's back staircase. Eugene followed, turning the sharp corner at the top of the stairs just in time to see the door of a bedroom close. His eyes widened at the site of stray guests milling about in the upstairs halls like drunken ghosts. He rushed to the bedroom door and knocked.

"Important phone call for L.P. Worthington. Worthy, are you in there?"

The woman opened the door with a gypsy's scarf wrapped around her head, fresh powder on her nose. She was quite tight. "He's not with me, Eugene," she said. "He's gone off to the library. If you find him, tell him I'm waiting, will you? And if you see my gracious husband, tell him he can order his mistress at his beck and call, but not me." She slammed the door shut on him.

Giving up on her, Eugene took to the central hall navigating through a crowd of guests to get to the new south wing. What was Worthy thinking? This was beyond a dare, more dangerous than the French lieutenant's wife thirteen years earlier. That episode had cost Eugene more than it did Worthy. With their fortunes evaporated on Wall Street, the estate was all they had. Eugene had had it good this last decade, he did not want to see it all dissolve by another insane affair. He approached the library doors. Finding it locked, he used his own key to enter.

At first glance, the room seemed empty. Then he heard Worthy having a conversation. He was used to him striking up a dialogue with no one else present. It was like eavesdropping on one end of a telephone conversation. He closed the door and re-locked it, slid himself behind a tall bookcase.

"You should've warned me about that crash, Memphis," Worthy said, leaning against a great oak desk, staring at the couch as if someone were sitting there. "Don't you have foreknowledge of that sort of thing? Yes, it ruined my relatives as planned, but also nearly myself as well. A little underhanded on your part, wouldn't you say? There is always some grand miscalculation or defect in the goods you deliver. Why do I always have this sense I am serving you more than the other way around? It's time I'm entitled to keep one for myself. Eugene, ol' sport! You scared the dickens out of me."

Eugene stepped out from behind the shelf, stood up straight. "Worthy, there's no time for distractions. Sir Thomas has his suspicions again. If I don't get back to him soon, he'll come looking for her himself––Worthy! What happened to your face? You look like you just returned from the pit of hell."

Worthy loosened his bow tie as he checked himself in a looking glass––his face had turned a blistery dark red.

"Hives!" Worthy said. "You see, you've given them to me again with all your worrying. Now what am I going to do, I can't go down like this, can I? Go find that fine fellow Buchanan who you love to 'sir' to death and tell him we've run off for a racy drive in the rain, and if he doesn't like it, he can come looking for us. Now, out of my way."

"Worthy, you're doing this to me all over again. Do you expect––"

"Go!" Worthy shouted.

"I'm not your servant!" Eugene said. "You can't order me around. We're supposed to be partners. I've always said, I'll never be treated like nor will I––"

Worthy rushed out of the room in an uncontrolled manner Eugene had never seen, scraping past him tense and frenzied. What would he tell Sir Thomas now?

He raced down the corridor to the grand staircase, passing the game room, its doors flung wide open. He popped his head in, alarmed to find guests standing on the furniture, couples lying on top of billiard tables, wine bottles and liquor being passed around like there was no tomorrow, great laughter belching into the hallway––no time to quell their raging soiree, no––he must get downstairs as fast he could.

He reached the grand staircase and made his way past streams of partygoers on their way up, couples looking for places of their own that were private and dark and spoon friendly. He hurdled past throngs of merrymakers filling the grand room now that it had started to rain, a warm refuge from the rain-soaked dance floor outside. The frothy flames of a fire danced alive in a colossal fireplace. He'd be forced to swim against the current of guests again.

The fluttering black and gray curtains of the French doors at the far end of the room showed the increasing strength of the on-coming storm. It had begun to pour and thunder and this had forced all but the bravest to dance their way into what space was left of the grand room, between sofas and lounge chairs, wet bars, buffet tables pushed against walls. A rowdy consortium of guests outside refused to evacuate until the orchestra played one last Charleston under the cover of a collapsing white tent, now ballooning. Sir Thomas was not where he had left him.

Looking out over a sea of bobbing heads, he spotted his flapper friend in billowing yellow dress pointing towards the tent's only bar still serving drinks. Eugene spotted the back of Sir Thomas' head, dashing his glass of champagne around like a baton while in conversation with another guest. As Eugene parted the density of dancers to reach him, someone tripped him, and he took a dive on the slippery wet flooring, sliding to a halt behind the bar. The bartender looked down; Eugene put a finger to his puckered lips to keep him quiet while he eavesdropped on Sir Thomas' one-sided conversation.

"I am not to be made a fool of twice!" Sir Thomas said. "This fellow Worthington is a fake! I know his true origins, and I'll let the whole world know. He was no hero in the war! He took those badges of honor from a wounded soldier, whom he left to die. Rather suspicious, don't you think? I've always believed he was a spy for the Germans. Worthy's a bastard all right, son of a trollop, and his father wouldn't have anything to do with him. He only passed through St Paul's and Princeton because of that sappy religious uncle of his. He's a lothario if there ever was one and if he's with my wife, when I catch those two—where the hell is that goddamn butler of his?"

Eugene hated to be referred to as Worthy's goddamn anything. He stood to his feet attentive to this arrogant son of a bitch, who controlled his wife's vast million-dollar inheritance invested in Chicago grain futures, saving this once celebrated polo player from

Yale from his own obscurity.

"Sir Thomas, she sent me to say that she might be a little––she said to say she's on her way down herself to see you," Eugene said.

"She is, is she?" Sir Thomas answered. "Why didn't she come with you, and where the hell is—" he paused. "Okay, I see through this masquerade. He's behind this, isn't he? Now Lequin, you're going to take me to them at once or I swear I'll see this place shut down or burned to the ground in short time."

"Of course, sir, follow me," Eugene said. "No, not through there, it's too crowded that way. I have a shorter route we can take."

"Don't think you can lead me down some stray garden path!" Sir Thomas answered, fluffing his mustache.

The two entered the estate house by means of a black steel bulkhead. It led to the basement of the new addition stocked with supplies––crates of wine, booze, other food stores. The two walked the length of the foundation in darkness until they reached the lit staircase to the back hallway at the end. Upstairs Eugene led Sir Thomas to the grand staircase which rose along its curved walls on both sides.

At the top, Eugene looked to see which direction he might lead his patron adrift. Sir Thomas darted in the direction of the room where his frolicking wife had been powdering her nose and Eugene followed.

"I know where to find them, Eugene," Sir Thomas said. "I have my own spies around here. Of all the flagrant acts they could have chosen to commit right under my nose." He quivered with righteous indignation. Eugene stood between him and the door and began to rap his knuckles on the door when Sir Thomas stopped him.

"No, I'll do this," he said, sliding Eugene aside, "before you have a chance to warn them with your sly signaling." He placed his ear to the door to listen; then, without warning, he broke the door open with all his weight.

Muffled noises in the dark. He punched on a switch that turned on a lamp, revealing a couple necking on the bed. "Judas Priest," he whispered aloud. A woman on top of a man screamed as she pulled her blouse over her exposed breasts, covering her mouth with her hand. The man sat up on his elbows and squinted, searching with one hand for his moon-shaped glasses on the table.

"What are you gasping at?" Sir Thomas snorted at Eugene. "It's not them, you idiot."

He prowled around the room in search of the guilty lovers, opening the closet and bathroom doors, flapping the shower curtain back, peering into the tub. He leaned out the window to scan the front of the carriage house where the cars were parked. Holding his hand to his brow to cut the light's glare, he spotted the wayward pair running through the downpour headed towards Worthy's red Stutz Bearcat coupe. He ducked his head back in. "I knew it! I knew it!" he chanted, marching out of the bathroom. "They better hope to God I don't catch up with them." He removed a small pistol from his coat pocket and raced out the room.

Eugene's annoyance at Worthy was replaced by a panicking need to warn him. Fortunately, Sir Thomas ran by the upstairs corridor to the grand staircase—a path which would force him to wade through careless drunks meandering about, while Eugene stayed a step ahead by taking the backstairs to the kitchen, nearly falling the whole way. He raced out the back-porch door. Worthy was just turning the steering wheel of his bright red sportster down the driveway when he caught sight of Eugene.

"Goodbye, ol' sport." Worthy waved to him. "We'll send a telegram when we arrive in Italy!"

"Worthy! Wait!" Eugene, sopping wet from the rain, jumped in front of the car. He looked up at the estate, saw Worthy's adversary on his way.

"We've got to fix this somehow!" A bullet cracked through the windshield.

"Out of the way, ol' sport, there's no time!" Worthy careened the car at Eugene who dove for his life. He hit the gravel face down. Sir Thomas pulled him up by his collar.

"Where are they going, Eugene, I saw you speaking to him, tell me where they're headed or I'll—" Sir Thomas held his pistol to Eugene's head.

"How am I supposed to know?" Eugene said, his head held down by the gun.

"Never mind," Sir Thomas growled, "I suspect I know." He let go of Eugene and hopped into his own bottle-green sportster in pursuit of the lovers. Eugene felt the blood on his lip mix with the rain as he looked down the drive. There was nothing he could do now but return inside and shut the night down and wait for Worthy's return.

By 4 a.m., the storm had passed. Sound of mating crickets outside. Guests had left or fallen asleep upstairs. A straggler or two passed out on a sofa or plush carpet. The band packed their instruments and the house crew finished cleaning. A police wagon arrived. Two troopers stepped out. Worthy was found dead; his car had skidded into the reservoir at Devil's Den. They held up two wet passports and soggy tickets to board a ship to Europe in New York. Loaded in the back hatch of the wagon were two dead bodies covered in blankets. This was no accident. Sir Thomas was picked up by state troopers for questioning. They found where his front grille was smashed in, it matched the dents on the back bumper of Worthy's car pulled out of the sink. The jealous husband admitted to nothing and his lawyers made sure his name was kept out of the press.

10

EUGENE FINDS A HOME

Country Estate Connecticut, 1930-1969

The Depression settled over the country like a heavy wet blanket. Eugene, like most, struggled to survive. With Prohibition ended, business at the estate dried up. The property was lost to the state for non-payment of taxes, and the ill-fated country manor died with the dramatic end of its shady proprietor L.P. Worthington. Stories of its notorious guests and parties entered town legend. Eugene boarded up the estate muttering of his misfortune. How would he survive the tough years of the Depression to come? His one consolation; having for years kept the officials supplied with gin, the town selectmen allowed him to stay on as caretaker of the vacant place, until a new owner could be found. That wouldn't happen until the end of the next world war.

When the estate sold, it did so in a snap. To a New York tycoon, whose fortune derived, not from the illegal trade of bootlegging, but by the legal business of selling lipstick and cosmetics -- it was the beginning of a post-war empire. Eugene was asked to stay on as the year-round caretaker, excited when he learned the plan was to restore the mansion to its earlier splendor. He thought he was going to be told to leave and the estate demolished. "Not even hell loosed could bring her down!" he used to say. The property was to be modernized as a country residence where the tycoon, his wife, and two young sons could retreat to from the city in the summers. After the carousing years of the 1920s with Worthy, this was an opportunity for Eugene to feel like a valued part of a family. He took to the boys, teaching them how to fish, hunt, and tie knots as if he were their Boy Scout troop leader.

By the 1960s, the boys grew into young men. With daring risk-taking the two took to the dangerous international sport of grand prix racing. That's how tragedy struck the family twice: the younger son Doug lost his life racing in Denmark; the elder Peter, in South Africa. Their deaths sent Eugene into a morose shell. Why was he, a man of eighty, allowed to live, and they, barely out of their teens, had their breath of life cut so short? He swore he would never let his guard down and grow close to anyone again. Their deaths provoked in him such thoughts of his own expiration that his favorite pastime became the construction of a coffin for himself, so sure was he that soon would come his fatal day. "Make it easy for everyone," he'd say. "Dump me in there and forget about me, no more attention than that."

One day in his quarters above the carriage house, the owner found Eugene planing the top of his pine box. "Finished yet with that morbid obsession of yours?" he asked. The man looked befuddled and confused, fumbled with his words. "Eugene, we have no more need of this place now that the boys have passed, you understand. We're going to sell."

He spoke weak with sadness, the voice of a broken parent.

"This summer retreat doesn't fit our world anymore. It's time to move forward, Eugene, begin a new chapter in life. Your day too has arrived."

Eugene hammered the last nail into the top with an emotionless response.

"You've been an important part of this family, Eugene," the man continued. "To show our gratitude we've arranged for part of the proceeds of the sale to go into a pension for you. That will provide a comfortable life at a retirement home in Norwalk." The millionaire patted him on the back and left. Eugene would never see him again.

11

REUNION WITH AN OLD PARTNER

In the heat of summer, Eugene slaved away in a white shed behind the carriage house. Sweating like a sprinkler, he pulled down from upper shelves heavy boards, the same used decades earlier to secure the estate windows. They would be used for that purpose again. He was much younger the first time, now it was a struggle. He wished he had someone to help. When he reached the highest shelf for the last remaining board, he did not see an anvil placed on top to keep it flattened. When he pulled too hard, the anvil slid off, striking a blow to his head, knocking him out cold.

Eugene awakened to the noise of an engine revving in the driveway. He recognized its sound as if it were music he had written. There was only one car whose pistons struck notes like that––the Stutz Bearcat he kept well-tuned in the 1920s, the same in which Worthy had plunged into the reservoir. Standing up, he felt woozy. At his feet, a dry puddle of blood stained the concrete flooring. He stepped out into dark night. Disoriented, his ears latched onto the engine's rambling. He steered his legs in its direction like a ship guided home by a foghorn. When he reached the gravel drive, he found not the Bear Cat purring, but the race car Pete Revson used to drive on the tracks in Lime, Connecticut, a silver Morgan coupe. After his death, Eugene had removed the tires and retired the car to cinder blocks in one of the carriage house's stalls. How could it be here again, idling on the estate drive with a couple sitting in it? The driver hopped out of his seat and opened the passenger car door for a blond woman. She stepped out on the gravel in red high heels, wearing black coat tails and a top hat, nearly tipping over with each step she took. She steadied herself against the windshield with one hand, clutched her glittering white purse against her stomach with the other. Staring at the ground, she looked as if she were going to vomit.

"Hello, sport. I'm home." The shadowy figure tossed Eugene the car keys. "Swing open the carriage doors and park it for me, will you?" The man grinned with a sparkle from his teeth and a wink from his ice green eyes.

Eugene's face turned white. "Worthy."

The stranger nodded to the woman, who headed up to the estate by herself, wobbling on her heels. The man took Eugene by the arm and escorted him into the carriage house.

"Come now, Eugene," the man said, "you know it's me, Lawrence, the youngest and last living son of the Revsons." He flipped on the light switch and the room filled with light.

Eugene blinked. Lawrence Revson, a son who he knew did not exist, appeared looking like Worthy, but dressed for the present year 1969, not 1930.

Eugene pointed towards the estate house. "Who is she?"

"Sharon Peters, a local divorcee. Scandalous, don't you think?"

"Everyone in this town's getting divorced these days," Eugene replied, pan faced. He felt the top of his head where the point of the anvil pierced his skull. "I must be dead," he whispered.

"Well I'm not, old sport," the man said. "Now that father has deeded me this place, I'm moving in." He moved about the musty beams in the carriage house, careful not to dirty his white dinner jacket.

Eugene held on to a cobwebbed timber support, keeping

himself from a dizzy spell, uttering Worthy's name over and over, repeating it like a magical incantation.

"You really must improve that memory of yours," the man said. "Don't you remember who I am?"

Eugene stood as motionless as a hollow statue. "The last day I saw you," he said, "was Independence Day, 1930. That was the night you sped into the reservoir with that dame, chased by that knighted polo player husband of hers."

The man caught his reflection in the windowpane, rubbed his white teeth with his finger. "I don't know what you're talking about, my man. Do I look that old?" He showed off his teeth.

"It's impossible," Eugene said, drifting closer to him. "If that's really you, you haven't aged a day."

The man pulled down on his suit lapels. "And don't I look swell too, a newer updated model." He picked a few fallen wood splinters off his dinner jacket. "Don't you know it is written, Eugene, you must die, in order to live?"

"But your body, the reservoir, Devil's Den––"

"Come now, old man, this is my body, this is my blood, standing before you now."

"Impossible."

"You're repeating yourself, sport. Someone should think you're growing senile."

Eugene pointed in the direction of the back gardens. "But I had you cremated, kept your ashes in—"

"If I were dead, shouldn't I know better than anyone?" Lawrence laid his hand on Eugene's shoulder. "I know this is all hard to take, and you're doing heroically, but let's be over with this worthless chatter, be a sport at last, and pull my automobile in before it rains. I shall retire to the manor to entertain my lady friend. You look like a spooked codfish, Eugene, and you're bound to scare the young thing. Stay away from the manor house for a while until she gets used to the place."

"I still can't believe you're alive."

The man placed his hands on his hips. "And I can't believe to find you still here breathing air! That woman is going to be staying with us a long time, Eugene, and you may stay on as the estate manager only as long as you don't cause me any grief with her."

Eugene frowned and crossed his arms. "I ain't nobody's servant, and never have been."

"Suit yourself. But it's my dominion exclusively this time around and I will share control of it with no one."

Eugene dropped his arms and leaned forward. "As if you ever treated me like a partner. You left me bankrupt with heavy debts I couldn't pay off. I was lucky the town let me stay. I can leave this place anytime I want. Martin Revson has a place for me to retire to as soon as I finish getting this place in shape to be sold." He paused. "Or I might go back to Maine."

"Have it your way," Lawrence said. "But you're older now and will die soon. If you stay you can prolong that meeting with death indefinitely. I know that doesn't make any sense to you now, but it will later." The man walked to the door and turned around. "Now be a sport and make yourself useful again by driving this car into the carriage house."

"I told you I don't take orders from no one."

Lawrence rested his foot on the threshold ready to step out. "If you do choose to stay, I'm to be addressed as Lawrence, the last remaining son of the Revson clan, and the new lord of these premises."

Eugene curled his fists. "Like hell I'm going to let you tell me what to do anymore." Eugene felt giddy and nauseous. If it were all a dream he must wake up, and these trespassers, the man and woman both, must disappear. He would stay as long as he pleased, leave when he decided it was time. He did not trust this new Worthy. Not that he ever trusted the old one, but he had an obligation to Mr. Revson who'd been good to him all these years to see that nobody entered the property to cause it harm. He would stay. For now. Without dwelling another thought on it, Eugene parked the Morgan inside just as he was ordered to do.

THE REVSON ESTATE

WELCOME, JAMES

12

A STRANGE AND MYSTERIOUS COUPLE

She leaned over him, his nurse nightingale, and brushed the fallen hair from his head. James woke up in a strange room, with a woman sitting on the bed beside him. Aching with pain, he asked what happened.

"You had an accident," she said, "hit by a car––"

"That's enough," a man's voice cut in. "He'll be better off, dear, without you hanging all over him." The man took center stage. "A few minor scratches and bruises are all you have really. By the morning, you'll be good as new."

There was a sparkle to the man's eyes. Dressed in beige linen trousers and an alligator polo, his ankles showed bare in a pair of bass penny loafers. Deeply tanned, his stallion black hair brushed back neat and trim above his ears. The woman was slim with a cosmetic smile, wearing a short-sleeved summer dress cut above the knee, in the modish colors of yellow and orange. She had a light white sweater draped over her shoulders. Side by side they appeared the perfect young couple, Barbie and Ken.

The man scratched his nose. "Honey, why are you standing there? You should be down preparing the sauna for us like I told you. Get going, love, and don't forget," he winked at James, "make it hot, just as we like it." The woman gave the man a cold stare, then left. "She's some peach, isn't she?" the man said.

Lifting his head, James glanced around the room and spotted his clothes on the floor. They were ripped and bloody.

"Those are yours," the man said. "We'll have them cleaned up by morning." He glanced at the bedside table. "We've left you some pain killers, which'll help you sleep." He turned off the bedside lamp. "May you rest in peace." He left the room, leaving a faint smell of gin in his wake.

James wiggled his way up to a sit. Who were these people, and where the hell was he? He caressed his body; bruised ribs which hurt when he breathed, a swollen eye, a lesion on his forehead that bled through gauze. Sore legs but no broken bones. Across the room, a warm summer breeze entered a window, jostling its muslin curtains. James pulled the bed cover off, slipped his feet down to a white carpet, and limped across the room. Leaning against its molding, he looked out the window; floodlights threw a soft glow down a driveway which disappeared into dark woods. He spied his clothes on the floor, indeed bloodied. He lifted his trousers when out from its pocket fell a chestnut in its thorny shell. Flinching in pain he picked it up, wondering where it came from. He removed its husk and rubbed the chestnut's imperfect lumpiness between his fingers. Suddenly he was awash in memory:

Through the disturbed ripples of a forgotten pool, the contours of a one-hundred-and-fifty-year-old Tudor residence ten yards behind a wrought iron fence. Two stone pillars tall as a man, silent and heavy, rose on each side of a slate walkway to the front door. Inlaid in one was a brass plate with the letters of a surname engraved like a tombstone: "Harris Residence." Behind each pillar grew a giant chestnut tree, whose branches entangled together near the top, shadowing a grassless front yard. It was late October and they were ready to burst with dead leaves. James heard a song which had forever wandered his mind: "Ride, Captain, ride, upon your mystery ship, on your way, to a world, that others might have missed..."

"You've risen," the woman said. She appeared at the door

wearing the same dress, her hair dry and untouched, as if she hadn't stepped in and out of a sauna. She walked towards him and stopped, controlling the distance between them. James steadied himself against the window frame.

"Where am I?" he asked.

"This is the summer residence of the Revson family," she said. "That was Lawrence who you just met, one of the sons."

"Such a familiar name." James took a step forward and collapsed. The woman rushed to his side. Placing his arm around her shoulder, she walked him to the bed. Her hair brushed his face and he smelled jasmine. She helped him climb back under the covers and rest his head on a high pillow.

"You look familiar too," he said, looking up in her eyes. Her face suggested a woman in her twenties, but her presence felt much older.

She glanced around as if expecting someone to appear any moment. "Do you know me?"

"I'm trying to remember," he said.

"You must try harder then," she said.

"Well, if you tell me your name." He raised himself up and felt pain in his back.

The woman helped him lower down again. "You need rest," she said. She motioned toward the pills on the table. She took two out and placed them in his mouth, following them with the smooth rim of a glass of water. He sipped, holding her hand steady to the glass; he felt the beat of her pulse quicken. She gazed into his eyes and lingered, until she broke eye contact and took the glass away.

"Now sleep," she said. "When you wake, I'm sure everything will come back to you as if this had all been a bad dream." She picked up his crumpled clothes. "That's how I feel every morning I wake up in this place." She turned off the light and left.

Feeling drowsy, James fumbled with the pill cylinder and read its label in the glow light: M Revson, Valium, 5 mg, April 1969. He wondered, being so old, if they would have any punch. He dropped the container to the floor as they knocked him out cold.

In the middle of the night, James heard the voice of a boy. "Jimbo, wake up." Numb and drugged, he tried to make out the face crouched by his bed. "Jimbo, listen. You gotta stay and help us escape from here. Promise you will, that you won't leave until we're out too." The boy looked about the room as if afraid someone would catch him, then disappeared. James barely registered the boy's presence before he fell back into deep sleep.

13

A STRANGE AND MYSTERIOUS PLACE

James woke to the light of morning sun shining through his window, catching a scent in the air that didn't belong. The man stood by his bedside accompanied by an eerie odor, as if he had ascended from an ancient wine cellar.

"Good morning, sport, feeling better?" The man held a pair of sunglasses at his hips. "Sorry we can't stay to entertain, but we must be on our way. We have a flight to Rome to catch. Always jetting off somewhere exciting." He pointed with the sunglasses at a tray on the bureau. "My wife has prepared a hearty breakfast for you. After you eat, you can dress yourself and be on your way." He walked to the door. "We wish you a safe journey out of here," he said, and left.

Out of here. Those words again. Where was he that he needed to get out of? He rose out of bed on his own strength, surprised to discover he felt no pain, as if all his sharp twitches and aches from the night before never existed. No swelling around his eye, no marks on his forehead. The pills on the table were gone. He spotted the breakfast tray and his clothes on the bureau. They were cleaned and folded with no signs of bloodstains. On the plate were warm scrambled eggs, bacon and toast, and a glass of orange juice. He ate like a hungry bear and didn't notice there was no flavor to any of it.

He entered the room's tiled bathroom, marveling at its outdated style. Beside the sink was an old-fashioned two-sided razor with an ivory handle beside a shaving cream bar. A tube of Head & Shoulders lay in the shower tray, in a bottle design he'd not seen since the 1960s. After showering, he dressed and buckled on his watch; it had stopped ticking. He shook it but the second hand didn't move. In the armchair by the window, he found the chestnut. Picking it up, he rubbed it between his fingers believing in its power of recall. Falling back into the chair, he slipped into vivid memory.

James sat behind the wheel of his sportster purring in neutral in the shade of trees. He gazed up at the top window of his childhood home behind the iron fence. The girgly voice of his baby brother echoed in his ears and he shuddered. A horse chestnut hit him on the back and distracted him from his thoughts; pockets of them dropped as they were shaken by a fierce autumn wind. His mother used to gather these for roasting, he remembered, despite his father's warning how poisonous they could be; she made James eat one just to test his father's theory. He deposited one of the chestnuts in his pocket. He would chew on it later, just for the memory of its bitterness. He glanced one last time at the house and zoomed off.

A revving engine without a carburetor exploded in the driveway. James dropped the chestnut to the floor and glanced out the window. There he saw an old man tinkering with a car engine in the drive and quickly ducked out of view. He sat back down in the chair with the nut and upon rubbing it, returned to his world of memory.

Leaving his childhood home, James drove up the road to the entrance of a grand country estate hidden from view by woods. He parked his car on the opposite shoulder of the road and stared at its gate, which leaned crooked and dented, rusted from years of abandonment. NO TRESPASSING BY ORDER OF TOWN POLICE DEPARTMENT. Other "No Trespassing" signs were nailed to surrounding trees. He grinned with boyish mischief—this was not his first visit to the property. He climbed over the gate as he had countless times as a boy. He followed its leaf-strewn gravel drive at a fast walk, anxious to see how this place had changed since his last visit.

When he reached the drive's bend, the weather became warmer. His stomach filled with butterflies and he felt lighter; how could the weather change so dramatically? Trees with shady green leaves waited for him ahead, flowers seemed to pop out of the ground as he marched on. With every step, the temperature became hotter and he perspired. He heard the roar of a car engine picking up speed and saw a sports car racing from the property. He waved at the driver, realizing too late that he was headed straight for him. Before he had time to jump out of the way its low bumper clipped his legs, flipping him over the road shoulder onto the jagged remains of an old stone wall. The next thing he remembered was waking up in this mysterious world.

14

IT WAS AN ACCIDENT

Fiddling with the chestnut between his fingers, James sat gazing out the window. A knock at the door startled him and he jumped from the chair. The door opened. The woman appeared.

"Are you all right?" she asked. "You look like you've seen a ghost." The woman glanced at the breakfast tray on the bureau.

"You didn't eat everything," she said.

"I couldn't taste anything," he said.

She held up the tray and shook her head. "It's the nature of this place. Nothing is real. But you get used to it."

"Real?" he asked.

She hesitated. "Nothing is fresh."

"You didn't leave with your husband yet?" he asked.

"He's running some errands; he'll be back soon." She lowered her arms with the tray to her waist. "Has your memory returned? Do you remember––" she hesitated again, "––anything about who you are?"

"My name is James, and I grew up here. I remember." He stared at the ceiling trying to grasp a memory. "I was walking alone when a car struck me––in your driveway. Strange," he poked at his ribcage, "I don't feel pain anymore." He touched his forehead lightly, the skin under his eye. "All my cuts and bruises are gone. But I know it happened."

She searched his face. "What else do you remember?"

"I remember I was walking in from the outside road for some reason, I don't remember why—but just as the estate came into view, I saw a sports car speeding away from it. I waved at the driver, who suddenly veered towards me. I just stood there like some fool, and then——I had no time to jump out of the way." He snapped his fingers. "That man was trying to run me over on purpose!"

The woman dropped the tray to the carpet and all its contents spilled out. She quickly knelt and gathered everything. "That's ridiculous," she said. "Nobody was trying to hurt you." She stood up with the tray. "The gate is locked for a reason. You were trespassing. No one's allowed to enter that's not invited."

James looked at the room. "You know what else I remember? This place. It was abandoned and burned to the ground years ago. It shouldn't be here anymore."

The woman carried the tray to the bureau. "Well, as you can see, it did not burn down and it's not abandoned. I'm real and I live in a real place and you should've heeded the signs and not entered. We don't like people disturbing our peace. We've had to keep that gate locked ever since Lawrence's brother was killed in that terrible crash. You might remember Pete Revson, the race car driver?"

"Yes, of course," James said, not realizing how he knew that.

Outside he recognized the revving of an engine identical to the car which hit him. At the window he parted the curtains to see. The man was back. He honked twice.

"That's the same sportster," he said. "And that's the same man driving——your husband!"

"He's not my husband," she said as she yanked the curtains shut. They were so close their noses could've touched. She brushed her hair back from her face and walked to the bureau. "He's wary of strangers who think they can just come strolling in," she said. "He meant no harm. He was probably just trying to scare you away by driving too close."

"Dangerously close."

The car honked again. "I must go, or he'll be upset." She picked up the tray. "After you've finished dressing, take these stairs outside your door down to the kitchen, and from there you can exit out the back porch." Before she left, she stared at him and added, "I do wish you a safe journey out of here, James."

He held the door open for her. She stepped out into the hallway and descended to the kitchen.

"Safe journey out of here, huh?" James heard the roar as the two drove off. He finished dressing and headed downstairs through the kitchen just as the woman directed.

15

THE ENCHANTED GARDEN

James, come back for me, it's time. The words floated like a whisper on the wings of a butterfly caught in the wind.

James skipped down the porch steps whistling a happy tune when he was halted by a wall of heat; even in the shade it was intense. He looked around the back lawn; neat cut grass, ornamental trees in summer flower along the property's west wall––what happened to the autumn of yesterday? He looked at his watch, shook it on his wrist, held it to his ear––no tick. Broken in the accident, like him. It was not his body which suffered the pain, it was his mind that took the damage. It was as if some giant hand covered his eyes the moment he walked onto the property and blinded him from seeing anywhere but in front of him. As the woman said, he needs to try harder to remember. The answers lay in his past. They'd flow back in bits and pieces and he'd have to fit them into a whole, like a puzzle.

He breathed in the familiarity of the place. To his north, the carriage house and driveway. To the south, a forest-size garden, as tall and wide as a giant tidal wave hovering above the mansion ready to crash down. He pulled out from his pocket the shell of the chestnut and sat on a kitchen porch step. With his eyes closed, he cupped the shell in his hands and blew. It would take him back to an earlier time in his life if he listened.

In the year James turned thirteen, the Revson estate was vacated and placed up for sale after the family's eldest son, Pete Revson, was killed racing in the Grand Prix circuit that spring. While the town grieved over the news, James the boy had his own grief to worry about. His brother had drowned in the pool the summer before and his parents divorced soon after that tragic episode. It was under this cloud which descended upon his starting teen years that James and his friends discovered a perfect refuge from the upheavals and naggings of a world expecting them to grow up too soon——the abandoned Revson Estate. They stumbled into it when searching for a quicker route to the school's baseball fields. To get there in short time, they'd need to sneak through the property; the "No Trespassing" signs posted everywhere around its edge merely served as invitations to mischief.

On the estate was a white-haired caretaker who chased trespassers away as if they were pesky crows, with shots aimed in the air from his two-barreled rifle attached to him like some third appendage. Accompanied by a silent dread, this roving pack of pent-up hormones sped over leaf strewn paths at the property's perimeters steering clear from open spaces where they'd be easy targets for him. They reached the gardens in back undetected, then lost themselves in a labyrinth of shrubbery and flower patches, skidding into unknown corners and dead ends, until by chance they came upon their newfound paradise; a shaded brick patio along the west wall, with a statue at its center. She was the most luscious reproduction of—Diana? Aphrodite? Cherubim cheeks, bursting lips, chiseled glittering jewel eyes; they marveled at her aliveness. The statue's face was not the only object of their adolescent adoration; her melon-shaped breasts splurged over the bouquet of roman ivy, which grew in circles around her curvaceous torso. In this silent, attractive, feminine presence, the boys found the first non-mother type of their life; a figure of the opposite sex they could approach with neither embarrassment nor shame, instead they greeted her in song with an overabundance of unnamed excitement; she physically grounded their pubescent curiosity.

These young sandlot athletes heard of the statue's glorious existence before they'd laid eyes on her, from gray-haired men who sat in the bleacher seats at their baseball games. Beyond the right field fence, a row of fir trees stood at attention at the top of a hill on the property's southern perimeter, as if guarding the estate from the outside world. The statue, the elder storytellers claimed, was behind there somewhere.

They too gave their hearts to her the day she arrived in town just after World War I, when their fathers––local tradesmen––liberated her from her packing crate. She'd been exported to America by some war hero tycoon who insisted on giving the estate a garish build up, a temple-sized overstatement to impress those who attended its magnificent parties. Guests from New York, Boston, Chicago and beyond kept its halls filled to the brim. According to these pensioners, who could remember seeing Babe Ruth and Lou Gehrig play (hadn't the Babe attended one of the estate's famously bawdy parties?), she was not just a piece of crafted, polished stone either. If one believed their tales, the statue possessed the imprisoned spirit of an enchanted gypsy princess once betrothed to a baron. Jealous of her alleged amorous escapades with other men, he had her turned to marble by a witch. Now here on the grounds of this estate she stood upon her pedestal, as if she were the prize trophy of a king who, after some great battle, ruled over her and this forbidden property. With these fanciful images in their heads, the boys visited the estate as often as they could, just to behold her beauty.

James' friends used to laugh at the amorous way in which he stared at her, absorbed in the beauty of her nakedness. On their last visit to the property, they dared him to climb up, pinch her puckering nipples, kiss her wanton lips. For a boy just discovering a world with women in it—sexy, naked, bouncy to the touch types–– James believed if he could prove his prowess before his friends, he'd be rewarded with a romantic magnetism to girls the rest of his life. With all eyes watching, he stepped over the wide-brimmed edge of the waterless fountain (had it ever spewed forth its clear liquid force?) to begin his ascent, of she who towered above him like Mount Everest.

He reached the top of her granite base in no time, but when he started to climb higher—bam! The caretaker shot his rifle in the air, scattering flocks of birds from surrounding trees. James' friends flew away on their bikes while he hung exposed, arms and legs wound tightly around her torso. Hearing someone approach, he shuffled behind her backside, shutting his eyes, as if that would make him invisible. It worked. The caretaker stopped in front of the statue, then took off in the direction of his friends' escape.

James continued his quest. He shimmied up her smooth surface, which gave him the sensation of reaching the top of the rope in gym class, tingling half in fear, half in dread of failure. Upward he climbed, rubbing his legs and stomach against her water worn stone, feeling an indescribable joy in his veins, which grew in fervor the closer he climbed to her top, until finally, like the tangy satisfaction from a slice of exotic fruit on a lapping tongue, he felt a soaring sensation within as if he were about to burst with delight— he reached her summit.

He stared at the statue's virgin face. Was she in love with him, as much as he was with her? No sculptor's art could've carved her expression so right. He cupped her bosom as a boy would for the first time––stone breasts cool to the touch––keeping himself up by their hold. Face-to-face he would now claim his prize. He closed his eyes to kiss her, then––bam! Again. James lost his balance and fell into the dry fountain basin. Any temporary happiness gained was replaced by pain.

He crawled to the outer rim and lay still. Curled up in a daze, he heard footsteps as they approached then stopped. Scared to insanity, he launched his growing mass upwards, knocking over the hovering caretaker who dropped his gun. James jumped on his bike before his downed captor could recover. "Wait!" the man shouted.

He thought he felt the man's reach miss the hair on the back of his neck. It was his frightened imagination, for James peddled south faster than the caretaker could run, catching the bumpy roll of the property's back hill down to the playing fields, where he skidded to a stop atop the mauve clay pitcher's mound. It had been no contest. Standing on his bike pedals, he gazed up the hill where he saw the figure of a man staring down at him from the shadow of the firs. By the time his friends gathered around, it had disappeared into the property.

Of course, James told the deserters of his successful mission; he touched her (truth) and kissed her (lie). Later in life, he relived the pleasure he felt during that climb many times. But he always remembered the statue's sorrow-filled eyes melting into him with abandon. Was love always a mixture of happy and sad feelings? As he grew into adulthood, he was sure it was one of the reasons he never married, for he would compare all potential partners to his fantasy with this statue, which felt so real. Despite all his rational scientific notions, he believed it contained the body and soul of this damsel-in-distress held by a spell that he alone could break. It always bothered him that he never returned to free her.

16

KISS THE STATUE

James leapt from the steps and smiled. He tossed the shell in the air and caught it. He remembered what he'd been sent there to do. Despite the couple's orders to leave, he'd stay to complete his mission; return to the garden to that statue, and if he found her—kiss her, kiss her, kiss her, free that princess' soul in its hollows forever. From the back lawn, he followed the white gravel path to the garden entrance, where there stood manicured shrubs the height of titans. His heart raced in his chest as he strolled down familiar walkways lined with flowers, colored orchids in bloom below a canopy of trees; leafy oaks, beeches, peeling elms, all evenly spaced to exact measurements; age had not added one ring to them since he was a boy. He followed the brick path free of weeds as it curved ahead to a shaded patio at the garden's center. Spread out was the outdoor furniture from years ago in pristine condition: white ribbed chairs set around clouded glass tables with orange ceramic ashtrays on each. Goosebumps shivered down his spine; how could it look so unchanged after all these years? He remembered twelve paths circled this center like numbers on the dial of a clock, each leading into an unknown part of the garden. Down which one would he find her? Standing at the noon hour, he followed bone memory. It was the path at nine o'clock––due west. His heart rose as he felt a longing to possess her other world beauty one more time.

He came within sight of the tall shaded west wall, then the statue as she stood at the end of the path in all her splendor. Did she sense his presence after such long repose? He snuck up as one surprising a lover, balanced himself on the rim of the basin, then jumped in.

"Hello, my love," he said, looking up. She was nowhere as tall as he remembered. "You probably thought you'd never see me again." In one fell swoop, he pulled himself atop her granite base. That face, such a beautiful work of art. Those eyes, the same ones which burned their dark impression into him long ago. "It's really me," he said. "I've come back to release you from your marble prison." He closed his eyes, leaned forward, and kissed, finally, he kissed her.

Bam! Dozens of birds scattered in flight in dark shadows. James lost his balance and fell. How could this be, the past repeating itself? He heard someone approach, so he rolled below the lip of the fountain rim. He peered over. A man stood there looking up in the trees. The same caretaker he knew as a boy, he was sure! He should be dead by now. The man aimed his rifle heavenward. Bam! He cursed and lowered his gun walking away. James stood and addressed the statue.

"Where are you?" he asked. "Shouldn't you now be free?" He brushed twigs off his sleeves. "Come on, speak, show yourself, something to let me know you were really in there." He held his arms up to catch her if she would just deign to come down from her pedestal. James closed his eyes and felt a cool wind. Another gunshot sounded in the distance and he opened them wide. "Well, all right then," he nodded his head at her, "at least I finally kissed you, didn't I?" He flew back down the path to the garden's center, ready to return to the outside world, where he was sure no other goddess was waiting to fall into his arms. Strangely, he felt free.

17

REACQUAINTANCE

Returning from the shadows of the lush green garden to the sun-soaked stones of the gravel path, James wiped his brow wishing for that puff of coolness, anything to bring relief from the heat. He reflected on having faced one of his demons down at last. Hadn't he been sent there for a reason, to save someone, and wasn't that now fulfilled with the release of the statue spirit? If that were it, then there was nothing left to keep him on the property. Removing the chestnut and its shell from his pocket he tossed them away, not wishing to conjure up any more memories. He was finished with his past. Time to go back to wherever he came from––it would all come back once he left––he was certain. But this property would not let him leave just yet.

A cool stream of air dive-bombed around his neck and spun him around before it swooped up to an open window in a colonial gable on the mansion's roof, flapping the curtains there like a distress signal flag. Glancing up, James saw the silhouettes of two children duck out of sight. He slid his hand down his cheek bone. This explained why his dream of the boy the night before felt so real––because it was. If there were children here, then this woman was their mother, and this couple was hiding something––no––this estate was hiding something from him. Which went far deeper than a statue needing a kiss. He felt determined to get to the bottom of it. He heard scuffling in the gravel drive, ducked behind a line of hedges separating the carriage house from the back lawn. It was the same caretaker unchanged in every detail, pushing a wheelbarrow. Why not go to him for answers? No. He was not ready to confront him. From the kitchen window, someone observed him from behind a curtain. It was the woman. Why had she not left as she said? He was not afraid of her as much as he was the caretaker. She, he rather fancied. He would go to her for answers.

SHARON'S FOLLY

18

IT WAS TIME TO
ESCAPE AGAIN

It was time to escape again. Wait. Start over. At the beginning. No,
slightly forward. To that southwest corner of Connecticut before he
was a corrupted boy, where country clubs and white church steeples
dominated the landscape, swimming pools behind patrician gates
and stone terraces and green lawns with fountains and statues
and garden parties with dark skinned help from Bridgeport and
Norwalk. This is the angst into which he had been born (where
he must return if he were to move on). Always on the run from
this place—children from whining broods fighting for parents'
attention, who, more concerned with tennis whites on mauve clay,
swung their racquets with vengeance but in style, splashing rye
and gin at court side with coddled lips and blood shot eyes. Junior
Leaguers who showed off their razzmatazz, posing for photographs
to appear on society pages of local rags wearing cocktail dresses with
hemlines a dollar bill above the knee, naked pumps in pastel colored
espadrilles and beads with Jacqueline Kennedy hairdos married to
Yale Republicans—the William Buckley kind—there was no such
thing as New Republicans nor the Religious Right -- just working-
class Democrats with jobs in the trades -- electricians, plumbers,
those who installed garage doors, cleaned swimming pools, tuned

foreign autos, who laid bored housewives -- whose husbands took their fantasies onto the Pennsylvania Central to Grand Central on weekdays to work on Madison or Park or Wall Street, then afterwards conspire to hang out in their favorite bars like cattlemen to stare, with white devil eyes, at flirtatious temptations, mistresses to-be, arrogant and self-righteous in their knowledge they deserved it, slaving away as they did, in that sweat filled city of untucked button-downs and dangling dark ties wrinkled gray flannel suits all so that their better halves could spend summer days fawning over bronzed club pros from San Juan or Johannesburg giving them group lessons or private whatever they preferred while their little beasts commingled as competing tribes of savages like sharks after fishes at poolside, under the unwatchful eyes of lifeguards, themselves spoiled sons and daughters of wealth who only half-disciplined their charges as if that too were a game, who wore long hair and protested war when both still meant something--a time when the generations were alienated from each other for a reason. Never trust anyone over thirty. James was thirteen then, what did he know about anything?

☙ † ☙

Social Committee Co-chairs Martha Grant and Mrs. Whiteside sat at the entrance to the great hall of the Seaside Yacht and Country Club checking off members' names as they entered the receiving line for the Mid-Summer Eve pool party. Spotting a new face in the line, Mrs. Whiteside put her pencil down. "Who did Anne say he was?" she asked Martha. She stroked the pearls on her necklace.

The younger woman squared the register book on the velvet covered table in front of her. "He's Lawrence Revson, Mrs. Whiteside," she said, "You know, his family owns the largest cosmetic company in the world?"

"But they're Jewish," Mrs. Whiteside said, never taking her eyes off the guest.

"And his mother's a hundred percent WASP," Martha answered. "I heard he appeared out of nowhere now that he's the only heir to his family's fortune. Didn't you hear the news? His brothers were killed racing in the Grand Prix. Apparently, he's the last surviving son."

Mrs. Whiteside sat back in her chair. "A Jew, Martha. Who seconded his membership?" She squinted her eyes. "The Hallorans I bet it was—they're the closest thing to communists we have in this club. They swim in the buff at their home pool you know. And at their age, octogenarians. We should black ball them outright."

Martha pressed her hands down on the table. "The Hallorans are founding members of the club, Mrs. Whiteside! Besides, Lawrence Revson came with Anne, whose family donated more than their fair share to get our sailing program going again."

"Mrs. Whiteside looked down, shaking her head. "Poor Annie, a divorcee, such an embarrassment to her family. What is happening to our class, darling?"

19

HOUSEWIVES OF
FAIRFIELD COUNTY

Connecticut Country Club, Mid-Summer Eve, 1969

Sharon stabbed the green olive in her gin martini. Ate it while staring at the reflections of blood orange flames from tiki torches dancing off the waves in a sapphire-colored pool. For her it was as if the water were on fire.

She was hungry, having eaten little while dining earlier at her fiancé's parents', an expansive estate overlooking Long Island Sound. Not speaking unless spoken to, hair in a tight bun, Sharon sat motionless in her lime green dress across from George's mother, who dropped unflattering hints about her. His mother had insisted she was an unwise choice, a recent divorcee with small children. Her son should take a prim and proper mate from their social class instead. Sharon, his father the senator decided, would do just fine.

Standing with her in the crowded hall at the club was short and pudgy George. Laughing like a hyena, he threw leis around her neck, wearing a dozen of them over his dinner jacket. "Come on, Sharon, why look so sad? Mummy and Daddy adored you tonight. Oh God," he turned his head away, "guess who just came in? Big

Deal Neddy Merrill. I'm surprised he showed his face here tonight. Did you know his family's broke? Some shady financial deal he was involved in collapsed. Left them penniless. He had to pull his four girls out of Greens Farms Academy––no debutante balls in their future, I'm afraid. You know what else I heard?"

While George droned on, Sharon spotted her friend Anne Godwin in the receiving line. She had been Sharon's roommate at Vassar until she dropped out to marry a Yale man. A year later, Sharon did the same. They did not see each other again until two children later when they found themselves living in the same town. Anne sponsored Sharon and her husband for club membership and the two became fast friends again.

Anne's date had movie star looks and a charisma one could feel ten feet away. He was trim with an athletic physique, a special savoir fare dressed in his white dinner jacket. As she caught the stranger's stare, the Andy Williams hit "A Summer Place" played through the club sound system. *"There's a summer place, where it may rain or storm."* Sharon's heart skipped a beat. *"Yet I'm safe and warm."* Thinking of Anne's date, she closed her eyes and saw herself in his arms, *"For within that summer place your arms reach out to me…"* She imagined being transported to another time and place with this man, to a dance hall, wearing a swirling red dress. *"And my heart is free from all care."* The two danced in circles, her heels twinkling on the parquet, his cheek pressed against hers as they swayed to the crooner's voice. *"In your arms, in your arms."* He bowed her down, leaned over to kiss her lips––

"Sharon, are you listening?" George nudged her back to reality. "And Mother, who sits on the club finance committee, says he's way behind on their dues," he glanced across the room again, "oh dammit, Ned's spotted us. He's making his way over. Not even his mistress wants to see him anymore. Quick, let's make a break."

The two walked out onto the pool balcony where a spotlight moon sparkled the tips of ocean waves in view beyond the pool. Below, his buddies and their wives lounged at a reserved deck. They waved up to him to join them. George pulled on Sharon to follow down.

Sharon stamped a foot. "Let go of me! I'm not going down there to join your tight little social circle!"

Members nearby stared. With a calculated jerk, George grabbed Sharon's arm and squeezed it while he took her off to the side. In harsh whisper through gritted teeth, he leaned up to her ear. "Don't you dare shout or disagree with me again in public like that." She stood captive, unable to move. "I know you're a real knockout, but the women in our family are there to make their men look good, not the other way around. Marriage to me is the best thing you've got going for you right now, and if you don't start towing the line, it's over." Members passed by and he smiled at them. "You don't want that to happen to you now, do you, and by God, you certainly never want to have me for an enemy. Now, when I let go, lean over, laugh, and kiss me." When he let go, he left bruise marks on Sharon's arm. She did as she was told, just as Lawrence and Anne joined them.

"Why, it's Sharon and George!" Anne said, sensing something had happened. "I want to introduce you to my consort for the evening, Lawrence Revson who—"

"We've met already," Lawrence cut Anne off. He kept his eyes glued on Sharon.

Anne turned her head. "Really? When?"

"Anne," George said, "aren't you going to introduce me?"

She rolled her eyes. "This is Lawrence, George, you probably recognize the family name."

"Of course, I do." George shook Lawrence's hand up and down. "Our mothers have been friends for a long time. I don't recall there ever was a third son. What boarding school did you attend?"

At that moment, George's friends hollered up from below on the grass verge. "Excuse us," he said, grabbing Sharon's hand. She nodded a bewildered smile at Anne as George tugged her down the steps.

They hurried past splashing cocktails at poolside, bumping into chatty men in dinner jackets and women in dresses with knee high hemlines. George's prep school buddies and their wives sat drinking Tom Collins and Harvey Wall-Bangers, lighting fresh cigarettes before they finished the last, ashtrays full of the forgotten ones left burning. The wives stared at their husbands as they stared drunkenly at Sharon, the prettiest of them all.

Sharon once belonged to their clique. Her first summer at the club, she and a few other wives were invited to model for a Junior League fundraiser at Compo Beach, attired in elegant dress and pearls while poised atop jagged rocks surrounded by a plashing high tide. The shots made the pages of *LIFE* magazine, the caption below reading "The Sirens of Fairfield County." It was a scandal when it printed, but other club members chuckled, proud for their girls. It made them the popular set that summer and they became known as the rule-breakers. They disdained tradition, pushed acceptability within the staid old Yankee club to its limits. To the satisfaction of the more conservative members, the group was disbanded after a few of them divorced. Swinging with each other's spouses was the popular rumor.

Sharon sat through the wives' catty conversation. Who could afford divorce today? They laughed. The rich with money to spare, or the poor because they had none. But for the upper class, it meant a step down to a middle-class existence. Gone would be the shopping sprees on 5th Avenue, summer homes in the recessed mountains of New England or by the cold Atlantic along the coast. No more yachts sailed to the islands and the Cape. Winter trips to Bermuda would be a thing of the past. And no more boarding school for the children either, unless a benevolent grandparent came to the rescue. Without that divine intervention, their offspring might be forced to attend public school. Far reduced would be their chances for admittance to the Ivy League. But the worst deprivation, the women agreed, was the loss of that most coveted and precious of all status symbols––membership at the exclusive country club.

Sharon's messy divorce didn't stop them from talking about it right in front of her. Cloaked in un-clever innuendos, they never asked for her side of the story (she was the unfaithful one, it was rumored) –– not that she would have told them anyway. Their tone reached deep into her guts and eviscerated her, but she never showed it. She put down her drink and excused herself.

Alone, she walked the length of the pool to its far end, which met the edge of the golf course under a line of cedar trees, and began to cry. She wiped her tears away with the back of her hand, sniffled as she caught the salty scent of a sea breeze blowing across the fairways from the Sound. Breathing in, she cleared her head from a liquor buzz, pulled a cigarette from her purse. As she searched for matches, a shadow figure appeared and lit it; Anne's date. He waved out the match, causing its smoke to spiral upward. Sharon blew a jet of her own in the air, which formed a bluish halo above his head.

"You've been crying," he said. "Why such a sad face?"

"It's none of your business," Sharon said. "Where is Anne? You should be with her."

"Come now, Sharon, you knew the moment our eyes met, we connected. So strong it transported us to another world where we danced, you in that red ballroom dress. I never did give you that kiss."

Shocked he could know of her dream, she stumbled. He caught her from falling and held her, until she steadied herself. "Please, I'm all right," she said. She smoothed down her dress and patted her hair.

"Once I saw that clownishly dressed fiancé of yours," Lawrence said, "I knew there was a mismatch if I ever saw one. The senator's son who plans to run for office someday, who knows marrying someone as beautiful as you would be a real feather in his cap. But from my own astute observation, he will never satisfy you."

Sharon felt her back rise like a cat. "I'm not going to stand here and listen to you insult my fiancé," she said.

"Don't presume it's official. He hasn't announced publicly."

"He will. Soon."

"Then you must put a stop to it before you ruin your life. You think you're unhappy now..." Lawrence spotted Anne with George and his friends. The two were looking around for them. "Over here, Anne, we're over here!" Lawrence shouted, waving his hand above his head.

"What are you doing?" Sharon asked. She lowered his arm. It was too late; they began to head over.

"Listen, Sharon," he said, "I'm headed into the city to a club I own in Greenwich Village tonight, why don't you join me?"

"The Village, with George? Are you kidding?"

"He's not invited. Neither is Anne."

"You mean we'd go alone."

"Don't worry, darling, we'll be gone before they get here."

"I'm not going with you," she said. "You came tonight with Anne."

"Why, we're just friends, I made that very clear to her."

"What do you expect Anne to do, walk home?"

"Anne's a big girl, she can take care of herself. Besides, she has George to depend on. You know this isn't your crowd."

They glanced over at the other two approaching. "It's time to take a new path, Sharon," he said, "the one you're on is leading to a miserable dead end."

George and Anne broke through the crowd and now had a clear path.

"You must decide, now."

A man spilled two Beefeater Gibbons on Anne. As she and George turned their attention to that mishap, Sharon took hold of Lawrence's hand and pulled him around the other side of the pool, walking him as fast as she could into the clubhouse. George kept shouting Sharon's name, but she did not answer and the two vanished out of sight.

"Dammit," said George.

Anne gave a smirk. "I'm not the first woman she did that to, George, and you're not the first man."

"Yes," said George, pounding his chest with his fist, "but she did it to *me*, a senator's son. She did it to me!"

20

CLUB HEAVEN AND HELL

Greenwich Village, Manhattan, 1969

Lawrence accelerated down the Merritt Parkway in his grey Morgan coupe, breezing down the West Side Highway through every red light.

"Slow down, for Christ's sake. Lawrence, you're scaring me." Sharon pinned her scarf to her ears. "You're going to get ticketed."

"Not tonight." He winked at her. "I've friends in high places." He jetted across three lanes to exit on 14th Street and stopped at a light.

Sharon hunted for a cigarette in her purse. "What kind of crowd is this anyway?" She pressed the car lighter in, but it wouldn't stay. Lawrence punched it in for her.

"Have you heard of the feast of Bacchus, my darling? You'll enjoy yourself so thoroughly, you'll want to stay forever. But you won't be able. At dawn's first light, the club will disappear in a flash, leaving no trace it ever existed. Not even God himself can divine its happenings."

"I hope I don't regret this," she said. The lighter popped out. He held its glowing rings to her cigarette until it caught fire.

They pulled onto Minetta Lane alongside a windowless building which took up half the block. Not one streetlamp to cast a shadow. The only sign of life was a basement entrance where two dandies stood outfitted in eighteenth-century garb––powdered wigs and pumps, ruffled shirts, red velvet coats––original Schiaparelli. At the bottom of the stairs read a sign: Club Heaven & Hell. Butterflies in Sharon's stomach fluttered; she knew she was about to step into another world.

A man with a pencil thin mustache and gelled back hair greeted them. He wore a tuxedo with tails and chaps over patent leathers. Leaning up to Lawrence's ear, he whispered, then clicked his heels. "Monsieur, mademoiselle." He bowed and ushered them in. A coat-check girl, slim and tall and dirty blonde, stood behind a counter. White powdered skin, dark painted lips, the same height as Sharon except for five-inch heels. She wore white gloves with black top hat and tails, pink lace lingerie beneath an unbuttoned jacket. Sharon handed over her summer sweater; the woman stared at her outfit, pearls and hair in a tight bun. "Aren't you dressed for the occasion," the woman said with a British accent. "That is, if you're attending one of the Queen's teas." She grasped Sharon's hand, smiling between mischief and mirth. Sharon froze. "Don't worry, I'm not going to bite you." The woman bit her bottom lip. "Unless you want me to."

"Velvet darling," Lawrence said and patted her on the cheek, "don't you dare."

Lawrence led Sharon to a closed curtain. Behind it was an exit door to a stairwell. Inside an arrow pointed up the stairs to Club Heaven, another down to Club Hell. She stepped towards Heaven, but Lawrence steered her toward Hell. "Devil's lair first," he said. She leaned over the railing and peered into a lightless abyss. "The lowest levels of Club Hell," he said, "where not even Dante himself can adequately describe what goes on." She hesitated. Lawrence took her arm. "I promised you an adventure tonight."

They descended a floor into a wide dark corridor. The only light to guide their steps was that which seeped out from beneath an endless row of doors lined up on either side. "Behind each of these doors is a unique Club Hell," Lawrence said, "all in a different place and time, which cater to their member's particular ravishings."

"So, this is Hell Central," Sharon said, "an underworld below city streets. No wonder it looks like the New York subway." Sharon heard accordion music from behind one door squeezing out a tune. She cupped her ear to it. "I want to visit this one."

Lawrence rapped on the door with his knuckle and a man, the night porter, peeked out. Recognizing Lawrence, he let them in.

21

INTO THE INFERNO

Dust covered air ducts hung from the cavernous ceiling, blades of overhead fans propelled slowly. Walls the color of cell block blue splattered with blotches of missing plaster had pock marks etched in by bullet holes. Other spaces were covered by World War II posters in French recruiting for the Nazi party. Flicker of black and white film footage played shadows upon Sharon's face as she gazed upon them playing on the walls in endless silent loops––German troops marching in the takeover of Paris, juxtaposed over the fire-bombing of Dresden. Men and women dressed in military uniforms sat drinking at tables under fluttering fluorescent lights, nimbus clouds of cigar and cigarette smoke floating above their heads. Waiters and waitresses walked around in army trousers held up by thin suspenders around bare breasts. They looked gaunt and pale, their hair dyed the colors of a dirty rainbow, cut short and uneven as if by a pen knife. One waitress straddled a patron's lap, pressing a Billy club to his choking neck; another led a man on all fours around the beer-stained floor, yanking on a chain leash which made him gasp for breath.

The piano and accordion players wore pig's masks with red Cardinal caps. As they played, a tall slim woman meandered about the room whirling a truncheon while singing German Cabaret in a low voice. She wore an SS officer cap tilted down to her eyes. "Psst."

A man with a handlebar mustache drew Sharon's attention to a hat box on his table. When she leaned over, he lifted the cover. Inside was a severed man's head, his eyes open and looking at her. Sharon jerked back against a wall, hiding her eyes behind her purse. "Get me out of this place, Lawrence, before I vomit." He followed her out. She headed for the exit.

He stopped her. "It was never my design that you should witness a place like that." He held her shoulders. "Sometimes you must descend into hell before you can rise to heaven. Don't give up yet, we've one more place to visit, then we can head upstairs to finish our journey."

They soon came upon wide steps which led to a landing where double doors lit by floor lights awaited their entrance. Lawrence straightened his tie, took a deep breath, and pushed open. Inside Sharon saw red.

22

THE MASTER

They stepped into a lounge wallpapered in red velvet, like a 1920s speakeasy. Patrons dressed in tuxedos and evening dresses were seated around small square tables drinking alcohol from tea cups, served by busy waiters and waitresses who wore bowler hats and red jackets held closed by one button, the women in black miniskirts and go-go boots. They flitted in and out between tables speaking French, selling and lighting cigarettes, serving oysters and champagne. Sharon noted how young and nubile they appeared, smiling at their customers with merriment, turning away in disdain.

Across the room on a stage, a French cabaret singer sat on a tall stool with a plush curtain back drop, legs crossed in fishnet stockings. A spotlight fixed upon her as she whispered into a microphone a tune of Edith Piaf, sung like Liza Minnelli. Sharon clutched Lawrence's arm as he hurried her down the length of the bar to the farthest end. People stared as she rushed by.

"One drink and we go," he said. He sat her on a cushioned bar stool and motioned his hand to the bartender. "Adolph, scotch and soda for my friend please." As he turned to leave, Sharon grabbed his arm. "Don't worry, my love," he said. "I have some quick business to attend to. Then we'll head up to the club you've been waiting for all night. Adolph, keep her safe, won't you?" The bartender nodded. Taking a top shelf bottle, he poured her a drink.

Sharon thought about deserting Anne and George at the country club dance earlier that evening. What had she done? Dumping the senator's son to run off with a man she didn't know, her best friend's date no less, to come to a place like this? It was a dark side of the city she wanted no part of; but she knew she would enjoy it.

A white cane rapped on the bar and she tensed up. Straining her neck, she looked up to find a man who towered above her, dressed in pressed white linens with a Panama hat and pointed beard. He wore a patch over one eye and a white rose in his lapel.

"Tennessee Bourbon Adolph," the man said, "you know how I like it." He tipped his hat to Sharon. "Allow me to introduce myself, Memphis Topheles, Master Magician, at your service." He handed her his business card. "You may address me as the Master."

She held it in both hands. "This is blank," she said. He poked the card's surface with his long finger and his name appeared in gothic letters. He started to sit down on the empty stool besides Sharon.

"Please don't," she said. "This seat is taken. My friend will be back any minute." She looked straight ahead and sipped her drink.

"Have no fear," The Master said. "I'm your friend's business partner." Sharon nodded and he sat down with a grin like Santa Claus. He held out his lapel with the white rose and Sharon watched it turn red. As she examined its petals a black rose appeared in its place. She took a pack of Virginia Slims from her purse and searched for her lighter.

"May I?" The Master lit it with a flame on the tip of his white gloved finger.

She blew a jet stream of smoke at him. "You're full of tricks, aren't you?"

"You've no idea." He brought his hand to her ear and pulled out a gold coin. It had the seal of Rome and a picture of Pope Leo X. She raised her brows in doubt, pushing her glass towards the bartender for another drink.

"Allow me to take care of that. Adolph," the Master motioned with his hand, "a wine glass of clear crystal water please." He patted the bar top in front of Sharon. "Name a wine from any region of any year, a Chateau Lafite, Moulin-Touchais, Cheval Bordeaux Blanc—an eighteenth-century Burgundy perhaps? I will turn this water into that."

She tapped her ashes into a cigarette tray. "How about the best scotch on the planet?"

"On just this planet? Spirits you prefer. We'll settle for a specimen from the cellar of King James the Fourth."

He hovered his Panama above the goblet, then lifted. The water changed to a caramel color, the goblet into a heavy tumbler. Sharon sipped and almost choked. She felt a wave of heat flowing through her veins. "How old is this?" she asked. She saw the Master in double.

"Centuries," he said. The Master sat down and leaned on his cane. "See those young waitresses out there?" He pointed his finger out to the floor without lifting his hand from his cane. "Guess how old they are."

She shrugged. "Not yet legal?"

"As young as the day I rescued them from certain death in the war to end all wars."

Her eyes widened. "You mean World War I?"

He nodded.

"A lot of bull crap that is. Adolph, can I have another of these?" She held her glass high.

"Sorry," said the Master, lowering her arm gently. "One per customer. But Adolph can serve you anything else you like." Adolph poured her the same as before.

"So," she said, feeling the effects of the liquor, "you're saying those women haven't aged?"

He slapped his thigh. "Not one day of wrinkle added to their skin. Lives immortal. Surrounded by men attracted to them like moths drawn to fire. How easy they control them with their magnetic beauty."

Sharon shook her head. "That didn't work out too well for me." She pulled out another cigarette and lit it herself. "My looks have been my curse. Even if I had them back, it would be the same result," she nodded towards the waitresses, "like them, serving men forever."

"You far underestimate yourself, Sharon Peters." He pulled out an ivory hand mirror from inside his coat and held it up. She saw a reflection of herself with a youthful complexion. Puffiness in her cheeks gone, not one worry line in her forehead.

"Is that me? If only." She peered closer.

The Master leaned forward on his tall cane. "You don't become younger, but there is a way to look young forever." Sharon drooped a strand of loosened hair over her nose to see if the woman in the mirror would do the same. She did.

"This must be some promotion of face cream by Revlon," Sharon said, "created by Lawrence's uncle, Charlie Revson, which you are testing on me."

He shook his head. "No, this is not some beauty cream concocted by snake oil experts." He pointed at her reflection. "Who you see in there is the self you used to be and could be again."

The reflection of her younger self winked at her; she slammed the mirror down on the bar. "This has all been very entertaining,' she said, "but I'm not buying. I'll wait for my date to return, thank you." She lifted her drink. "Alone, if you don't mind."

The Master tossed his cane up and caught it. "Lawrence, my young protégé! I would wager you to be more beautiful than any of the women he has brought to me in decades. You have that same spunk and daring he prefers in all of them."

"Other women? Decades? How long have you known him?"

The Master pulled his stool in closer. "The question is not how long have I known Lawrence, rather, how long have I known you."

23

A GOOD OFFER

"First, little girl, I am going to tell you about your past. Your father was a naval doctor who you didn't know until you turned four and he returned from the Pacific War. You lived a comfortable life, the sort afforded to an officer of his rank, in the Presidio in San Francisco. He preferred you to your sister and mother and spoiled you like a princess, but when he got drunk, he could be as cruel with his tongue to you as he was to them. He died of alcoholism before you turned seven, and your mother, jealous for the love he gave you instead of her, treated you with such enmity that when you won a scholarship to a prestigious women's college back east, you jumped at the chance and never looked back."

The hair on Sharon's neck rose. How could he know so much about her childhood? Must've had access to her psychiatric records. She felt dizzy, his words intoxicated her more than the alcohol.

"Free from your mother's put-downs, and the nun's restrictive control at your all-girls high school, who punished you for even looking at boys, at college you discovered how beautiful and attractive you were to the opposite sex. Discovering physical pleasures for the first time in your life, you gave yourself to those who flattered you most and broke many hearts, until you had yours broken by an older man. You realized you were going about it all wrong. If you were to achieve the American dream of a respectable life with a husband and children behind a white picket fence, you needed to mend your loose ways, follow the path straight and narrow."

The Master finished his glass of bourbon filled with flames. He patted his lips in satisfaction and continued.

"Your friends introduced you to the refined world of the elite by teaching you the right manners and how to compose yourself so you could, like them, land a well-to-do husband of good breeding. You reigned in your wild lifestyle and your strategy paid off. Wielding the power over men your looks gave you, you attracted many suitors, learning not to accept the first proposal, but to hold out until you found the man that best fit your needs and desires; handsome, educated and ambitious, someone into whose life you could pour your own, erase that painful past you wished to forget."

Sharon pushed her drink away. "No, none of this is true." But there was doubt in her voice. All she could do to keep her balance was hold onto this steady flow of dark song as it poured into her through the medium of his hypnotic voice. She slid off her stool to leave before she was sucked in further.

The Master held up his hand. "I'm not finished. Sit."

Addicted to that voice, she obeyed and sat down again. She stared at his lips as they continued to pour forth his spell on her.

"That was your past. Now I'm going to tell you about your present," he said. "You thought you were safe and happy in your suburban bubble. Yet there still existed deep inside an emptiness you thought this new life would fill. Though you smiled at everyone on the outside, your inner sadness grew. You resented it when your husband insisted on starting a family immediately. You wanted to live as a socialite, not the cloistered life of a pregnant wife with morning sickness and cramps. After bearing two children by the age of twenty-five, your figure lost all its sex appeal for your husband. Once so insanely jealous of other men's stares, he no longer cared who he saw flirting with you, and began to spend longer nights at the office in the city. When he showed up late one evening from work, his dinner in the oven which you allowed to burn to a crisp, you spotted lipstick on his collar and confronted him, and when he denied everything, you punished him by your cold silence. The estrangement between the two of you began in earnest. You fought more, and as you tried to hold onto him tighter, he pulled away from you further. To regain his attention, you tried to play the role of the obedient wife, but that just made him bully you more, so that finally you realized you had chosen the wrong man, one who could be as abusive to you as your mother. He stopped loving you, his feelings grew closer to hatred. He tolerated you in his bed with silent disgust. The biggest insult was when he left for a younger woman."

Sharon covered her ears and closed her eyes. "Stop it! None of this is true! Lies!" But it was all in her head. She could not deny the grasp this overbearing man's words had over her. Now she must hear all. She gripped her glass in hopes of crushing it, while waiting for his river of words to drown her. The Master savored his success with a Cheshire grin.

"The veil began to lift from your eyes, and you admitted to yourself this new world into which you had stepped was an illusion. As the divorce proceeded, your uncertainty grew about your future in that quaint Connecticut bedroom community. Without a husband in which to invest your own identity, you returned to your old ways of drinking and began to sleep around. Your husband used your erratic behavior to wrest custody of your two children. Watching your social status evaporate, with no economic security, not knowing how to take care of yourself, you surrendered your free will to your mother's wishes. You resigned yourself to marry her choice of another self-centered, ill-tempered man, who would help her control you."

That dreaded emptiness in Sharon which remained vacuous for so long filled up with each phrase spoken, making her heart heavier, weighing it down. She felt worthless.

"Smile my lovely. That is only your present. Now I am going to paint for you a glorious future." The Master snapped his fingers and she blinked.

"What were you saying?" she asked.

"I was saying I am about to offer you the deal of a lifetime." Sharon's heart pounded. She felt as if she were about to be given a treasure chest of gold that would cost her nothing.

"What is it you want more than anything else in this world?" he asked.

Her face muscles relaxed, her eyes lit up, her tongue tasted pleasure. "If I could start over, I would never marry or have kids. I'd travel without a care in the world. I'd live as I pleased, never beholden to a man again."

"I can offer you all that and more." He patted the mirror. She picked it up and held it with two hands. The Master spun his Panama hat around on the bar top. Sharon followed its dizzying turns. "Come work for me and you will look like that rejuvenated self as part of a higher order, no longer a submissive housewife who dutifully obeys, but an empress who leads and commands. With your newfound confidence and looks, you'll help me recruit an army of able-bodied men who will fight with each other to be with you. Then you'll convince them to pledge their loyalty to me."

From his breast pocket he slipped out a scrolled document, laid it out on the bar placing a glass on each corner to keep it flat. "By signing this contract," he said, "you'll be able to travel the world wherever and whenever you choose."

She read down to the fine print and stopped. Her shoulders sagged; her gaze softened.

"Why so sullen?" the Master asked.

"My two children would grow old while I stayed young. If I am crazy enough to agree to this, promise me you'll wipe me from their memories."

"What, and relieve them of their pain and suffering from a mother's abandonment? Never. But I can wipe yours from remembering them."

"No," she said, "I want to feel my guilt forever."

The Master viewed Lawrence approaching. He put his finger to his lips. "He's coming back." While she looked over her shoulder, the Master folded up the contract and slipped it deep in her purse.

Lawrence patted the tops of Sharon's shoulders. "What happened, my darling? You look sweaty and pale." The Master was gone. Sharon slapped the bar with both hands.

"Adolph, where did he go?" Shrugging, the bartender took her glass and soaped it in the sink. She picked up the mirror, saw herself as a wrinkled old woman, then slapped it down on the bar top, cracking it. "This is one big snow over," she said. "Nothing but a dirty old man trying to pick me up."

"Who?" Lawrence asked.

"He sat right next to me." She gripped the bar edge. "Adolph, you served him a drink!" The bartender dried her glass with a towel.

"You look out of sorts," Lawrence said.

"Nothing is wrong with me," she said. "He sat right there and bought me a drink. He performed magic tricks and told me things about myself nobody could know––I smelled a faint wisp of sulfur about him the whole time."

Lawrence pulled on his ear lobe. "I'm afraid you just met my partner Memphis; I take it he did not make a good impression."

"Certified lunatic."

"Did he try that clever water into wine trick?" He clicked his tongue and shook his head. "Should have guessed he'd seek you out with me not present. I should never have told him you were here, crafty devil."

"What did you tell him about me?" she asked, adjusting her shoulder strap. "He seemed to know everything. It was Anne, wasn't it!"

He held up his hand as if swearing an oath. "She told me nothing, honor bright. Besides, what should I care to know about your past, we all have one."

"A real charlatan. He offered me to look like—" She pointed her purse at the Frauleins on the floor. "Like—" She picked up the cracked mirror and gazed at herself one last time. She saw her familiar face. "Ha! See, I haven't changed at all. There's no younger me. It was a cheap illusion. The things he said about me, lies."

"He's not such a bad tyrant," Lawrence said. "Misses the mark now and then but if he promises you something, he means it."

"Why do you defend him, what did he do for you to keep you so loyal?"

Lawrence patted his heart. "He saved my life in the war."

Sharon's eyes widened. "Vietnam?"

"Never mind that, it's boring." He nudged her elbow. "What's important is that you saw right through him. You can never tell what he's scheming, his motivations and reasons for doing anything cannot be fathomed."

Sharon rubbed her arms. "It's cold here. I'm through with this place. When are you taking me to heaven as promised? Or is this really all there is?"

"You can't have heaven without a hell." He stared at a ray of light bouncing off the varnished bar top. "A mod crowd for sure, full of life in a place where Memphis is not allowed to step."

She stood up. "Why not?"

"Because the Master once did God a very bad turn and didn't keep his end of a bargain." Lawrence knocked on the bar three times. "Now he is banished, from heaven, forever!"

Sharon's eyebrows lifted. "God in a bar?"

"Seeing is believing." He pointed up. "Club Heaven, where he rules at the end of a long banquet table surrounded by an entourage of hand-picked angels. Adolph, thanks, ol' sport."

Lawrence left him a gold coin. Sharon left hers too. The bartender slipped them into a slot, registering a double chink as they dropped in a box below.

Down a dark hallway, Lawrence escorted Sharon to the back of Club Hell where a light shone down upon them. Bathed in its yellow beam, they climbed a spiral staircase to heaven.

24

STAIRWAY TO HEAVEN

They reached a door at the top of the stairs and knocked. A slit opened, a pair of buggered eyes appeared. They were escorted into a black box theater with all the seats removed. Colorful neon crosses hung on wires from a baroque ceiling; a multicolored body of a plastic crucified Christ appeared to levitate out from one wall. The nature of the music playing was foreign to Sharon; it wasn't the Beatles, or Beach Boys, but something stranger––Lou Reed and The Velvet Underground. A woman greeted them, filming with a hand-held 8mm camera, Sharon had to block its light from her eyes. Lawrence led her up silver chrome stairs to a higher platform where a party was in full swing. There were so many people, it was hard to see how nobody fell off; there were no rails. People grabbed at the corners of her dress as she and Lawrence walked by.

"Look, it's Sandra Dee visiting an opium den," said one.

"Groovy, she's so square, she's in," said another.

They sat on plastic stools at a long white table positioned down the center of the room. Lights strobed within its interior.

"How do you like it?" Lawrence asked, shouting over the noise of the music.

"I wouldn't call it heaven!" she shouted back. "But certainly better than that hell."

She saw white dust snorted through dollar bills off tabletops.

Lawrence lifted two martinis from the tray of a passing waiter and handed one to Sharon.

"Memphis that old man, such a nuisance, isn't he?" he shouted.

"Yes, very weird." She lifted her drink to her lips. "You came just in time to rescue me." Flinging her head back, she downed the martini in one gulp.

"Harmless old crow really." Lawrence waved to some people he knew. "What other tricks did he perform?"

"Lame ones if you ask me," she said. "My eight-year-old could do better. The illusion with that mirror was incredible. I looked as young as before I had children, it gave me chills."

Sharon looked around at the crowd dressed in bright colorful outfits. All so young––had they drunk from the fountain of youth, too? At the end of the long banquet table where they sat was God holding court, God, who wore thick glasses, a turtleneck and leather vest, who kept pushing his bleached yellow hair out of his face with a complexion that was pinkish. He looked to Sharon like a mad man.

She squinted. "I know him."

"That man would be God," Lawrence said.

"That man is Andy Warhol," Sharon said.

"One and the same." Lawrence drained his martini.

Warhol whispered into the ears of one of his girls who started to walk towards them. Sharon recognized her as the one who took her sweater at the door. She touched Sharon on the shoulder. "Is this handsome devil bothering you?" she asked.

"Hello Velvet," Lawrence said with a grim smile, "off duty for the night?"

Velvet bent down to Sharon's eye level. "Lawrence, you're keeping her all to yourself, that's very selfish of you. Aren't you going to introduce her to me?"

Lawrence took a sip of his drink. "Why bother, Velvet, you're just a coat check girl."

Velvet stuck her tongue out at him. "There is a frolicking good time going on, yet you keep her glued to the chair, old goat. Jesus Christ up there would like to meet her. Let me borrow her for a while."

Velvet took the pin out of Sharon's bun, tussled her hair so that its ends dropped to their natural length. Together they looked like twins. "Take this," Velvet said, handing Sharon a flute of champagne, "and take these." She handed Sharon two small capsules. Sharon looked down in her hand. "For the journey we are about to take down the rabbit hole," Velvet said. Sharon's expression was like that of an uncorrupted girl about to enjoy doing something unbelievably bad.

"I'd think twice about taking those pills if I were you," Lawrence told her, sipping his fresh martini. Staring at him in defiance, Sharon downed them with a long swig, then placed the empty flute glass on the table and locked arms with Velvet.

"Velvet," Lawrence shook his finger at her, "promise me you'll behave. I need Sharon back before midnight, before she turns into a pumpkin and the cowboy lassos the moon."

The two joined the dance floor where everyone danced with nobody. Some wiggled wildly, others stood in a trance or stupor. On the walls and ceiling, black and white film clips of Edie Sedgewick flickered in endless loops; Edie laying naked on a bed with furs, Edie bouncing around a kitchen high as hell–, Edie hovelling in an abandoned dry pool in L.A. like a heroin addict. Sharon learned from others how to dance more than the twist and started to let go. Someone led her to a table and offered her a wafer from a jar which said EAT ME; so, she ate it. She was offered a tiny bottle of liquid which said DRINK ME; so, she drank it. She smoked marijuana for the first time in her life. Later Velvet took her to another room, and from there the rest of the night was a blur.

25

MORNING AFTER

The Revson Estate, Connecticut

Sharon woke atop gold silk sheets in a four-poster bed. Her head ached and she felt nauseous. She looked up at the reflection of a naked woman in a mirror above the bed, much like herself, except younger. She sat up with flashes of the night before——pool party, cabaret, psychedelic hall filled with light and energy. She remembered rolling around in a bed, not sure if it had been with a man, a woman, or both. Stills from the night before flipped through her mind: a head in a hat box, man growling on a chain, French cabaret with waitresses in bowler hats, bartender soaping a glass, the slap of a white cane; a yellow haired man they called God surrounded by models with names like Viva and Nicki. She pulled herself out of bed and walked about the room; floral wallpaper, antique bureau, Louis XIV chairs, windows covered by full length curtains around which light edged in. She lifted a silk sheen robe from the back of a chair and slipped it on, continuing to browse the room.

On the bureau an ivory plated hand mirror with a matching hairbrush of soft tentacles laid out on a lace doily. Beside it, a photo of a woman kneeling between two boys dressed as cowboys, their toy pistols in raised-up hands. She scuffled off to the bathroom to make herself new.

She found some aspirin and swallowed a few. Turned on the water in the tub, threw in bath crystals, dropped her robe. As she waited for the water to fill, she gazed in the mirror; that younger self again. Plush breasts, smooth skin, gone were the stretch marks and scars of childbirth. Her cheeks showed no indents, no dark shallow rings beneath her eyes. She leaned over the toilet and threw up. When the tub filled, she stepped into the bubbles and laid down. Under the water, her hands explored her body, curious to discover what else might have changed. She fell asleep.

She was aroused by knocks on the bathroom door. She grabbed the robe and wrapped it around herself. "Who is it?" she asked. No one answered. Dripping wet, she opened the door a crack and peeked out at a man rolling back the curtains to let in the light of day.

"Good morning, my love," Lawrence said. "How did you sleep?"

She smoothed her wet hair back and stepped out. "Not much, what time is it?"

He brushed his hands together to rid them of dust from the curtains. "Almost noon hour. I didn't think you'd ever wake. Dead to the world you were."

She held the robe closed at her neck. "Where am I?" she asked.

"My estate in Connecticut where we're safe."

"Safe, from what?" She sat on the bottom edge of the bed. "What happened to me last night?" She bowed her head to her knees. "I'm still dizzy."

He sat in an armchair in the darkest corner of the room. "You should have seen yourself, good girl gone wild." He whistled.

"I remember leaving the country club party with you, abandoning George and Anne at the club pool!" She hid her face in her hands. "God, I'm going to catch hell for this. I'll never be able to show myself there again."

Lawrence swung out of his chair. The late morning's sunlight beamed down upon him but cast no shadow. "Forget them, my love. Everybody you met last night adored you, they all wanted a piece."

Sharon stood and crossed into the sunlight, shook her fist at her own shadow. "I remember taking pills, smoking marijuana!"

He touched his finger against his nose. "And cocaine. You were naughty, but you enjoyed it."

"What else did I do?"

"I don't know," he said. "I wasn't with you every minute. As it got late, I tried my best to pull you away, and I almost succeeded, but then," he snapped his fingers, "that mischievous Velvet stole you away again. Very fond of you, she was. You two were inseparable."

She looked at the dance of light on the carpet. "Whose room am I in?"

Lawrence strolled over to the bureau, smoothed out wrinkles in the doily on top of it. "My mother's." He held the framed photo. "My two brothers with her when they were young. Sadly, neither are with us any longer. I doubt my mother will ever return to this place. Too many painful memories."

"I'm sorry," Sharon said. "It's not easy for a mother to lose her children."

He put down the frame. "Let's not talk about that, it's boring."

She pulled her robe tighter. "Where're my clothes?"

From around the room, he picked up loose garments. "You exchanged them with Velvet. Here's what you returned in." He held up the coat tails, lingerie, and ruby red high heels. He walked to a closet and opened the doors. "Now, let's get you dressed in something presentable."

The dresses and shoes all appeared to be for a woman her size. "Where did you get these?" she asked. She felt the fabric between fingers. "They're not the sort an old woman wears. I see, clothes left behind by your high couture girlfriends you invite home. What did you do with my purse?" He motioned her towards a side table. She took out a box of Virginia Slims and lit one, exhaling the first puff. She gazed into a long mirror at her younger self. "Is that really me?"

"One hundred percent. Younger than when you walked into the club last night."

"I don't know how it's done," she put down the cigarette and opened her robe to the reflection, "but I like it." She turned to see her front and back. "How long before it wears off?"

"It doesn't have to, if you're willing."

"Willing?"

Lawrence clasped his hands together and stretched his arms out. "This very evening we'll fly to Europe where we'll join my friends. We'll have the time of our lives; gamble in Monaco, lie on beaches in the French Riviera, ride camels in Morocco. All this you'll enjoy with the added pleasure of looking as young and beautiful as you see yourself now."

"Wait a minute." Sharon returned to the bed and looked up at the kinky mirror. She glanced at the wardrobe with the perfectly sized outfits. "I'm not buying it." she said. "This little scheme of yours, tricking gullible women to go along with your plan, believing if they do they will look young again. Then you whisk them off around the world to disappear and never be heard from again."

Lawrence shook his finger in her direction. "That's not the way this works."

Sharon blew smoke in the air. "What woman wouldn't sell her soul to the devil to remain young forever?" She set her cigarette down. "And for those who turn down this offer? What happens to them?"

Lawrence shrugged his shoulders. "They return back to their dull ugly lives. Few rarely do turn this offer down though. Living out the rest of one's life with a fresh new body and new face most find too valuable to resist."

"I could, resist." Sharon marched to the bathroom where she grabbed a towel and handed it to Lawrence. "Here, dry my hair." She sat down at a vanity table and gazed with fascination at a guild-edged box filled with gem studded pendants, bracelets, necklaces and other jewels. "Your mother's?" she asked. "May I?" She scavenged through and picked out a heavy emerald and gold necklace studded with diamonds. She held it up to her neck. "This is stunning," she said, "must be worth a fortune, if it's real."

"From the treasures of royalty," he said, "given to my mother by her father as a present on her eighteenth birthday." He whispered to her in the mirror. "Once belonged to Marie Antoinette."

Sharon looked at his reflection with a grim lip.

"It's true," he said, "allow me." He fastened its clasp behind her neck. "It is stunning," he said, "especially on you."

"I couldn't wear this." She unclasped it and laid it down. "It's your mother's, she'd be crazy to part with it." She looked in the vanity and applied some lipstick from her purse. "If I go with you, will I always look like this?" She puckered her lips.

Lawrence stared at her in the mirror. "In the flesh."

She put the lipstick back in her purse. "Your partner scared me last night, the things he knew about me. I don't trust him, Lawrence, and you shouldn't either."

He crossed his arms. "I never have and never will."

She lifted her dying cigarette, held it between her lips and walked to the closet to browse through more clothes. She pressed an outfit to her body before the dressing mirror. Lawrence titled his head and gazed. "You cut a slim figure for that one. You'll fit right in with the jet set."

She hung the dress back up and selected another which she threw on the bed. She snuffed her cigarette out in an ashtray. "Please turn around, I don't care what you may or may not have seen of me last night." She slipped on the dress. "Zip me please." He zipped. She walked to the mirror. "This'll do." Lawrence applauded her choice. She chose a pair of espadrilles and tried them on. They fit as perfect as Cinderella's glass slipper.

"You're in bad company with his kind, Lawrence. If I was within his orbit, I'd see as little of him as possible." She clipped a burette in her hair. "If I were left alone with him for one minute, I'm afraid he'd twist things around and before you knew it, I'd dutifully do all the tasks he asks of me."

Lawrence placed his hands on her shoulders. "I'm no slave working for him, why should you be?"

"I'd regret it," she licked the end of her finger, "or enjoy it too much." She tucked her hair behind her ears and stepped towards the door with her purse.

"Okay," she said, "I'm ready."

"To come fly with me?"

"Ready for you to take me home." She held her purse down by her waist and smiled. "You don't really expect me to believe any of this is true, do you?"

He opened the door and bowed like a gentleman. Standing in the doorway, he watched her descend the back stairs.

26

SECOND THOUGHTS

Down in the kitchen coffee percolated, a blue china bowl of eggs waited to be whisked, a glass pitcher of orange juice with ice to be poured. Sharon reached in her purse for another cigarette. As she scrounged around for a lighter, she discovered the folded up scroll the Master had presented to her the night before. She heard Lawrence skipping down the stairs and slipped it back in her purse snapping it shut. She held her cigarette up and he lit it for her.

"Before you go," Lawrence said, directing her attention to the breakfast, "won't you have something to eat first?"

"No thanks." She stared at a bottle of vodka on the counter and sat down at the kitchen table. "But I'll have a drink."

Lawrence poured the vodka into the pitcher of orange juice and stirred. He filled a glass and reached over the table to hand it to her. She put her cigarette down in an ashtray, accepting the glass. She thought about the contract in her purse. Leaning back in her chair, she ran her fingers down her arms. "How does he do it, Lawrence? Not one sunspot or bump."

"They'll return the moment you step foot out of here. Poof!" Lawrence gestured an explosion with his fingers. "Back to that old worn self again." He sat down in the chair sideways opposite her. "You're only getting older, Sharon."

"And no wiser." She took a long sip of her drink. "Why do you associate with him, Lawrence?" she asked.

He scratched behind his neck. "Who, Memphis? Well for one thing, he's made me a rich man."

She sucked on an ice cube from her glass. "What do you need his money for?" she said. "The Revsons are multi-millionaires, one of the richest families in the country."

He looked at the back of his fingernails. "Doing business with him keeps me free from family control. I like it that way."

"You don't need him, Lawrence, you could live very well on your own. We could." She took a puff on her cigarette and watched the smoke climb.

He looked up, "You said we."

"Let's get something straight." She leaned over the table towards him. "I'll take this crazy trip with you as long as I don't ever have to see that partner of yours again." She sat back. "Take us some place where he'll never find us."

He laughed. "You don't accept a gift from Memphis without giving something in return. He'd never let you get away with it. He'd never stop looking for us. He'd always be waiting outside the gates of this estate when we returned."

Sharon stood, leaving her cigarette burning in the ashtray. Her heart sped up its rhythm. She took a deep long breath. "Then let's never come back."

Lawrence stood up erect. "What about your children?" he asked.

A cool breeze flowed through the window above the sink and circled them before exiting through the backscreen door. Sharon followed it, walking to the porch window where she looked out at the back lawn. Dogwood trees in summer bloom lined the ivy-covered wall which separated the estate from its fields to the west. A whip-poor-will cooed.

Lawrence came up behind her. "You didn't answer me," he said. He placed his arms around her midriff. She lifted her hand and stroked his cheek, never taking her eyes off the idyllic view. Such a calming place. She could get used to living here.

He whispered in her ear. "Sharon, something happened to me when we danced together last night in our own world. No woman ever stirred my heart and imagination like you. If you're willing to come away with me and forget your world then," he paused as if frozen in time, "then I'm willing to do the same with Memphis. I'll guarantee you'll never be subjected to his control ever."

She gripped his arm around her waist. "It will be just us?"

"Just us."

"Looking as we do now, forever?"

"Forever."

"Then I'll cut my ties with the world too."

She turned around and rested her head on his chest.

"We'll be the perfect pair, you and I," he said, stroking her hair. "We'll travel to exotic lands where he'll never find us––Thailand, Polynesia, the undiscovered islands of Fiji. Then we'll sneak back here where you'll always be safe from the likes of him."

She leaned back on him and looked over the west wall. "I've always wanted to go to India," she said.

"I have friends who live beneath the Taj Mahal who would hide us."

She turned her head up to his eyes. "They're like you––us, I mean?"

"They've kept hidden long before you and I were born."

She stroked his hair. "What do we do when we just want to grow old again?"

He felt the smoothness of her neck. "I suppose one could make another deal with Memphis, but God knows the price he'd exact."

"Maybe I will wish to change back someday. But not yet." She danced past Lawrence into the center of the kitchen. "For now I'm going to enjoy this!" She hugged herself and twirled around. "Now, take me home so I can pack." She stepped to the porch door and opened it. He shut it.

"I need to go home for clothes."

"We'll buy you a new wardrobe wherever we go."

"I need my passport."

"You don't need a passport the way we're going to travel."

"Then I need to leave a note for my children, explain why I'm doing this."

"What for?" he asked. "I've no intention of telegraphing my intentions to Memphis. We're leaving. Now take my hand."

She opened the porch door to leave. The wind breezed in and flapped papers off a hall table.

"Don't fight this, Sharon. I'm putting a lot on the line for you."

She stood silent.

"Once you step foot out of this place, you'll lose your youthful appearance forever."

"Lawrence, I won't take more than a minute, I promise."

"That's not the way it works. If you step back into your world, you'll return to your old self and this estate will become a boarded up mansion ready to be sold. You'll never see me again."

"That's crazy," she said, lifting her purse and pointing it at him. "Somehow, you pulled me into believing this was all true. If you're not going to come, then give me the car keys and I'll drive myself." He held up her palm, taking the keys from his pocket and dabbling them in the air above. Then he dropped them in, wrapping her fingers around them. She walked down the porch steps. "You're really not coming?"

He leaned against the door jam and crossed his arms. "There's a great life waiting for us in my world, Sharon. Remember I'd be giving up just as much as you are."

She held her chin up at him.

"Well then," he said. He watched as she followed the grey gravel path to the carriage house, looking back just once. He did not follow.

27

SHARON MUST DECIDE

She took in the panorama of the place. A clear blue sky, vibrant green trees. The wind blew gently in the heat of the day. What was making her shiver? The place was starting to cast its spell. She felt lonely with the absence of people. As big as it was, Lawrence lived here alone. Who was he really? That master magician partner of his, who offered her eternal youth, she just had to sign a piece of paper. Ridiculous. The grey Morgan coupe was parked facing down the drive, engine humming. She stepped into its low-lying seat and felt the vibration throughout her body. She started to back up when she caught in the rearview mirror the reflection of a man standing and slammed on the brakes. It was the gardener in overalls and floppy hat, holding a rifle. He glared at her as if she were an unwanted trespasser. She put the car in gear and drove down the drive without a word or apology for almost hitting him.

At the front gate she peered out at the road. To where would it lead? To a home she couldn't afford in a wealthy town; a custody battle she was going to lose in a world she had little confidence she could survive in without a man. A second marriage for love was not practical, she agreed with her mother on that. But marry the senator's son, to whom she felt no attraction? Whose irritating personality and unpredictable temper she must put up with? It would place her closer to the top of the social ladder again. No.

Truth was that George path closed the moment she blew him off and left the party with Lawrence. If she drove out now, she'd be shunned at the club and must bear the acid criticism of her mother. She'd drink more when she felt depressed and become more depressed when she realized how much she was drinking. No. What waited for her out there were the consequences of bad decisions. She could run away to the city, get a job modeling. No. She was too old for that. Her best option was to stay with Lawrence and see where that would lead. Last night was new and exotic; she loved it, though she couldn't remember it all. Yes. Enjoy the type of life she always dreamed of, yes, enjoy the pleasures her body and spirit craved. Lawrence Revson from a renowned international family would remain her guardian angel whom she could trust to put up with her impulsive behaviors and excesses, keep her safe from herself, and—he promised—from the Master. Perhaps her white knight was not out there waiting to rescue her, he was in here. The kids were with their father until the Fourth of July. Nobody would miss her until then. If she were to run away from all responsibility, now would be the time. She felt a pang in her heart. Timmy her son would understand why she did it, he alone knew her suffering. He would watch over his sister in her absence. She took a deep breath. The mirror lay in the seat beside her. She gazed in at her younger self. What a trip if this youthful illusion were true, how stimulating it would be. Imagine, thirty years from now, a body free of cellulose, unblemished skin, no wrinkles or varicose veins--stay young forever--just like those waitresses in hell. She unclasped her purse and removed the contract, holding it in both hands. Return to the estate, her heart demanded. No, don't, it's too high a price to pay, her inner self warned. She ignored its wisdom as she had her whole life, turned the car around and headed back in.

THE REVSON ESTATE

ALL TOGETHER NOW

28

YOUNG MOTHER
AND CHILDREN

James marched up the front steps of the estate below the shaded portico and rapped the lion's head knocker, its golden mane shaped like the flames of a blazing sun. The woman looked through the side window.

"Did you leave something behind?" she asked.

He looked through the glass. "No, I need to ask you something."

She unlocked the portly door, which sounded as if it hadn't been opened in years, opened it a sliver to allow the morning sunlight carve out a flattering slice of her figure. She stood at an angle, lock of fine blonde hair dangling in one eye. She smiled but then quenched it; responded with a grimace instead.

"What is it you want? Why haven't you left?" she asked.

"Why haven't you? Do you have a boy?" He stared at her through the breach.

She shooed him down onto the lawn before she stepped out and closed the door. "What are you talking about?"

He wiped sweat from his forehead. "There was a boy who came to visit me last night." He rubbed the sweat on his pants. "He called me Jimbo. Only my friends call me that. Do you have a son?"

Two children burst out the door before the woman could stop

them. A boy with straight brown hair over his ears screeched to a halt on the landing above James. A girl smaller and younger with dimpled cheeks and spring-like curls stared at him with one finger in her mouth. The woman yanked both children back. They resisted but her strength was too much, and she shoved them inside. They cried to be let out. James lifted one foot onto the first step when she warned him not to come any further.

"You don't have to keep them locked up like little beasts on account of me," he said. "I assume they're yours?"

"Sometimes I wish they weren't," she said. She struggled to hold the door closed as the children struggled to open it.

"That's the boy I was telling you about. He told me I must help you get out of here, escape––from this place."

"Help us?" the woman said, holding the doorknob with both hands. "We're not prisoners."

She lost her grip, and the children flew out. James backed up falling onto the bouncy grass where he drowned in the children's chatter, each pulling on one of his arms to lift him while continuing their nervous babble. A chill shot down his spine. "Wait a minute." He climbed to his feet and pointed at them. "You're Timmy and Sally. My god," he looked up at their mother on the top landing, "it's you."

Sharon darted like a deer to get inside, but he got to the door first and blocked her.

"Tell me who you are, tell me who you are really," he said.

"Let go of me!" she shouted. "Out of my way!"

She thrust her elbow in his side and he buckled, grabbing her down. She fell on top and cried in pain. He rolled over and sat up, reaching out his hand to help her.

"Don't touch me." She stood up by her own strength. "I'm used to nursing my own bruises." She hobbled to the top step and sat.

"It is you," James said, his body tingling. He took an agile stand a few steps below. "You look exactly as you did years ago, you all do, how is this possible?"

"This was not supposed to happen like this," the woman said, rubbing her ankle. "You were supposed to leave. You're trespassing. Now go. Please."

Clasping his hands to the back of his neck, James squeezed his head between forearms as if in a vice. He walked in a daze down the expansive sloping lawn; the gravel driveway to the left, dense woods to the right. At the bottom, tennis courts in a deep wood which hid the property from the road and the outside world. He looked up at the surrounding trees, saw their tops swirling, twirling, whirling, hearing nothing but the twitter of birds bickering from their highest perches. He stumbled forward as if drunk, the summer heat pulsating at his temples, walked through a dense blanket of humidity until he reached a large circular flower bed at the lawn's center. Not paying attention, he walked into the middle of it and stopped. Down beneath his feet were flowers woven together in broad bands of color like a well-knit quilt: vibrant violets, phosphorescent blues, fuchsia reds; silky yellows, pillowy whites, burning oranges. Bumblebees zagged, hummingbirds darted, a dragonfly levitated. A sundial rested at its center, the triangular point in the middle of its face broken off––that piece lay flat under his shoe. He looked back at the estate––so well preserved after it was purported to have burned down to the ground; how can any of this be?

Kneeling in the flowers, he yanked out handfuls without being conscious of it, pressing some to his nose. He sniffed their aroma, not registering that the flowers were odorless, so absorbed he was in her, the youngest and prettiest of all his mother's friends. Sharon Peters. Why wasn't she an old woman by now? They had an affinity for each other, she never treated him like a child. For his tenth birthday, she gave him a set of Sherlock Holmes mysteries. After her divorce, Mrs. Peters had a reputation for being one of the hottest divorcees in town. One year over thirty, she was an easy catalyst who could ignite all men's sexual desires. His heart had thumped whenever he was in her presence, his throat turned dry when she spoke. She stirred in him the same urges he felt when he climbed the statue that spring long ago. Except with her those urges exploded.

She dated a lot and for that needed a dependable babysitter, one she could trust. She chose James.

The last night he saw her was in the late spring of 1969 before he and his mother moved to Boston. She asked him to spend the night, knowing she would arrive home late. After he tucked the children in bed, he watched an episode of *Love American Style*, then looked for something to do. He entered her bedroom and snooped around. In her bathroom he sprayed perfume, imagined what it would be like to see her in the shower. In her closet he inspected dresses and shoes, could hear her in clacking heels. He peered into her top bureau drawer and closed his eyes, smelling the fresh washed scent of her underwear and blouses. Hidden in a lower drawer he found a copy of the *The Joy of Sex*, with its charcoal sketches of men and women exploring each other's hairy naked bodies. He imagined seeing Mrs. Peters that way, and in this state slept under her silken sheets. Until she returned and found him in her bed.

Her. Here. Now. Why? Was he sent here to relive that night she stole away his youth? This place makes no sense, of course it's not real. More a lucid dream. Or maybe because of injuries sustained in the accident he lay comatose in a hospital, fragmented memories floating around in his brain to keep him alive. Perhaps he was already dead, transported somewhere between heaven and hell, a ghost, as the others here must be. This his one unresolved life issue he needs make peace with to move on in the nether world. He watched Mrs. Peters order the children back inside, then limp on her ankle down the lawn toward him. Her flowery scent caught in his sweaty nostrils. As she approached the flower ring, he stepped out the opposite side. She looked down at the trampled flowers.

"You've made a serious mess here," she said.

"It is you," he said. He walked around to where she stood but did not come full circle, keeping distance between them.

"I'm not dreaming this, am I?" he said.

"No, you're not," she said.

"And I'm not dead?"

"Of course not. Nothing else may be here, but we are real.

That is Sally and that is Timmy. All the same, except nothing has changed, just as the last time you saw us before you and your mom moved away."

His throat constricted with shortness of breath. "Yesterday. You told me; I was. Accident. Today I wake--no pain--how is this?" He bent over and rested his hands on his knees, "That caretaker, he too. The same. Too. All of you. The same. Only I--seem. Changed."

She placed her hand on his back. "Breathe slow, breathe deep."

A pause, a silence, a blank thought. He stood and gazed at her with renewed scrutiny; arms, face, not one wrinkle for a woman five-years younger than his mother. He touched the back of his hand to her cheek--at his touch she pulled away—as if she'd just been shocked. She picked up the decapitated heads of flowers and twisted them apart.

"When did you know it was me?" he asked.

"Immediately," she said, dropping the flowers.

"I feel so lost," he said.

"We're the ones who are lost here, James, not you."

He pointed towards the mansion. "That man, your husband—"

She lifted her hand. "He's not my husband."

He wiped his brow. "He said you're his wife."

She wiped her brow. "He likes to act as if I am. Think twice before making a deal with the devil," she said. "You may just get what you asked for."

James felt his chest rise. "Why did your--partner--try to run me over?"

"Jealousy," she said, throwing her head back. "He thought you were an old lover of mine." They stared at each other. Around them the wind rustled the green summer leaves, revealing their backsides the color of mint blue.

"You're shaking," she said.

"I'll be all right," he said. "I just need some time to figure this out. Seeing you again, just as you were back then. Except now you're younger than me." He wondered if he should say something more about their sexual encounter. He chose to stay silent.

The caretaker approached from the carriage house. "Come James." She held his shoulder and pushed. "You've had a terrible accident, now you're okay. It's time for you to go."

"I'm not ready to leave," he said. "Not until I understand what's going on. Why are you here anyway? Why am I? Why are we?"

"Never mind," she said, staring at the approaching man, "we need to get you off the grounds." She pushed him in the direction of the estate. He walked as if in a trance.

"How can I leave?" he said. "I can remember parts of my past, but don't know where I came from, much less where I'm going! I need to stay and figure this all out."

"I'm sure once you step out of the bounds of this place, it will all come back to you, now come, hurry."

He trudged forward, then stopped. "You need my help."

She stopped and looked up in the air. "Every time someone tries to help, they make things worse. Let's get going." The gardener reached the flower bed. "Dammit," she said. "He's here. Stay quiet. Let me do the talking."

A clatter banged. The man on the far side dropped his bucket of garden tools on the ground while holding a hoe over his shoulder. He looked at the flowers in need of repair and shook his head.

"Even if we could leave together," Sharon said to James, not taking her eyes off the old man, "we would never make it."

"Why not?" James asked. "What's to stop us?"

"Not what," she said. "Who. Him."

29

THE CARETAKER

That brittle tin man. James stiffened at the sight of him. Dressed in mud-covered boots, faded blue coveralls, canvas hat with a hoe over his shoulder instead of a rifle. For James and his friends, the caretaker symbolized a foreboding adult will. Incarnation of the boogieman, wrinkled guardian of the gardens who took neighborhood children that strayed too far on the property into the barn, where they imagined he did ungodly things like blow off a limb or chop off a head. James and his friends could laugh and make fun of him from a distance, but none of them as young boys ever thought to unmask the enemy up close, find out what sort of human being he was really—just an old man with bad aim.

The man walked up to Sharon about to say something when Sharon addressed him first. She curled her arm in James'. "Eugene, this is Mr. Harris, our latest guest." Eugene remained silent. "He's still not well from the accident, Eugene. He's lost his bearings and we're responsible. He's going to need to stay a little longer." The old man remained tight-lipped. "Eugene, he knows what's going on." Eugene took off his hat, rubbed his jaw and chin with one hand. "Don't worry, Eugene, we can hide him."

"Hide me?" James eyebrows lifted at the thought.

"Lawrence will be back soon, Eugene. Then he's going on a long trip. When he leaves our guest can come out and leave on his own when he's ready. Please Eugene, although I hardly care at this point if you mind or not." She balled her hands into fists at her side. "Eugene, I'm asking as kindly as I can, do not say anything to Lawrence. Think of the children. Please."

Eugene returned his hat to his head, left his bucket of tools where they lay on the grass. He walked back to the carriage house in even step without having uttered one word.

"Sorry about your garden, sir," James said to the man. But he was out of hearing distance.

30

TO GO OR TO STAY

Timmy and Sally meandered out to their mother from the front steps as she and James walked across the lawn. "What's Eugene gonna do?" the boy asked. "Is he gonna tell Lawrence James hasn't left?"

"I don't know Timmy," she said, "I've never trusted that man. He's always been a loner."

"He didn't say much. He didn't say anything," James said.

"I'm always careful what I say around him. He was a bootlegger once you know."

They reached the circle of the drive. Sharon pointed down the driveway. "Now please go."

"Why? You just said—"

"I just said to see what kind of reaction I could get. It's too dangerous." She looked at his chest and straightened out his shirt lapels, picking off a few white flower petals stuck to the sweat of his cotton shirt like daintily pinned medals. "Lawrence was proud of the way he handled you," she said. "But if Eugene tells him you're here—"

James placed his hands on the children's shoulders. "Then let's leave together, before he returns."

She shook her head.

"Do you want to be free or not? Let's go." She wouldn't budge.

149

"What's wrong with you?"

Sharon stamped the gravel. "We can't leave!" She strode away and hugged herself in her arms, squeezed the bridge of her nose. Tears dripped down from her eyes and wetted her cheeks. Sally wrapped her arms around her mother's waist. Timmy stood on her other side taking her hand. Sharon placed her hand on the girl's head, kissed the boy on top of his. She wiped her eyes and sniffled. She nodded toward the drive.

"Timmy. Show James the border of the property with the road down by the front gate. Show him why we can't leave. Tell him everything and don't take forever, Lawrence will be back soon."

Timmy took James' hand and led him down the drive. Sharon took Sally's hand and led her to the estate. "Come Sally," she said, "we have a meal to prepare for our trespasser, if he stays. Until the tasteless food convinces him to leave otherwise."

"But mommy, wad' about La'wence?" Sally asked. "Won't he be mad if he finds him 'till heah?"

"I'll handle Lawrence," she said. "James could be our last chance. But first he must know everything."

31

CAUGHT IN A LOOP

James and Timmy walked down the drive, their shoes crushing the gravel with each step. As they moved, the sky narrowed between the treetops.

"Gee Jimbo, you look a lot older than I remember," the boy said, "your face is like canvas."

"And you don't look a day over eight years, kiddo."

"Hey!" Timmy shook his fist. "I'm not so many years younger than you."

"Let's not bring up the subject of age anymore, shall we?"

Timmy picked up a handful of gravel and sprayed it in the woods. His unreleased bounding energy made James think of a tightly wound pocket watch which never missed a tick but had no hands. Longing to grow up, the boy was powerless to move the hands forward.

"What's it like to live here?" James asked.

Timmy picked up a brittle branch. "It must be like when you're dead." He broke it over his knee, whisked the pieces into the woods. "I'm alive but I'm not. I'm growing on the inside, but nothing grows on the outside."

James grabbed a branch and tried snapping it over his knee, but it was too thick. He held his leg in pain. "That didn't feel like I'm dreaming," he said, hobbling. He wiped his forehead with his sleeve. "Jesus, it's hot here."

"That's because it's always summer," Timmy said. "There's no school, which is good. But the worst part about being stuck here are the people you miss. Like my father."

James thought of his own father. He didn't know how to comfort the boy. They trudged along.

"What do you do with all your free time?" James asked.

"I like to go exploring," Timmy said. He fixed his gaze upon some unseen land. "I pretend I'm in Sherwood Forest with Robin Hood or on an island with the Wild Things." He waved an imaginary sword. "Or I'm a valiant knight like Ivanhoe."

James raised his arm as if holding a medieval sword. "And you're waiting for King Richard to return to claim his rightful throne from his evil brother. Fie on Justice!" Timmy handed James a stick and the two battled. The boy made as if he stabbed James in the heart, who then keeled over. They laughed and tossed away their wooden weapons.

When they reached the bend in the drive, Timmy made a pirate's spyglass with his hands and peered through it at the gate entrance. "What I like to dream about is the sea," he said, collapsing the imaginary spyglass. "My father was going to let me sail solo this summer. I can handle a rudder, hug the wind on a beat, tack and come about by myself, even let out a spinnaker, jive ho! I know my knots too, the half hitch, the cleat hitch, and—" he stepped into the woods, "bowline, watch." He pulled a piece of clothesline from his pocket and formed a loop at one end, holding loose the other. "The rabbit hops around the tree and down the hole." He threw the loop around the other rope end and twisted it over. Out came a tied bowline. He lassoed the top of a white birch sapling and bent it down in a flexible arch. He let go; the sapling sprung back to life. Timmy held out his chest. He untied the rope and shoved it back in his pocket.

"You know what I'm going to do the day we get out of here? I'm gonna join the merchant marines, then build my own boat and sail away. I'll disappear, never setting foot on the mainland again."

Just then, something in the woods caught Timmy's eye. "Look, that white shed, see? Something smells in there. Eugene won't go near it so neither do I."

James stared at the shed. "Why doesn't Eugene help your mother more?"

"He prefers to keep to himself in his gardens," the boy said, "he won't even eat with us."

"He shouldn't cause her so much grief," James said.

"He doesn't mean anything by it. I think he's afraid of this place as much as we are. Lawrence has nothing on him, he can walk out anytime he wants. But he doesn't."

"Why not?"

The hollow knock of a lone woodpecker echoed in the woods.

"Cuz he's old," Timmy said. "If he leaves and joins the world of time, he will die."

They reached the end of the drive. "I still don't understand," James said. "If Eugene can walk out," he opened the entrance gate, "what's stopping you from doing the same?"

The boy stepped into the ferns growing by the stonewall which separated the property from the road. He laid his arms on top and nestled his chin on his hands. "Can't do it."

"Of course you can." James tapped his temple. "It's a mental mind game. Watch."

Before he could take one step out the gate, Timmy tackled him.

"Don't do that again, James, please I'm begging you!"

"What are you getting so excited about?" James said. They stood up, brushing the dirt off their clothes.

"If you walked out, you'd return to the time and place you came from." The boy curled his fists. "Nobody who's left has ever come back. You'd be just another trespasser who didn't stay."

"There've been others?" James asked.

Timmy nodded. "Lawrence says they come to steal my mother away."

"That's why he tried to run me over."

"Listen!" The boy pointed at a navy blue and white Chrysler as it passed. It had the shield of the town police department detailed on its side. Timmy swung on top of the wall and gave the finger to a long-haired cop driving, who gave one right back. "Did you see that?"

Timmy jumped off the wall. "Every day he passes, I give him the finger. You'd think he'd stop to yell at me or something and then I could ask for help. But he never does stop, just fingers me back every time." The boy walked to the gate, held the bars as if looking out from a prison. "Now and then a driver in a car model I don't recognize sees me. Those are the ones I wave down. They turn into the property to see what I'm fussing about. I convince them to drive in. But Gene gets gruff, tells 'em they're trespassing, or says, 'Pay no attention to that boy.' They leave with no idea where they've just been."

The two watched the traffic pass, James amazed at the old makes and models not uncommon for the 1960s. A red VW beetle, grey Karmen-Gia, light-yellow Datsun; he gaped in awe. A maroon Peugeot wagon followed by a white VW van with the classic peace signs spray-painted on, a silver Mercedes sedan with winged bumpers, and a station wagon with wooden panels on its sides. A dark blue 356 SC Porsche raced by, loud and low to the ground. It was James' father––a younger version—with those terrible bushy sideburns he grew after the divorce. "Jesus," James said, slipping down against the stone wall to sit on the ground.

"That world is not real, James. You're seeing a rerun of the same day we arrived."

"You mean time is frozen in a loop here. That's why none of you have grown and this place hasn't changed."

Timmy hurled a stone into the woods, which ricocheted off a hard elm like a shot. "Lawrence says this is a forbidden place, cut out and frozen in time with few windows to look out of and see the world we left." The boy dropped a handful of pebbles onto an ant hill like a slow drip. "But I know how you can help us break that hold on time." The boy flattened the ant hill with his shoe. "Lawrence thinks he's got you beat, but you can be the one who beats him."

"How?" James asked.

"Win my mother's trust, which you've started to do already. Then you'll see things change quick."

"There hasn't been one trespasser yet she's trusted?"

"One," Timmy stared at nothing. "But it ended badly."

"That's going to make it twice as difficult for me then."

Timmy crouched in front of James. "Not if you fall in love with her."

James stared at the shadowed crevices between the stones in the wall where spiders built their webs. He listened to baby birds chirping in their nests. He stood up and wandered into the drive. "I could never, Timmy, even if I believed, even if I tried, in a real sense love her. Then if we did leave, what would I do? Do I un-love her then?" He held the gate by its bars and gazed out. "Why would she have anything to do with me?"

Timmy took James' hand. "Because you two have a connection."

James nodded, knowing they certainly did. He wondered how the boy knew.

A crack of thunder ripped the cloudless sky. "That means Lawrence is returning!" Timmy tugged on James' hand to return to the estate, but he just stood as if his feet were lead.

"How exactly will things change, Timmy, because of our connection?"

Timmy didn't wait to answer. He shot off in a run back to the estate. James watched as the boy grew farther away.

A soft wind blew down from the oak and whispered, *Follow the boy, James.* He looked out at the road. Why stay for a woman he had tried to forget his whole life? Why stay with a megalomaniac who tried to run him over, with a caretaker who fires his shotgun at children? No. Let the cop rescue them.

He opened the gate as wide as it would go, where did the road lead? To his own world, the boy said. What's stopping him then? Purpose, for a greater good. He remembered he was sent to help a woman leave, to make her feel safe. Someone must have cared so much about her that they chose James for this gargantuan task––for a reason. His reward must be great. The gypsy princess in the statue, he helped her leave, with a kiss. But that was only a harbinger of something greater. Sharon. He was sent to save Sharon. Perhaps with a kiss too.

Thunder boomed like a cannon ball projectile. If James were going to stay, it would have to be done one hundred percent, not half-assed, not taciturn, no looking behind his back to see what spirits hovered, no running away no matter how frightening. It is a calling. Gain Sharon's trust and love her. Or there's the gate, he could leave. Now. The thunder boomed and he ran.

By the time he caught up with the boy, Sharon and Eugene stood in front of the carriage house waiting. Timmy took his mother's hand and the two walked inside with Sally. Eugene held the carriage house door open and waved James in.

"Get in this utility closet and wait," the old man said. It was located beneath a low slanted ceiling following the angle of stairs leading up to Eugene's apartment. James crowded in with an oily lawn mower. He couldn't sit or stand. Eugene closed the door.

"How long do I have to wait in here?" James asked from inside, his voice muffled.

"Until he leaves," Eugene said.

"I could be in here a long time," James said.

"Don't worry," Eugene locked the dead bolt on the door. "You won't get any older."

Sharon kept busy with the laundry off the kitchen while Eugene kept digging a hole in the back garden, when Lawrence appeared back on the scene.

INTERLUDE:

THE DAY ANNE APPEARED

32

ARRIVAL

The day Anne appeared in her jade-colored Jaguar, the world in which their lives were trapped changed forever. The porch screen door slammed shut and Timmy ran into the kitchen. Sharon was in the middle of preparing deviled ham sandwiches for lunch. She laid four slices of bread on the counter.

"Mother, guess who's here?" he said.

She dug the knife into the can. "Who is it this time, Timmy?"

"Mrs. Godwin."

She raised her brows.

"I swear it."

Sharon parted the lucent green curtains above the sink and saw her friend's car breaking to a halt in the drive. She dropped the can of spread and went out onto the back porch; it was Anne. She pulled her apron off and ran.

Standing by her car, Anne waved. She wore giant-lens Ray-Bans and a paisley headscarf dressed in tennis whites. Sharon dashed up and gave her a smothering hug.

"Woah, don't you seem wound up," Anne said. "You'd think you hadn't seen me in ages. And you look ten years younger if I say so myself." Sharon was shaking. "Is everything all right, dear?" she asked.

Sharon glanced over her shoulder. No sign of Lawrence. "Anne, you've got to help us," she said. "We need to get as far away from this place as we can."

Anne closed her car door. "You two did hitch up rather impulsively," she said.

"Big mistake," Sharon said.

"Honey, if that's how you feel, why don't you just pack up and leave?"

Timmy and Sally arrived. Anne patted the girl on the head. "Hello Sally, isn't this place gorgeous?"

"Why did you do it, Anne?" Sharon asked. "Why did you tell Timmy I was here?"

Anne tried to keep a smile. "Because I thought you'd be happy to see them, Sharon! You could say thank you. What was I supposed to do when Timmy called yesterday? It was the Fourth of July for Lord-ee sake. Would you have preferred I called the boy's father after you insisted on having them for the big holiday?"

"They should've never come, Anne," Sharon said. "You put their lives on hold forever."

Anne shook her head. "Sharon, I didn't want to see or talk to you after the club party. But here I am and all is forgiven. Show your friend a little kindness. Did Lawrence take you to Europe for that wild time he promised me?"

"Two scary weeks. We had to hide wherever we went."

"He is a celebrity after all," Anne said. "No wonder you had to travel incognito the whole time."

"We tried."

Lawrence stepped out the front door under the shaded portico wearing tennis whites and carrying a racquet. Anne waved to him.

"Anne, please stay," Sharon pleaded. "Stay and convince him to let us go."

Anne fixed her eyes on Lawrence. "Lookie-do, handsome!" She breezed by Sharon and wrapped her arms around his neck, giving him a great kiss. "What are you doing to this woman?" Anne said. "You have her acting like a scared chicken waiting for the axe to drop. You didn't take her to Rome as planned?"

"We never made it," he said. "We flew to Bora-Bora instead. In fact, we traveled to many destinations trying to shake off this harsh weather which seemed to follow us around. And that caused this teensy-weensy fight." He held a pinch in the air. "She's still miffed, but hey, that's a boring story you need hear nothing about." He sized them up, side by side. "Look at you two, the dynamic duo back together, friends again, I hope."

Anne patted him on the chest. "You really have Sharon confused, Lawrence. She told me they're being held here against their will."

Sharon looked at Anne with panic in her eyes and mimed the words "don't say anything" with her lips. It was too late.

"Shame on both of you," Anne said, shaking her finger, "we were all shocked by your surprise escape from the club. George swore he'd never talk to you again, Sharon. I don't suppose it matters now with you two shacked up together. If I were you, I wouldn't show my face there for a while."

Sharon glanced at Lawrence. "That's not going to happen anytime soon."

Lawrence placed his arm around Sharon's waist and pulled her to his side. "We're just two love birds fate has drawn together to live happily ever after." He looked down into Sharon's eyes. "Isn't that right, darling? Forgive us our past indiscretion, Anne. Let us make it up to you with a game of tennis."

"I only stopped by to see how you all were doing," Anne said. "I'm on my way to the club."

Lawrence waved her idea away like a gnat. "Forget that boring club crowd, Anne. Stay."

"Yes, Anne, stay," Sharon said. "You can watch the town's Fourth of July fireworks on the back hill with us tonight."

Anne's eyes opened wide. "I hate to point out the obvious to you, Sharon, but the Fourth of July was yesterday."

Sharon and Timmy looked at each other. Years had passed on the estate for them, but for Anne in her world, it was just one day.

"Do stay, Anne," Lawrence said. "If not for the fireworks then for an afternoon of cocktails and fun."

"I don't know if I should interrupt this repeat of a family holiday."

Lawrence put his arm around her shoulders. "Anne, here we're all family. If it weren't for you, Sharon and I never would have met." He looked down at Timmy and patted his head. "Go put your tennis whites on, son, and we'll play a few sets together. Afterward we'll throw some meat on the grill beside the pool and the adults will have a few drinks."

"All right," Anne said, "but no more than one set."

Lawrence held up his finger. "And one cocktail."

Anne held up her finger. "One cocktail."

"And one quick dip in the pool," Lawrence said, "then Sharon will throw you out of here herself, I promise." He took Anne's hand. "Sharon, you and Timmy get dressed while we head down to the courts. Don't tarry or we'll have to start a game without you."

Sharon's composure relaxed. With a bounce in her step, she returned to the kitchen with Timmy and Sally.

"Are you sure about this?" Timmy asked.

"Be positive, Timmy! Mrs. Godwin is staying, and Lawrence is happy to see her. And you," she touched his nose, "get to play tennis." Sharon tickled the boy's side and he skirted away.

"I don't trust him, Mom. He's never invited me to play before."

"Don't be suspicious," she said, "we've got to keep him in an agreeable mood. If anyone can convince him to let us leave, it's Anne." She climbed the porch steps with Sally.

"Don't you think it was strange they both dressed in tennis whites?" Timmy asked.

"Anne said she was on her way to the club, now stay positive!" She and Sally stepped inside, allowing the screen door to slam shut behind them.

Outside, Timmy felt a crush of cool wind as it swooped down and up into the surrounding trees, tussling their tops with a violent shake. He witnessed the color of flowers in hanging pots on the porch deepen, their stems stand taller. Change was in the air.

33

TENNIS ANYONE?

Down at courtside Eugene finished sweeping the courts free of twigs and other wind-carried debris. He picked up his wheelbarrow and fixed his gaze up. The trees swayed in different wind patterns, a change that was not supposed to happen in this world, where every day was an exact duplicate down to the movement of a breeze. He scratched his head; like Timmy, he too suspected something was amiss.

Sharon placed a pitcher of iced lemonade on the table against the court's chain link fence, which towered up to stop errant shots. Lawrence and Anne stood at the net in quiet conversation, stopping their chatter when Sharon greeted them.

"You two seem to be getting reacquainted," she said.

"Do you realize, darling," Lawrence said to Sharon, "if I hadn't met you, it could have been Anne standing there in your place?"

"I wouldn't wish that upon my worst enemy," Sharon said, "let alone my best friend."

"What was that, my love?"

"I said, I'm lucky it happened to me, and I hope it'll never end!"

"Hey, sport," Lawrence said to Timmy. "Boys against girls, you're playing with me." They headed to their side of the court while Anne and Sharon to theirs. Sally took a can of balls and made up a game rolling them against the fence by herself.

All that afternoon, they laughed and screamed whenever there was a close shot. Lawrence, who never spoke a kind word to Timmy, showed great calm and patience, taking the time to improve the boy's game, encouraging him when he hit out of bounds or into the net. When they played together, he complimented Sharon on her good shots, shrugged off the easy volleys she let by. Her self-confidence was growing, and the boy felt it.

As they played, Eugene walked back and forth along the lawn perimeter with the trees, trying to figure out why birds chirped different songs, cotton tails and squirrels rustled different patches of dead leaves. Just before the last serve of the game, Timmy watched Eugene clutching the fence's metal links, his eyes fixated upon his mother. Sharon was having more fun than any of them. Eugene's eyes opened wide and his mouth fell open. He looked at the trees, then at Timmy's mother, then––took off faster than Timmy ever saw him run. A ball whizzed by.

"Timmy!" his mother yelled. "Pay attention!"

They won the break point. Lawrence called it quits and they walked off the court, wiping their sweat with towels dropped at the base of the net poles. They tightened their racquets in their wooden presses.

"Now, how about that fresh dip in the pool, Anne," Lawrence said. He was the only one with not one drop of sweat. "And not a few icy cocktails to wet our throats, and then a patriotic barbeque feast. How about it, ladies?"

"You've sold me," Anne said, leaning on her knees.

"Me too," Sharon said. "I'm famished."

They started walking up to the pool when Timmy cried and fell. Sharon rushed over to him, kneeling down at his side. The boy rubbed his thighs. "I don't know what's happening, Mom," he said. "The bones in my legs hurt. It's like they're trying to stretch."

Sally fell next to her brother. "Me too, Mud'dah, my legs hoa'ht too."

Sharon waved Lawrence and Anne to go on without them. "I'm sure you're both dehydrated," she said to the children. She rubbed

Sally's leg until the discomfort stopped and the girl stood up. They gathered their things and started to walk back.

"Wasn't Lawrence nice out there today?" Sharon said. "I think it's Anne softening him up, didn't I say she could do it? Finally, to be free of him at last."

"I don't trust any of this, Mom," Timmy said. "Don't get your hopes up."

"Will you stop?" she said. "We'll leave tonight and be rid of this place forever, you'll see."

"What about the Master out there waiting for you?"

"It's time I take responsibility for my actions, Timmy. I will deal with him later. What's important is to get you and Sally home where you belong. The wind is blowing in our direction. I can feel it."

"But Mother!"

When they neared the pool entrance under a small grove of cedar trees, Timmy broke off to join Eugene in the gardens. Sally and her mother stepped through the pool gate.

34

POOLSIDE CHATTER

Sharon and Sally passed into the pool area and heard an explosion of music blaring at them; the voice of the 5th Dimension. They walked down poolside to the other end where Lawrence and Anne chatted under the shaded porch patio outside the French doors. Lawrence mixed drinks while making Anne laugh. Neither helped Sharon carry in the tennis gear, towels, tray with the empty pitcher and cups. With arms full, she veered away from them down the service path to the kitchen hidden behind tall hedges.

"Sharon!" Lawrence shouted. "Hop into your swimsuit and join us." He held his stomach. "And don't forget to pull some meat from the ice box, will you? I'm starving."

With a deep breath and forced smile Sharon turned around. "Anything else, Lawrence, my love?"

He smiled back. "Nothing at all sweetheart, by the time you return, I'll have the coals burning hot, and your favorite cocktail mixed and waiting."

Sharon returned in a yellow bikini and a tray of seasoned steaks, foiled onions and potatoes, summer vegetables and other accoutrements. By then the other two adults were in the pool splashing each other, Lawrence in his speedo and Anne in a one-piece suit with a flowered bathing cap. Sharon laid the tray down; the Weber grille was empty, no drink waiting for her. She curled her lips tight and poured herself a scotch. When they saw Sharon, the other two climbed out of the pool. The album, *The Age of Aquarius,* played on the stereo.

Sharon shouted over her shoulder, "Lawrence, it's deafening. Turn it down!"

"But this is the dawning of a new age!" He sang along with the tune, "When the mooooon is in the seventh house…and Jupiter aligns with Mars." He grabbed a towel off the rack and approached her drying his hair. Anne peeled off her cap and tossed it onto a ribbed pool lounge chair, pulling her hair back and wearing her Ray-bans. Lawrence nodded at her. "Isn't Anne the splitting image of Diane Cannon, Sharon?" he said. He snapped his fingers, *"This is the dawning of the Age of Aquarius––the age of…"*

"Why are you so interested in what she looks like?" Sharon put her glass down.

"No offence, Sharon, but her beauty captivated me before I ever laid eyes on you. I could've left with her that night from the pool party."

"Maybe you should've." Sharon closed her eyes and slurped down her drink.

"Come on, love, you know you're my only angel." He tugged on her hand to join Anne in a dance. Sharon didn't budge. He dropped her hand. "Have it your way."

Lawrence handed Anne a martini glass and she held it high above her head, swaying like a serpent. Sharon pulled up a lounge chair beside Anne's, searched her friend's bag for a cigarette, found one and lit up. She laid back and downed her third scotch, listening to Diana Ross and the Supremes sing "I Hear a Symphony." She got up to pour herself another.

"Baby, Baby…" Lawrence and Anne sang in unison. Sharon gulped down a shot of rye. She knew it was only a matter of time before Lawrence cut her off. Alcohol was scarce unless there were guests. She held up the bottle to pour another when he came up from beyond and grabbed her upraised arm, forcing her to lower the bottle.

"Careful, Sharon," he whispered in her ear. "I'll not let you drink yourself into oblivion again. It's okay with annoying trespassers we toy with, but not with your friend Anne visiting. Either you stop or I'll—"

She ripped the bottle away. "Or what? Tell Anne what a charade this is, that you're a fraud holding us here by some strange mystical authority?"

"Keep your voice down," he said. He looked over at Anne sipping on her drink and dancing, as if lost in some dream. "You know why I can't let you go, it's for your own good."

"I'd rather take my chances out there than stay inside here with you."

"You'll never convince the Master to let you out of your arrangement." Staring him in the eyes, she finished off her drink. He shook her off and dove in the pool.

The Blood Sweat and Tears hit "Spinning Wheel" began to play. *"What goes up…"* Sharon lay down in the lounge chair beside Anne. *"Must come down…"* Anne took out a box of Paul Malls from her bag. *"Spinning wheel…"* She offered Sharon one. *"Got to go round…"* They lit up together.

"Did you talk to him yet, Anne?" She watched Lawrence swim at the other end of the pool, ignoring the children playing on a raft. "Did you tell him we want to leave?"

"Yes," Anne said. "Now, about that, Sharon." She put her cigarette down and sat up straight. "Lawrence did in fact tell me everything, so I know what's been going on."

"Thank God. At last someone—"

"And I know what the problem is. But the problem is not him."

"What do you mean?"

"The problem is you."

Sharon sat up straight. "What?"

"Listen, sweetheart, I didn't just come here to see if the kids were all right. Lawrence called me. He needed to talk to someone who knows you well. Tell me, Sharon, why are you so mean to him?"

"What?"

"Why do you treat him like a doormat?"

"Is that what he said? That's a lie, he's lying to you, Anne."

"He's a broken man, Sharon. Are you in love with him or not?"

"How could we be in love? We weren't together long enough to find out! It was physical attraction, pure and simple."

"Did you kick him out of the bedroom already?"

"Yes."

"Won't let him touch you?"

Sharon gritted her teeth. "There is no sexual pleasure to be had in this place, Anne."

"Not if you withhold it from him."

Sharon sat up. "I mean literally, no physical pleasure here can exist!"

Anne shook her head. "And so soon after the honeymoon."

"Is that what he told you? We're not married!" Sharon stared at the chlorine filter flapping by the waves of the pool. She held her hand up to Anne's face. "Do you see a ring on my finger? No."

Anne pulled her hand down. "I've seen you do this before, Sharon; ruin men's lives. That professor at Vassar who was married, remember?"

"I can't believe you brought that up. He took advantage of my innocence. You know that."

"And the Harris boy? You took advantage of his innocence."

"And I regret that now."

"There's no forgiveness for what you did, Sharon."

Sharon laid back. "I should've never told you."

"Listen to me, Sharon, you asked me to stay and I did. Now I'm trying to help, and you are making it awfully difficult. Lawrence is very distraught, but he's forgiving. You can still save this relationship."

"Anne, I'm the distraught one! Lawrence has this place so rigged we can't step foot outside even when we try––nobody comes or goes without his permission. You must convince him to let us go."

"You're right, he doesn't want to let you go. He loves the children and was thrilled when they arrived. He said he had to convince you to let them stay."

"He said what? Anne, don't you see what he's doing—"

"If you left him now, he'd feel empty without you and the kids. He wants to make this work. Don't you?"

"I suppose he told you it was all my idea to ditch you and George."

"Well Sharon." Anne shook her head. "We all saw you lead Lawrence away from the pool and disappear with him."

"It was his idea first."

"Like all men, he got caught up in your beauty. You bewitched him."

"Anne, he's not human like you and me. He's a ghost!"

"He was going to run away with me that night. At least I would have loved him."

"What goes up..."

"You think he would've really loved you?" Sharon said.

"Must come down..."

Anne stood up ripping off her glasses. "Why should that surprise you? You think you're the only love object in this town?"

"Spinning Wheel..."

"Wake up, Anne!" Sharon stood up. "He's a sham, this place is a sham, none of it is real! None! I told you, it doesn't exist!"

"Got to go 'round..."

"Don't raise your voice at me, Sharon Peters!" Anne shouted.

"I didn't hold a grudge against you that night, so don't start getting mad at me."

Sharon shouted louder, "If you don't want to stay, then Jesus Christ, leave!" She thrust her arm and pointed to the other end of the pool so hard she almost stumbled and fell. Lawrence caught her.

"Now now, girls, stop this fighting," he said. He led Anne to a pool chair in the shade and returned to Sharon.

"What did you do to her?" Lawrence asked.

Sharon pointed her finger sharply at Lawrence. "What did you do to her?"

"Having some fun with an old friend is all," he said.

"Yeah, by getting her drunk," she said.

"Don't be old-fashioned. Besides," he shook his finger at her, "we both know you love to drink more than anyone. So why should we stop because of you? And another thing, what you told Anne about my feelings for your children was a lie. You know I adore them."

"Bull crap. I can't believe I'm even listening to this."

"Come now, I try ridiculously hard to be a father to Timmy and Sally. Look how the boy and I got along today? Maybe I'm not particularly good at it, but I try."

"Oh, don't start with that slop. It was all show, and you know it."

"And where's our food which you were supposed to cook?" he asked her. "Why isn't it ready by now? Why don't you take care of that instead of lounging around sulking?"

She peered around him at the Weber. "Oh, and you did such an excellent job preparing the coals."

Lawrence picked up the whole bag and dumped the coals in. He squirted vast amounts of lighter fluid on them, lit a match, and dropped it in. Flames jumped into the air.

"There. Does that suit you?" he said.

"I'm not cooking a goddamn thing," she said. Sharon called for Timmy and Sally and the three made their way down the side entrance into the estate house, leaving Lawrence and Anne the pool to themselves.

35

THERE WILL BE FIREWORKS

Sharon climbed the stairs in the empty great hall. The smack of her sandals on every cold marble step echoed. At the top she leaned against the banister holding her stomach then ran to the nearest bathroom and threw up. She fell on her bed and didn't wake until it was dusk, when Timmy came in and shook her.

"Are you all right, Mom?" he asked. "I guess things are not going so well."

She jolted up. "How long have I been sleeping? Is Anne still here?"

"She's still here, making mushy with Lawrence."

"That bitch."

"Mom."

"I know I shouldn't care but I do. Come on."

She changed into a long white sleeve pullover and linen slacks. The two grabbed blankets from the laundry room and collected Sally.

"Are you sure you're all right, Mom?" Timmy asked.

"I'm fine. We're not going to miss the fireworks because of them."

They stopped at the pool terrace on their way. Someone had finally cooked the food and left a mess on the table. Lawrence and Anne were slow dancing to bossa nova, more like lovers than friends.

Lawrence smiled over. "Ah, there you are. We wondered where you had disappeared to. Is it time for the fireworks already?"

Anne picked up glasses and plates and left them by the grille. "Sharon, let's not fight," she said. "I promise I'm not going to steal Lawrence back from you."

"You can have him as far as I'm concerned."

"Don't be that way, honey. How can we make it up to you?"

"Come to the fireworks with us," Sharon said. "Now."

Lawrence rested his arm around Anne's shoulders. "Anne needs to get out of her wet suit first," he said, "and so must I. You three go ahead and we'll join you shortly."

Anne laughed. "Incredible, you all still believe today's the Fourth of Joo-ly."

Lawrence sang, "And the rockets' red glare, bombs bursting in air…"

"Hurry up you two or you'll miss them." Sharon stared into Lawrence's eyes. "I want Anne to see for herself, so she'll know everything we told her is true."

When they reached the back hill, Sharon and the children laid down their blankets. On the other side of the fence the town's Fourth of July celebration gave off bright lights which reflected a colorful glow upon them. Sharon kept looking behind for Lawrence and Anne to arrive. When the fireworks started, she stood up. "Wait here," she said to the children, then took off to the estate house without them.

PART II
LIFE ON THE ESTATE

1

In his stealth manner, Lawrence appeared to Eugene digging by the greenhouse, its glass paneled roof broken in a checkered pattern. He brushed the dirt off his Madras blazer, its dazzling patchwork of orange and yellow mirroring the day's eternal heat.

"You did a fine job back there, sport, tuning that engine. That trespasser never knew what hit him." He stared at the gardener's rough-cut rectangle in the ground. "What is this, Eugene, are you ready to rest in this grave of yours and leave my paradise for good?"

Eugene rested the smooth grain shaft of the shovel inside the shallows of the grave. "Why not? I owe you nothing." He staked his boot up against its soft earthen side, leaned his arm upon one knee, and spat.

"You owe me, sport, and a great deal at that." Lawrence extended his index finger at Eugene like a bayonet. "Out of the depths of my own mercy I clothed you and fed you and, oh, why do I even bother?" He batted his hand at Eugene like sweeping away a bad smell. "Useless man, why this droll manual labor, you know nothing progresses here, tomorrow you'll just have to start all over again."

"The exercise justifies the effort," Eugene said.

"Remember whose prince of this palace," Lawrence said, "nobody gets in or out without passing by me."

Eugene stared at the bottom of the grave. "I'll leave when my own chosen time has come."

Lawrence bowed. "Of course you will, Sir Eugene, our privileged guest. But you never will. You're too afraid of what awaits you in the real world. Death."

Eugene slipped off the red bandana around his neck and wiped his brow. "It used to be hard for me to let go of this place," he said, "spent most of my existence here."

"That's right, the only home you've known. For which you've got me to thank."

Eugene looked at Lawrence. "What about you? You're more attached to this place than any of us."

"And why shouldn't I be? I'm the rightful owner, aren't I? This estate belonged to my mother's family for generations. Now a safe haven to where I retreat from the affairs in the mortal world––where people grow old and die. Folly, Eugene. All is folly. You are guilty of the worst sins, and if you ever do depart, it will be for a more fiery place."

Lawrence shoved his hands into his pocket and whistled, strolling back and forth in front of the grave. "So how are you planning to do it, old man, knotted rope over the barn rafter, sharp knife to the flabby throat? Gas stove?"

"Nothing so fancy," Eugene said. "I'll go by dying of good old-fashioned old age."

Lawrence removed his hands from his pockets. "Where do you find the time to fill your brain with such nonsense? You know the revolution of the sun and moon here are still. Eugene, I believe you are hiding something."

"What have I ever hidden, Lawrence, that you have not found?"

"Let's see." Lawrence patted his chin. "Why the sudden interest in—what has happened that you should begin to think." He snapped his fingers. "The trespasser––he hasn't left, has he?"

"No, he has not."

"I knew it." Lawrence's eyes expanded like hot blown glass; his pupils enlarged within them. "So, he's the something to do with your sudden declaration of independence." He crossed his arms.

"I am worn out and old," said Eugene. "He's youthful

and energetic."

"I knocked that trespasser off his feet too easily, didn't I? Could death enter, I should take great satisfaction to see life in him cease." Lawrence lifted his foot upon the crumbling stone wall and stared into the empty woods. "It is always the defeated one must watch out for, who wait to fight another day."

Eugene held the shovel across his waist. "Lawrence, go away and leave this to me. When you come back, he'll be ready to do anything you say so he can stay."

Lawrence returned to the grave side. "And what would draw this gent here, keep him bound and obligated? What makes you think this sport will serve my every whim?"

"Because he's made no more peace with his past than you have."

"And what would that past be?"

"I don't know," Eugene tossed a shovelful of dirt into the wheelbarrow, "but he shows a strong interest in this young mother of yours."

The air filled with the stench of sulfur which emanated from Lawrence. "What makes you think I would ever permit him to replace you?"

"Because if you don't, he may replace you."

"Enough!" Lawrence kicked over the wheelbarrow filled with fluffed up dirt. He tightened his jaw and spoke down close to Eugene's ear. "You think you're so smart, that you can trick the great Lawrence P. You and I are of the same nature, old man, though you pretend superiority."

Lawrence pounded his fist in his hand. "This is my kingdom for my use which I paid for dearly with my own mortality, do you think I don't know the cost? I shall not give it away to just any sucker, and if you or this trespasser think otherwise, Beelzebub himself shall appear and turn you all into mindless shades."

At that moment, a strong torrent blew down from the trees. The decrepit greenhouse groaned as its weathervane turned in ceaseless spinning. Lawrence shielded himself with his arms from the strong gust. He finally relented, letting it muss up his hair. "Oh, why should

I care? All right then, I shall allow him to stay." The wind ceased and he combed his hair back in place.

"One is as good or useless to me as another. I measure only in terms of how well all serve my purposes." Eugene held his heart, leaning against the edge of the grave.

"You see? You are too old for this place, Eugene Lequin, I've kept you round long enough. I welcome your replacement, not mine. Go off then, be fulfilled and bury yourself in this ditch, or have the trespasser do it for you. I shall never fear to be alone, for I embrace the emptiness the living run away from."

Lawrence rubbed the dirt off his white bucks, brushed down his sleeves. He showed not a drop of sweat. "Keep the turn of the screw tight on them old sport, as you do with all who dare to trespass against us." With a cold rush of the wind, Lawrence disappeared into thin air.

2

Lawrence arrived in the kitchen with arms full of dirty clothes. "Sharon!" he shouted. "Sharon, where are you?" She appeared at the door of the washroom with rubber gloves on.

"I suspect our latest trespasser left, as planned?" he said.

"Of course, why should it be otherwise?" She stripped off the gloves and returned inside. He followed her.

"You played your part well; he didn't suspect a thing. Here," he dumped his laundry at her feet, "I need these washed and pressed right away."

"Lawrence, you don't need a housewife to spend eternity with, you need a maid." She separated the colors and stuffed them in the washer while he sat on the utility table against the opposite wall.

"Come now, Sharon, you have all these labor-saving devices of our modern century, you're forever young, and you're with the man of your dreams. What more could you possibly desire? Oh, that." He roamed over to the window and stared out at the front lawn, stroking the hairs of his forearm. "There are greater satisfactions in life than physical pleasure," he said. "Did you ever stop to consider, ever stop to think that I wish it were different too? Things didn't turn out in that department as I expected either." He turned around. "Memphis is such a cheat."

Sharon nodded at a detergent box near him and he grabbed it for her. "There's a lot of things about this kingdom of mine he never came clean about." He handed her the box. "Sex being one of them."

She poured a cup into the washer. "Don't blame him, Lawrence." She slammed the top shut. "I could tell this trespasser was more of a man than you ever were."

He drew nearer. "What did you say, woman?"

"You heard me." She cranked the dial up and the water pressure built. "You were so afraid you just had to try and kill him," she said, "even though you knew it was impossible. You know nothing can die here. Coward."

He held his finger up like a knife. "Watch your lip, Sharon, I'm warning you."

She leaned back against the machine. "What are you going to do, try and kill me too? At least he had the scent of a real man."

"Enough!" Lawrence grabbed her by the wrists, held them to her chest. She stiffened her arms. "What's going on, Sharon?" he said. "You've not spoken this boldly to me in a long time, What's going on?" She stared at him in silence. He threw her arms down. "Damn you!" He pressed his hands on the tabletop. "Suddenly you're acting awful peculiar."

She came to him and touched his shoulder. "I'm sorry, Lawrence, it was this trespasser's presence today. He was so different from the rest."

"You've never paid much attention to a trespasser before." He turned around. "Why this one now?"

"His bloody fall unsettled me is all. Please don't be cross." She raised the backside of his hand to her lips and kissed it. At the touch he jerked it away, as if he'd just been pricked.

She touched her lips. "Did you feel that?"

He rubbed his hand. "You haven't had this effect on me since the day you arrived."

He jingled his belt buckle, then walked to a wall mirror and looked at himself. He smoothed down the sides of his hair. "Look," he said, "I didn't just come here to ask you to prepare my clothes for another trip. There is something more important I have to tell you."

She lifted a basket of clothes to fold on the table. "Yes?"

"I have a plan which will allow us to leave this cursed place forever without Memphis ever having to send his henchmen after us."

She frowned. "You've been saying that since the day I arrived."

Lawrence took a box of buttons from the shelf and sorted through them. "I'm serious, are you ready to leave this place for good or not?"

Sharon folded a blouse she'd worn a million times yet showed no wear. "What makes you think the Master will go along this time?"

He spotted a brass button with an emblazoned gold anchor and placed it in his pocket. "I found something of even greater importance to him than you."

"Which is?"

"This trespasser."

Sharon dropped the basket on the table with a thud.

"He's here, isn't he?" he said. "Don't worry, I'm not angry. You've every right to crave a little companionship what with how I've kept you cooped up here so long. I'm feeling in a generous mood." He walked to the window to let in fresh air. "What if I allowed him to stay and keep you company until my return?"

Sharon's brows creased. "What are you getting at, Lawrence, you were ready to do away with him yesterday."

He slid his hand in his pocket and played with the button. "He's shown some great cunning not leaving like the rest. I can make good use of him, to our benefit."

"Why? What are you going to do with him?"

He patted his chest with his hand. "It's not what I am going to do." He pointed his finger at her. "It's what you will do."

"Me?"

"Keep him here, until my return."

"And how am I supposed to do that?"

He looked at her figure. "Use that feminine mystique which teaches all women how to land a good man using all the natural resources at their disposal."

"Meaning?"

"Seduce him with every trick in the book."

She threw the shirt down. "I can't believe the day's come when you'd willingly throw me into the arms of another man."

He leaned against the door frame and crossed his arms. "I'm not asking you to sleep with him, for Christ sake, just make him think you're in love with him."

"Lawrence!"

"Not for real, pretend. Do it for me, do it for us."

She pushed the basket of folded clothes against the wall. "Leave him be, Lawrence, and we can remain in peace the way we've always been."

He stood up straight and took a step towards her. "Can't you see the world you've missed is waiting for you out there? To walk among the elegant and handsome people of the world as one of them, show off your youthful good looks, have your photo snapped a million times, fashion magazines who will compete to have you on their covers and learn your beauty secrets. You'll have your own brand of perfume named after you. Travel the world the guest of royalty, play host to celebrity because you'll be celebrity too. We'll travel from city to country to sea, tropical beaches to Swiss chalets, we'll own estates in all the chic places to be seen—the French Riviera, Rio De Janeiro, Venice, Milan, Barcelona, Lisbon, Paris—never set foot on this cursed estate again."

He raised her hand above her head and spun her around like a ballerina in a music box. "You and I--we'll feel love and sex like we've never known or tasted before, women will see you on the arm of the great Lawrence P and die of envy."

Sharon covered her face in her hands. "You're overwhelming me, Lawrence. Yes, I wanted that once, but now that I can have it, I don't any longer. There's the children to think about."

"Yes, think of the children. What if I told you that Timmy and Sally could return home to their lives as they were meant to be?"

Sharon's mouthed dropped open. "You'd allow that?"

He nodded.

"Oh Lawrence," she started to embrace him, then stopped. "Wait, you've promised to let them go many times, why should I believe you now?"

"Because Memphis must have this trespasser within his grasp at all costs and will trade dearly for him."

"What makes this trespasser so valuable that he'd give me and the children up?"

Lawrence held her hands. "It's really none of our affair, Sharon. Let him have his reasons. Now, kiss me, on the lips this time."

She closed her eyes and leaned up to him. At the moment their lips met, she was repelled back as if some hoarfrost had escaped from his heart into hers, then crystallized it to ice. She broke out in cough.

He rubbed his lips. "I feel as if a great freeze has been lifted from my heart," he said. "With one kiss, you've brought me back to life. I can feel my blood pumping again." He walked to the door, dazed. "Wash and iron my things. Pack them neatly too. I have half the globe to cover."

He hesitated at the door. "Oh, and Sharon, start cleaning yourself up for our trespasser, you can look quite unattractive when you don't take care of your appearance. Remaining young doesn't always mean looking pretty. Sometimes you must work at it."

She threw the box of soap at him. He ducked, laughing as he left, whistling a carefree tune. As soon as he was out of shout range, she stomped on his white clothes. "I hate you!" she said.

What was making her so passionate? James' presence was stirring up and inflaming her emotions. In the events of one morning, he'd made her feel like a real woman again, beautiful, desirable, strong. She could feel her self-esteem rising, lost confidence regained. But of all trespassers to arrive, why did it have to be him? The boy-not-quite-a-man who'd sprouted sooner than most his age. If only he'd been ten years older when she found him sleeping in her bed. Perhaps God was in on this too, tempting her with James a second time. Ironic, he was now older than she. If Lawrence knew their history, he'd never have asked her to lure him into a seductive trap.

Lawrence said James was the price that must be paid for them to have their freedom to roam the world free as immortal stars, and now there was another good reason to go along with this deception: Timmy and Sally would finally be able go home. But how could she do this to James and betray him? What was it that made the Master so interested in him in the first place? James should have left, instead he decided to stay. Why must she now have to choose?

Her heart jumped a beat thinking of the two men. She must make sure they never meet. She touched her lips; they were cold to the touch. She rubbed color and warmth back into them, then pressed ahead with her chore. Excited by the intermittences of her palpitating heart, she hummed a forgotten love song.

3

Hours later, James spilled out of the closet, a twisted daddy long legs.

"Get yourself up, sonny, he's gone," Eugene said.

"That was a hell of a thing to do to a guy," James said. "Leave me like that. One hell of a thing."

"What's the matter, too fat to exercise in there?"

James stretched down to his toes. "Where's Sharon?"

"Forget her," Eugene said. "You'll be needin' to make yourself useful if you're stayin'." They headed back to the gardens. As they strolled, James took it all in; trimmed rows of colorful flowers, the greenery appending the swept pathways.

Eugene winked. "Bet you've never seen a prettier garden than this."

James winked. "Bet you I've seen this one."

Eugene shrugged. "Yeah, well, you were a kid then."

James skipped ahead of Eugene. "You knew it, didn't you? How we used to sneak in all the time without being detected, until we heard your gun shot." James slapped his hands together like cymbals. "Then we scattered like birds." He shook a low hanging branch of a primrose tree. It emptied a cloud of chickadees. All flew away, except one. "All took flight, Eugene, except me." He watched as the little creature bounced up and down on a low-lying branch alone.

"I didn't bring you here to brag about your childish antics. I just need you to do some heavy lifting. Now hurry your pace." They stopped at a shed stripped of its paint, the door barely hanging on its hinges. Inside was a rusted cart low to the ground. With it, they headed east along the property's south perimeter through tall bamboo-colored grass.

"Where are we going?" James asked. "What exactly is it you need my help lifting?"

"Something I've been procrastinating about for ages," Eugene said. "Some unfinished business which cannot go un-faced a day longer. Help me move a heavy stone."

They reached the greenhouse in the back corner of the property. Inside the dilapidated structure, James set the cart beside a table of mauve clay pots filled with seedlings. The old man pointed at a bulky object on the floor.

"Go ahead, uncover it," he said.

James pulled away a paint-stained burlap tarp from a pink marble tombstone. Eugene pointed at its lettering:

Eugene Lequin b. 1889 d. 19—.

He guided his finger inside the curves and cuts of the letters. "I did all that when the Revsons were here before Lawrence appeared to retake possession. I got so far, then wham!" He slapped his furled handkerchief atop the marble with a snap. "He shows up and stops me from getting any further with my favorite pastime. Couldn't do anything about it after that."

James examined the engravings. "Who chisels their name and date on their own tombstone?" he asked.

Eugene took off his hat and wiped his brow. "Who am I, but an old man? What am I doing here? Avoiding death, what is. Now Sharon and the children, they've been robbed of their lives. Held in captivity without the wherewithal to leave. I could'a helped them escape long ago but I didn't, cuz' I would'a had to leave too, and then I would'a surely died. You see, in here, I knew I could always live in my flesh a little longer. Now I can admit it. I've been cowardly and selfish." He returned his hat to his head. "I'm ready to finish this and you're gonna help me."

"Finish what?" James asked.

"Prepare for my burial. Time to make things right."

"When did you start thinking like this?"

"Back in the beginning, when *this* started, when she showed up and then the kids did too. When the universe proved it didn't always have to exist with perpetual motion, when I knew I'd never finish my coffin. Now you're arrived and it's a brave new world. Things are gonna start to change around here quick."

"Change, how?"

"You'll see soon enough. We'll haul that tombstone out another time. Now grab this wheelbarrow here and help me finish digging my grave."

"I can't believe what I'm hearing."

They heard the faint tinkling of a heavy cow bell being rung.

"That's dinner, son. They're calling fur ya."

"Yep, the day is done Eugene."

"The day's almost done. But not yet."

"I'll help you dig your grave tomorrow."

"Tomorrow? What if there isn't one?" Eugene grabbed a shovel and marched out alone to the grave.

What was so obstinate about this man and his obsession to die? James watched the gardener disappear out the door. The faint echo of the dinner bell reached his ears again.

"All right then," he said. Rather than head back to Sharon and the children he decided to catch up with the old man and help after all.

❀ † ❀

James came upon Eugene digging in a small clearing between the stonewall and a row of pines. The old man stomped his heel down on the spade lip and slung a shovelful of dirt in the air which landed square in a wheelbarrow.

"Okay, Eugene, I'm ready to help," James said.

Eugene held up a shovel full of dirt. "Why are you here, son?"

"I don't know. Maybe because we're all part of some bigger plan."

James helped Eugene climb out of the hole with the shovel. "You've no idea what you're taking on by showing here, do ya?" Eugene said. "This isn't a game what you can leave when you grow tired of. You could get stuck here forever." He waved his hand at James like a swarm of gnats. "You don't belong here."

"Belong?" James grabbed the shovel from Eugene and jumped in the grave. "I've never felt so at home in my life. This is my destiny as much as it is yours, and I'm damn sure not going to let you or anyone else take that away from me." He picked up a large stone and with two hands tossed it out where it rolled to Eugene's feet. "See, I can do this." He shoveled a mound of dirt in the wheelbarrow but missed. There was a slight grin on the crusty senior's face. "Maybe you don't like it," James said, "maybe you're cross because I know what's been going on here in your timeless space."

Eugene pulled down on the brim of his hat. "Oh, you do, do ya? Think you've got it all figured out."

James shook the head of the shovel towards the estate house. "There's a young mother up there with two children, who've been terrorized by that man for god knows how long. And you apparently have done absolutely nothing to stand up for them. She is edgy, unsure of herself, deprived of her own identity. And you, who's been a part of their lives all this time have been, by your own admission, nothing but a guilty bystander." He continued to shovel, his aim into the wheelbarrow improving. "So, do I have a purpose for being here? Damn right I do."

Eugene spit into the pine needles covering the ground. "Don't let her fool ya, son, no matter how he treats her, she's in love with him."

James yanked out plant roots hanging from the grave wall. "Yeah well, after a while, we'll see who she loves."

"Do you really think you could take him on and resist? You've no idea who you're dealing with."

"He's not so strong that I couldn't take him on," James said.

"He's no longer one of us, like you and me!"

James stopped to catch his breath. "My mother came under the dominion of men like him, bullies all. I learned their tricks. And I made up plenty of my own to rid her of them."

"Careful young man, he has powers you haven't begun to see."

"I can hide, I can survive, while I figure this out."

"Not if you have a cocky attitude like that. He'll smell your scent soon enough. Then he'll try to get rid of you, and then if you won't leave, he will destroy you."

"You're just trying to scare me."

"I'm trying to wake you up! She's not worth it, go! At least you can walk out freely still, if you leave now."

James tossed the shovel. "There's your damn grave." He hopped out wiping his sweaty forehead with the back of his hand. "I'm not going anywhere, Eugene, until I see them leave. You better get used to that."

Eugene scratched his hair under his hat. "If your goal really is to get 'em out, don't be a stupid ass and try to do it all yourself."

"So, you're finally coming around."

"Oh, I wasn't talking about me," Eugene said. "I was thinking of Lawrence. He'll be the one to help you."

"What?" James lost his footing. His arms whirled in the air and he fell backwards into the hole.

"Understand mind you," Eugene said, "Lawrence will need to know you're here; he will need to think—"

James stood and steadied himself, a little shaken. "Forget it, ol' man, I'll win her trust, by my own terms, you just keep Lawrence away. Then between the three of us––you, me, Sharon and the power of," he fumbled with his words, "and the power of love, good over evil––"

"Yeah, the power of peace, love, and all that hippie shit. When that doesn't work, come back and I'll teach ya how to really beat Lawrence." He started to walk back to the greenhouse.

James pulled himself up out of the grave. "Okay! I'm listening."

Eugene returned. He squared off his stance like a coach giving out field plays. "First, never, never try to out lie him. He is the master of deception and will always win that one."

James nodded.

"Second, always confront him with the truth, then he'll use his own wits against himself."

"Makes sense."

"Finally, don't try to do it all on your own. Cuz if you try to go up against him with just your own strength and cunning, you'll lose every time."

"Got it."

"Do you really?"

"All up here." James pointed at his temple. He slapped his hands and rubbed them. "Now are we ready to eat? Because I'm starving."

"You're not gonna follow one word of my advice, are ya?"

"I'll make a deal with you," James said. "Give me space to call my own shots, beat this place in my own way. If I don't succeed, then you can call Lawrence in and," he rubbed the back of his neck, "I'll face him straight on, however you say."

"This is not the place to be making deals, son," Eugene said. "When I see you slipping—"

"I told you, I don't need help from anybody. What success I have is because I've achieved it on my own. You just gotta give me some space. And time, you gotta give me that."

"There's plenty of that here," Eugene said. The dinner bell from the estate clanged louder.

"Get goin', whipper snapper. Your supper's probably gone cold by now."

"Aren't you going to come too?" James asked.

"I never eat, and if I did, I wouldn't with them. I'm not going to start just because you're here. Go on, get your fill of her cookin' yourself. If you can keep it down."

"Thanks, Eugene. I'll haul that tombstone out for you tomorrow all by myself. I promise -- with superhuman strength." He walked down the path which led into the thick of the gardens instead of the path along the stonewall which would have led him straight to the estate house.

"Wait, son, you're taking the long way!" Eugene pointed to the shorter route but James was gone. He lifted the wheelbarrow full of topsoil and parked it under the shadiest of pines. James was right, Eugene could've helped Sharon long ago, if he'd let himself grow closer to them, something he swore he would never do after the death of Worthy and the two Revson sons. "Pshaw, I dug my own grave," he said out loud to no one in particular, "you might as well dig your own too."

❀ † ❀

Wander wrong paths, get lost in the process. James thought he knew where he was going, but sometimes memories are as made up as a dream. Every path led to another, crisscrossing crossroads taking him to dead ends. Physically the garden hadn't changed, but he had; it was no longer a playground paradise where a boy, now a man, could go to indulge in mischievous games. He let his mind wander, and in so doing, it led him straight to the statue at the center of her waterless pool.

"Hello, old friend." A breeze picked up and a swirl of leaves encircled her. "Are you in there still or not?" A flying kite's tail of titmice and thrushes twisted and turned in the air, settling upon the statue's head and shoulders. "Sharon is going to walk by and when she does, I need you to sprinkle a little fairy dust on her, enough to plant a subtle glow in the heart so that when she looks at me, she sees what I see in her. You'll do that for me, won't you?" The statue didn't answer, the birds fluttered away. James left down the path to the garden's center where he would regain his bearings.

4

In the kitchen, a pot of water boiled at a simmer, ears of corn laid in a row ready to be dropped in. Vinegar potato salad with mustard seed and dill, chicken pieces crisp and golden nestled in a cotton cloth while burnt breadcrumbs smoked in a cast iron pan. Where was everyone? It was as if they'd been taken in the second coming. He was hungry. He leaned over and inhaled, expecting to smell the bouquet of different aromas, but there were none. Strange about this place, no odors or tastes. He turned off the stove and climbed the kitchen staircase to his room where he heard weeping.

Sharon lay across his bed atop a thin summer quilt bunched up beneath her, her face buried in it. She sat up, tearful, her fresh mascara running down her cheeks. To James she was beautiful as ever. Not the cupid doll beauty he adored in her as a boy, this newer version had a harder edge to it; no more life's illusions. But what a lovely scent in the air she gave! Washed hair, moisturized skin--did she freshen up for him? Another Sleeping Beauty in need of his kiss to be freed from this place. She motioned for the box of Kleenex on the bureau and he handed it to her. "You're late for dinner," she said, sniffling.

He sat on the edge of the bed. "Are you crying, because of that?"

She wiped her eyes of the smudged mascara, rubbed her nose. "I thought you'd left for good."

He seated himself closer. "I was with Eugene," he said, "helping him in the garden."

"You mean helping him dig his grave."

The children screamed. The two raced out. James shadowed the quick-footed Sharon who knew every corner and turn. In the game room, the children lay writhing among board games as if possessed by demons. Sharon knelt on the plush orange carpet.

"It's okay Sally," she said, stretching the girl's legs out straight, "it'll pass."

"Take slow deep breaths, Timmy," James said, kneeling at his side.

Sally wiped her tears away with the back of her hands. "Timmy says dis' pain is good, he says dis means we ah gwowing."

"It's not going to happen again," her mother said.

"But it will," Timmy said, "as long as James stays, time will move us forward and make this place and everything in it alive again."

"How revolutionary." James walked to the pool table and rolled a ball to the other end. "That's the new plan, stay put and let time take its course. Maybe it will liberate you from this psychological torture you put yourselves through, and you'll come to your senses and walk out of here free."

"Psychological?" Sharon threw her arms up. "Timmy, didn't you show James the world beyond the gate?"

"I saw everything," James said, tossing the cue ball between his hands. "Car relics from the 1960s, some from the 1950s even."

"That's not the world I'm talking about," Sharon said.

"She means the wun wheah da flowahs die," Sally said.

"Timmy, you didn't tell him!" Sharon shouted.

Sally squeezed a doll and it wheezed.

5

One day early in their arrival when Lawrence was away, Timmy convinced his mother they should try to escape. He took them down to the entrance to take that fateful step. Timmy pushed the gate wide open. The three stood on the edge of the drive with the outside world, held hands and stepped forward together.

The estate as they knew it was gone. Sky overcast, dark and grey. Trees like zombies, hollow and dead but still standing. Same road, but with bleached grass grown up through raised ripples of tar. Abandoned cars strewn along in both directions, burned out or overturned. The marshland across the road flattened and dried up, and on the hillside across from the property, a split-level house with a horse pen sitting like a caved-in lump without a roof, thorny vines engulfing its rooms.

The estate gate lay crumpled in rust, the property's trees stripped of leaves and ashen as if raked and bruised by fire. Visible through this forest of skeletal arbors, the mansion was burned and fallen to rubble. Sharon's stomach churned and she began to panic. Did this mean they were stuck in this other hellhole for good? She breathed in deep and controlled her inward panic. They must look for an escape hatch somewhere. She tied Sally's red scarf to a fallen tree, marking the point where they entered, hoping if no other way were found, they could return to the placid sunny estate as it was before they made their leap. She told Sally to hold onto the scarf while she and Timmy explored.

They headed for the cars. Perhaps they could get Eugene to fix one of them. Most were scorched shells. The wood panel sides of a station wagon had peeled off, windows in its doors broken, the roof bent in. It smelled as if there was something dead or rotting inside. The tires were cracked, had no air, the engine under the hood had been fleeced for parts. Lawrence was right, there was no physical escape from this world. They were staring at a post-apocalyptic end. Timmy and Sharon began to cough.

Across the marsh, they spotted a dark grey cloud rolling toward them, dispersing poisonous chemical vapors. Sharon called to Sally, but she had disappeared out of sight. The red scarf was missing. Panic rose in her chest and this time exploded out. She turned in circles looking for her girl, not knowing what direction to start in. Sharon yelled for Timmy to do something.

Sally appeared. She had taken the scarf down and placed it around her neck and returned inside the bounds of the Revson property. She returned with a bunch of bright flowers. She said this yukky place needed them. Sharon shook her hand until she dropped the flowers, which wilted and died as soon as they hit the ground. The poisonous chemical cloud was now bouldering towards them closer and closer. They ran back inside the property gate, and never tried to escape again.

🌀 † 🌀

James rose to his feet. "Wow, this place is one mysterious layer over another."

"Why would you want to stay then?" Sharon asked. "We are literally at the end of the world."

"Maybe that's how we escape, with gas masks." Out the west window, he watched the sun drop off the horizon. "How could I not stay? I'd never be able to live with myself."

Sharon sat on the couch and hugged a pillow. "It's too dangerous, James. You've no idea what Lawrence could do to any of us if he discovers you're still here."

The children ran over and clung to her. "Mother, please!"

"I was sent for a reason, Sharon, and I think you know it," James said.

She noticed how her shadow darkened the shag rug from the sunset, thought of her deal with Lawrence; if it succeeded, it would not end well for James.

"I'm not leaving unless you throw me out," James said.

Sharon nodded her consent. The kids jumped on the couch on top of her and they all rolled to the floor laughing.

6

They descended the curled marble staircase together to the dining room set for twelve. Fresh cut fuchsia with yellow forsythias down the center of the table in vases, hurricane lamps with tall white candles in-between. Sharon placed James at the head while she and the children brought out dishes. She took the first bite, then James began to devour everything.

The children watched in disbelief as he consumed the fried chicken, ears of corn, potato salad, green beans, cold beets and carrots. He slurped down glass after glass of tasteless milk and ice-cold lemonade. No matter how much he ate, the food did not quell his appetite. For dessert, she served him chocolate cake decorated with strawberries. He stuffed whole slices in his mouth until the cake was gone. When Sharon had no more to give, he leaned back on the legs of his chair and rubbed his stomach. "I ate like a glutton yet I'm still hungry."

"Nothing in this world will ever leave you feeling satisfied," Sharon said. "There are no real sensations." She poked at the vegetables on her plate. "We may as well be eating wax. The reason we eat at all is to maintain a daily routine for a sense of normalcy."

Sally put down the salt and pepper shakers she was playing with like figurines and looked at her mother. "Mommy, ahh' we going to show Jimbo de fiah wohks tonight?"

"Fireworks?" James asked.

"Tonight is the 4th of July celebration in this town," Sharon said. "Every night is. It's as if a snapshot of this day were taken and frozen in time."

"That's what Timmy explained down at the gate." James pushed his plate away. "Of course! The town fireworks shoot off today on the school baseball fields south of here." He stood up. "If we sit on the property's back hill, we'll have front row seats!"

"Not tonight, Sally," Sharon said. "James is tired. Tomorrow."

"But if tomorrow really is tomorrow," James said, "it may be the last time you'll ever see them. Let's go."

❀ † ❀

As dusk turned to darkness the four headed to the hill in back. They laid their blankets below the line of fir trees. James stared at the vibrant life beyond the school fence; red painted Ferris wheel spinning endlessly; carousel horses still as statues whirling ceaselessly; gyrating rides spinning perpetually. A world in constant motion moving towards the future. Yet time on the estate never leaving the present. So they keep believing.

James searched the crowd at the fair. He imagined seeing himself, a budding teenager walking around with his friends, having a forbidden cigarette, impressing the girls, maturing foolishly—but maturing. If he could jump the fence and find him, what advice would he give his younger self?

The sky darkened, revealing stars the size of pin holes. Were they too an illusion? Or like the road traffic beyond the front gate just a snapshot in time, carbon copy of that one day and night they were trapped on July 4, 1969? The children's bubbly giggles and bodies knocked and rolled against him as the first fireworks shot into the sky. Sharon took James' arm and squeezed it with every loud burst, laying her head against his shoulder during the soft sprinkling explosions. The place started to work its spell on him.

What if he were never to return to the world he left? If he couldn't remember it, did it therefore cease to exist? Not such a bad idea, as long as Lawrence could be kept out of the picture. Enjoy this as a respite from the cares of the real world. The clouds of sulphur from the fireworks descended upon them. The children screamed and laughed and danced like this was their last day in the estate's forever present. He looked down upon the carnival lights as they blurred with screams of fun. When the missiles soared in the finale of the town's Independence Day display, the children looked up at their mother and saw her smiling and crying at the same time, not for sadness, but with unwrinkled joy.

7

From the earliest hour, it poured heaven. James woke to the sound of wet laughter spilling through the window, Sharon and the children dancing round the flowerbed outside. And why not? For him it was the next day, but they'd woken from the sleep of a quarter century. The sensation of rain bursting cool upon goose-bumped skin until now a distant memory, felt only in dream. To witness change in the direction the wind blew, flight patterns of birds, advance of flowers in bloom--to feel and observe these minute changes of movement in the natural world must also imply they felt the same invisible influences working inside themselves, an ineluctable force so sublime it was only felt by poets, artists, and holy men of their time.

James stuck his head out the window and waved, shouting at the others through foggy drizzle, but they couldn't hear. Anxious to explore this new world, he hopped in his wrinkled clothes from the day before into a maze of crisscrossing hallways on the second floor. From the north of the estate overlooking the carriage house, to the south side facing the garden, he wandered until he came upon a pair of tall white doors trimmed in gold leaf, over above which read an ancient inscription in gilded letters: "Eritus sicut Deus, scientes bonum et malum/Be like God, conscious of Good and Evil." Through doors slightly ajar, a ray of light streaked into the hallway brightening his path, beckoning him to enter.

He stepped into the warm expanse of slanted light pouring through a broad picture window. The sun broke out from the rain, painting him a glazed honey. Standing on an oriental at the center of the room he looked up at shelf after shelf of books surrounding him two stories high, above a railed walkway circumscribing the room. To his left below the winding stair, an oak refectory table covered with artifacts of clay, bronze, wood and glass. To his front, a red velvet Victorian settee facing the large picture window, tables with cranberry glass lamps on each side; the room felt as though nothing had changed since the early twentieth century.

He roamed to the side of the room overlooking the lawn, found an unlit fireplace surrounded by reading chairs with lamps. He thrummed his fingers along a row of classics he recognized and loved: Homer's *The Odyssey,* the dramas of Aeschylus, Sophocles, and Euripides. Those in the Latin tongue: Ovid's *Metamorphoses* and Virgil's *Aeneid.* On a shelf below, the earliest English sagas such as *Beowulf* and the tales of King Arthur, followed by the works of the renaissance writers Dante, Boccaccio, Petrarch and Chaucer. James wandered back to the center of the room, craned his neck up to take it all in: books on every subject known to mankind. This library, the safeguard of Logos, all the knowledge of the universe contained in one place. He shook his head at them. Of what value are any of these works, if they do not inspire the reader to take action and change for the greater good?

James drifted across to the other end of the study, which overlooked the fields beyond the west wall. There a wide and tall gilded mirror hung above a display case of wood and glass from the Bauhaus art deco era, standing on spindly wooden legs. Below the glass, James found rare leather-bound volumes open to brittle pages; the celestial discoveries of Copernicus and Galileo, an alchemical text of Paracelsus, parchment scrolls of the Kabala, texts of Nostradamus in a mix of languages, a book on symbols and pentagrams entitled the *Druid's Claw*. Laid flat on the velvet bottom was a dull blue volume with a frayed spine, the words on its cover written in gold swirling letters of medieval calligraphy: *Tales of the Daemon Lover*. He lifted it out as if handling fragile china, opened to a veiled page of rice paper, behind which read a quote from Milton's *Paradise Lost*: *"Subtle he needs must be, who could seduce Angels."* James sat on the couch bathed in a wealth of sunlight and began to read.

❀ † ❀

The doors of the study opened and closed with a crisp click and snap. Sally appeared, hair beaten down, clothes damp from the rain.

"I'm not the lit'tew guel you see he'ah, you know," she said. Without taking her eyes off James, she glided past the refectory table cluttered with trinkets, pulling off her favorite seashell and caressing it in her hands. Fondling it, she walked up to James, then threw it down to wrap herself around him like a starfish. He patted her head and felt something heavy inside. What thoughts lived in the mind of this child, to be kept so young forever? He peeled her off and she climbed up on the sofa, patting the cushion for him to sit beside her.

"I am so gwad you ah he'ah James," she said, swinging her feet over the sofa edge.

James sat next to her. "Me too, Sally."

"Wha's dat you ah wea'ding?" she said. He opened the book and they glanced at a medieval illustration of the devil surrounded by an entourage of horned creatures.

"Stories older than Grimm, Sally," he said. He turned the page to an illustration of a seaside cottage upon a cliff, below which read "The Coast of Scotland, a lover's Cottage." A sailor stood at its door knocking.

"Is it a love sto'wy?" Sally asked.

"Let's find out." He began to read in the three different voices.

Woman: Oh, where have you been, my long-lost love, this seven years and more?

Sailor: I've come to seek my former vows, ye granted me before.

While James read, the library doors opened, but James and Sally didn't notice, absorbed as they were in the story.

Woman: Oh, do not speak of your former vows, for they will breed sad strife; do not speak of our former vows, for I have become a wife.

Narrator: He turned her right and roundabout, and a tear blinded his ee.

Sailor: But I would never have trodden upon this ground, if it had not been for thee.

Woman: If I was to leave my husband dear, and my two babes also, what have you to take me to, if with you I should go?

Sailor: I have seven ships upon the sea, the eighth brought me to land—with four-and-twenty bold mariners, and music on every hand.

Narrator: She'd taken up her two little babes, kissed them on cheek and chin:

Woman: Oh, fare ye well, my own two babes, for I'll never see you again!

"That's tew'wible," said Sally, with barely audible breath.

"There are women who do that, you know," James said looking at her.

"She set her foot upon the ship, no mariners could she behold; but

the sails were of the taffeta, and the masts of the beaten gold.

They had not sailed a league, a league, a league but barely three, when dismal grew his countenance, and drumlie grew his ee.

They had not sailed a league, a league, a league but barely three, when she espied his cloven foot and wept right bitterly."

James interrupted himself. "—oh,"
"What?" the girl asked.
"He's the devil," James said.
"Lah'wence," Sally said. The clouds covered the sun and the room darkened. "My muth'a." She pushed off the couch and sat on the rug grabbing the toes of her shoes and began rocking. She spoke an incomprehensible chatter while James continued with the story.

Sailor: Oh, hold your tongue of your weeping said he, of your weeping now let me be, I'll show you how the lilies grow on the banks of Italy.

Woman: Oh, what hills are yon, yon pleasant hills that the sun shines sweetly in?

Sailor: Oh, yon are the hills of heaven, he said, where you will never win.

Woman: Oh, what other mountain is yon, she said, so dreary with frost and snow?

Sailor: Oh, yon is the mountain of hell, he cried, where you and I will go.

He struck the topmast with his hand, the fore-mast with his knee, and he broke that gallant ship in twain, and sank her—sank her— in the sea.

Sharon and Timmy stood behind the sofa, Sharon with a wan look on her face. Timmy led Sally to the door, but not before his mother turned on him.

"Timmy! Did you leave that book out for him to find?"

"It wasn't me," the boy said.

"You know you're not allowed in here," she said. "If Lawrence finds out, I'll catch hell for it."

"But Mommy, I promise."

"Sharon, it's not his fault," James said.

"You are forbidden to step foot in here again, Timmy, do you hear?"

"Sharon."

She turned on James. "You too!"

The children left. Sharon stood at the window staring out above the gardens. "That's me. Seduced away by my own vanity, swallowed up to the bottom of the sea."

"It's an old fisherman's tale," James said.

"No, it's true. It's my fault we're stuck here, I did a terrible thing."

A moth flittered about on a windowpane trying to escape. Sharon slapped at it, catching it between the palm of her hand and the window. It smudged on her palm but didn't die, so she slapped the window again to kill it. It remained alive so she slapped again and again until she slapped so hard with both hands, James had to grab her around the waist and swing her away from the window, holding onto her until she stopped resisting. He relaxed his grip and she moved away.

"I left them, James," she said, "I didn't want to at first, but I gave in."

"Because he forced you."

She punched her chest. "Because I wanted to."

"But they needed their mother—"

"They had their father."

Outside the trees waved in the wind, brushing shadows over Sharon.

"I never wanted to be a mother," she said, "after they were born it was like they belonged to someone else. But I never treated them badly."

"You mean you never loved them."

"I didn't say that." She lifted a plush cushion from the sofa and hugged it. "I just wasn't a very good mother. Timmy always took care of his sister. He acted more responsibly than I was capable of."

"How did they end up here with you?"

"Anne Godwin sent them."

Her name sparked a memory and he remembered. James had met Anne at the top of a skyscraper—where she slyly tasked him with visiting the property.

Sharon brushed the wet grass clinging to her dress. "Their father dropped them off at my house on the Fourth of July. He didn't bother to make sure I was there first, son of a bitch! Left those two young kids alone to fend for themselves. What kind of parenting is that?" She threw her hands up. "It was two weeks after the club party and Anne knew I had moved in with Lawrence. Timmy called her looking for me. They came straight over in a town car. It shook me to the core to see them arrive. Lawrence was furious. He ordered them back in the cab, and me to return inside." Sharon knelt on the sofa and gripped the back edge of the settee. "I walked away, turning my back on my own children, covering my ears so I wouldn't hear them cry. I followed Lawrence inside. But they wouldn't leave." She turned around and sat limp, gazing down at a sun beam coloring the floor. "Instead Timmy sent the taxi home and they sat in the drive crying. I finally disobeyed Lawrence and brought them in."

James walked away, hands over his head. He circled back, stood by the side table. "It must be a horrible thing to live with," he said. "Abandoning your children like that." He straightened the lampshade.

An older memory: he remembered his baby brother drowning in a pool while his mother lounged not far away.

"Everyone has their dark moments. Mothers are no different." He clicked the lamp on and off.

Sharon wiped her eye with the back of her hand. "You can hate me now if you like."

"I'm not going to hate you," James said, standing up straight.

"This isn't your fault, it's that narcissistic keeper of yours who pushed you to it. Why do you let him control you like that?"

She leaned back, fingered the swirling circles on the settee's curved wood trimming. "He can do whatever he wants with me. I've been here so long, I no longer care."

Sharon stood up from the couch. She pointed at herself in the giant mirror. "See that young woman? Once upon a time she made a deal with the Master to look young and beautiful forever, expecting it would lead to happily ever after. It didn't turn out that way."

James nodded at the woman in the mirror. "She's nothing but a phantom reflection, Lawrence can have her. But you must return to the outside world you left."

"How? For years, Master sent trespassers in to steal me away from Lawrence. Some brought me hope, until they left. Then I was the one who suffered. That's why I no longer trust anyone who offers to help. Not even my best friend."

She sat down resting her hands in her lap. "But James, you're different. I can trust you, can't I?"

Another memory. The Chairman. Money. Lots. Why? To convince a woman it was safe to leave. What happens if he doesn't succeed?

He sat beside her. "I understand why you can't leave. I promise I will never, ever let anyone out there touch you, not even the Master. Somehow, we'll find a way to leave this place together and escape his reach."

He took her hand and squeezed it. When she squeezed back, an intensity of attraction bounced between them like an electrical shock. She let go of his hand as if it were a live wire and slid to the other end of the couch. The two sat like that without speaking, until their breaths normalized.

8

The next morning, James was wakened by the slide of a window frame, its lattice shades riding a breeze. He smelled coffee. Sharon stood pouring a mug of it on a breakfast tray which she lifted off a table and balanced on his lap. She bent down and pecked him on the cheek.

He sat up. "What was that for?"

"For learning the truth about me yesterday, and not running away."

"And how many times have you already insisted I leave?" He lifted the coffee to his nose, breathed its aroma, took a sip. "That deep richness." He picked up a piece of bacon and crunched on it. "Salty."

"This place is alive with taste and smell now, James!" She twirled around in her flowered dress. "Timmy and Sally can't stop eating Fruit Loops downstairs, eating peanut butter and jam straight from the jars. I smoked a cigarette I had hidden and tasted the tobacco." She gazed out the window onto the front lawn and sniffed, the smell of flower pollen floating in the air. "We live another new day, James, and we owe that to you."

"If you're truly grateful," he lifted the tray, "then show it by taking this away and letting me sleep. What time is it?"

She took back the tray. "We stopped telling time long ago."

He rolled onto his side towards the wall and closed his eyes.

Sharon pressed the tray down on the bureau so that its contents shook. "James Harris, how can you waste one more waking minute of life asleep?"

She jerked his shoulder back, and when he turned his face up to hers, the two were so close, he could have kissed her. "All right," he said.

He pulled the covers off and stood up in his boxer shorts. She stared at him, then quickly looked away.

"What?" he asked. "Oh."

He looked down at his erection showing through his boxer shorts.

"You're pale," she said, without looking, "you need a tan."

"Sure," he said, "take advantage of this endless summer." With his back to her he pulled on his wrinkled suitcoat pants from the chair.

"No, don't wear those," she said, "it's too hot." She pulled the top off a wicker hamper Timmy had hauled in. In it were summer clothes. She pulled out a polo shirt and handed it to him. "Try this."

"No thanks," he said, "I'm not interested in wearing your partner's hand-me-downs."

"They're not his. They belonged to the Revson brothers."

"Now I'm going to wear the clothes of dead men."

"Kind men," she said, "who died young."

Sharon poked through the basket and handed him bathing trunks. He held them up. "A tan and a swim?" he asked. "Perfect."

"Every morning," she said. "Lifts our spirits for the day. It'll be a treat for the children to have someone else to play with besides me. Lawrence never pays attention to them." She walked to the door. "See you at the pool." She stepped out. "And do not go back to bed, promise?"

"Promise."

✿ † ✿

Wearing what she gave him and a pair of Ray-Ban sunglasses he found in the basket, James roamed down the hall to the top of the grand staircase. Holding the banister, he eyed the crystal chandelier hanging down from the glass atrium, sparkling free of dust. He felt the spaciousness rise from the black and white tile floor below. How could so few people live in such a large place? He made his way down the stairs through the grand living room to the far end where the French doors opened out to the pool. Timmy and Sally were laughing and splashing.

He walked up to pool's edge, gazed around. To his left, a row of flower bushes in bloom along the edge of the manor house, now giving off a magical fragrance. At the opposite end, a tree-shaded lawn enclosed by beech hedges and on his right the bathhouse extending the length of the pool, its windows with clapboard shutters. Connecting the bathhouse to the sunroom of the estate was a latticed arbor covered with grapes. Through it a brick walkway led down to the side lawn. James felt safe; he belonged here. A splash of water wet his feet.

Sharon climbed out by the ladder in a neon orange bikini with thin laces tied around her neck. The water rushed off her body, her tanned skin dripping with beads of water. He stared at her.

"What?" she asked, pulling her wet hair back in a pigtail.

He took his Ray-Bans off. "We all noticed you back then," he said, "my friends and I around the club pool. But then you knew that, didn't you, the way all men looked at you."

She squeezed the water from her hair, standing in her own puddle. "The club didn't permit bikinis," she said. She asked him to hand her a towel from the rack under the shaded portico. She wiped down her arms and legs and laid down on one of the ribbed lounge chairs.

"Come in, Jimbo, we want to play!" Timmy shouted, arms flat

on the curb of the pool at James' feet.

"Yeah, Jimbo, we want to pway wid you," Sally said, floating in a bubble ring next to her brother.

James looked at Sharon rubbing oil into her arms, then removed his shirt and sandals and dove in over the kid's heads.

Together the three splashed and laughed while he pushed them around on the plastic raft, tipping them over, letting them stand on his shoulders and jump off. After a while, the children tired and got out. They wrapped towels around themselves. Timmy took Sally's hand and led her into the house through the service entrance hidden behind the hedges. Avoiding the ladder, James lifted himself out on the strength of his arms, hands pressed down on the curb of the pool. Dripping, he grabbed a towel and sat on the edge of a lounge chair opposite Sharon.

"Eerie this place," he said, wiping his chest. "Quiet, so peaceful." He stared at her curves glistening with droplets of sweat rolling between lines of coconut oil.

"Too quiet, too peaceful," she said. "The longer you're here, the harder it is to leave." She grabbed a bottle of Coppertone under her chair. "You need some lotion." She squirted a stream of the white liquid on his back. He arched away from its warm gush. She rubbed it in deep. He felt each of her fingers move down his backbone, rubbing the lotion into his lower back, circling up to the creases of his shoulder blades, the nape of his neck. "You have beautiful skin," she said, "youthful like your mother's." She walked back around, dabbed a bit of lotion on his temples, rubbing in small circles. "You've become a truly handsome man, James Harris, even in middle-age," she said, looking him in the eyes. "I always thought you'd grow up to become one." They soaked in the sun.

❀ † ❀

After a while, James felt the excessive heat and stood. "Join me for a dip," he said, extending his hand. She stood up and before James could react, she punched him in the gut and dove in.

He dove in after her and the two splashed each other like kids. He reached to grab her, but she was too slippery from the coconut oil and glided away. When he was about to catch her, she kicked at him and tried to swim away, but he caught her leg and reeled her in and dunked her. She surfaced and screamed and tried to dunk him back but couldn't, and instead like a mermaid with giant tail fins swam out of reach to the far side of the pool. She looked at him as if she were a dangerous siren who could wreck him if he came too close. He swam to a spot along the wall and rested his elbows behind him on the curb of the pool. With eyes closed, he nodded to the sun. She inched nearer, held herself floating in front of him.

"Must be hard not having adult company more often," he said. He reached out, picked some stray wet hairs off her cheek. "A beautiful woman like you, forever young, trapped by a louse who leaves you alone constantly. Isn't he concerned someone might show up and take you away from him? Certainly, I'm not the first male trespasser to walk into this paradise with genuine concern," he said.

"You're the first who ever stayed," she said.

"Because you chase them out."

"Because Lawrence does."

She pulled herself out of the pool and sat on its edge. "They only appear when he's here, which is why he stays away as long as he does. Doesn't want the constant battle of keeping trespassers' hands off me, never knowing which were sent by the Master and which simply wandered in." She dangled her feet in the water.

"This past spring in the real world, you might remember, the property was placed up for sale. Young couples would show up from the city on a house hunting mission. They'd drive in having no idea they'd just entered a timeless world. Lawrence would insist we walk out to the drive to greet them holding hands. If he found the man glancing at me too often, he'd invite them to stay for a cocktail at the pool. Lawrence did all the socializing, I just lay there enjoying the loud music and sun on my skin, my chance to drink and chain smoke cigarettes. Lawrence filled these trespassers with booze, flirted salaciously with the wife, told them how oversexed I was and that I tired him out. Then he'd go inside. This gave the husband a chance to flirt, eventually making a pass at me. That's when Lawrence would appear and humiliate the husband until he took a swing at him. Lawrence is a trained boxer. He'd knock the husband over and then run them out."

"I can box too," James murmured. He lifted himself out of the water and sat beside her. "There must have been one visitor who he didn't get to." James circled his toes in the water creating a whirlpool. "Not one decent man?"

"Once," she said, staring at the sun's reflection in the wavy surface. "It was the last time Lawrence ever allowed a trespasser to stay for an afternoon. The man was Ned Merrill, you might remember him, he was friends with your parents. In fact, he was friends with everyone. His family was one of the longest standing members at the club. Old New England money from ship building in New London. He was close to fifty yet appeared ten years younger, fit as Jack Lalanne, a face like Burt Lancaster. That's why I remember him so vividly. But his end was rather tragic."

James stopped kicking at the water and the whirlpool disappeared. "Tragic?" he asked.

"It's a long story," she said, "do you really want to hear it?"

"We have all the time in the world here, don't we?"

9

"One day Ned Merrill came strolling up the driveway in his bathing suit and bare feet," Sharon said. "As he passed, he nodded at the dead pan Eugene, who just stood there holding his rake, suspicious. Ned had left an all-night party at the Balridges across the street. After their morning mimosas, the guests began their trudge home. Ned was about to catch a ride with the last stragglers when he decided on a better idea. He knew where all the pools in the neighborhood were and decided he would swim home through all of them. He told Lawrence he knew the Revsons well, they were good friends of his. He was certain there was never a third son."

"I'm sure that didn't go over well," James said, raising his eyebrows.

"Lawrence was not going to allow that to go unchallenged. He began to scheme at once how to entrap Ned in his games of masculine one-upmanship. I thought, 'Oh-oh, here it's coming.' He invited Ned to take his swim but only after he stayed for a few cocktails and Ned gladly accepted.

"Lawrence gave him double shots of whiskey, glasses of scotch on the rocks. He accepted every refill, but it never affected him. He ignored Lawrence whenever he taunted him, instead focused on me, not to flirt, but to talk."

"About what?" James asked.

"At first it was about common friends and acquaintances we knew and recent club events and activities. But as the alcohol relaxed him, he began to pontificate on long discourses about the death of the American dream and the deteriorating moral fabric of our community. More couples having affairs and getting divorced, which was quite hypocritical since I knew he had a mistress. He complained of teenagers wearing longer hair and protesting a war they didn't understand. He leaned back in his pool chair totally at ease. I could see Ned was making Lawrence tense, who kept walking in and out of the pool terrace, appearing to mope, all the while my friend chattering away. Lawrence kept handing him drink after drink, hoping he would either fall over in a stupor or make a pass at me. But he did neither. I'd never seen Lawrence lose a match before."

James gripped the pool curb. "Especially on his own turf."

"I could tell Ned really needed someone to talk too. I didn't say one word the whole time. He spoke of his wife and how swell she was, and his beautiful daughters, two at Greens Farms Academy and two in boarding schools up north. That's when he surprised me."

"He finally put Lawrence in his place?" James slugged a fist into his palm. "That's what I would've done to him by now."

"That never happened. He began to talk about how happy he and his wife Lucinda were, major renovations at their colonial estate, a cocktail party they were soon to give, a trip to Europe they were planning with their girls before the end of summer. That's when I started to wonder about his sanity.

"I knew his real story. He'd been the most envied man at the club, inherited money, eight generation WASP back to the Mayflower. With his background, looks, athleticism and charm, he was one of the most sought-after cocktail guests in the county. But he'd been financially ruined, something about a scandal, nobody ever knew what exactly. He lost everything. A stigma attached to him. Overnight he became a social pariah. His wife filed for divorce and took their kids away from him to the west coast. Their home was boarded up by the state for taxes and placed up for auction. It was then that I realized he was living in a fantasy world."

"Like you," James said.

Sharon nodded. "So sad really, one thinking he still has it all, I felt sorry for him. He must have been lonely."

James slid into the pool holding the curb.

"Lawrence became so fed up, he marched up and took away my drink, berated me in front of Ned as if everything was my fault. Called me horrible things. Ned stood up, and with a gentle hand moved Lawrence back, warned him to treat me better, Lawrence shouldn't pick on women from his own insecurity and cowardice. Lawrence was livid and ordered him off his property immediately. That's when Ned took my hand, looked me in the eyes and said, 'Sharon, you don't have to put up with this anymore.'"

James lay his arms on the pool curb at Sharon's side.

"He told me to grab the kids and my things and leave with him. My heart rose and beat hard and I started to believe I could. 'You have no reason to be treated like this,' he said. 'You can leave him anytime you wish, you must take courage.' I looked in his eyes, soft and tender, and that's when I recognized that for all his fantasies, he was more grounded in reality than I was. 'No,' I said, 'I'll be okay, Lawrence and I just have our spats now and then like any couple, but most of the time he's a real gentleman.' Lawrence beamed. Quietly and with perfect poise, my friend stood up. He'd several more pools to swim through, he said, and if he was to make it home to his wife and girls before dark, he'd best get going. He downed his last drink and dove in the pool. Hopping out at the far end, he grabbed a towel off a rack to brush the water drops off his arms. He tossed the towel aside and with a great wistfulness stared across the pool at me, knowing what I was feeling––trapped and isolated––like him––alienated from a world that no longer believed in us, the same ritzy crowd of Fairfield County to which neither of us anymore belonged. Slowly he waved his hand goodbye, then disappeared through the beach hedge gate."

Sharon lowered herself in the water next to James.

"I always wondered what would have happened if I tried to leave with him, James," she floated in front of him. "What if because of the Master we can't ever escape? Would you be willing to stay here with us, if Lawrence were out of the picture, even if it meant you might never be allowed to leave too?"

"If it meant taking Lawrence's place then yes."

She leaned in and pecked James on the lips. Then she pushed off the pool wall with her long legs and glided away. She spurted water in the air like a fountain, then swam to a ladder on the opposite side and stepped out. Wrapping a towel around her waist, she grabbed her hairbrush and coconut oil and walked to the side entrance. She waved goodbye to James, looking like her friend the swimmer, wistful. James waved his hand back goodbye, continued even after she disappeared inside.

10

The initial months of James' stay passed like this, picnics and outings in the fields under great oaks and elms, barbeques by the pool. Each day was different than the one before with its own novelties for them to notice. The manor itself registered new creaks they could detect.

The excitement of the natural and physical changes they witnessed were tempered for Sharon and the children by an internal dread. The day Lawrence would return. James--as the others grew restless--grew more relaxed, accustomed to the idea of staying as long as it might take to get Sharon and the children out safely. He enjoyed teaching Sally how to read and write, tutoring Timmy in math and the classics. He never planned a great escape, believing somehow it would reveal itself naturally as the days passed into the future. And neither Sharon nor the children pressed him on it since, every day being new, they too began to believe that was the only plan, a flowing momentum which would sweep them over a waterfall of time, like following the arc of a rainbow, drop them back into their real worlds--one where life was evidenced by growth, change, death.

For Eugene, it was the curse of time that creeped across the property. Everything was growing again. The estate's lawns and gardens, surrounded by the forest which hid them, were too wide and broad for an old man like him to keep up with anymore. No longer could he cut all the grass and trim the hedges, upkeep the special fringe trees such as golden rain, late blooming summer dogwoods, ground cover such as wisteria and juniper, nor paths of brick and slate and flagstone winding through the back garden. The sweeping of tennis courts, keeping the pool water filtered. He abandoned the most strenuous labor for James and Timmy to handle. With time moving ahead, Eugene began to feel the strain of age more acutely than the rest. As the summer passed, he withdrew more, dedicated his days to his only love, the care of his bulbous beauties, replacing July's blooms with August's perennials and the rest of the ocean of flowers in the back garden.

James continued to feel Sharon's growing affections for him and his for her. It slipped out in the smallest physical ways, which they pretended not to notice; when Sharon applied lotion to James' sunburns, cut his hair short as she preferred, soothed his skin with her fingers. When he lifted her in his arms to reach a high spot on the wall for cleaning, or pulled straw from her hair while they hunted for berries the birds had missed—these were the stolen scenes they cherished. Misplayed opportunities to attain a stronger, physical union left unattended. James reminded himself he was there to support her, not become romantically entangled. But it was not working. The hot days of July passed into the dog days of August, and Sharon's vegetable garden, which Eugene helped her seed, she kept free of weeds, and so cultivated by her hard work and sweat, grew to its maturity.

11

Enjoying the last cool sip of his iced lemonade, James rested bare back in the shade of the garden hut watching the sweat-full curves of Sharon in her halter top as she raked down rows of vegetables. He shook the remnants of ice in his glass. "Sharon, of all the flowers surrounding your garden, which is your favorite?"

She stood by a column of sunflowers, smoothed over with the tip of her finger one of their soft centers, millions of minute brown tentacles surrounded by yellow petals.

James smiled. "'The sunflower, weary of time, countest the steps of the sun: seeking after the sweet golden clime, where the traveler's journey is done.' William Blake."

"I would be this flower itself," she said. "Willing to worship the sun, climb into its arms if it promised not to burn away my petals, fragile, soft and long. You see I can be a poet too."

He fondled a petal. "This sun, does it have a name, someone special?"

She looked up at the afternoon sun, covering her eyes. "Such as who, James Harris?"

He rubbed the back of his neck. "Lawrence, perhaps?"

It was as if the moon appeared and eclipsed the sun. Sharon erased her smile, marched away to work in the farthest end of the garden.

James followed. "You move away just because I mention his name." He sat back on his heels beside her. "Do you know what

Eugene thinks our best chance is to get you and the children out of here?"

She lifted a droopy carrot top. "No, what does he think?"

"When Lawrence returns, we meet face to face, and I have it out with him."

Sharon pushed James back so hard he rolled over in a somersault. She stood up. "He's trickier than you think, James. He'll smooth talk you into taking his side, then use you against me somehow. No," she pulled her hair back in a knot, "I'll take care of him when he returns. I know his weaknesses. Just leave it to me."

"But Eugene said—"

"Forget Eugene, he's in cahoots with him. I should've never gone along with your staying. We're better off without you here to make things worse. Promise you won't dare mention his name again—"

"I promise."

She bent down with ties for the tomato stalks. "—or meet him without my presence." She tied them tighter than they needed to be. "This is his kingdom, and he's the one who sets the rules."

"Sharon," James said.

"He will con you, James, into some deal that favors him, not what you think you're getting. Just like that partner of his. You can't win with them, nobody can."

"I won't, but Sharon––watch out!"

James slapped a spade upon the neck of a copperhead slithering along the garden's edge, trapping it against the ground, body wincing and coiling like the tail of an angry cat. Sharon brought the metallic blade of her hoe swiftly down, severing the snake in half. She continued chopping at it, nearly slicing James' hand off. The body danced and squirmed before it lay limp. James swept Sharon away with his arms around her waist and stopped her from any more chopping. She struggled in his arms but finally gave in and held him tight, crying on his shoulder.

"I don't love him, James. I never did."

"I know." He held her back and looked into her eyes. "I'll be

your new sun to burn his shadow out of your memories forever."
He took a shovel, carried the messy massacre and tossed it over the
stone wall into the woods. Sharon wiped her red eyes and runny
nose on the back of her canvas gloves, then stripped them off. The
clouds passed, and the sun shone down on them again.

"You know that snake would never have died before you
arrived," she said, approaching him.

James threw the shovel down and approached her. "And time
would never have started to tick forward if your hopes did not rise."

Sharon walked her fingers down James' tan arm. He watched
as her finger followed his lines of sweat. He held her arm down to
her side. Kiss her, kiss the statue. She took his hand and wrapped it
behind her back and their lips moved closer together.

They kissed and kept kissing deeply until they were breathing
hard. James slipped one blouse strap off her shoulder, then the other.
Sharon untangled herself from him and stepped back. "The hose."
She gave him a frightened stare. "I left the water overflowing in the
melon patch." She ran behind the sunflowers out of sight.

12

Dark of unknown night, unseen clouds blocking the light, from a host of moons and suns sucked into a void, of rain-filled wind, thunder, and lightning. James and Sharon laid on the beds of the children, reassuring them Lawrence was not behind this, just nature getting used to expressing itself in different moods again. With the lights out, they distracted the children from the ferocity of the storm by telling stories under the dim glow of dying flashlights until the lightning ceased and the thunder dissipated into a distant bark. The children drifted off to sleep under the soothing pulse of rain.

In the hall James whispered in Sharon's ear. She kissed him on the cheek, and the two said good night, walking in opposite directions. In his room James laid undressed on top his bed, cooled by the rain-filled air flowing in from the window. He fell into a deep sleep and dreamed.

He dreamt he was a boy again on the grounds of the estate traipsing through on his way home from the baseball fields. The sky darkened and down from the dark flew a winged creature. He thought it was a bat. But it was much larger than that; wings straight and wide, tips dipped in gray, she was an owl, a Great White. The creature swooped down and up gliding over his head into the rafters of a faded red barn standing at a slant. He headed into the barn where the owl floated in effortlessly.

James sauntered across the hay strewn floor, discovered at its center an open hatch, with stairs descending into a lightless tunnel. His heart swelled as it rose into his throat. He was curious how deep the hole went. Reaching the bottom, he walked towards a dim light, visible through the open portal of a thick wooden door, iron plates fastened to ancient wood of such rough texture that, if grabbed carelessly, would leave penetrating splinters in a clumsy hand. Through the barred window, the light pulsated like a flame. He pulled the door open by its iron ring handle and the light leaped out and blinded him. A man held a torch above his head, casting a shadow down upon himself: Lawrence.

James woke and found the power back on. The bedroom lamps shone broad. He threw on his clothes and wandered barefoot turning off lights; Sharon's room where she slept, the children's room––Sally had kicked off her blanket, so he covered her with it. He turned them off downstairs in the kitchen, dining room, front hall atrium, finishing in the expansive grand living room. A rhythmic double tapping broke the silence.

The French doors at the opposite end of the room were open, their muslin curtains rippling in a sudden gust. Closing them, he took in the luminescent glow from the sky. Clouds had cleared making way for a bright moon. Was it too held hostage here? Or just some devil memory? Soothed by the hum of the pool pumps in the bath house, he stepped out onto the patio to view the heavens. He felt eerily at peace, but it was short lived. He spotted a shadow escaping below the grape covered arbor between the bath house and sunroom down the side lawn. He followed, in time to see it dart behind an apple tree, a great wrinkled arbor which should have been cut down long ago, but instead stood self-consciously along the edge of the garden as if it had been given special consideration by an indebted gardener, a place of honor among younger trees—above the status of the pear, the dogwoods, all growing elsewhere on the fringes of the manicured property. The tree split into two halves: one dead, no longer bearing fruit; the other, though of no great bounty, still alive. Surrounded by the trim and raked grounds, it emanated a halo with an aura of suspicion in the sparkling due of the predawn. In the moonlight, James felt exposed. A single glistening red apple hung in plain sight. He reached to within an arm's length of the tree's branches to pick it, smelled fermented cider, then––a voice spoke. Startled he tripped backward over a root, fell on his back to the ground.

"Who's there?" James shouted.

"Nay, answer me," said a dark silhouette as it stepped into the light, "what are you still doing here?"

It was Lawrence, leaning against the tree. He played with a long piece of straw between his teeth, a hand in his tuxedo pocket, bow tie undone.

"I see you chose not to take my advice and leave," he said. James inched away on his elbows. "You're a bold man to stick around like this." He gazed up at the night sky. "By god, ol' sport, what have you done to the weather? We now have rain. Things may actually start to grow around here. And die." He crouched beside James, placing his hand on his shoulder. "Floored by my presence, are we?"

"Surprised," James said, raising up on his elbows, "I didn't think—we didn't think you'd return this soon."

"We? Or just you?" he said.

"What do you want from me?" James said.

Lawrence laughed. "Why should I want anything from you, when I already have everything I need?" He picked a few blades of wet grass from James' hair. James knocked his hand away and jumped to his feet.

Lawrence stood up. "Be not afraid, my friend. I already know all about you."

"Eugene, the snitch," James murmured.

"Don't think the worst of Eugene. He thinks very highly of you, ol' sport. To think I was jealous of you when you first arrived."

"Is that why you ran me off the road?"

"Obviously, you were no lover of Sharon's in her time. Would've been a boy then. Fancy you coming to this place a grown man. With an obvious romantic interest in her."

"I just want to see her stand up to you and find the courage to walk out on her own."

"You mean leave with you."

"I didn't say that."

"So, you fancy yourself the protector of our beautiful damsel in distress. Tell me, James, how much do you adore being with her, how much does she make the blood in your veins quiver when she walks by? The butterflies in your stomach dance?"

James felt his stomach. "That's not what I'm here for."

"You're in love with her."

"I know she's not in love with you."

"She told you?"

"She hates you."

"God bless her," Lawrence said.

James stiffened his arms at his sides. "Whatever you're planning to do to me, get it over with now," he said.

"Ha! What makes you think I came to do you harm? Perhaps I've come to do you some good!"

"I'm not going to stand here to find out." James turned and walked briskly back to the estate.

"Young man, you can't walk away from me like that!" Lawrence ran ahead of James. "You know I could tear you to shreds for disobeying my orders and staying."

"You can't hurt me, Lawrence," James said to his face. "You're not what they say you are. You're just a man, flesh and blood like me. Now out of my way."

Passing Lawrence, James marched up the slight roll of the hill back through the arbor to the pool patio and the French doors. Finding them stuck, he crashed them in at the end of their hinges with his shoulder and fell through. He checked to see if Lawrence had followed, and when he saw that he had, he walked to the far end of the grand room to the fireplace. A painting hung above the mantel, of a pack of dogs tearing apart a wild boar. His heart pumped.

Lawrence stopped in the doorway, half in the moon light, half in the dark of the interior. He strolled towards James, heels and toe tips tapping the floor with each ordered step. He stopped on the edge of an oriental behind an orange couch, the only barrier keeping the two apart.

"Ordinary man, did you say? Flesh and blood? I'm a man much greater than you in every way." Lawrence said. A fire burst out of the fireplace spitting out embers onto James' shirt.

"No little trick like this is enough to scare me," James said, pulling off his polo shirt. He jumped on the couch, the hairs on his sweaty chest tingling. "I'm not afraid of you." He tightened his fists.

Lawrence stepped closer. "I see right into you, James Harris, further than you ever shall. I could tell you things about yourself so scary you would drop into a catatonic state in an instant, bundle yourself up into a ball and slip your thumb into your mouth and rock back and forth in perpetual motion forever. And it would be forever. Sharon and the kids would feel so afraid they'd never come near you. Locked away in one of the hidden alcoves of this cavernous mansion, nobody would find you ever. Soon you'd be forgotten, a dream in their minds not sure if you ever existed. That you ever came into this world to rescue them in the first place. A world which is really my world."

James cocked up his fists. "It'll take more than that to scare me away," he said. "I know what you are, just a cruel, phony, abusive lout."

Lawrence smiled. "I see Sharon and the children have spoken well of me."

"They didn't have to tell me anything," James said. "I could sense it the first day we met. I've known men like you my whole lifetime, worthless cowards who lived only to serve their own interests and no one else's." In a split second, he saw all the authority figures whose control he resisted his entire life--his father, who left angry without a goodbye; two stepfathers who were jealous of him, a prep school teacher who punished him for spite, bosses who did not promote him because he refused to play into their Machiavellian dramas. When he left corporate America to work for his father in the family investment firm, it lasted only until the two were ready to kill each other. James hated Lawrence now as he hated, at one time, all of them. It showed in the darkening of his pupils, in the heavy exhale from his nostrils. His body tremored.

"You are powerless over me, over any of us here," James said. "Jesus Christ All-Mighty. I can beat the crap out of you anytime. Just tell me when you're ready and I'll do it without hesitation."

Lawrence lost his grin. "You're no longer welcome here," he said, "get off my property."

"You'll have to throw me out."

Lawrence tensed up his stance. "I gave you a chance, now I'm going to destroy you."

"What, with special demonic powers?" James said. "Let's see you fight like a real man."

Lawrence pulled off his dress shirt and drew his fists along his jaw line. "Okay, come down from your perch and just try to take the first swing."

James jumped off the couch and snapped a quick jab to his opponent's face. Lawrence rubbed his nose. "A southpaw, the hand of the devil, didn't the nuns teach you anything?"

"I'm not Catholic," said James, throwing two more jabs, one knocking Lawrence over an end table and breaking a ceramic vase.

Lawrence righted himself. "Don't use all your energy in the first round ol' sport." He needled a jab to James' nose, followed through with another and then a sharp bullseye swing to James' gut.

James backed Lawrence into a wooden cabinet which cracked, splintered, and broke. Its contents of gold and silver tinkled across the floor. Lawrence smacked James' mouth, who bear hugged him into the wall against a regal coat of arms. As it crashed like cymbals, the iron nail which held it pierced into Lawrence's skull. Would such a sharp sting not kill a man? Lawrence felt behind his head where the nail struck, drew his hand to his face, saw red––he didn't believe he could bleed anymore. He went berserk. He picked James up and threw him to the floor where James lay stunned.

"We'll see who the real champion is. Get up." Lawrence said.

James steadied himself. He lunged forward, punching a quick one-two to his rival's face. Lawrence tackled James to the floor and began pummeling him. Shielding the hits, James tripped Lawrence down. They wrestled, knocking over floor vases and plant pots and light stands. Two shirtless bodies fastened together like magnets of opposite poles, sweat mixing with sweat, foreheads knocking, arms and legs fixed in lock.

Upon the gold oriental, they rolled to a stop. James had Lawrence pinned down by a full body press, their hard breaths commingling as they stared into each other's eyes. He raised his arm to give a departing shot when Lawrence shouted, "Enough!"

Breathing hard, his fist still cocked, James kept his superior position on top. "Get off me now," Lawrence said. "You've proven your virility."

The two laid on their backs catching their breaths. Lawrence sat up first. He felt the cuts on his face. "You've got spunk, ol' sport," he said, "I'll give you that. You certainly made mincemeat of my face. God, am I going to hurt tomorrow." He stood. "Is it really Sharon you fought me for? Do you really believe she's worth all this trouble?" He held his hand down to James who took it and climbed to his feet.

"You get no pardon from me for the way you treat her," James said, touching his lower lip.

"Aren't you the cock now," Lawrence said. He swiped his dress shirt up from the floor.

James leaned against the top of the couch, felt the heat of the flames in the fire dry the cold sweat off his back. "What did you do to make her this way?" he asked.

"Nothing," Lawrence said. "She did it to herself. I just bully her now and then to remind her who's in charge."

"Why?"

"Because she lets me." Lawrence buttoned his tuxedo shirt which clung to the sweat of his body. "It's the only way she's ever known to be treated by a man," he said. "She provokes it intentionally to bring down wrath upon herself."

"No woman lets a man bully her on purpose. Tolerate it for survival, maybe." James grabbed his shirt off the couch and wiped the sweat off his face with it, avoiding the bruises and cuts.

"I confess I am not without sin," Lawrence said. "I haven't always treated her the way she deserves, I leave her alone quite often and she's upset for a while but eventually she comes around."

"Do the right thing," James said, holding his shirt in a ball, "let her go."

"It's not that easy, ol' sport." Lawrence fitted on his tux jacket. "Once in possession of an object of such perfect beauty, no man can give it up willingly."

"I could." James pulled his shirt down over his head.

"Could you?" Lawrence darted a stare at James. "What if you were the lord of this manor in my place, with all the same powers over Sharon as I have. As her master you could force her to do anything you please, be your servant, your cook, your seamstress, why you could even make her the ox to furrow your fields. Some men call that a wife."

"I was taught differently," James said. He crouched down to a broken plate and held its two halves up. He tried to fit them together.

Lawrence felt the back of his head. "What about the softer pleasures a woman can afford a man? With this place now alive to the senses those possibilities are bountiful."

James cut him off. "A man has many needs," he said, "why do you think about the basest of them all? What about man's desire to improve himself and his world? Why didn't you bargain for the knowledge and power to do that instead of serving as the devil's footman?" He pointed one of the sharp plate edges at him. "Have you always been so self-absorbed you never cared to know how you could improve the lot of others, those who haven't had the advantages you've had?"

"Stop your crusading," Lawrence said. He shoved his hands in his pockets and paced the rug. "How do you know she wants to leave? I've given her the chance many times, and every time she's turned it down."

"I doubt that very much. She still has that partner of yours to reckon with."

"Even if he let her off scot-free, it wouldn't matter." Lawrence waved his hand in the air. "She'd never survive out there alone."

"Not if she were with me."

Lawrence huffed. "If she were to leave, she'd be old and ugly in an instant." He tapped a cigarette filter on his gold cigarette case. "A shock to a woman worse than death. You'd stay as far away as you could. She'll never be this beautiful and desirable again." He lit up and blew smoke above James' head.

James watched the smoke tumble down. "I'm not so superficial that I see beauty skin deep." He walked to the edge of the rug, watched as the wind blew across the tops of the hedges outside the windows. "At least she would be free from you."

Lawrence stepped on the neck of a fallen swan vase snapping it in two. "It is clear to me you are not going to leave willingly no matter what I do. I therefore have a proposal to make."

He took out a folded paper from his vest pocket and laid it on the wet bar at the center of the room. It was the deed to the property. "Would you risk never returning to your world if it meant ridding me from her life forever? What if we were to present Sharon with a simple choice? She can leave here now, with me, keeping her beauty intact and free to travel the world. Or she can stay here with you confined to this cursed property."

James froze. He was not prepared for that. He gripped the edge of the bar with both hands, arms stiff, and lowered his head in deep thought.

"What happens to the one she doesn't choose?" he asked.

"If she rejects you, you'll be left here alone forever," Lawrence said. "Knowing a woman you sacrificed so much for did not care for you."

"And if you lose?"

"I would never see her again and my partner would send me to the underworld for good."

James leaned over and read the conditional endorsement Lawrence had written on the back of the deed. He took up the pen in his shaking hand.

"It's not worth the risk, ol' sport. Leave while you can."

"I'll sign anything to get you out of her life." James' hand wavered above the signature line.

"She's only using you to get back at me, my friend. She doesn't warm to trespassers kindly. I'm surprised she hasn't thrown you out herself already. She's done it to others."

James touched the pen nib to the signature line yet still hesitated to sign.

"Not so confident when your existence is on the line! Tell you what, set ink to paper and be done with it. Then take the day to think about all this. If your cowardice trumps before dusk, you can leave out the gate and return to your world with nothing lost. However, if at that hour you're still here, the borders of this world will close to your exit, and you'll be bound to the outcome when I return at midnight."

"How do I know you'll live by the outcome?"

Lawrence hunched his eyebrows. "My partner has strict rules when it comes to honoring deals. I don't come to this agreement lightly."

"I have no intention of leaving then." James signed the frayed parchment and flipped the pen down. Lawrence tucked the deed inside his breast pocket while he walked to the far end of the grand room. He saluted James with a flick of his wrist at his brow, then departed into the last hours of the night. James returned the salute with no one there.

✿ † ✿

Walking back to the apple tree, Lawrence watched as one of the gates to the garden swung open. He strolled through the interlocking paths in wonder at how plush it remained. This was Eugene's world––everything in bloom, an eternal spring. Floral scents floated in clouds of perfume. He breathed in their ardor, savoring the smells. Not even Memphis could stop life's progress here now, nor what was happening inside of him.

A whoosh of cool air swirled over his head like a comet down one of the paths. He chased after it like a boy again, grasping at its icy blue tail always out of reach. It led to the fountain, where the comet twisted around the statue's physique, and like pulled taffy twirled up around her like a cyclone and vanished. Lawrence stopped at the rim of the dried basin and gazed upon her in the dark.

"My dear," he said, shaking his head with a smile, "my, my dear." He placed a finger on his lip. "You have been here this whole time and I never suspected it once." He sat on the rim, his back to her. "If I hadn't climbed the cliffs to Memphis' cave that day, I might never have met you. Then you might've lived a full life as someone else's companion, become someone's mother, grandmother. To think if our fates had crossed in another fashion who knows, we might've grown old together, with grandchildren of our own." Lawrence laid one foot on the knee of the other and leaned back holding the raised knee. "To think you were here since the day Eugene uncrated you. Of all statues in Italy to choose from, how is it I chose yours? You emigrated to America after all, didn't you? Your mother would be proud." He craned his neck up. "Luludjka, have you too been re-awakened to life like everything else here?" He stretched his legs out straight and crossed his ankles. "I can't be totally dissatisfied with how it all turned out, your tragic end notwithstanding." He slapped his thighs and stood up. "I'm still in my prime you know. The rest of my generation fought a war and died or grew old with aching limbs bent over sticks like Father Time. But not me," he shook his finger, "not me. I side stepped death and remain in my prime." He circled the patio. "I'm a success all over this globe. I own cotton plantations at the foot of the Himalayas, rubber plants in the rain forests of Brazil, a castle above the Rhine. I have an in with the Pope. The rulers of the world, they know who's got my back. And what do I do for a living? Steal children's mothers away from them for Memphis, those so dissatisfied and chained to domestic servitude that they are willing to run away with me to a faraway place, where I dump them and watch as they suffer unrequited love in the face of my rejection. Having given up, they listlessly submit to the service of Memphis like the walking dead. The braver ones kill themselves. Like you." Lawrence gazed up at her in the dark. "There was nothing but pure love in you, Lulu, it was I who murdered you and the baby, it was not your fault." He stood up and breathed deep. "It was easier to deliver women to his doorstep after that. But how I suffered when I heard the news of your deaths." He searched for a reaction from her. "I understand, no need of a reply, I don't deserve to be in your presence any longer, I am an unforgivable soul." He turned his back and began to walk away. "Sharon, she'll be my second chance to do what is right." He felt the bloody bump on the back of his head. "To be human again and feel pain. Maybe I won't stay immortal much longer." As the sun crawled over the curvature of the earth in the east, brightening the trees and their flushing leaves, Lawrence walked into the mist and dissolved into the light of dawn.

13

MASTER AS BISHOP

(The curtain opens with Memphis dressed as a Catholic Bishop behind the altar of a cathedral wearing red liturgical vestments and a miter cap. He takes the host out of its box and lays communion wafers on a silver tray as if they were crackers. He takes a can of American Cheese Whiz and starts swirling gobs on them. As he picks one up delicately to nibble on, Worthy appears from stage left. Cuts are visible on his nose and cheeks and he sports a black eye.)

MEMPHIS: Care for a wafer? Incredibly good with this American imitation cheese in a can. *(Worthy turns it down but Memphis munches on them one after the other while speaking.)* Good Satan, what boxing ring did you step out of? *(He hands Worthy a cloth to wipe his face and it heals up everything immediately. His face looks like new.)*

WORTHY: An exhaustive tussle with another trespasser. A long story. *(Sits down on the stage edge before the audience, smoothing his once again handsome face).*

MEMPHIS: *(Strokes his bearded chin and walks about).* Spare me
            the details. Worthy, you must quit these cat and
            mice games with visitors, raising their libidos and
            hubristic tendencies to uncontrollable heights then
            exposing them to ridicule. It may prove your male
            prowess but will serve you to no good end.

WORTHY: Hah! We both know it's your doing, sending rivals
            into that protected palace to steal Sharon from me.
            They enter like water through a sieve. What else do
            you expect me to do?

MEMPHIS: She's impossible for any man to resist, and that's
            why I want her. I knew from the moment we met
            she'd make one of my best recruits, right up there
            with Helen of Troy.

WORTHY: I hide her away from you to keep her from such a
            degrading fate.

MEMPHIS: Why this double standard? It's all right for you to
            draw in forlorn women, but not her to attract down-
            trodden men. You hide her from me to keep her for
            yourself. Sooner or later, all you demon lovers fall
            in love with one of your prey and try to hide them.

WORTHY: I'm not one of your demon lovers. I have no hooves.
            I was born human. I think I'm becoming more
            so again.

MEMPHIS: That's why you're bleeding. Something happened.
            You know nothing can live; nothing can die there.

WORTHY: Mother Nature arrived, that's what happened. She
            shows no intention of leaving. It wasn't supposed
            to be possible. Everything has started to grow. Not
            even you can stop it now.

MEMPHIS: That's because you let Sharon gain hope! A powerful anecdote when one has almost lost belief entirely. Not even I can change the course of the spirit once it's released from bondage, it lifts and spreads like a mighty wind. (*A wind blows through a church window and Memphis nervously ducks, watching it swirl around until it leaves out another*).

WORTHY: Now I understand why Eugene was so insistent on letting this trespasser stay. He knew if life took hold, so would death. Crafty fox. Growing older and feebler, he waits to be buried in his grave.

MEMPHIS: You let a trespasser stay this long? Get rid of him and hand her to me. Then I'll restore everything back to the way it was before time ever stepped foot in there.

WORTHY: (*Worthy stands*). Are you joking? It's all part of my plan. This trespasser is my bargaining chip.

MEMPHIS: With whom?

WORTHY: With you.

MEMPHIS: For what?

WORTHY: Our freedom!

MEMPHIS: What would I want with him?

WORTHY: Because with him, you can turn the tables on Him. (*He points a finger up to heaven*).

MEMPHIS: How did you know about that little wager of mine?

WORTHY: You get mighty boastful when drunk.

MEMPHIS: You're exploiting my highest desire, Worthy; you've tempted the great tempter with the opportunity to win a wager at last with that high-seated Lord. I'll let you keep hundreds of your women to win this one soul of His elect. Tell me, how do you plan to entangle him in this web of yours?

WORTHY: I didn't have to do anything. Sharon the seductress has him so enamored he has already accepted my offer to stay with her there in my stead. Naturally, that will never happen.

MEMPHIS: What's your play?

WORTHY: (*Holds up the rolled deed and hands it to Memphis*). At midnight tonight, Sharon shall choose, to stay on the estate with him and the children and grow old or leave with me looking young and beautiful forever.

MEMPHIS: (*Reads the back of the deed*). This is a dangerous game Worthy.

WORTHY: She loves me Memphis. When we kissed, I felt a surging delight of energy like never before. Not even when I walked the earth a mortal. So, do we have a deal or not?

MEMPHIS: Very well, but if your plan backfires, your own hourglass fills complete. Then it's to hell with you! The only way you could save your skin then will be by killing her with your own two hands. To quote Edgar Allen Poe, "There is nothing more poetical than the death of a beautiful woman."

WORTHY: I'd burn the whole place to the ground before I harmed a hair on her head.

MEMPHIS: You really think you are capable of loving another
human being?

WORTHY: Perhaps I too have changed.

*Worthy steps to the front of stage. All lights switch off and a spotlight
appears on him. A cane and top hat are tossed to him and he begins to
dance soft shoe singing Sinatra's "Bewitched".*

> She's a fool and don't I know it?
> But a fool can have her charms
> I'm in love and don't I show it?
> Like a babe in arms
> Love's the same old sad sensation
> Lately, I've not slept a wink
> Since this silly situation
> Has me on the blink
> I'm wild again, beguiled again
> A simpering, whimpering child again
> Bewitched, bothered, and bewildered am I
> So, I'll sing to her, bring spring to her
> And long for the day when I'll cling to her
> Bewitched, bothered and bewildered am I.

*Worthy exits stage left wearing a dreamy smile, the cane over his
shoulder. The stage lights up again.*

MEMPHIS: The battle for heaven begins!
If you've been listening all this time.
Then you know that victory is always mine.
Either way this story ends
I'll be dancing, watch me friends!
Imagine winning over you know who.
For a devil like me it's a dream come true.
If Worthy's plan works out well,
The one the Lord chose I'll take to hell.

If Worthy loses, I still win
For his life will stay an unpardonable sin!
Beware of making a deal with the devil.
It seals your fate which makes him revel
Every soul he's able to steal
Strengthens his hand and sweetens the deal,
I'll storm the gates of heaven yet,
on that God All-Mighty himself can bet!

(Curtain.)

14

CHANGE IS IN THE AIR

6 a.m.

The savory taste and smell of Folgers coffee, a sensation which Sharon experienced afresh, like the pleasurable stimulation of all her senses now. With caffeine shooting through her veins, she was wide awake, the vestiges of sleep swept away––if only she had a cigarette, she'd be her old self again. Standing on the back porch, she breathed in the moistness of the dew not yet burned away, watching birds flutter from bush to tree to bush again, chirping to their mates. If she had her way, she'd spend the whole day in her garden, the one place where she felt in complete control. With it now fully ripened, she could begin her first harvest. She'd waited all summer for this. She laid her coffee cup on the porch rail and headed over.

While she worked in the garden, a gunshot sounded beyond the boundaries of the property. She searched for its source. A thrashing of underbrush grew louder. A tall figure emerged from the foliage dressed in hunting gear, lugging a canvas cover with the large carcass of a deer inside. The figure stopped short of the stone wall which marked the line between the outside world and the estate grounds. It was the Master, dressed like a hunter.

"No makeup, no jewelry, no rings under your eyes," he said, "this place really becomes you, Sharon Peters. Even with all that

243

dirt and sweat, you are glowing."

Sharon raised a rake in self-defense. "What are you doing here?"

"Standing at the edge between two worlds," the Master said. "One an illusion created in the imagination and timeless, the other real and decaying." He dropped his cargo to the forest floor and approached the wall. She jabbed the toothed rake at him.

"You know you're not allowed in here," she said.

He raised his hands and stepped back a few feet. "I know, I cannot go where I am not welcome. Nice to see you back to your old spunky self again."

"What do you want?" she said.

He sat up on a high moss-covered log. From his composed seat, he lit a pipe with a flame on the tip of his finger. "I've come to warn you this trespasser's intentions are not as pure as you think."

"What do you know about him?" She pointed the rake head at the Master.

He bit down on the pipe stem and lifted out a watch from his vest. He held it up to his ear and listened to it tick, nodding in approval. "I always found the absence of time here rather annoying." He shrugged. "Last night your hero James met with Lawrence," he said. "You were the topic of discussion."

"I don't believe you. James promised he'd never meet Lawrence alone." She lowered the rake head. "What did they say about me?"

"It's not what they said." The Master jumped down from the log. "It's the deal they made. Tonight at midnight, you will be forced to decide with which man you prefer to spend the rest of your existence. You can choose to stay there," he pointed his pipe stem at the estate, "with your children and James and grow old together, or out there," he pointed his pipe over his shoulder, "with Lawrence and remain young and beautiful forever."

"Are those my only choices?" Sharon pounded the ground with the top nub of the rake. "Maybe I don't want to say yes to either of them!"

"Precisely," the Master said. "That is why I offer you a third option. Say no to them both and I'll send you and your children home."

"You never give anything for free," she nodded her chin at him, "what's in it for you?"

"I'll gain two able souls instead of one."

Sharon stepped back shaking her head. "No matter how unheard my opinion goes or as invisible as I might appear to them at times, I will not be the cause of their eternal deaths."

"You owe them nothing. They did it to themselves."

"I'm not like you. I may have been selfishly vain and a bad mother at times, but I'm sorry for it and ready to make amends. You are pure evil."

"Isn't that the crux of the matter?" the Master said. "I am evil because it's my nature. Mankind chooses to be."

"I won't do it."

The Master chuckled. "All this time, you've seen me as your enemy. But them? They will never see you for yourself. Throughout centuries, men have depicted women in art and literature as symbols of their own aspirations and desires: Dante with his vision of Beatrice, Petrarch his Laura, Botticelli and Venus. So-called enlightened men who never saw women as living breathing equals, but as representations of their own concept of beauty to be exploited for their own means to glory and gain. To Lawrence and James, you are the same. As long as men view women as a fantasy to possess rather than a life to imagine, they shall always belong to me. You can't do anything for either now. They've made their choice. Now make yours."

"Get out of here."

"The offer stands, reject them both and go home. I'll even throw in keeping your youthful beauty intact if you prefer that to watching yourself age."

"How do I know anything you say is true? You are the father of lies."

"Why don't you ask the trespasser yourself?" The Master spotted Eugene approaching the garden. "Or ask him."

Sharon turned around and saw the gardener approaching with

chicken wire. She shook the rake head at the Master. "Go!" she said. "And never return."

The Master tipped his hunting cap at Sharon before he disappeared into the dark woods.

15

12 p.m.

James woke to the sensation of pain. Cuts to the faces, twitches to his side. While this place had kept them young, it did nothing for him. He thought of last night's dream: swooping owl, deep passage under the barn, torch, Lawrence, apple tree, Lawrence—bare knuckle fist fight. That was no dream. He stared down at the carpet and dressed, mind clouded with the recognition of what implications this confrontation raised. What was he doing fighting with a demon? What trap did he just step into? The irrational fear in the supernatural he chided Timmy for now took root in him. The dread from his mind spilled into his heart.

Maybe love cannot exist here. Maybe Sharon is incapable of it. He still has his free will, he could exercise it and leave—but how would that go over, could he explain it to her face? No, better write a letter instead. How would it start? ~~Dear Sharon, Sharon my sweetest, My love, Dear Mrs. Peters my boyhood crush, I'm a phony, I'm running away, so long~~—Would she reread the note a thousand times, rip it up and forget, turn her heart to stone? He'd be no better than any others who came and left. Worse, because he'd sent their hopes soaring, then crushed them after they'd offered up their tightly guarded trust. The cruelty of cowardice. The smile which would widen on Lawrence's face knowing he'd eliminated another suitor after his Penelope.

247

No. Today will be a decisive and beautiful day because he will decide he loves her. With this deal, he'd gone all in when Lawrence thought he'd opt all out. He must stay and back his claim. Lawrence, living in a fantasy world within this fantasy world, how could Sharon choose him over James and her children? What if she did?

James would live a long, lonely existence for nothing. Shall he back out now? No. A decision made is a decision not to be altered. Fate did not lead him here to lose. Sharon shall choose James and Lawrence will be banished to the underworld for good and they will stay here in this bubble of an estate living happily ever after. In the bathroom, he dressed his cuts then skipped down the backstairs, whistling.

Downstairs the house was peaceful and serene. James' pains were mere tinges of discomfort. He peeked into the grand room from the great hall's arched entrance. His heart expanded against his chest –it showed signs of a late-night brawl: shards of glass, flattened end tables, loose dirt from caved-in ceramic pots, their flower stems limp in a puddle. His morning confidence began to erode. Sharon must have seen these shambles already. He lifted the coat of arms from the floor and returned it to the nail on the wall, rubbing the still moist blood of Lawrence between his fingers. How was he going to explain? Let truth be his guide. Except in this case. He righted chairs, returned unbroken items to their original place. He would clean up the rest later. He exited out the French doors to the pool where Timmy and Sally were swimming.

He found the two splashing around with their usual playfulness. They looked up at him and stared. He pointed at his face. "What, this? I'm okay. Just something I ran into last night." The sky darkened. A chill wind swirled around the patio swiping cold the back of his neck. The three heard distant thunder and gazed up at a darkening sky.

"Better get out of the pool, kids," he commanded. "You don't want to be caught in there if lightning strikes." They wrapped themselves in towels and lied down on the stone terrace absorbing into their bellies its warmth.

He gulped. "Where's your mother?"

They pointed him towards the garden. "Be caeh'ful, James," Sally said, "she's mad at you wight now."

A rush of particles cascaded down his spine like sand. "Everything will be all right, Sally, I can explain."

James stepped out beneath the arbor overflowing with edible globes. Sniffing the ripe scent of Concord grape, he bumped into Eugene passing by with rings of cage wire.

"What happened to you?" Eugene asked. "Fall in the bathtub or somethin'?"

James touched his face. "No, nothing like that."

Eugene tightened his grip on the wire as it attempted to unravel. "He sparred with you, didn't he?"

James blinked. "How would you know?"

Eugene scratched his head. "Ain't it obvious?"

"I took the bait, Eugene. I threw the first punch."

"That's what he wanted you to do," Eugene said. "He loves a good fight with his foes, sizes them up and learns their weaknesses. So, what kind 'a deal did you make with 'im?"

"Why would you assume we made a deal?" He flapped his arms. "We agreed to let Sharon choose. Leave with Lawrence or remain here with me. That simple."

Eugene scratched his chin. "Harrumph. You make it sound like some sort of horse trading just went on."

James searched the trellis for a plump grape, "He's smitten with her, Eugene, he's so convinced of her love he bet everything on it. She'll never choose him. He's doomed." He dropped the grape in his mouth.

"And what happens if she does choose him?"

"She won't."

Eugene raised the coil of wire in the air. "It was your own vanity which got you into this. I told you all along don't try to handle this yourself."

"I know what I'm doing," James said.

Eugene pulled up his sagging trousers. "That ain't gonna sit well with her when she learns the truth. She's in a mood right now."

"Angry about the mess in the grand room?"

"Didn't say," Eugene said. "Looked as if she'd bite my head off. Better go see her and confess your sin."

"No." James shook his head. "If I told her the truth, she'd end up hating me more than she hates him."

"Son, now's the time to be honest whatever the consequences. Remember what I said about trying to play his game of lies."

"I'll be fine, Eugene, we'll be fine." He walked down the curved brick path to the side lawn, rehearsing in his mind what he was going to say.

16

Gangly sunflowers stood like sentries to her garden; James had to brush through them to enter. He was astonished; it was the end of August and two wooden baskets sat filled with the bounty of her hard work; heads of broccoli and cauliflower, carrots, onions, potatoes, turnips, tomatoes, rutabagas. Tin pails of weeds lined the perimeter between plantings covered by dominant leafy greens, their bouquets flopping over on the ground. Sharon kept her head down as she handled the spade among the plantings as any master gardener could.

James crouched down beside her. "You've been busy," he said.

She glanced at him with disinterest and continued in her labor. He stood up.

Sharon sat back on her heels. "We need to put a fence around this. The rabbits are going to eat everything before we have the chance to pick it all."

"Did you see what happened in the grand room?"

"Eugene's hammering wire grills to a wooden frame now. He and I'll have it up before nightfall."

"When I woke, I had these cuts and bruises all over."

Sharon looked up at the sky. "Looks like it's going to be another wet one. Eugene says a nor'easter."

"Last night I came down after the storm and found the French doors open. Something scared me and I went berserk. I must've been half-dreaming about wrestling with a demon or something."

She wiped her brow with her garden glove. "I don't know if I can get used to this change in the weather anymore. At least before, it was predictable."

James touched her shoulder. She repelled his touch.

"What's the matter, Sharon? If it's about the shape of the grand room, I'm sorry."

She stood. "I'm too angry to talk about it right now."

He viewed the pointed spade she held up in her hand.

"Sharon, talk to me please."

She shot the spade down and it stuck in the ground. "What is it you want to hear? That I forgive you, because you're our gallant hero come to rescue us?"

"Calm down, Sharon." He pulled out the spade and tossed it out of reach. "You're overreacting. Splintered furniture in a place like this is no big deal."

She removed her gloves. "You're right, what do I care about a bunch of broken antiques and fractured pots in a place like this?"

"Exactly. Boy, this hurts."

She yanked the red scarf off her head. "Sorry you're hurt, but pain comes along with the days here now too." She picked up tin pails full of weeds and started dumping them in the wheelbarrow. James helped her collect them.

"Something else is bothering you, Sharon, not just the mess I made."

"It's the mess you made all right," she said. "Of our lives."

She cuffed the pails on top of each other and set them down.

"Hey, I came and stayed to help."

"So, help."

She lifted one wooden basket filled with vegetables and shoved it in his arms. She lifted the other and they headed for the estate. James followed her up the curved hill to the arbor entrance. When they reached the pool area, she lowered her basket and turned on him in front of the children.

"Those aren't cuts from wrestling with a phantom last night, are they?"

"Well." He patted his cheek and felt the pain.

"What you really dreamt about is keeping us prisoners here for your own pleasure."

"Hey." He lifted his chin. "You know I'd never do anything like that."

"Apparently, I don't know."

Sharon walked to the edge of the pool and stared across as if it were an ocean. "I don't need you here anymore," she said, turning back around to face him. "Not after you betrayed me."

"Betrayed you? What do you think I did?"

She shouted from the pit of her stomach. "You saw Lawrence last night!"

Thunder rumbled, and the sky darkened further. The children stood frozen, watching the fight unfold.

"I know all about the little deal you made with him."

James threw his hands up in defense. "You're misinterpreting my intentions. It's not like that."

She raised her chin up at him. "Is it true or not?" she asked. "Did you meet with him last night or not?"

"Yes," James said.

She stamped her foot on the stone patio. "You lied to me!"

"Yes," James said, arms limp at his side.

"I trusted you," she said, her hands on her hips.

"Then go on trusting me," he said. He watched her pick up the kids' wet towels from the concrete. "I did it to give you more control," he said.

"You mean, give *you* control," she said.

Sharon stuffed the towels in a canvas bag. "You're no better than he is, bargaining for possession of me, as if I were some prized meat you could wrap up and sell. He gets to everybody, no matter how close they are to me! I'm sorry, James, I'm not going to stay here with you if I have better options. Just forget your little scheme." She headed towards the service path with the bag to go inside.

"You're not going with him, are you?" That stopped Sharon in her tracks.

James stood behind the children. "You certainly can't say yes to him and leave the children behind." The children ran up to Sharon. Sally grabbed her shirt tail.

"Is that true, Mother?" Timmy asked. Sharon stared at James, tight-lipped.

"I'm beginning to think you used me from the beginning," he said. "That was the plan all along, wasn't it? Trap me here so you could leave with him!"

"If you think that's true then you still don't know me," she said.

"You're right," he said, "I don't. Because maybe you've been in love with him all along. Haven't you?"

She marched up to him and slapped his face. "Leave!" She pointed at the far end of the pool.

James stared at Sharon while rubbing his cheek. "Timmy and Sally, looks like you're on your own again." He marched down the side of the pool at a brisk pace.

"Wait, James, no!" Timmy shouted. "You can't leave us, you can't!" He moved toward him, but James held up his hand to stop the boy from following.

"It's not me," James said, "it's your mother who pushes everyone away when they grow too close."

Sharon threw the bag of towels down, spilling them into the pool.

When he reached the beech hedges and cedars, James slammed the gate shut, bouncing it on its hinges. He hurried across the front lawn with tense muscles and stiff limbs. "I was so sure of myself. I thought she trusted me, I thought I could trust her!" He reached the driveway and heard hammering coming from the second-floor window above the carriage house. Eugene, that worthless goat. Before James left, he'd give the old man a piece of his mind.

❀ † ❀

James climbed the rickety stairs to Eugene's quarters and kicked open the door. Eugene stood placing the finishing touches on his coffin.

"You didn't tell me everything," James said. He sniffed turpentine and pine.

Eugene put down the plane he used to scrub the coffin's beveled seams and picked up a screwdriver. "Next time knock," he said.

James pointed towards the estate. "He tricked me, and you knew all along."

Eugene tightened the last screw into a tin hinge of the lid. "Finished," he said.

"I'm no better than he is," James said, "and you're to blame for letting me think I was."

Eugene ribbed the edge with his thumb. "Sturdy and tight as a drum, water'll run right off her. Your mistake, son, was pretending you were never afraid. I told you, with Lawrence, it's all a mind game. That's how he gets to you." He blew sawdust off the top of the coffin, smoothed it with his hand.

"That's what he did to Sharon, not me," James said. He pointed at himself. "She's afraid of him, not me."

"Pshaw. Who are you fooling?" Eugene said.

"I did all I could, all I was capable of," James said.

Eugene placed the screwdriver and plane into his wooden toolbox. "Tell her that, she's the one you've deceived."

"I only did what you told me to do. You said if I faced him squarely everything would work out in the end. Well I did, and it didn't."

"I also told you what not to do. Now leave me alone."

"Pshawww," James mimicked Eugene. "What do you know about relationships anyway?"

He slammed the door behind him, tripping down the stairs

to the garage, bracing the railings to keep from falling head long. Shaken, he stood at the bottom in the dark. The side door to the carriage house opened and in stepped the two children.

"James, you can't leave," Timmy said.

"You heard your mother," James said. "I can't save someone who doesn't want to be saved. I'm sorry." He walked past the boy to leave when Timmy grabbed him.

"James, you just can't yet, you can't. Please!"

"I told you there's nothing I can do now." James tried to jerk his arm away, but the boy wouldn't let go.

"You've got to stay and help fix this," the boy pleaded.

"I said let go of me!" James pulled the boy off and Timmy fell and banged his head against a timber support and crumpled to the floor. Sally ran in.

"What did you do to my bwuthah?" she said. "And Mommy too? Ah you so bad as Lawence now?"

With heart racing, eyes welling up, James ran out the door down the drive. He didn't look back, and his mind raced with him.

17

Run James run, get out of this place and forget you were ever there, climb that gate and fall into whatever world you land. Run so hard you incinerate your thoughts, obliterate your feelings of guilt, anger, sadness, frustration—burn them all away. Keep running until your throat swells and you begin to suffocate. You wish you could go back and defeat Lawrence, rescue Sharon, but you can't. The moment to act is gone and you know you can't change the past. No one can.

James reached the gate and rested his arms on his knees. "I've made such a mess," he said. Out on the road, the hot afternoon traffic moved lazily by. Slow at first, their numbers increased as they picked up speed, breezed right by, faster and faster non-stop, one long blur at such a dizzying pace James couldn't tell where one car ended and the next began. All filled with townsfolk anxious to escape, in search of what hell they did not know, lives going nowhere but in circles. Empty hearts, marriages gone bust, ghostly children whose parents relied on the unsure glue of alcohol and pills to keep the illusion they were one big happy family living the American dream. Like those 1950s highway billboard façades which towered the sky, of the model couple with two children loving the suburban life, until the signs collapsed showing how flimsy and short-lived was their existence. James wondered who was more real, the people in the cars out there, or those who were inside here? He covered his ears and screamed so loud he could have flattened all the trees with the force of his voice. But he didn't. He shut up and closed his eyes.

Then. All. Went. Silent.

When James opened them again, not one car was in sight. The unhitched gate anchored open as if inviting him to leave. He slid his hand up its cold metal post, unsure whether to close it or open further. He stared out at the quiet empty road and wondered, if not back to his world, where would it lead?

To that world of his youth where he'd return as a boy. What's the first thing he would do? Track down his father and confront him for abandoning them the summer his brother died. His father was home that day, lost in his bottle of whiskey, but refused to share in any of the blame. James didn't see him again for a decade. If he could find his father and sit him down, would the man listen to an angry son who expressed his feelings with the maturity of an adult? What if his father had been a different person, stronger, not run away from his family duties? Would he have been able to show James how to hold a family together through a tragedy such as the one they suffered? Could his brother's death have served to transform his father into a better father and husband, and by extension transform the kind of man James would become? Would he then have grown up with a different feeling about how to love a partner if he'd learned how first from his father? Perhaps he would've started a family by now. But he didn't, and that's not what happened, and he can't change any of it, least of all not what kind of person his father turned out to be: one who did not know how, or did not care, to guide his son with love. Instead he chose to rule over him with the power of his ego––and money. A man from whose grip James had yet to be totally free. But there was still time to change that by changing himself. He felt the push of the property trying to nudge him out the gate. His body repelled it and his stubbornness would not allow him to yield to fear.

A cool forceful wind whistled over his head, feathering the fine hairs on the nape of his neck as it whispered his name––*James.* It moved him like an underwater current flowing at the bottom of his heart.

James, you fought with Sharon and you fought with Eugene. You must not leave now because you think you failed them.

He knew to whom this soft flowery voice belonged. He turned around and was immediately struck with blindness. "My eyes, statue." He rubbed them. "What happened to my sight? Please restore it so I can see your legendary beauty."

It is not I who block your sight, James, but your own ideal of beauty. I shall always remain invisible to you so long as you seek my physical perfection rather than the substance of who I am. True beauty inspires reflection of the heart, not desire of the body and mind.

"I've never imagined you as anything but a beautiful soul," James said. "Why are you still here? This place is evil. Maybe I deserve it, but you don't. I freed you with a kiss. You should've escaped by now."

I shall be free, James, when Sharon is freed. Our fate depends on what you do.

James crumpled to the ground. "I just had to do it on my own, the trespasser who thought he'd be the one to beat Lawrence. He taunted me and instead of calling him out on it, I fought back." James hugged himself. "Here I was sent to make her feel safe to make her own decision about leaving. Instead I decided what was best for her, which was to be kept here under my thumb instead of his. I'm not the hero you think I am, I'm no better than he is, nor am I the man I aspire to be." He stood up, maintaining an unstable balance. "No, Sharon is better off without me. You all are. I'm leaving." Unable to see, he felt his way toward the gate.

James, how can you strand those who depend upon you the most?

James stopped. "Because that's what my father did to me."

Dwell not on the scars of your past. Live fully in the present despite the pain, which although may never fully heal need not determine your future.

"It's too late. Sharon would never allow me to return."

She is angry because you broke her trust. It's been so long since she could trust anyone that she's forgotten how. Resist your desire to run, do not fear an outcome which you can neither see nor hear. Harness your goodness for the benefit of others and do not try to do it alone anymore.

James turned around. "Any goodness I had disappeared the moment I stepped foot in this place."

When you were a boy, you snuck onto this estate and rode through uninvited. You thought you could fly in and cause mischief, then leave after you had your fun. Now back as a man, the novelty has worn off and you do the same. You have faced your true nature, flawed, mortal and fragile and found yourself wanting. It is not this place you run away from but yourself.

"I'm not running away, she kicked me out!"

You let her chase you out. You tested her limits and she failed, so you have an excuse, you can blame leaving on her. You must not give up believing you can be loved and forgiven even when your mistakes hurt others. You need to seek their forgiveness, then forgive yourself.

"I'm not the man for this job I told you, can't you see? Please just leave me alone!" He gave a monstrous kick to the gravel, and his eyesight returned. There was no spirit of the statue standing before him, just a numinous cloud of dust floating upward.

He gazed out the gate unable to decide whether to leave or stay. He slid down to the ground against the stone wall and sat motionless. Too tired to feel or think, he fell asleep.

18

When James woke, Timmy was shaking his shoulder. He noticed the bump on the boy's forehead from when he pushed him.

"I'm sorry about the bump on your head," he said.

Timmy nodded quietly. He swung up on the wall by the tree limb and began skipping stones into the on-coming traffic. He cracked the windshield of one. James picked up a few stones and started skipping them too. His bounced across a car roof.

"You don't have to leave, Jimbo."

James shook his head. "It's better me leaving than your mother separating from you and Sally and leaving with him. I bet I'm not the first trespasser with a connection she's thrown out."

"No." Timmy jumped off the wall. "That was her best friend."

"Mrs. Godwin."

"Yes." Timmy found an acorn and peeled the nut out of its shell. "Mrs. Godwin showed up looking for Sally and me," he said. "When she saw we were all right, she was ready to leave. But my mom begged her to stay and help us, and then when Lawrence showed up, Mrs. Godwin fell right under his spell." The boy blew on the shell between his thumbs and let out a piercing sound. "I told my mom it was a set up but she so wanted to believe."

"Quite the charmer, isn't he?" James said.

"We played tennis with Mrs. Godwin and swam in the pool. It was fun until the adults started drinking, and that's when things got bad."

James leaned against the tree with stiff arms. "How do you mean?"

"Lawrence got Mrs. Godwin so drunk, she flirted too much, and it really upset my mom. The two argued and didn't talk to each other the rest of the afternoon. Lawrence and Mrs. Godwin sat on one side of the pool drinking and my mother on the other, until she ran inside and threw up. When she returned, they were dancing."

"Is that when she threw Mrs. Godwin out?"

"No. Lawrence and Mrs. Godwin promised to join us on the back hill to watch the fireworks after they cleaned up but they never showed. When the fireworks started, my mother couldn't sit still. She ran back to the pool. Sally and I followed but we couldn't keep up. When we finally made it, they were arguing."

"Lawrence and your mother?"

"No, my mom and Mrs. Godwin," Timmy said. "My mother pulled her off the lounge chair where she was lying on top of Lawrence half-naked and pushed her into the pool. She screamed at her to leave the property immediately. Mrs. Godwin did, and we never saw her again."

James caught the movement of grey matter fomenting behind the marshlands across the road. "There went your chance of escape," he said.

"There was one good thing which came out of it though," Timmy said, oblivious to what James was staring at.

"What was that?" James asked. The billowing dark tide drew closer. He watched as flora shriveled to their roots, birds fell from the sky, leaves on tree limbs turned brittle.

"It was because Mrs. Godwin visited, I learned time could move forward here. Our growing pains started when she arrived. Eugene noticed too. He clipped the heads off his roses and tulips, dumped whole pots of flowers on the ground. Then he ran outside and began to dig his grave. I thought he'd gone crazy."

Seeing what hideousness was approaching, James could barely focus on Timmy's words. "What does any of this have to do with your mother?" he asked.

"Don't you see? For the little time that Mrs. Godwin was here, my mother believed we would be rescued. She hoped. That's when everything started to grow again. It all stopped when Mrs. Godwin left. When we woke the next day, it was the Fourth of July, same as always. The flowers in the greenhouse were standing in the same pots, Eugene's grave was never dug and Sally and I didn't feel any more aching pains. Nobody has stayed long enough since for my mother to regain her hope of escape. Until you."

The odious black and grey cloud swiveled towards the estate like a serpent and the transformation of what was once a colorful world on the other side of the wall was now complete. James clasped his hands over his head.

"Don't worry, Timmy," James said. "I couldn't leave even if I wanted to." He pointed above the boy's head.

The boy turned around and looked out the gate. "Holy—"

The heaving blanket of darkness stopped at the gate. Its smokestack puffs churned, unable to advance any farther, as if the property were protected within an invisible transparent dome.

"Yes. Holy shit," James said. "It happened just as Lawrence warned, at dusk."

"I'm scared, James," the boy said, grabbing James' hand. "What are we going to do?"

"It's up to your mother now. Whatever she wants will happen next."

Drops of rain hit their heads. Shadows above the trees darkened from storm clouds sailing past like overloaded ships ready to spill their cargo. "Let's get back before that noxious matter seeps into this place and suffocates us all."

19

Reaching the carriage house, the two found Eugene pacing back and forth with a sledgehammer over his shoulder. Timmy ran to the estate; James approached the old man in silence.

"Eugene, about what I said in your room earlier."

The old man spat. "Looks like your way didn't work after all, did it?"

James raised his chin. "I'm back, aren't I?"

Eugene dropped the sledgehammer head on the gravel with a thud.

"What's that for?" James asked. He lifted it up by its long wooden handle.

"Something I'm not strong enough to do myself," Eugene said.

James felt the weight of the double-faced head in his hands. "Eugene, this might be some heavy-duty chore you need done, but first we need to come up with a plan for Lawrence's return."

"What do you think I'm inviting you to do? Play croquet? You don't have a chance with him later if you don't deal with this first. Now let's get."

The two walked across the back lawn to the gardens. James glanced over at the estate.

"Why don't you just go in and apologize?" Eugene said.

"I don't think she's ready to see me," James said.

"You mean you're not ready to see her."

"I didn't say that. God, this is heavy." The hammer began

to slip off his shoulder, but he caught it. "Don't worry, I've got so much fear and adrenalin, I could handle anything now with super-human strength."

Eugene led them through the garden until they reached the fountain patio. With James following, the old man stepped over the rim of the basin. He leaned down to feel the contour of the statue's base. It had been cemented over years ago. He marked it with chalk.

"That's where I want you to strike, sonny."

James lifted the hammer off his shoulder. "You realize this blow might knock her down."

Eugene pulled taut the rim of his hat. "She'll understand."

"No." He stood the tool on its head. "She may be a hunk of marble to you, but to me she's a living breathing thing. Why am I doing this?"

"Because it's your best chance at getting them out of here." Eugene lifted the hammer and handed it back to James. He took it.

"What could destroying this statue possibly have to do with Sharon and the kids?"

"It's not the statue herself what have to do with. It's what's so valuable hidden inside her which counts."

"I don't like this."

Standing before the spot marked X, James crouched at the knees. He took a short practice swing, then a deep breath then bam! The statue shook, but there was no damage to her.

"You're gonna have to swing harder than that," Eugene said. "Take all that super-human strength and really give her a whack."

James spit in his hands and rubbed them together then raised the hammer. This time he gave it everything, blow after blow, grunt after grunt, sweating, jerking, heaving. Chips flew as he crushed plastered stone, weakening the statue's support such that she lurched forward. He hesitated.

"Don't stop!" yelled Eugene.

With tired arms, James swung at the statue's base like a lumberjack to a tree. He slammed with such violent force, the stand finally buckled in and she toppled into the fountain basin. Her limbs broke off upon contact. James dropped the hammer and ran to her.

"Statue!" he knelt at her side. A crack ran across her face. He traced it with his finger. "What have I done?" He turned his head to the old man. "Why Eugene, what's inside her that so important we had to––destroy her?"

Eugene had his head submerged inside the hollow of the base, reaching through green oxidized pipes bent out of shape. He pulled out a box made of cherry wood and stood it on the basin rim. With a pair of pliers, he twisted off its rusted lock. Inside, encased within a velvet lining, was an alabaster jar with a patina enameled top.

"This is the secret of the statue," he said, holding it up to eye level. "What I've been hiding for nearly a half century."

James took hold of the decorative urn, admiring its beautiful design of baked in colors—blue, white and gold—stars swirling around in constellations around the sun and the moon. He began to unscrew the top with a full hand grip.

"No, don't!" Eugene said. "There you go, always jumping two steps ahead. It's not time."

"Time for what?"

"To bargain, with this."

"With whom?"

"Lawrence."

"What's in it that he would care?"

"His own human ashes what is."

James took back the jar and examined it in wonder, while Eugene kept close with hands stretched out to catch it should it fall.

"Mr. Revson always asked me to fix the pipes inside her to get its water flowing again but I told him it couldn't be done. It was in here I hid Worthy's ashes after the fatal car accident which took his life. If he were to come in contact with what's inside, he'd turn to dust in an instant."

"So, we have the advantage now. What is the next step?"

"Follow me," the old man said.

20

The next step was to hide the urn in a place where it could be kept safe until Lawrence's return. Somewhere he'd never go. Eugene had the perfect place. The two walked down a wood chipped path, pushing Eugene's wheelbarrow with the cherry wood box, along the west wall hidden from the estate by a thin line of trees and brush. They didn't know they were being followed.

They reached the white shed behind the carriage house. A faint putrid smell surrounded it. Eugene pushed the thin plywood door in, but it was stuck. He leaned into it with his shoulder and when it opened a slither, out escaped an effluvium of organic rot. They had to clear their throats and noses of the stench. Eugene pushed on the door again, but something was blocking it.

"That boy," Eugene said, "probably fiddlin' around and broke somethin', always pokin' round where he don't belong." He kicked at the door's bottom. "Feels like something's heavy blocking it, a sack of fertilizer or somethin'." He wiped his brow. "Boy, do I feel faint."

James leaned in with his own weight and shoved whatever was on the floor out of the way so that the door opened wider. "That smells more like a dead animal Eugene," he said. He pushed in further, enough that Eugene squeezed through.

"Judith Priest, this is no sack of fertilizer," he said, looking down in the breach.

"Yeah?" James peeked over his shoulder. "What is it?"

"It ain't nothing Timmy done or knocked over. It ain't no

animal neither. A dead body, what is." Eugene crouched down, coughing from the revolting smell. "Someone's suffered a horrible blow to their head," he said. A bloodstained anvil lay beside the body on the concrete floor. Eugene turned the body over towards himself, so he could see the face. He gasped and looked straight up into James' eyes.

"Who is it, Eugene, who is it?"

"It's me," said Eugene, and faded into his own corpse.

James fell backward off the door landing. He turned over onto his knees and pounded the ground with his fists.

"This place! I can't take it anymore, I can't do it, I can't save anybody! Get me out of here, get me out!"

Timmy ran from the bushes where he'd been hiding. He peered in at the bloated body, the deformed face of Eugene puffed up like a balloon. He backed out, holding his stomach, and vomited.

The two laid in a state of shock until James crawled over to Timmy, who smothered him with a hug.

"What happened to him, James?"

"I think he died before Lawrence inhabited this place, Timmy, before you arrived. I think he died, and his spirit became trapped here like Lawrence and the statue."

"How do you know we're not all dead too?" Timmy asked.

James felt a creeping chill down his spine. It made sense. He was dead. They all were. Restless spirits trapped between heaven and hell on the Revson estate, itself the spirit of an age that once was, in a world known to death. Eugene *was* a ghost. It's probably why they never saw him eat. To think of it, he never even changed his clothes. James examined his hands, felt his heart beating, touched the cuts on his face. This can't be the afterlife.

"Can the dead laugh and cry, Timmy? Swim? Can they eat, shit, sweat, sleep, blow their nose, get themselves dressed? Of course not, but we can." He looked Timmy up and down, his pants bottoms higher on his shin, his shirt sleeves above his wrists.

"Look at yourself," he said. "Spirits don't grow out of their clothes. Here. take this." He lifted the urn from its wood box and handed to the boy. "We've going to finish this, Eugene's way."

"What do we do with that?" the boy asked. He pointed at the body.

"We're going to give Eugene his last wish and bury him, in that hole of his, in his own coffin." James firmly held the urn in Timmy's hands. "Stash this in the bulkhead of the basement where it opens into the back lawn. Then get your mother and sister, and meet me in front of the carriage house, we're going to need their help."

"Help for what?"

"Leave that to me." A bolt of lightning lit the sky followed by faint thunder. The wind howled. The storm which had teased them all day showed signs of coming alive.

"What if that's Lawrence?" the boy asked. "What if he finds me with this?"

"Stick to the woods. And watch that you don't let that spill. Hold it like this." He showed the boy how to hold it under his arm like a football. Timmy pulled it into his side and ran along the west wall path.

🍠 † 🍠

With Timmy gone, James lifted the stiff body and yanked it through the shed doorway, the smell repugnant to him. He dragged it to Eugene's wheelbarrow and laid it in, limbs hanging over the sides. He went back in the shed for the anvil which gave the mortal blow and threw it in too, then carted off the corpse of someone who had become dear to him. He did not stop until he reached the front of the carriage house. By then darkness had fallen. Floodlights from the estate roof shone down their beams, lighting up nascent granules of raindrops as they blew about in the wind. He wheeled Eugene inside the carriage house and set him down. Then he climbed the wobbly stairs to what had been the loyal caretaker's rooms for a half century.

Sitting on its horses in the large room, he lifted one end of the coffin to the floor. While he looked down the narrow width stairs wondering how to get it down, a breeze fluttered papers in the room where Eugene slept, drawing his attention. Inside James found faded color magazine pictures of the Stations of the Cross tacked up on the walls and slanted ceiling. Around the mirror prayer cards of the virgin mother and her haloed babe neatly tucked in. He ripped down some of the pictures and pulled out some cards and slipped them into the coffin. He spotted rosary beads on the bedside table and jammed them in his pocket, then turned the pinewood box on its side and slid it down the stairs.

At the bottom, a long white cart for gardening was filled with fertilizer bags. He removed them and positioned its open front at the foot of the stairs. Then he slid the coffin in and lifted its top wide open. He grabbed burlap blankets off a shelf to line the inside of the pine box and spread the religious cards and pictures on them. Then he lifted Eugene's body from the wheelbarrow and laid him on top of the religious keep sakes. He placed the rosary beads in the dead man's crooked fingers and clasped the coffin shut. Eugene's rifle hung on a hook on the wall, and he threw that into the cart along with the anvil which caused the fatal blow. Then he wheeled all outside through one of the open garage doors. Sharon and the children stood lined up in the rain waiting for him, dressed in yellow slickers. Sharon handed him a slicker to put on and the four of them were reunited again.

21

James lifted the handles of the cart and started pushing forward when Sharon stopped him. She wanted to see the dead body for herself. He unclasped the top latch. She raised the lid and pulled back the burlap cover from Eugene's disfigured face. She stepped back in fright as the lid dropped down hard.

They headed across the front lawn to the stone wall path past Sharon's garden. The rain and wind splashed in their faces and the electrifying air felt as if it may ignite any moment. A streak of light blinked above them followed by thunder.

"Lawence!" Sally screamed. She fastened herself to her mother.

"We should turn around," James said, looking up into the low hanging clouds dripping water like sponges.

"No, we'll finish this," Sharon said.

They reached the grave. Two shovels stuck in the mound of dirt leaning across each other like a cross. James removed the plywood cover off the grave. They tilted the cart and the coffin slid in. It was not a snug landing and James had to jump into the hole to straighten it. Timmy and his mother took up a shovel after James hopped out. They began slinging dirt, Sharon with sharp thrusts into the mound.

"What did he do all the time but help Lawrence push us down? I hope he's in hell now. I'll never forgive him. I hate him!" She began stabbing the mound of wet dirt when James held her arms until she released the shovel. Sharon took Sally's hand and the two stood under the older pines for shelter while James and Timmy continued. After a few feet of dirt covered the coffin, James threw in the anvil. Before they reached the top he threw in Eugene's carbon rifle too. They shoveled up to a heap above ground then patted down the final layer of earth. Shots of thunder followed rhythmic flashes of lightning.

"Timmy, take Sally back to the estate and change," Sharon said. "Start a fire in the grand room and wait. There's something in the greenhouse James and I need to take care of before we come in."

"Sharon," James said, soaked to the bone despite his raincoat, "this is a hurricane."

"Go children," she said.

They obeyed. Timmy took Sally's hand and they ran at the girl's speed. The adults threw the shovels into the cart and rolled it back to the greenhouse. Tree limbs broke and fell while bushes loosened from their roots and walloped by like tumbleweeds.

❀ † ❀

Inside the greenhouse, the wind picked up and rattled the windows. Rain streamed in through the missing panes of glass on the roof. Lightning flashed intermittently, thunder cracking louder each time. Sharon lit a kerosene lamp on the worktable.

"You came back James," she said.

"I had to," he said. "I've been leaving behind people I care about my whole life. I'm not going to anymore."

"You really shouldn't've."

"That tombstone," he said. He leaned down upon it with outstretched arms. "I promised Eugene I'd cart it out to his grave before the time came." He pushed hard without a budge to show for it. "As if I thought I were up to such Herculean task." He removed his slicker and tossed it on the table.

"What are we doing here, Sharon?"

"James, I'm sorry."

"For what?"

She zipped off her slicker, opening to a wet soaked blouse clinging to pink breasts. She smoothed down her wet hair. James approached, caught a raindrop off her perfectly carved nose on his finger. She kissed him, wet tongue, wet lips, wet chest pressed against his, and they kissed, deeply. James picked her up and they picked up the pace while she enfolded her legs around his waist and the two knocked heads.

"Sharon," he said.

"Don't stop," she said.

He swung her around, swung her around, then sat on the tombstone with her wrapped around. She un-snapped his pants, ripped off his shirt, unbuttoned her blouse, stripped off her skirt. Glued in his lap she slid him right in, and the two didn't separate, even when he lifted her up and pinned her down, where they melded together on the dirt covered ground. She arched her back and closed her eyes and screamed as if caught in a wondrous surprise. In heavens of pleasure, she sunk right in, rolled beneath James with her sweaty skin. He collapsed on top, his wet ears ringing, felt her pulse, heard breath singing. He brushed her hair and she brushed his.

"Hold me tight, James," she said. "Please hold me until there's no more time."

"Silly, we have all the time in the world together now."

"No James, we don't." She squeezed him with full force.

"People, people, enjoy not the living, grieve for the dead." They were no longer alone. It was Lawrence.

22

"Eugene, poor Eugene, we cannot, we shall not pity him." Lawrence sat atop the pink marble tombstone in a cavalier manner. Not a drop of water touched his sailing cap or navy-blue blazer with brass buttons. "He's in a better place now," he said, "where we shall all go eventually."

He slipped off the tombstone and paced back and forth, his fist clenched behind his back. He peered down at the two naked bodies fanned out on the floor. "Eugene, that senile specimen, who planned from the first day of your arrival to depart from me." He threw his hand up in the air. "Fool––he's changed one prison for another, as if he thought dying would relieve him of the heat of this place."

James scrambled to buckle on his pants while Sharon took cover naked behind him.

Would you like to see me raise him up?" he said. "Worms of decay crawling in and out of his belly, every seething slippery sucker turning him inside-out in the earth, he'll bear through a natural cycle until he's nothing but bone crumbled to dust. The earth cries with the voices of the dead, even as they are now used to grow the fruits of the land!" Lawrence clicked his heels together and bowed. "Sharon, my lovely Sharon, we have finally come to this."

From a leather traveling bag on the table Lawrence removed a lime-colored dress. It was the same Sharon wore the night they met at the country club. "Here," he said, "I recovered this from Velvet." He held it up with an out-stretched arm. "Step over and get dressed, so we can be on our way."

"Don't," James said, holding his arm before Sharon like a closed gate arm. She paused, then stepped around it to Lawrence's side and took the dress. Lawrence straightened the cap on his head.

"Silly mortal," he said to James, "you thought you could prance in here and steal her away from me, something that was never yours to begin with. Whose destiny did you think you were going to change but your own? We gave you the chance to leave, ol' sport-- instead, you played the hero and returned. You misread her." Lawrence pulled a pair of espadrilles from the bag and held them up by their straps over his shoulder. Sharon reached and took them.

"Sharon, what are you doing?" James said. She didn't answer. Holding onto Lawrence's shoulder for balance, she slipped on the shoes.

"We may not always act like it," Lawrence said, "but Sharon and I have been in love from the start, waiting for this moment."

"Never, never, did I think it would end like this," James said.

Sharon turned her back to Lawrence holding her hair up above her back neck so he could hook the top of her dress. "You played your part well, darling," he said. He clasped the hooks. "You almost had me convinced you weren't acting anymore."

"I gave up everything for you," James said. "My life, my future. I fell in love!"

Sharon squeezed the remaining water from her hair and held it back with an elastic.

"We shall leave this place no longer with any fear of the Master," Lawrence said, "because James' ego grew larger than his heart. He shall be damned to stay here forever while the children return to the outside world to live their normal lives as promised."

James waved his hand over the floor where they'd made love. "Was this all an act too?"

"A last hurrah, James," Lawrence said. "That's all you were to her before her new life begins. Now princess," Lawrence turned to Sharon, "you're getting my suit all wet. It's time you apply some makeup and look all slim and handsome for the trip." He handed her a makeup bag and a small hand mirror. She began to apply lipstick. "We'll go to New York," Lawrence said, "stop in the Village for a drink at Heaven and Hell before it vanishes to the other side of the world with us in it. We'll trot around the globe, visit my vast holdings, then afterward join Velvet and the gang in Monte Carlo. She can't wait to see you again." He lifted the travel bag from the table and looked around. "My, we certainly have outgrown this place. I can hardly stand to be here a moment longer." He grabbed Sharon's arm to leave.

"Sharon, wait!" James said, his eyes fastened on hers. "I must hear you say it first. Say you never cared for me and don't ever want to see me again." He reached a hand up grasping at air. "Sharon." When she gave no reaction, he curled it into a soft fist and lowered it to his side, face expressionless.

"Darling, let's go," Lawrence said. Transfixed with pleasure he pulled on Sharon's arm. But she resisted.

"Come, darling. We haven't time to stand here in the presence of a doomed man."

Sharon looked up straight into his eyes. "I'm not going with you, Lawrence."

Lawrence chuckled. "This is no time for kidding. We're going to be late if we don't hurry." He embraced her, but she shook his arm off.

"No," she said. She walked over to James and entwined her fingers with his.

"All right, you made your point," Lawrence said. He extended his arm out to her. "Take my hand." She didn't budge. "I'm not going to say it again." She stood staring at him; mouth shut tight. "Now!" He waved her over with his fingers. "Or I'll come over and get you myself!"

When she didn't respond he stepped towards Sharon, but James shielded her. "Forget it, ol' sport," James said. "Looks like she's not going with you after all."

Lawrence stood back. "Very well. First woman, then man, rebels. They were banished from paradise, you might remember, as I will now have to do with you. James, that was a dangerous risk you took trying to rise above me, you who lusted for the chance to take my place and keep Sharon under your own command. My, you two do make for such dull company. You are more compatible than I give you credit for." The ground shook for seconds knocking plant pots and benches over, James and Sharon with them. When it stopped, they steadied themselves and looked around; Lawrence was gone.

"The children!" James dressed as fast as he could. They ran back to the estate against the blowing wind and rain. When they arrived, they burst through the French doors in panic.

23

Lawrence held the children to the flames in the giant fireplace, Timmy with a red-hot poker to his neck, Sally under his shoe, they struggling to slip free. James and Sharon stopped behind the back of the long orange couch separating them from Lawrence.

"See what my own mother did to me as a boy his age," Lawrence said. "I didn't do a thing to displease her, except be found wanting of her love, even though I strove to protect her from all men."

James grabbed the couch top ready to jump. "I'll destroy you before I let you harm either of them," he said.

"Such the romantic hero, aren't you?" Lawrence said. He released the children, stabbing the searing hot poker into a burning log. Sally ran to her mother, Timmy out of the room.

Sharon nudged Sally over to James. "Go," she said, "take her."

"Yes, James, go," Lawrence said. "This is between Sharon and me alone, as it's always been."

"Sharon, don't," James said.

"Just take her," she said, staring at Lawrence.

James walked Sally to the arch of the great hall entrance. When he saw Sharon wasn't going to come, he disappeared with the girl.

Lawrence pulled the poker out of the fire, wood carbon caked on its tip and glowing. "So, it's come down this." He waved it at Sharon in small concentric circles.

"Lawrence, don't, please," she said.

He slid the poker across the floor to the windows with long

drapes and they caught fire. He slow-stepped his way around the couch to Sharon, who circled around the other way until she was in front of the fire. Crack! Air pockets in the sap-filled logs exploded, propelling Sharon into Lawrence's arms. He gave her a soft hug and buried his nose in the scent of her neck. She tensed up, as still and stiff as the fountain statue.

"There my love," he whispered, "you can relax now, no more loneliness for you to endure, no more suffering because of me. I'm going to change. Do you know why? Because I've realized just how much I genuinely love you."

She squirmed in his arms and he relaxed his hold and she darted away.

"You're upset about the way I treated the children," he said.

Keeping her eyes on him, she took small steps backward toward the great hall.

He followed at her pace. "I wasn't going to harm them, I wanted to have your attention. And now I do." Lawrence backed her up against the column arch.

Lightning flashed above the glass atrium of the great hall, the wind hammering rain drops upon it like nails. Lawrence took Sharon's hand and led her into the center of the hall beneath the chandelier whose lights dimmed and flickered.

"Let's start fresh," he said, grabbing her hands to his heart. "We'll leave and have a family of our own. I'll be the kindest husband and father you could imagine."

She tried to tug her hands away, but he wouldn't let go. "I don't want to go with you," she said, "I want to go back to my old life the way it was."

"How would you ever do that? Memphis would never allow it."

Smoke and heat billowed from the grand living room as it became engulfed in flames. When thunder cracked, Sharon jumped into Lawrence's arms. The lights went out. In the glowing dark, Lawrence pulled her closer into himself, holding her with a quiet strength.

"Even if you could go home, do you really think, Sharon,

that you're so strong and independent-minded you could survive out there without me, the person you've depended upon for so many years?"

"If you really ever loved me, Lawrence, you would've let me and my children leave long ago."

The chandelier snapped from its hanger above. Lawrence pulled Sharon out of the way before it smashed on the marble tile floor where they were standing. He walked her backwards to the wall on the opposite side of the hall which led to the kitchen.

"You see, Sharon? You are safe with me." He took out of his pocket his mother's gold and emerald necklace and clasped it around her neck. "How beautiful you look in this. Mother's most prized possession. It's yours now." He braced his arms flat on the wall above her head. "Kiss me," he whispered. She moved her face down away from his lips. He lifted her limp arms around his neck. "Forget him," he said. "If you stay with him, the romance will die a quick death. He'll grow bored and restless with you. Imagine that, being stuck here for eternity with someone you know doesn't love you." He turned her chin up to his. "But I, your faithful Lawrence, wherever we go in the world, will always shower you with love and affection. Kiss me, Sharon, like you did in the laundry room that day, find the real me again."

She closed her eyes, fearful of another boost of frost but fearful too if she didn't kiss him.

At the moment their lips touched, lightning bolts shot through the hall dome obliterating floor tiles, splashing glass and marble everywhere. Startled, Lawrence knocked Sharon's head hard against the wall. She slid down to the floor. He grabbed her hands to raise her up.

"That was some kiss," he said.

The walls of the hall caught fire and the wind blew the rain down as pellets of hail.

Sharon came to and threw his arms off. Rubbing the back of her head, she yelled, "You monster!" Pounding him with her fists, she pushed him back onto the broken glass and he slipped. "You beast!"

she shouted. "All this time we've been here you've only hurt us and humiliated me! If you think for one vain moment, I ever cared about you, would ever choose you over a man like James, you are a gullible fool!" She picked up one of the iron rods from the fallen chandelier and swung it at him.

"Now Sharon," he said, holding his hands in front to protect himself. She swung the rod again. "Let's not lose control and do things we'll regret." She wacked him with the sharp edge of the bar, cutting a line of skin across his face.

Lawrence felt the bloody trail and pushed her to the floor. He pinned her down with his knee, taking her by the throat. She gasped, trying to pry his hands from around her neck, but she couldn't, her face turning red. He watched her cough for breath, snarling with his teeth. She tried to speak.

"Pleeees—let—me—" Lawrence squeezed harder as she grabbed his hands to lighten the force. "Pleeees, le—m—luvv, let—me—luv—"

He loosened his grip wanting to hear her say it, that she loved him, but love was not on her lips.

She said, "Live, please let me live."

Lawrence let go. His arms dropped limp and he stood back. Sharon sat up holding her neck and throat. She rolled over on all fours gasping and heaving.

He stared at his two hands, fingers still crooked from their tight grip around her neck. The tenseness in his limbs disappeared. Rings around his eyes darkened, his eyes stared contrite. She stood wheezing. She sniffled with tears. She cast a last glance at him then ran down the back hall which had not yet caught fire.

Lawrence remained in the center of the hall in tender composure. Fire evaporated the rain, its tongues rolling down the two grand staircases until they collapsed. He looked through flickering flames at the spot where he last held her against the wall, almost won her back with love; she made him feel human again. His cheeks wet, not from the rain but from salt tears leaking down his warm skin. In a cracked wall mirror, he watched as the curls of flames created an aura of black and orange that consumed him. He knew momentarily he had returned to a mortal life, but it did nothing for him.

24

At the top of the basement stairs, Sharon was grabbed in the dark; she thought it was the end of her; it was James. She buried her head in his neck while he guided her down the stairs.

"Where's Sally?" she asked. "Where's Timmy? We've got to hide them—"

At the bottom of the stairs, he held her squarely. "They're safe. We all are."

"No place is safe from Lawrence," she said.

The basement was damp, cold and moldy. With the power out, the only light emanated from two candelabras James lit atop a mantelpiece above the fireplace built in an alcove of the cellar. Their quivering light reflected upon a giant photograph hung above the fireplace of the Revson brothers––Pete and Douglas––the last photo ever taken of them together, at the Danish Grand Prix where Douglas was killed. Their trophies, plaques, ribbons and pendants, ornaments celebrating their racing victories––surrounded them like a shrine built by a forlorn mother. Framed pictures of the two growing up hung about the alcove, arms always around each other's shoulders; at summer camps, racetracks, galas, restaurants, clubs.

"Where's Sally?' Sharon asked in a hoarse voice.

James pointed. "The wine cage, below one of the racks."

"That won't do," she said.

They were interrupted by a loud voice from the other end of the darkened basement. "Tisk-tisk," Lawrence spoke in a slow even tone, coming into dim view as he walked toward them. "There's no hiding from me by anyone, any more than you think you can hide from God."

He was dressed in white—turtleneck, flannel suit, on his head a white navy cap and on his feet white bucks. He passed the billiard table and stopped to roll the white cue ball to the other end; it returned to kiss the bumper where it started. He crouched down, smiled at Timmy hiding beneath the table.

Making his way to James and Sharon, he stopped at a pinball machine, slapped its glass top causing it to tilt and play circus music. The red light in its display, the nose of a sinister clown face, flashed while it grinned at its skilled player who'd just won the game's jackpot.

Lawrence reached up above a smooth varnished mahogany bar which ran the length of the cellar, slid an upside-down crystal champagne glass off a rack, tossed it in the air in somersaults, as an expert knife thrower might his favorite cutlery. As he neared their end of the cellar, James slipped into the wine cage to protect Sally. Lawrence glanced at James behind its cell-like bars. "What do you plan to do to me from in there, James Harris?" he said.

"I beat you once and I'll do it again," James said, clutching the bars.

Lawrence bent over and laughed. "Beat me? Again? By your own cunning and strength? You didn't win any fight I didn't let you."

"I beat you, Lawrence, because I had something to fight for that was real."

"Real? Who are you to judge the reality of one state of existence over another? Do I not control this manor and the surrounding land and all life within its borders? Were there an ocean attached to this place I should drain it and rule the sea bottom too. What's real that you have control over?"

Lawrence glanced at the wine cage door and its lock clicked secure. James shook the door but could not get it to open, holding him and Sally as prisoners inside.

"James, James," Lawrence said, "you should have a look at

yourself—modern man, on the cusp of the next millennium, confined by his own doing in a cage like an ape."

"And you, Lawrence, a man born in the nineteenth century, who acts like one," James said.

Lawrence walked past Sharon who reached out to touch him. He pulled away from her. "Don't touch me, woman!" he sniped. "It is not yet time." He trolled past her to the fireplace surrounded by regalia and rested his arm with the champagne glass in hand on the mantelpiece.

"My mother spent part of her childhood on this estate," he said. "Forced to feed pigs and fowl like child slave labor. But not for long. At the command of her father, she moved up in the world."

The basement ceiling above his head creaked and sagged like the bottom of a buccaneer ship caught in a storm with a heavy load. Strands of smoke began to trickle down the stairs with the scent of burning timber.

"Good riddance to this place I say," Lawrence said, waving the glass. "Looks like if you two stay, you'll have little room left in which to reside." His eyes glazed upon Sharon and he smiled.

"Be not afraid, my love, come take a seat. Listen to what I have to confess, what will be the last words I ever utter to a live audience."

"Careful. Sharon, it's a trap!" James yelled from the cage. She stepped forward and sat on a pew-like wooden bench facing the fireplace.

Lawrence raised the crystal glass, eyed its bottom as if looking for some rare watermark, then shattered it against the edge of the stone mantelpiece, leaving its flute in jagged edges. He waved the broken glass by its stem in a nonchalant manner, the candlelight twinkling upon it.

"This stately mansion, our humble abode for so long," Lawrence said, looking around, "it will soon settle, and its ashes and debris blown about by the wind, thanks to the annoying intrusion of this malevolent trespasser, the true agent of destruction. What burns above foreshadows the fate of us all!"

He held the slivered flute glass up like a sword in front of his face as a fencer might prepare his foil for the start of a match; he lunged forward in a striking fashion, laughing hysterically as he stood up straight. Sharon winced but did not leave her seat.

"Sharon, step away from him!" James shouted. "He's crazy, and dangerous."

Lawrence flipped the sharp glass in the air, catching its stem. "You are afraid because I wave this?" he said. "I assure you it has sentimental value for me only, the weapon which caused my mother's own death! Did I never tell you, how she—no, of course not. I wouldn't have, why would I? Sit back now and relax. It's time you heard the saddest, most tragic confession ever told, from a boy who saw his mother die by the likes of such a fragile thing."

He stood the jagged-edged flute on the mantel, then faced out as if he were on stage ready to perform a one-man show.

25

"Where shall I begin? My name is Lawrence P. Worthington III, born in 1898, the illegitimate heir to two fortunes. For the first years of my life, I lived with my mother, because my father would have nothing to do with us. We lived all right mind you, Washington Square in Manhattan, that Gotham City, thanks to the beneficence of my father's brother who, to the chagrin of his family, considered it his Christian duty to provide for a fallen young mother and child abandoned to their fate. And so we lived, the two of us, until I reached my tenth birthday, when it was time for her to find her own way, or a willing husband to support her.

She started her search for a suitor of fine pedigree and means, for it was her secret hope that someday she should rejoin the high society from which she came but was banished from years earlier, living now on its fringes. Marriage, such a buttery word, what does it really mean anyway? That antiquated institution in which no woman truly counts but must depend upon a man for subsistence.

"Her betrothed was a confirmed bachelor, an extremely handsome one I recall. He did not love her, nor she him––it was a business arrangement––marriages were all about convenience back then. His family needed an heir and she was the prized bitch to be sired. They only insisted she fulfill her end of the bargain by having the baby first, out of wedlock, as stipulated in their contract. Thus, my baby brother was born, and I, no longer of any monetary benefit to my mother, was to be cast aside like some worthless old toy."

Lawrence took an aged, browned paper from his breast pocket.

"The telegraph she sent to my uncle, the night before her wedding day. Listen up!

Wedding tomorrow STOP Leave for Europe on honeymoon STOP Please wire boy's month of support to the American Express office in Paris and keep him STOP We shall not return for a long time STOP

My uncle replied:

Congratulations on tying the knot STOP From me you shan't receive another cent STOP Keep the boy you are his mother STOP Godspeed STOP STOP STOP

"He nearly fainted when I showed up on his doorstep later. But that's getting ahead in my story."

James and Sharon looked at each other, bewildered by the hypnotic state into which Lawrence had fallen. Timmy left his hiding place below the billiard table and James unjammed the cage lock and led Sally back to her brother. He whispered to the boy who then took his sister's hand and the two disappeared into the darkness at the other end of the cellar even as the estate above their heads burned in the ravaging storm. Not once did Lawrence break his self-absorbed trance, even when James crept forward to listen.

"You know, I hated the dear curmudgeon at first, the way he stuck his tongue out at the only brother he was sent to torment. I wanted to kill him. Until one summer day when the nursery maid needed to run an errand. She took the baby out in his carriage and I was allowed to tag along. We went for a stroll through Washington Square, needing to visit an apothecary on the other side of the park. The nurse left the carriage in the shaded lawn beside the duck pond and ordered me to watch my brother while she ran her errand. When she was out of sight, I leaned down in the carriage and made a nasty face, scratching the air around baby with my hands as claws like a hungry beast and growling. He began to cry. At that moment, a mother duck waddled by with her ducklings. She must have sensed my intentions for she took to the water with each of her little ones behind, except I grabbed the last stray by its tail and held him tightly over the carriage so my brother could see."

Lawrence held an imaginary duckling in the air while he gazed down into an imaginary carriage.

"Do you know what happened? He calmed down and giggled, so I laughed too––I could never make my mother happy, I didn't think I could make anyone else either. Maybe he wouldn't be so bad to have as a little brother after all. I pressed the duckling upon him, and it snapped, which scared baby. He began to cry again and as I tried to shush him, the nurse ran over and crowned me so hard on the head, I dropped the smelly thing. She threatened to tell my mother who was very protective of baby, not because she loved the little devil but because he guaranteed her future security. The nurse never told her, since she knew she would be blamed for leaving the baby alone. Especially with me."

Lawrence picked up a framed photograph of the young Revson brothers dressed in racing slicks and ascot scarfs, their arms around each other.

"Tragic," he said. "They both raced to their deaths in a dangerous sport of speed. Pity both brothers who died so young. Would that I had died at the same time as my brother."

He stood the frame back on the mantel.

"Everything was moving swell. To avoid scandal, my mother would be given a considerable sum of money upon delivery of the infant to her in-laws who would be waiting for them in Europe. Our flat that day was filled with wardrobe trunks and other baggage packed for travel. Her fiancé was to pick her up at noon and take her to City Hall for the civil wedding, then return for baby and take me to Grand Central Station and ship me off to Boston. I was shaken and out of sorts. I thought I would never see my mother again. I accepted my fate, but my heart hardened. I vowed when we separated, I would not cry. Excuse me, I have a rather parched throat."

Lawrence lifted a gold trophy from the mantel, took it by both handles and drank a hardy amount of red wine found miraculously inside, its dark blood color dripping on his cheeks. He wiped his mouth clean with his coat arm and belched, then sat down cross-legged on the edge of the marble hearth, holding the trophy nonchalant with one hand like a jug of moonshine.

"Now, where was I? Mother woke up in the morning extremely irritable. Too nervous to sleep or eat, she drank cup after cup of coffee, with not a little spike of rum. She spent the morning smoking incessantly while she decided what she was going to wear for the ceremony, and the journey across the high seas afterward. She must have changed a dozen times. I watched her--keeping my distance--snappy as she was from too much coffee and cigarettes, and not a little tight for the rum. If she looked at me at all, it was with indifference, as if I were already gone."

Lawrence finished the rest of the wine, wiping with a handkerchief what more trickled down. "Excuse me but I'm not feeling as myself in this moment." He touched his forehead feeling dizzy.

"Well then. We waited and waited for her fiancé to show up. She rang up her imminent in-laws, but the butler continued to make excuses for them all afternoon. She kept herself busy, packing and unpacking her wardrobe, eating nothing, wondering where he could be? At the tailor's for a needed alteration? Buying flowers? A last-minute haircut? At four o'clock in the afternoon, she decided enough was enough. I had already missed my train and must now take care of baby while she left to go look for him. If anyone arrived, she said I was not to allow them in. When she left, I was thrilled and hopeful because maybe now I would be able to go with them. Baby and I laid down on the bed in the nursery spreading his toys out and playing until we both fell asleep, remaining as such until the dark of night."

Lawrence appeared to grow sleepy, almost couldn't keep his eyes open. He yawned and fell over, but Sharon caught him in time to help keep his balance straight.

"Lawrence, are you, all right?" she said. "Lawrence?" At her touch, he opened his eyes widely and blinked. Looking at Sharon he said in a frightened voice:

"Mother?"

"No, Lawrence, it's me—"

He stood up. "Mother, is that you at the door?"

He straightened his clothes out and acted like a little boy, brushing down the sleeves, combing his hair with his fingers. He stood straight at attention with a smile, showing how eager he was to please.

"Mother, are you back at last? Are you married now? What's wrong with you? You look, sick. Are we leaving now?"

Right before Sharon and James' eyes, Lawrence's whole appearance and figure transformed as his trance placed him in a deeper state. His eyes closed and his face drew as blank as a death mask, while his body slimmed down, moved in subtle ways, a shiver there, a wiggle at the hips, a stretch of the spine, until it no longer acted like his body but one with someone else's mannerisms. A black shadow stepped into his body as if a spirit from the dead had taken over. When he looked at Sharon, his eyes were hollow and lifeless. Then they darkened, and he spoke in an angry feminine voice:

"Leaving? Leaving where? To the new estate? The one filled with banquet tables and drawing rooms and libraries and servants? Or to the poor house, the one with slivers of bread and gruel to eat and rats that crawl over you when you're sleeping at night with four to a bed and nibble your cheeks? Where's your cursed brother?"

"He's sleeping."

"Good. Now start the bath water."

"'Why am I taking a bath, Mother?"

"No, you idiot, it's for your brother. He needs a bath because he stinks and smells and is rotten to the core. How could I love any child whose father is a coward who deceives and lies to me? First your father, now his. Stop standing there. Just get the damn water ready."

"I ran to the bathroom and turned on the water, getting it just the right temperature, dipping in my elbow as I watched the nurse do. When I returned, Mother lay on the sofa pouring herself drink after drink of brandy. When I dared attempt to lay my arms about her, she shooed me away with a frenzied hand gesture."

"'But what happened, Mother, what happened to make you so sad and angry? Didn't you get married to baby's father?"

"She fumbled with her purse for a cigarette, tried to light it, and in her frustration threw the heavy table lighter at the mirror over the fireplace, fracturing it. She struck a match and lit up, smoked and puffed, smoked and puffed, then told me what happened. She never looked at me once, only stood and paced the floor back and forth, back and forth."

"I looked all day for the baby's father. I took a horse-driven hansom and arrived at his parents' home, but they wouldn't even let me in the gate. I knew where he had his own secret apartment down in Greenwich Village. I had never been to his place before, and only knew the street. I arrived and asked a pushcart peddler stationed at the corner if he saw any man that day in a wedding suit. He said he had but he did not know where he lived. A florist with a stand on the same street knew who I was talking about because he had just bought a white wedding corsage. Of course, I thought, that must be him. He said he saw him walk down the street into an apartment house but did not know which one."

"She poured a drink from a crystal decanter, but it only gave her its last drops. She drank all it had to offer.

"I waited in front of the brownstones asking anyone who passed if they might know of him. But no one did. Then a taxi pulled up and an elderly couple got out and stood while the driver carried their luggage to the steps. They said they had just returned from a long trip and yes, they knew of a man who fit the description who kept the apartment on the top floor. A handsome dandy. There were two men who came often. I climbed to the top floor as fast as I could. I reached the top step and found two doors. Before I could decide which to knock, I heard laughter coming from inside one, and recognized my fiancé's silly high-pitched voice. I was about to knock when I heard two voices, his and a younger man's. I listened at the door. Here are their words which continue to unnerve me even in hell where I relive the final hours of my life over and over:

'Look, how late it is,' said the young man. 'You've missed your own wedding.'

'But I couldn't! I just couldn't go through with it,' my fiancé said.

'We've been through this already, you dumb-dumb, we are going to meet up in Greece.'

'It's too late, the Justice of the Peace is probably gone. What do I do now? She must be fuming.'

'Forget the ceremony. You both signed the certificate yesterday.'

'But it's not legal until it's witnessed.'

'I'll sign the damn thing. Now pick her up and let's get you on that ship!'

'And sleep in the same bed with her again? Thrilling. It was bad enough carrying out the dreadful deed the first time, my parents in the parlor room below waiting for us to finish. Thank God she impregnated the first time. Exceedingly difficult to hold that erection—'

'It's getting really late, now go!'

'What excuse do I use? That I spent the afternoon with you?'

'Straighten up and be a man. You are going to stick to our plan.'

'I told you I can't!'

'Think of your parents, if they learn you never boarded, boy are they going to be cross with you.'

'That's another reason I hesitate. You know as soon as they get their hands on the baby, they don't plan to give her a dime! Such a sweet girl too. I feel terrible for her.'

'Forget about her. You're doing this for us. Get on that ship! Do it for us!'

'Very well…'

"When I heard that, I banged on the door furiously. Their voices went silent and I began to yell. I was outraged. Then I knew what I was going to do.

"Back now in the apartment, Mother hurried past me to the bedroom and I followed. She fixed her hair and reapplied her lipstick and creams. She poured herself another drink from her own bottle on her wardrobe chest. She lifted from her jewelry box the heavy emerald and gold necklace her father gave her and wore it around her neck, beholding it in the mirror. I went to hug her."

"Mother, you're all dressed up, are you going to go out again?"

"Don't touch me! Now go get baby and give him a bath!"

"She took me by the ear and led me into the nursery, releasing with a hard-nasty tug."

"*Now take him and place him in the bath. Go on I said, take him!*"

"We marched to the bathroom and my mother stopped at the door pushing us in. I hit my head against the sink and dropped baby. He started to cry."

"*You klutz pick him up and drop him in the bath.*"

"But the water level, it's too high!"

"*Pick him up, Pick him up! Good. Now lay him in.*"

"In the bathtub?"

"*Yes, in the bathtub, of course. LAY HIM IN, WILL YOU?*"

"I carefully picked up my little brother, who quieted down and cooed at me with a smile, content in the arms of his kindest and last caretaker he would ever know."

"But it's too deep, mummy, he'll drown."

"*Just do it, do what I say! I'm your mother, aren't I? Do you love me or not?*"

"But mother!"

"I couldn't do it. As I stared at her motionless, she looked at me, and began to cry. Her face smeared in uneven mascara running below her eyes and she leaned against the door frame. Then she smiled at me and I thought she was going to call it off. But that wasn't what she had in mind."

"*Do it, baby, then it'll be just the two of us again. I'll sell this antique piece of jewelry and we'll leave this town for good. We'll have only each other then, I promise. Remember, this will make your mother very happy and she will love you for it. Always, honey.*"

"She kissed me on the forehead and left the bathroom, and I was filled with a new zest to please. I no longer felt it to be a cruel act, but the most natural thing a boy could do for the love of his mother. I thought he must have done something awfully bad, otherwise why would she make me do this to him. I placed my hands around his throat. I closed my eyes and buried him into his watery grave. He was not that strong, and his little body collapsed under the water quickly. I could feel it. Then, it was over. He hardly struggled."

Sharon sat completely motionless. James stood in shock behind her at the tale they were hearing.

"You have to hold them down long afterward," Lawrence said. "Otherwise they wake up and grab you. I saw my neighbor Charlie do it to an alley cat once. He thought he was finished drowning it in the rain barrel and let it go just when the animal jumped out and fastened its claws to his face. So, I knew I had to stay there a good while, holding baby under, thinking of those scratches that cat left on my dear friend's face. Finally, it was finished. He sank to the bottom and landed on his back. He looked up at me so peaceful, I thought I saw a smile, he wasn't even mad with me."

Lawrence kneeled, grabbing the iron mesh curtain around the fireplace like a security blanket.

"I ran to my mother's bedroom afterward as fast as I knew how. 'She's going to be so proud of me,' I thought. I was not prepared for what I saw next. I found her lying face down on the bed. At first, I thought she had fallen asleep. 'She'll be happier in the morning when she sees what I have done,' I thought. I began to draw the covers over her and that's when I noticed. The bedspread was stained and darkened. I stirred a finger in the warm red liquid, it was so rich and thick. I tried waking her up to see and succeeded in pushing her over, then blood spurted out of her neck all over me like a fountain. She had slit her throat with a broken wine glass. Do you have any idea how much guts and determination it takes to cut your own throat like that? Her eyes looked at me. Glassy and colorless."

"Oh Lawrence." Sharon knelt beside him. Staring into the fireplace void of flame, he cleared his throat and stood up. Brilliant flashes of lightning shown through the cellar windows which looked out on the side lawn to the garden, followed by rolling thunder. At the other end of the basement there was a crash and a scream. James left Sharon alone to see what was happening to the children. Lawrence continued with his confession.

"I returned to the bathroom and pulled brother out of that cruddy tub. I dried him and changed him, told him how we were both mistreated, but it was over now, mommy would make up for it by taking us both away with her. I brought the baby with me to her bed and we laid beside her. I knew if we all just cuddled together and slept, in the morning everything would be back to normal again.

"I was the first to wake up, cold, and sneezing. I decided it would be my responsibility to cook breakfast, so I proceeded to the kitchen. Broke a dozen eggs over everything, including myself. It was a mess, I tell you. I went downstairs to the neighbors to borrow more eggs, but they just stared at my yellow and red stained appearance and would not let me return. The police arrived with a nice woman who said she was going to buy me the same candy which my mother always promised."

Worthy embraced one of the two Greek columns framing the alcove, one hand reaching to the carved flowers at its top. "I was never suspected in what happened," he said. "My father had to take me, or the police were going to scandalize him. Of course, his brother stepped in and took me instead.

"I felt betrayed. I did exactly what I was asked, pleased to do it for her. But she lied. She abandoned me, and I hated her for it. You promised it would be us but it's just you and baby again, together, forever. I swore I'd find her someday; death would not keep us apart! I never saw her again, even after I passed to the nether world."

Sharon approached him, her arms raised and open for an embrace. "Lawrence are you all right?" she asked, crying. He looked down, focused his attention on the necklace around her neck.

"Mother?"

He saw Timmy approaching in a slow procession from the other end of the basement. "Brother is that you? Brother!"

Sally followed behind her brother holding James' hand. Timmy stopped in front of Lawrence and held up the alabaster urn with the lid off. Two white sauna towels that James had used to dry him from the rain were draped over each of his shoulders such that he looked robed in a religious vestment.

"Lawrence, I'm sorry, I didn't know," Sharon said. She reached up to touch his cheek.

He pulled away. "No! I must face my end alone."

In solemn silence the procession halted before Lawrence. The two candelabras burning on the mantelpiece behind him glowed like silent prayers. Timmy stepped forward, despite Sharon's attempt to pull him back.

"Allow him to pass," Lawrence said. "He has something which belongs to me." The boy held the urn up. He took it like a priest receiving a holy sacrament and said, "This is my body." He lifted it high with outstretched arms and said, "This my blood." He gazed heavenward. "Mother, please, I forgive you! Brother, please forgive me! *Pater, in manus tuas commendo spiritum meum!*"

With one sweep through the air, he swung the urn out in a wide arc above everyone's heads. The ashes flew out floating in one great sanctified puff. As they fell, each granule of ash metamorphosed into a moth the color and texture of white rose, and numerous, such that the air became a dense mass of wings flapping together in great balls like chrysanthemums, so brightly lit they all had to cover their eyes. The moths darted and swerved, then shot back into Lawrence, each pricking a hole in him, causing an infinite number of light rays to emanate outward, until suddenly reaching such a tremendous concentration of light his whole body exploded in a white flash. They saw the outline of Lawrence shrouded in nimbus and then, saw him no more.

26

3 a.m.

Lightning bolts struck the estate like a Van de Graaff machine, thunder pounded the ground like cluster bombs, the bulkhead took a direct hit. It was if the weather itself were trapped in this unnatural world expurgating its last kick of energy, sighing its last breath. In the quiet that followed, the four lay on the floor trembling.

They helped each other up. In the mirror behind the bar, they saw ghost-like figures huddled together, tainted in a powdery substance, as if they had just passed through some primitive rite of passage. They wiped the grey ashes from their eyes, brushed it out of their hair, off their clothes, wiped it from their mouths and lips.

"Lawrence is gone," Timmy said. He stared at the fireplace. "Blown to smithereens."

"I'm scaeh'ed," Sally said.

"Don't be," said Timmy. "He's gone––forever."

Sharon started laughing. The others followed, but she laughed the loudest, so hard she had to hold her rib cage and abdomen while crumbling to her knees. Her laugh turned into a silent utterance with tears; nobody knew whether they were from joy or anguish. Most of all it had been her burden to bear. She heaved a breath. Lifted at last were feelings of guilt, shame, relief. A happiness returned; dignity restored; but Sharon would always live with regrets. The others knelt and comforted her. James helped her to her feet.

"He couldn't have conjured this up as another trick, could he?" Sharon asked. She wiped her eyes and nose with the back of her hand.

"Why not?" James said. "With that partner of his, he could do anything."

They heard timbers falling upstairs.

"We better get out of here and we better hurry," James said.

"But the sto'am!" Sally said.

"Don't worry, sis," Timmy held her shoulder, "the storm's over. We're free!"

They felt their way through the semi-darkness to the cellar bulkhead, smelling its smoldering metal. One iron door plate had been blown open, the other bent in on its hinges. James picked up a two-by-four and knocked the bent door loose and it fell out of the way. They walked out into a softened wind. The rain washed their skin clean from the ashes and they dripped back to their original colors. They smelled burning pine and cedar.

"Get yourselves to the kitchen," James said. "It looks like that side of the estate was spared. And wait for me. There's one last thing I must do." He took off to the gardens.

Flames danced atop globe-like bushes, giant trees lay across tops of smashed tables and flower boxes, pine needles crackled and floated in the air like fireflies. Tall hedge walls collapsed. James found the statue laying in the fountain basin. "Spirit!" he cried. He gazed into her jeweled eyes twinkling like diamonds, reflecting the chaos of the surroundings. He touched her brow with his hand but quickly pulled it back for the singe. "Rest now, you whose life was trapped here far longer than our own." One of her inlaid eyes popped out and he caught it, tossing it between his hands until it was cool enough to deposit in his pocket. He looked down at what was left of her, "Fare thee well and if forever, still forever, fare thee well." A burning oak tree collapsed above him and he scampered out of the way running out of the garden.

James stopped at the garden gate. In the distance he saw the others on the kitchen porch, water gushing from broken gutters hanging off the roof. They must be anxious to leave. Why wasn't he? He wished that the summer for them had never had an end. Hands in pockets, he strolled up to the porch where they stood wrapped in quilts they pulled from the laundry room. The children lay against each other on the swinging porch bench.

"Don't fall asleep, children," she said. "We've got to get to the gate before something else happens or it closes." They had already closed their eyes.

"How do you know you can leave?" James said. "You can barely see ten yards in this fog. Besides, there could be some of the Master's minions watching the gate. We'll wait for the light when we can see what we might be up against. At least we'll have a fighting chance if there is. Here we're safe."

Too tired to argue, Sharon opened her quilt to him. Wrapped together, the two reclined in a wide Adirondack chair. She laid her head on his chest and dozed as James watched the flickering dying flames in the garden, before sleep overcame him too.

27

6 a.m.

No flashes no rumbles, rain dissipated to a spray. A cotton-like cloud had crept up the drive encompassing the carriage house and lawns in a shroud. No birds sang, no mice scrambled, nor rabbits seen hopping out of site. Arising, the children stepped from the porch toward the cloud, dragging the edges of their quilts through dewy grass. Hearing them on the creaky stairs, Sharon woke and followed them.

Rising on the porch, James yawned and saw them heading out. He yelled for them to stop. Sharon did, but the children kept trudging on. As they disappeared into the velvety puff, James ran past Sharon after them until the prickly pebbles of the gravel pinched the bottom of his feet and he eased up.

"Call them back, Sharon. Lawrence's partner could be outside the gate waiting for them."

Sharon mashed down the gravel with her wet shoe. "I'm not worried about him anymore."

"Call them back Sharon." He walked up and took her hand. "Stay with me here, please."

She withdrew her hand. "James, there's nothing left. Look behind you, it's in ashes!"

"Trust me," he said. "It'll revert back to the way it was when I arrived."

301

"Are you crazy, James, after all we've been through?"

"We can be happy here. I don't want you to leave. This is home now, this is where we belong."

"James, you're scaring me." She turned to walk into the mist, her shoes scuffling the gravel.

"Stop!" James shouted. "I command you!"

That stopped her. She turned around with a guarded calm. "I'm going to forget I heard that. I said no to one controlling man and will not be ordered around again by another. James, you came to get us out, remember?"

He rushed forward and fell to his knees, clinging to her, burying his face in her stomach.

"Please, Sharon, I'm begging. I'm not ready to return to the world. Relationships to mend, promises to keep, expectations to meet. I can't go back, I'll fail, I'm not ready. I won't!"

"Oh Jimbo, you didn't fail us, and you won't let anyone else down either." She crouched down to his level and stroked his cheek. "I am afraid too and not ready. But this is my last chance for freedom and I'm taking it! I have a lot to face, my life was a big mess when I left. You will return to people who love you and care about you, they don't expect you to be perfect, just that you try. I don't know what's happening to you in here, but you're not thinking straight."

"Here it's blissful." He spotted a white bird gliding above her in the clouded sky. "And I'll always have you."

Sharon stood up. "James, I am leaving. Now do the same."

James stared at her neck. Sharon grasped the necklace in her hand. "I'm keeping it if this place will let me. It's too valuable to leave behind."

"Not the necklace." James pointed. "The red marks, on your throat."

She touched the painful red ring gently. "I'll be okay."

"Don't go, Sharon, please, don't go."

Her eyes fixed upon his. She breathed in and slowly exhaled. A dove swooped down and fluttered in place above her head. Before it flew off it startled her back to her senses. The ground swelled, buckling up between them.

"James, hurry and join us!"

The property shook and Sharon did not wait for him any longer. She ran into the mist, alone. James watched as the white whale-like cloud swallowed her up. Then it enveloped him in its opaqueness along with the entire estate. He held his head in his hands and lied down flat upon the rough gravel and cried.

❀ † ❀

The children reached the end of the drive like fleeing refugees wrapped in their sopping wet bedspreads. The white cloud opened to reveal the gateposts as two wary sentries. The outside world they knew was back. Was it real this time? A great white owl glided out above their heads and they saw it land on a tree branch across the road, its big eyes staring at them, as if waiting for them to escape too. The gate unlatched, and Timmy pushed it open. But they did not step out yet.

"What will happen to us out day-uh, Timmy?" asked Sally.

"It's like visiting Never-Never Land," Timmy said, "except you get to grow up."

The patrol car Timmy knew so well sped by, until its driver screeched to a halt. A police officer with his long crop of thick chestnut hair and bushy sideburns leaned over to the rolled-down passenger window and shouted at them.

"What are you kids—what—" his voice changed from a harsh bark to one of wonder. "What are you two doing there alone after a storm like this, where are your parents?"

"I'm here," a voice said from behind them, "I'm their mother."

He smelled smoke rising above the trees in the direction of the manor house. "Another fire. Not the only place in this town to be hit by the storm of the century. Step closer to the car where I can see you better please." He called the dispatch on the police radio to send for help.

Sally looked up at her mother out of the hood of the blanket. "Whe'ah's James?" she asked.

"He's taking care of himself," she said.

The patrolman looked up to question them further. They were gone.

28

A cacophony of orchestral sound from a flock of morning birds woke James. His cheeks were imprinted with the pebbles on top of which he slept. James rubbed his eyes; the estate had transformed back to its original form, just as he expected; beautiful and clean, no sign of smoke or ashes blowing about a burned-out shell. As the sun began to create the dawn, James stood somewhere between its light and darkness. He looked at the sprawling front lawn with its rainbow-colored flowers blazing at its center. He remembered that first day standing there when he recognized Sharon and the children for the first time. *At least we've got this place to ourselves. Wait.* The blood escaped from his face. Sharon and the children had left. He heard the children's laughter. *No, they're in the pool having fun.* Smiling he wandered to the portly front door and let himself in. He could barely keep his eyes open. Too tired to comprehend his predicament, he drudged up the staircase. Perhaps she lay in bed waiting for him. When he reached her room the bed was made, with her empty silk slip laying on top, but no sign of her. He sniffed its arousing scent and fell flat on the bed, its sheets steeped in the lingering sweet perfume of her body. He whispered her name and nodded off. Out of his pocket a glittering gem, the eye of the statue, fell to the floor, just as the rising sun peeked in from the east. A shadow covered him.

"Mr. Harris." The Chairman hovered above. "Will you sleep forever?" A twinkle of light caught his eye from the floor, the statue's eye, glistening in the red ruby sunrise. He picked up the stone and examined it under a jeweler's lens before slipping it into his pocket. He lit a cigar and seated himself in a chair resting his feet upon the cherry wood desk. Blowing smoke, he stared down at the body of James sprawled out sleeping like the dead. "Just as I thought, the property may not be through with you yet." He would wait for him to wake.

PART III
GOING HOME

BOSTON

DEATH COMES TO THE FAMILY

1

RETURN

Boston, 2000

*He's, he's coming to--Who are you, where am I?--The McLean Asylum
for the insane -Where?-- You're on the grounds of Mclean's Psychiatric
Hospital--Why? What happened?--You were nearly hit by a car and
fell, hitting your head--I feel off balance--You need to see a doctor, you
may have a concussion--I'm as clear headed as I'll ever be. Where's my
mother?--She left, this morning--But I was supposed to pick her--Are
you the son?—Yes, who else?--Her lawyer picked her up--Why didn't
she wait for me?--She was afraid you'd re-commit her.*

*Stop. Red light. Roll down window. Boston sea air, involuntary
memories of--so cold it hurts my nostrils. Green light. Go. Left down
Belmont Street through Watertown past Mt. Auburn cemetery (coffin,
dead people, shovel), past boat houses and football stadiums and
business schools on the Charles (Harvard, not Yale, we're in enemy
territory now); down Soldiers Field Road onto Storrow Drive, past
Nickerson Field and student dorms, university chapel, Kenmore
Square, the Citgo Sign and Fenway Park (that heartbreak team, Yankee
rivals), past the burned down church turned into condos (where she
said, mother said, she and dad were married, before it burned). Take
right into tunnel, exit to surface opposite Hatch Shell on the Esplanade
under Arthur Fiedler's pedestrian bridge. Brahmin territory. Red light.*

311

Stop. How did I get here? Green light. Go. Take left on Beacon, right on Arlington. Past Public Gardens. Halt. Public alley number 422 behind Marlborough. Home. Hers. First floor condo of immaculately brushed and re-detailed brownstone. Back door painted royal blue; Indian corn wreath hung on knocker. Bottom panel cracked and splintered like it's been kicked in, a hole the size of my fist where the knob used to be.

2

HOMECOMING

James reached through the hole and turned the indoor knob, wobbly connected that it was. The heat of the apartment escaped to mix with the windy cold until he closed the door and trapped it in. Down the hallway's hardwood floor, a disheveled oriental runner laid like a long languid serpent twisted and dead. He straightened it out with his foot, walked the long dim corridor to the front landing of the apartment.

Along the way, James glanced at pictures he hadn't seen in years; a Currier and Ives print of skaters on ice, lithographs of colorful birds from the nineteenth century, two Wyeth prints and towering photos of the tall ships from the '76 bicentennial. He heard voices speaking, glasses clinking.

When he turned into the high-ceilinged living room, there was no one. Just a hodgepodge of furniture from different homes he grew up in––grandfather clock with the sun and moon dial to tell the hour, oriental floor vases and plants, end tables and colonial chairs––remnants of his mother's voided marriages. Smoke rose from a burning cigarette in an unattended ashtray, two armchairs faced a fireplace with birch logs burning. Above the mantel piece hung a painting he remembered from his youth, a late-Victorian scene of a woman with her hair pulled in a bun sitting at the keys of a grand piano. Her curls dangled from each ear like long earrings and she wore a yellow dress with a hemline down to her ankles, frilled sleeves and a scandalous low bust line. As she played, she gazed into the eyes of a gentleman leaning against her piano, handlebar mustache, turn of the century dandy. He returned her gaze with a devilish grin. From a varnished table with a cranberry-colored lamp, James lifted a silver-framed photo of his mother wearing tennis whites in the prime of her playing days, standing at the net with her Japanese doubles partner holding the tournament trophy they won together.

"She's a beautiful woman, your mother." A voice spoke from across the room. "Still looks as young, how does she do it, some mysterious elixir given to her by the devil maybe. Jimbo, you finally made it, we didn't hear you come in. How the hell are you, boy?"

"Nice to see you again, Hawke." He folded his coat onto a chair.

The man stopped in front of a mahogany credenza in a corner of the room, lifted a liquor bottle, and poured two drinks. Starting toward James, he tripped over the edge of a white knotted rug, a glass of scotch in each hand. He spilled neither as he handed one to James. Hawke, a family friend from Connecticut, dressed in a button-down and navy-blue blazer with the gold crest of his prep school emblazoned on the breast pocket. On his head a Greek sailor's cap, a red and navy cravat patterned with anchors around his neck, whale prints on his trousers and an embroidered canvas belt with nautical flags sewn in for his initials––the kind sold in Marblehead.

Hawke was handsome and rotund. No one ever had a clear idea what he did for a living except that he often flew to Venezuela, something to do with oil, or gold––part of a family fortune which would someday be his. After his divorce, Hawke returned to Boston where he reconnected with James' mother, and together they visited their favorite Boston watering holes––Joseph's, Marliave's, Lockobers. Not long after, Hawke proposed to her, but she turned him down for a local politician (her father, a former New England governor). Years later after her divorce she and Hawke ran into each other at the Charles Street Grill at the bottom of Beacon Hill. She was ready to marry him then--but it was too late. Hawke inherited that large sum of money and married something much younger. It didn't stop the two from becoming best drinking buddies again.

Hawke and James rested themselves in the wingback chairs by the fire. "You've settled down on the west coast, your mother tells me, how long since you last saw her?"

"Too long," James said.

"She may not act like it but she misses you." Hawke lifted his heavy glass to James and the two sipped in silent toast.

"My eldest son, come home." James' mother entered from the kitchen and the two men stood up. She carried an ice tray and vodka bottle from the freezer and placed both on the coffee table. She greeted James with a kiss on the cheek. "To what do I owe this honor?" she said. "Did you finally miss your dear mother?" She waved away his answer before it was uttered. "Never mind." He gave her his seat.

"You remember Hawke from our Connecticut days."

"Of course I do," James said, "and you shouldn't be drinking."

She stared at his scotch-filled glass. "That's right, Jesus, you go right ahead."

James set it down. "Why did the lawyer sign you out of Mclean's?"

"I wasn't going to stay there any longer than I had to. I can take care of myself, thank you."

The conversation between James and his mother ended. Hawke filled the void. "James," he said. "How's the ol' town in Connecticut?"

"He lives in California now, Hawke," his mother said, "I already told you that."

"I know that, Maddie, you think I'm an idiot? But your sister told us he was driving up from there today. I heard the place hasn't changed, frozen in time, still has one stoplight. Did you see anyone we know?"

James thought of Sharon and the children. "No," he said. "Only our old homestead and then a quick drive by the club. That was it."

"It's getting to be paddle tennis weather. Do they still have those raised, cloistered decks?"

"Hawke, James doesn't want to be bothered with memories of that place, so stop asking."

"It's okay, Mom," James said. "It was cold and empty. The club house was closed. I climbed Trap Shoot Hill, that was still open. What a beautiful view in autumn it still has overlooking the pond."

"Your mother was the best shot in her day."

"Come off it, Hawke, I only shot a few times."

"Yes and hit every clay pigeon too. You should have seen the embarrassment on the men's faces."

"He loves to tell that story."

Hawke plopped his glass down. "Well, Maddie, time I go, it's getting dark outside."

"It's early, Jimbo hasn't seen you in a long time."

"Maddie, you knew I was going to turn into a pumpkin early tonight, your son has arrived, and my turn of duty to which your sister reluctantly agreed, is over. I'm sure James doesn't want an Irish drunk like me hanging around."

"It's my house and my rules, now sit."

"What would we continue to do but drink? We promised your sister not a drop and we broke that promise long ago. Besides, you're almost out of booze."

"We can send James to Deluca's for more." Hawke wasn't going to be influenced to stay. "Oh Albee, you know how I'm afraid to be left alone."

"Christ, your son is here, you two must have a lot of catching up to do."

"I don't know what I'll do, you know I can't sleep."

"Take the pills I gave you, Mad, that's what they're for. And not too many this time. Now, goodnight!" Hawke walked to the front door with a jig, singing an old sailor's tune before letting himself out.

3

MOTHER & SON

James sat in the armchair Hawke vacated while his mother grabbed the vodka off the table. She kept her eyes on him, guarding the bottle like a baby he might take away from her. She emptied the tin ice tray onto a cheese plate, took up the melting cubes with her fingers and dropped them in her glass. "James darling, get a ginger ale from the fridge for me please?"

Her refrigerator was sparse; a jar of grain mustard, open cup of yogurt, mealy apple, half a dried-out lime and limp lettuce leaves stuck to the glass shelf. In the cupboards, there was less; squiggly pasta, chocolate candies, water crackers. He returned with her soda and she diluted her vodka with it.

"What happened to us in Connecticut, we were such a happy family, remember? Then your father turned weird, smoking marijuana and pushing me to do that wife swapping thing. There was no way I was going to do that."

"Don't worry, you didn't," James said.

"Your brother, he was so quick after he learned to walk. I couldn't keep up with him."

James stared at the burning logs. "I used to chase him around the house for hours." He pried the logs loose for air with the poker. The reflection of the flames danced in his eyes.

"He was getting into everything," she said. "There were no

child locks on cabinets then." She closed her eyes. "I shouldn't have left that glass door open."

James stopped poking and stood straight. "I've been here five minutes and already we're talking about this."

"If that accident hadn't—your father would never have left, and we'd still be the most popular couple in town." She began to cry in her drink.

Hands behind his head, elbows out, James walked behind her. He stared at the shadows on the opposite wall where light from the flickering flames cast shadows. His mother glanced up from her chair looking for him.

"They said I was a bad mother, was I, James?"

Letting out his breath he walked back around the chair to face her. "No, you weren't."

"Despite what you believed, I loved you and your brother equally."

"I never believed otherwise."

She poured herself the last inches of the vodka. James took the glass from her and tossed its contents in the fire, which hissed like holy water thrown upon the head of the devil. He splashed his own in the fire too.

"What did you do that for?" she said.

"I thought you'd finally turned the corner. I come back and look what state I find you in. You need to stop—"

"You don't know what I need," she said. "You've never taken the time to get to know me."

"That was your job as the parent, to know me."

"I'm a person too."

"Better start admitting you need help, or you'll never get better."

His mother squeezed the padded arms of her chair. "You think you can barge in here and tell me what to do. Why don't you just say what you've always had on your mind, that you blame me."

"All right," he said. "My brother drowned that day because you were on the other side of the pool drinking and gabbing on the patio phone, not paying attention. I heard the splash and I heard you scream and by the time I ran downstairs and pulled him out, it was too late. And there sat dad in a drunken stupor in his study and didn't do a damn thing except blame you."

She raised her hands in the air. "Enough."

"Isn't that what you want to believe? That you're guilty? You love to hear it over and over to punish yourself."

"But it was my fault."

The fire popped a bouquet of sizzling embers. James extinguished them with the back of the grate shovel before they could catch the rug on fire. He separated the burning logs and stared at them. He listened for a long time to their hiss before he spoke again.

"We all thought it was a major success you pulled off when you backed the new governor," he said. "No one thought he had a chance. Why did you leave your job in his office so abruptly?"

"I couldn't cope anymore," she said.

"Because of your drinking."

"Because something happened you don't know anything about." She picked up her cigarette pack, saw it was empty, and laid it down. "Someone from work walked me home one night. He invited himself in for a drink and wouldn't leave. He got me so drunk, I passed out but not before feeling the humiliation of him forcing himself on me. I cried all night."

James was stunned. "Did you report it?"

"For a year, I shut up about it."

James walked up and stretched his arm out before her. "Why?"

"It would have caused a scandal and I was too embarrassed. After that I couldn't function and they were going to fire me, so I told them. They gave me a settlement and my pension early."

James crouched down by her chair, laid his hands over hers. "Why didn't you tell me, I would have come home."

She drew her hands away from his. "Of course, you wouldn't have. Once you joined your father on the west coast you stopped caring."

"That's not fair." He walked to the front window and stared

into the street where autumn leaves swirled around the lamp post light. "It wasn't easy growing up with you," he said. "Men coming and going, the nights you cried on my shoulder, asking me whether you should marry this one or that. You should've married Hawke when you had the chance. At least he loved you."

James turned and looked at his mother for a response. When there was none he looked at his watch. He lifted his coat off the chair and put it on.

"You belong back in Mclean's."

She laughed. "Yeah, they were real helpful."

"Didn't you learn anything while you were there?"

"How to fool the staff," she said, with a subtle grin. "Many of us forced to go in there against our wills because of some goody-good in the family. It was like a prison, but we knew how to get out. We played their game."

"I'm sure you were one of the leaders." He buttoned up his coat.

She leaned back and smiled. "I was their queen. They looked up to me because I knew how to break the rules."

"You're going right back in there tomorrow," he said.

"You sound like my sister."

"I'm your son."

"You don't control me."

"I can get the courts to say otherwise." He walked up to her, his hands in his pockets. "After you're well, you'll come to San Francisco and stay with me. You can meet my girlfriend." He scratched his nose. "If I still have one."

"Maybe I don't want to go."

"Maybe you don't have a choice—"

"I'm not going back in there, James. Don't force me."

He turned on the TV for her. "You need something to eat." He walked to the front door and unlocked it with a click.

"Where are you going?" she asked.

"To Deluca's, like you asked."

"Buy me a bottle of vodka, darling, won't you do that for your sweet mom? Charge my account if you don't want to pay for it yourself."

"Absolutely not. You're too skinny and need to put something in your stomach––food––not alcohol."

"I'm so tired," she said.

"Go lie down," he said.

As he opened the door into the building vestibule, she looked at him in her girlish way, smiling as if she were softening towards him.

"James," she said.

For a moment he thought she was going to say those words—I love you—and if she did he would do anything for her.

Instead, she said, "Sweetie, buy me a carton of cigarettes, please. I'm all out, Carlton Green 100s."

He walked over and kissed her on the forehead. "You can be such a pain. But despite it, I love you, Mom. I just wish we got along better than we do."

"James," she said, "I love you. Always remember that."

His heart warmed and he left, locking the front door tight.

4

AN ERRAND TO RUN

James gallivanted down the stone pudding steps. The smell of burnt autumn leaves peeked his nostrils as a mighty wind swept them off the street into a cyclone. James followed it down Marlborough Street toward the public gardens until it dispersed itself into the passing traffic on Arlington. If only he'd stayed nearer to her all these years. He knew how she struggled and drank too much, especially when alone. When the opportunity presented itself to go to college out west, he thought of staying local, but his aunt urged him to go and start a new life for himself and be happy. He didn't have to agree with her so quickly.

The pedestrian light flashed and he crossed into the Gardens. From there he took the path which led to the statue of a doctor towering above a fountain. A famous Boston physician who invented ether in the early nineteenth century, carved out of grey stone. Portrayed as a sage in the classical tragic pose, he held a dying young man in his arms. The doctor looked with anguish as if he were the one suffering, because he knew all he could do was relieve his patient of his last pain before his exit from this world.

James continued on the path over a bridge, to the swan pond where the park lamps cast eerie shadows across his path into the hanging branches of willow trees. He expected Lawrence to appear from behind their trunks any minute. Didn't he say you could never leave that place without some of its evil following you? He quickened his step to the "Make Way for Ducklings" brass statuettes. He thought of Lawrence holding that duckling above his brother's carriage. He remembered his own. Why couldn't their brothers have lived? If they had, would he and Lawrence have turned out different men, grown up more whole?

He exited the park across Charles Street to the entrance of the Boston Common. A pair of mothers pushed baby carriages up an asphalt path. His own mother, sexually assaulted while James was three thousand miles away. His aunt had alluded to some traumatic experience last year but never shared the details. She didn't want him to worry. If only he'd been there, he could have protected her. Like he always did, after his father left. Truth was she never wanted to be saved, not then and still didn't now. Just taken care of and loved. He crossed Beacon and walked down Charles Street until he reached Deluca's, where he'd buy her food that wouldn't rot.

He bought carrots, cod fish and parsley, potatoes, onions and broccoli, and at the register cigarettes--she should be allowed at least one vice while she's trying to kick another. As James walked back, he took a peach from the grocery bag and bit into it, relishing the taste of a sweet tangy fruit he knew was real. Afterward he threw its pit into a bush for the grey speckled squirrels and returned through the gardens to his mother's apartment.

He arrived at the front door but had no key. He rang her bell. Looked through the curtained window, saw the TV on but no sight of her. He walked around the block to the back alley and let himself in. She was asleep in her bedroom. He decided to cook dinner. When the potatoes were boiled, buttered, and seasoned with parsley, the fish peppered, oiled, and broiled, he called her to dinner. He set the table and called again and again after he laid the food on the table. He went to wake her. She was pale. He shook her, no response. He checked beneath her eyelids. She was breathing, but he could not rouse her. Under the bed, a half-filled bottle of vodka laid spilled on its side. On her bed table two pill vials knocked over, their contents mixed in a pile. He called 911. Paramedics arrived.

One of them remembered the apartment from the previous rescue a week earlier. They rushed by James with a clutter of emergency equipment and tried to waken her, but she did not respond. They fed her an intravenous solution while she lay on a stretcher.

"Take her to McLean's," James told them. "They know her there."

"Yes, we know," the paramedic said, "we were here the first time. But there's no time. Mass General is closer."

Less than an hour later, his mother was dead. From the hospital, he called his aunt to give her the news. Then he called Pamela.

5

THE LAST HURRAH

A memorial service was announced in *The Globe* obituaries. To be held at First Unitarian on Newbury Street, between Arlington and Berkley. James' relatives came from all over New England, some from the west coast. His mother's political friends showed, as well as some of her drinking buddies who left their Back-Bay cave dwellings to attend. Hawke sat in the front pew beside James, red-eyed, red-nosed, and solemn. James hoped his mother's friends from Connecticut would show, like Anne Godwin––he had a lot to say to her. And what of Sharon—would she resurface again? If she did, he wondered, would it be as a young woman, or her true age?

One of James' nieces, a girl no older than Timmy, stood up and read an Emily Dickinson poem—"The bustle in a house, the morning after death…" James' aunt stood at the podium and told thoughtful and heartwarming anecdotes about her sister. His aunt's performance betrayed her down-to-earth New England stock; her plain talk. Not once did she bring up his mother's drinking, allude to or intimate her failures––just showed how much she loved her. Why couldn't he love her, his own mother, like that, so blamelessly?

As others spoke, James' mind kept drifting back to the Revson estate. Its memories and images attached themselves to his brain like barnacles to a boat. Was it real or not? By what proof? He was not inclined to chalk it all up to his imagination; he could not refute the richness of the colors his eyes had seen, weather his flesh felt, scents his nose smelled.

When it was his turn to speak, Hawke nudged him. Upon stepping to the microphone, he thought, "My mother's dead, and we are all guilty of doing nothing to stop her from destroying herself, least of all me." But instead he took hold of the podium, looked as if he were about to throw up. "We will miss her," was all he could muster before his emotions overwhelmed him.

The service ended with a church hymn and a prayer. The crowd dwindled to a few as it passed James in a dissipating stream of sincere condolences. He said goodbye to the last of his relatives then sat on a bench in the front hall stirring his black coffee in its Styrofoam cup. Hawke appeared.

"I can't help but to blame a little of myself for this tragedy," he said, sitting beside James, "those sleeping pills were mine."

"I didn't notice she was unconscious," James said, "barely breathing." He stared into his coffee thick as tar. "Instead I cooked dinner."

Hawke slapped his thick thighs and stood. "It won't do either of us any good to confess our sins, better we ignore and repress them with liquor. Come with me, my boy, we can grieve later. We must go to your mother's favorite watering hole and celebrate her life, The Last Hurrah beneath the Parker House. A toast to the dead, an ancient Irish tradition."

A Joycean celebration––why not? It would fit his surreal state, not wholly present. Conjure up Sharon if he wanted, drunk himself to death and reunite with Eugene and Lawrence. And, as Hawke said, drown out the pity and sadness he was feeling for his mother.

They exited the church onto Newbury Street. James stared at the top of the John Hancock from where a brisk wind blew, catching in its path a familiar scent. From that other place. He spotted a woman in a black dress, scarf and dark glasses opening the door of a cab. "Sharon? Sharon!" He ran up to her. The woman turned around and removed her glasses. "You," James said.

"Anne Godwin, how the hell are ya," Hawke spoke up. "After

all these years, I didn't see you in the chapel."

"I was there," she said, "standing in the back. It was too emotional for me to mingle afterwards. You were busy, James, I didn't want to interrupt—"

"We were just going for a drink," Hawke said, "why don't you join us, in tribute to ol' Maddy-Mad-Mad?"

"Thanks, Hawke," Anne said, "but I don't think that's a good idea right now."

James took her by the elbow.

"Of course, it's a good idea, Hawke," he said. "She'll come gladly. Because not only did she come for the service, she came to see me, isn't that right, Anne?"

Anne entered the cab first, followed by Hawke, then James. Hawke squeezed them both to the sides with his large frame and did all the talking until they arrived at the Parker House on Beacon. James paid the fare, then scrambled down the stairs after them to the basement level pub. Taking a table in the back corner against a mirrored wall, their own images reflected dimly down on them.

"Where's the waitress?" Hawke said, "Never mind. I'm good at guessing what drinks people like. Anne, a cosmopolitan? James, a Guinness? I'll have my favorite, a double martini."

He hummed the sailor's tune he sang when he was nervous and disappeared.

❀ † ❀

With Hawke gone, it was their opportunity to talk, but James and Anne sat in silence. At a nearby table, they overheard a discussion about car racing by a group of businessmen.

"Sad at the Indy this year. Adam Petty was so young. Such a great racing family too."

"That's open wheel racing for you."

"Senna, Brayton, Marcelo, the gods have not been good to the sport of late."

"It was worse racing in the sixties and seventies, the cars were flimsy back then, tinder boxes made of tin on wheels."

"Weatherly, Sachs, McDonald."

"Sad deaths, all of them."

"Swede Savage at the Indy. Remember that one?"

"Who could forget? The weather that day, strongest winds and rain, hail even. I don't know why they didn't postpone. Called the race with six laps to go. Swede Savage's fatal crash, that's what everyone remembers, not the winner that year. Devastating."

"Then there was Pete Revson."

"Oh yeah. That rich kid. Heir to the Revlon fortune. His uncle was Charlie Revson. Engaged to Miss Universe, Israeli, what was her name? Jesus God, someone worth millions like that boy shouldn't have been racing in the first place. Bought his way onto the circuit for sure."

"False," said the other. "He wasn't some celebrity driving as a hobby. He was the real thing, a true pro, he could've been one of the best ever."

"Oh yea, what did he ever win?"

"Are you kidding? Three Grand Prixes, the last American born driver to win even one. Came in second at the Indy one year."

"How do you know so much about him?"

"We were classmates at Hotchkiss before he got kicked out. We all followed his racing at Lime and Watkin's Glen. That's where he and Gurney first raced each other. Sad family story. His brother died racing too, many years earlier and much younger.

"And that didn't stop him from driving? How old was he when he died?"

"Thirty-three."

6

A RECKONING WITH ANNE

"James, you're shaking," Anne said. "Are you all right?"

"I'm all right. It's been quite a day. And you know where I just came from." He stared at her as if made of heavy stone. "You wanted me to go there, didn't you? To do what you couldn't." He sat back. "Now I bet you want to know where she is."

"She?" Hawke showed up with the waitress. "Who she?" he said.

"Sharon Peters," James said, staring at Anne. The waitress set their drinks down and left.

"Now there was a pretty gal," Hawke said. "Married to that self-proclaimed Town Republican Party leader of ours––what was his name? I remember that son of a bitch. The time he tried to drive the senator's hippie son out of the party, just because of his long hair and a few other antics. You remember, the lifeguard at the club?"

Anne, still in her trench coat, laid her arms on the table and laced her fingers together. "Okay, James, where is she?"

"Finally, you admit you know what I'm talking about," he said. "How did you know I'd get in?"

Anne sat back all the way. "I knew all about your teenage fantasy with Sharon come true."

"We all had our fantasies about Sharon Peters," Hawke said, "but they didn't come true."

James leaned forward. "She told you about us?"

"She used to tell me everything," Anne said.

"If I were to go back to visit Connecticut," Hawke said, "I'd stop by the club first thing."

"I don't know if I'm angry," James said to Anne, "because you deceived me, or grateful that you did. You were her best chance of anybody to help her escape but instead you ran out."

"Is that bartender at the club still there?" Hawke asked. "Gray haired and old then, he must be in his grave by now. If he were still alive, I'd find out from him what happened to everyone we knew, after I'd had a few drinks of my own first."

"She kicked me out," Anne said.

"With good reason," James said.

"Whatever happened to that theatrical family at the club?" Hawke said. "The father was a Broadway producer. They had all those boys."

"I don't blame you for running out," James said.

Hawke suddenly stood. "I have a matter to attend to. Can I get you two another drink?"

"No thanks, Hawke," James took a sip of his Guinness he'd hardly touched.

"Then I'll have to drink for us all." Hawke pushed back his chair and left.

Anne stirred her cosmopolitan. "I know I could've done something to help, but I wasn't in my right mind."

"I almost ran out on them myself," James said, staring at the lather running down his beer mug, "but I didn't. And you shouldn't have either."

"He took advantage of me. Got me skunk drunk then seduced me right in front of Sharon. Words came out of my mouth I didn't place there. Let's not talk about any mistakes made. The point is you succeeded, you got them out. James, you really earned that ten million!"

He stood up. "You were the mysterious investor who sent that posse of bankers to find me at Hearst Castle. Sent me into that abyss without forewarning. You could've flown out or picked up the phone and asked. At least then I could have gone in prepared."

"Would you have believed me?"

He sat back down. "No."

Hawke returned. "Sorry for my extended absence," he said. "I had this biological matter needing attention regarding my kidneys." He leaned down and finished Anne's untouched drink, then promptly sat down and dropped his head onto the soft-pillowy feel of his chubby arms.

"How did you do it, James? How did you convince Lawrence to let her go?"

"It was Sharon who figured it all out. I really thought in the last act she was going to leave with him."

"What do you mean?"

"Too bizarre to explain," he said. "Lawrence wasn't all to blame for the way he was. Made quite a confession of his own in the end. Accepted his final fate with great contrition. As bad as he was, there may be a place in heaven for him yet."

"James, if Sharon and the children made it out, why haven't I heard from her?"

"She hasn't contacted me either."

"You really don't know where she is? Wouldn't the two of you have made plans?"

"They left in great haste. She pleaded with me to leave with them, but for reasons I can't fathom, I chose to stay. Somehow I think that infernal place cast its own spell upon me. I was too caught up in its pathos--or mine--to resist." James slapped his glass down spilling beer and suds. "Anne, we're going back. Right now."

She sopped up his beer with napkins. "What for, what does it matter anymore?" she asked.

"How do I know it wasn't just a dream?" he said, throwing his hands up. "The only way is to go back and search around for clues to another world. There's got to be some hard evidence we can find."

"Can't you just accept you did it?" she said. "You got her out, isn't that all that matters? You're a hero for god's sake!"

"I won't believe it until I can prove to myself it wasn't a dream."

"I have no more interest to go on," Anne said. "My feelings of guilt have been reduced to the size of a little pea, and I'm not one to be kept awake by so small a thing."

James stood up. "Is that all you ever cared about? You did this to assuage your guilt feelings?"

"Guilt?" Hawke lifted his head up off his arms. "Let's not talk about guilt." He sat up straight and bug-eyed like the mouse at the table of the Mad Hatter after a long sleep. "We all let Maddie down, did or said things we shouldn't've, not done what we said we would or could've. That's why we're here now, to commiserate in our failings. Let's not talk about guilt anymore."

"We're going back to Connecticut, Hawke," James said, slipping on his coat. "You can join us if you want to."

"I haven't said yes yet," Anne said.

"You will," James said, "because you're going to drive me back with you." He fiddled in his pockets and pulled out a key. "I just need to stop by mother's place first."

Hawke stood up, "Yes, to Maddie's we must go!" He raised his finger in the air to make his point. "Your mother, I know where she keeps the booze hidden from your aunt, who most certainly has already combed the place trying to remove every drop––that temperance queen." He pushed in his chair, put on his black woolen overcoat. "We'll go and have a final nightcap, in her honor. We will drink to your mother's spirit, then drink some more, abolish all this nonsense of Connecticut. I heard what you two were talking about. Forget there ever was such a damned place with devilish people and––where is that waitress?" Hawke left to pay the tab, as if there was no more time left in the world. Anne and James waited at the bottom of the stairs until Hawke returned singing to himself an old Nantucket sailor's tune.

"We'll drink tonight with hearts as light…"

"Anne," James said, "decide quickly."

"…to loves as gay and fleeting…"

"Very well."

"...*As bubbles that swim, on the beaker's brim...*"

"It's settled!" James said. "Hawke, will you come along too? An adventure to another place you couldn't make up."

"What, what? To the mouth of that fiery hell? I'd sooner leap from the deck of the Pequod. I have no interest stirring up old ghosts as you say."

"...*And break on the lips while meeting...*"

He sang all the way into the taxi.

"...*Fa, la, lira, skirra...*"

CONNECTICUT

A MYSTERY LONG
HELD REVEALED

7

WARD STERLING

Connecticut, 2000

Ward Sterling unlocked the rusted gate to the long abandoned Revson Estate. The dull metallic sign stretched across it read: NO TRESPASSING BY ORDER OF TOWN POLICE. He chuckled; it was he who posted it years ago. Once the wizened protector of the public, he had been kicked off the force in the summer of '69 when he wouldn't stop investigating the fire which burned the estate house to the ground. He was the patrolman who drove by in the wee hours of the pre-dawn after the storm and spotted the woman and two children at the estate entrance. No sooner did he step out of his patrol car to help than they disappeared. Smelling fire, he drove into the property to investigate. Discovering the mansion burning, he called the volunteer fire department to come and dampen its smoking ash to slosh. The state fire inspector declared the cause an act of God, due to the hurricane, which went into the record books as the worst in the town's history. Ward was not convinced.

Standing at the gate on this chilly October day, he zipped up his patchy black leather jacket, wrinkled white at the elbows due to years of wear. While he waited for Anne Godwin and her friend to arrive, he remembered why he had been kicked off the force. Doubting the official report, he'd brought unanswered questions to the attention of the police chief. Why had no serious search been made to find the caretaker, Eugene Lequin, who'd lived on the property since World War I and why had no one made the connection between his own sighting of the woman and children with the missing Sharon Peters and her two young ones? The chief reprimanded him. The fire on the Revson property was not his domain. The inquiry was over in the eyes of the town's selectmen, no less because the Revson family wanted to keep it that way. The chief ordered Ward to let it rest. But the detective in him would not stop.

He returned to the property to have a look around. In the carriage house, workshop tools hung orderly on their peg board, parts of an engine left to soak in a pan of kerosene. Upstairs in the living area of the caretaker's apartment, two carpenter's sawhorses were fallen over on piles of wood shavings among a box of spilt nails and scattered loose sheets of paper filled with sketches and the dimensions for a coffin. In the bedroom, magazine pictures of the Stations of the Cross were pinned on the slanted ceiling, some of which had been ripped down, their corners still tacked up. An empty trunk and suitcase up in the loft. This caretaker didn't go on vacation or run off after the fire. He more likely perished in it. But no charred bodies were ever found.

Ward walked the grounds of the property. The renowned garden was unrecognizable; fallen trees, crushed flower boxes, fountain statue lay in the basin decapitated, its head scorched black. In the greenhouse, a tombstone with the caretaker's name chiseled on it with an open date of death. Clues would suggest this caretaker had been planning his own burial. Behind the carriage house, a white shed. Inside a familiar odor brought back memories of Ward's tour in Vietnam. He crouched down and rubbed a dark red stain on the floor. It tasted of blood. He sent a sample to the lab where it tested positive as human. That's when all hell broke loose. The chief was forced to declare the property a crime scene. A reporter found out and the story hit the paper. Someone leaked to the press that Ward was a habitual smoker of marijuana and the chief suspended him from the town police force without pay, indefinitely.

8

A SUSPECT

Ward took his army lighter from his top pocket and lit up a filterless cigarette, only to throw it down as soon as Anne Godwin pulled up in her Jaguar with her friend. She introduced the two. Ward extended his hand for a firm shake. James took it with guarded reserve. Together the three walked the gravel drive overgrown with brush in silence until they reached the bend in the drive, the property visible at the far end.

"So, you're the young man I've heard so much about," Ward said. "The one who claims to have made it in and freed the property's tortured spirits at last." James gave him a skeptical look. "It's not that I don't believe, Mr. Harris. Over the years dozens have come through claiming to Mrs. Godwin they could see the unfortunate souls trapped and for a fee rescue them. Now you come along and claim you already have."

James stopped the caretaker in his tracks. "I didn't come to prove anything to anyone other than myself that the other place existed. Then I'm out of here and this god-forsaken town. Forever."

Ward scraped gravel with the heel of his alligator boot. "I want proof as much as you do, Mr. Harris. From all eyewitness accounts, one theory suggests the estate existed in a parallel universe, a replica copy of the real thing, but in a Twilight Zone. Over the years many reported strange sightings, myself included; hell, some claim they drove into the property and were entertained by a young couple as alive as you and me. Others swore they saw a boy standing on the wall waving at them to stop, and when they didn't, he threw stones at their cars, sometimes with the help of a mysterious man who was with him. Would you know anything about that?"

James slowly shook his head no. Ward lit up another cigarette. "I want to know for certain," he said. "If we weren't all afflicted by the same hallucinogenic mist in different amounts, a psychic miasma emanating from an ancient crack in the earth spilling out within property borders. Perhaps when you trespassed, you too were lulled into a dream state."

They walked up to the edge of the tree line where it met the bounds of the front lawn, now a fallow field. "Before we go any farther into the property," Ward said, "I have a few questions I need you to answer, and then I'll stop asking for good."

James looked at Anne. "I didn't come back here to be questioned as if I'm a suspect in someone's murder."

Ward looked at Anne and raised his eyebrows. "Who said anything about a murder, Mr. Harris? I understand how you might feel that way. Rest assured, I'm only trying to find a rational possibility which could explain the events as you claim they occurred in that supernatural world, and perhaps solve the mystery of what really happened to the missing Sharon Peters and her children."

"Fine." James crossed his arms in the cold. "How can I be of assistance?"

"First of all, what was your relationship to Mrs. Peters?"

James looked up at the leafless trees. "I babysat for her occasionally. That was it."

"No other connection?" Ward asked. Anne cleared her throat and walked towards the carriage house alone.

"None whatsoever," James said.

Ward shook his head. "Yet there she was, in need of a white knight in shining armor to rescue her from a deranged boyfriend."

"Nobody before me was up to it." He glared over at Anne.

Ward lifted off his cowboy hat, rubbed his balding head. "Where are they now?"

James rubbed his cheekbone. "I don't know, I didn't leave with them."

Ward and James strode ahead to join Anne. "When her ex reported her missing with his children," Ward said, "there was no trace, her home left empty. Car was gone. They took nothing. Nobody has heard from them since. We suspect they fled to Europe with her boyfriend who had posed fraudulently as a Revson."

"I can't help you there."

"Can't or won't?"

James skidded to a halt on the gravel. "Where's all this questioning leading, Mr. Sterling?"

Ward returned his cap to his head. "I'm merely trying to protect Anne Godwin's interests, Mr. Harris. And so far, you have been unable or unwilling to fill in any of the details which could help me locate Mrs. Peters and her children in the real world. Now, last question, I promise. What do you conjecture may have happened to the old caretaker Eugene Lequin?"

James stared into the woods where the white shed used to stand. "He died, poor soul. He knew death was the only thing waiting for him in the real world."

"What happened to his body? It ain't here on the property, I searched everywhere."

"Maybe if you dug deep enough, Mr. Sterling, you would find him."

"And how would you know that?" Ward asked.

James smiled. "Because I buried him."

9

WHAT IS REAL

A dense thicket of chestnut trees separated the carriage house from the remains of the estate. James wandered into them, while the other two stayed behind talking. "Chestnuts grown from the seed I dropped." He picked one up and pried it out of its husk. "This proves I was here!" He looked over at the other two, but they'd disappeared.

He looked up. The afternoon sun burned down from a blue sky, the estate stood in its original state; fresh white paint, shutters forest green, surrounded by green lawns and ground cover. Towering trees protecting this hallowed property from the outside world again. How was this possible? But it was real. He was back. Same eastern songbirds swooping down screeching from their nests, sparrows and chick mouse gathered in the feeder by the kitchen. James climbed the front steps with great strides, slammed down on the gold lion knocker. No answer. He peered in the side windows; the front hall was empty. Where were Sharon and the children? He heard laughter coming from the pool. He smiled a big grin and ran around to the side as fast as he could. He reached the gate under the cedars, brushed the top of the beech hedges with his hand, no question they were real. He heard water splashing accompanied by youthful shrieks.

After he passed through the gate and closed it, the noise in the pool quieted. The lounge chairs lay empty, the pool surface still as glass. The pump in the bath house hummed, the arbor passageway hung heavy with Concord grapes, but he saw no one. He leaned against the French doors and peered in through the glass panes. Even the grand room was vacant. Where was everyone? He heard the shrieks and laughter again splashing from the pool. He turned around to find Timmy and Sally inviting him in for a swim. He couldn't take his clothes off fast enough. He ran up to the pool's edge and was about to dive in, when––he was grabbed and wrestled to the stone patio, someone sitting on him. He must fight for his life.

"Lawrence, let me go!"

"James!" A woman's voice shouted.

"Sharon!" James shouted. "Get him off! It's Lawrence, please!"

"James! You're reliving the past!" Anne Godwin's voice broke his spell. The blurry mass on top of him came into focus; it was Ward. The detective gave James a hand and pulled him to his feet. "Look what you were about to jump into, sonny."

The pool was an empty oblong crater, a cement grave. Blankets of leaves in rain puddles, broken skateboards, scattered beer cans, a scorched black spot where someone had lit a fire.

"Holy cow," Ward said. "This place really has a hold on you."

James stood in his boxer shorts shivering. Anne handed him his clothes to dress.

Ward looked up at a darkening sky, the wind picking up speed. "This place is getting spooky," he said. "Better take us to where Eugene's buried. That should give us all the proof we need before we run out of here as fast we can."

10

DIGGING UP THE TRUTH

James led the truth seekers to the side lawn. No flowery fragrances floated from the garden paradise; here in the real world it had long since turned to swamp, the smell of skunk cabbage clinging to the air. The bad half of the apple tree had since rotted off, while the good half burst with apples hanging from sturdy branches––they could smell the mash of fallen fruit on the ground.

In Sharon's garden, there were no sunflowers or corn stocks, no vegetable bed either, just remnants of a termite-infested shed, collapsed in prickly thorns entangled in vines. He led them along the stone wall until they stopped at a cluster of pines all grown to a mature girth and height. James searched the pine needle-covered ground for Eugene's grave, pressing down his foot where the earth might be soft.

"There's no sign of a grave here," Ward said. "There would be a sinking of the earth where he was buried."

"You wouldn't find a depression because his coffin was beveled on the edges." James said, "Eugene told me the soil above a coffin with beveled edges does not depress the ground above, instead the earth will sink down around the coffin's beveled edges first." James traced with his foot two parallel depressions, a slight mound between them. "This is it," he said. "This is where he's buried." He took a shovel from Ward and the two started digging. Nobody spoke, it was like opening a holy sepulcher which demanded solemn respect.

They soon hit something. Ward crouched down and reached below the dirt with his fingers, pulled up a rifle not greatly rusted.

James staked his shovel in the dirt. "You see? Proof! Eugene's rifle."

"So, we have the alleged murder weapon." Ward cocked the gun to see if it still worked.

James stepped forward. "Let me hold that—"

Ward pointed the gun at James. "Put your hands up in the air where I can see them."

James patted his chest. "You think I killed Eugene?"

Ward took aim. "You did it for Sharon Peters. Now raise your arms."

Anne raised her hand. "Ward, stop joking. You know James was just a boy then, how could he have?"

"Because the two were lovers. He helped Sharon murder her rich boyfriend then took care of Eugene too. I bet you know where she is now."

"Ward, you promised you wouldn't bring up any of your paranoiac conspiracy theories, you're scaring me."

"When Anne told me about your relationships with Sharon Peters," Ward said, "I had her lure you back east here."

"Don't listen to a thing he's saying, James. He's crazy."

"This is the story everyone can believe, not all this talk about ghosts and demons."

"Ward! All these years I trusted you!"

"Sorry, Anne, but justice must be served. And I have a reputation to regain. Now son, step away from the hole." Ward cocked the rifle. "It's been many years for me living with this. Cost me two marriages. At one point I stopped looking at this as some supernatural occurrence. I realized I had to go back and investigate it for what it was in the real world, a crime scene. That boyfriend is probably buried somewhere else on the property too." James rushed for the gun. Ward stepped back holding the barrel up and laughed.

"I'm sorry, I couldn't help it," he said, "you should have seen the look on your two faces. For a moment I thought James was going to confess."

James tightened his lips, balled his fists. "You could've killed me."

"Nonsense, this thing doesn't work." Ward aimed it in the sky and pulled the trigger. Bam! Birds scattered in flocks of feathers everywhere.

"Oops, my bad." He emptied the cartridge and handed it to James. "But it's the best real-life explanation there is, you must admit." James tossed the rifle far away.

"Ward, I'll never forgive you for this," Anne said.

James shook his head and waved Ward back, preferring to dig alone. Flashes of that first day he helped Eugene dig, memories of the last day when he helped Sharon fill it in. He hit another object with the tip of his shovel and stopped. He lifted out a rusty anvil stained in blood. "That," James said, "is the fatal weapon, if you must have one." He handed Ward the shovel and lifted himself out. "I proved he's down there, joker, now you finish it."

Ward took on the task with purpose. After a while, he hit the top of the coffin with a thud. He scraped away the last inch of dirt with the shovel and pressed down with his foot on the pine wood coffin top, bouncy and soft. Holding the shovel high with two hands he drilled it into the lid, and it caved in, releasing an effluvium so pungent it knocked them all back. Ward pried off the top with the shovel. Inside remnants of flesh stuck to fragments of Eugene's clothes and bones. Ward reached in, pulled the rosary beads from the deceased man's grip. He stepped back and the other two peeked down and saw the contents inside, beetles and earwigs trudging over the remains of a barely clothed human skeleton.

"That's Eugene for you," James said, crossing his arms.

"I'll be damned," Ward said, his face brightened as if lit by a hallowed grail.

"God," was all Anne could say, before she threw up not ten yards away.

SAN FRANCISCO

NO PLACE LIKE HOME

11

A MYSTERIOUS
PACKAGE ARRIVES

San Francisco, winter, 2001

Bitter wind clapped down Telegraph Hill as James climbed the steep street home. He pulled open his camel skin coat, inviting in the cold. The San Francisco winter was never extreme, it could not match the opposite intensity of that sultry searing light of that first blistering day of stolen sun, eternal Fourth of July on the Revson estate, which squeezed the sweat out of him relentlessly. He hated that day for which there was no other adequate expression of feeling. But he'd been initiated into that other world then, and that made it bearable.

The further in the past that other world faded so did its inhabitants. Had they been real? Or were they just a cast of characters locked in an unfinished manuscript tucked away in a drawer in the back of his mind, lost in the recesses of his imagination, a story the world would never hear? A midsummer night's dream contained in one autumn night of sleep. What's done is done, what's not visible did not exist.

Upon his return he confided in Pamela that he indeed had had a boyhood encounter with an older woman, who turned out to be the troubled woman he was sent to rescue in Connecticut. That was an unusual happenstance, but it was eclipsed by his mother's death. A painful reality Pamela's love softened. From her he learned the lesson his stubborn will resisted, that emotional dependance could be both humiliating and healing.

An eventual reunion with Sharon James knew must come to pass someday. Then Pamela could meet her and form her own opinion what happened. And if Sharon returned as an eternally young woman? Well, Pamela might come to a different conclusion entirely. No need to hurry that day on, especially if he could know neither the date nor hour of its arrival.

James entered the vestibule of his home red-cheeked. On the hall table lay a brown paper package included in the day's mail. A glow from an overhead chandelier brushed it in gold, his name mapped across it in sparkling strokes of indigo ink, each letter shaped as a swirling work of art. James removed a letter opener from a drawer and slit open the wrapper. A thin book bathed in a familiar scent slipped into his hands. It entered his nostrils, returning him back to the estate; green treetops in a blue sky encircled by a kaleidoscope of colors. He dropped the book to the floor, bracing himself against the hall table for balance. A hard knock brought him back to his world––the jerking of pipes in the wall. Pamela had just turned the hot water off upstairs. He crouched down to pick up the book when an envelope dropped out. Coat sleeves sagging down to the elbows, he began to read the letter when he felt a wisp of rain.

"James, you're home." Pamela stood above him wrapped in a white chamois robe with his monogram on the pocket. "What are you doing down there?" Water from her straight blonde hair dripped on him. Slipping the letter in his pocket, he stood up and kissed her, returning the book to the table. Pamela leaned over and read the title inlaid in gold thread, *Trespass in Time*.

"Who's it from?" she asked.

"Her."

Pamela looked up. "You mean the woman from Connecticut?"

"Yes." He handed her the book and crept towards the front closet to hang his coat. "I don't feel well." He turned up the narrow stairs.

"Wait," she said, "take this." She handed him the book. With head bowed, he ascended the steep steps to bed.

❀ † ❀

That night James lost himself in an old Gene Kelly movie while Pamela readied herself for bed. "Watching *Brigadoon* again?" she asked. "A man suffering for the love of a woman trapped by time in another world."

"It happens," James said, head against the backboard.

Pamela stepped out of the bathroom perfume fresh. "Such the romantic," she said. She clicked off the TV. James stared at its blank screen. "Did you read any of the poems yet?" she asked. He shook his head. She turned off the light, slipped under flannel covers, and pressed her flat strong abdomen against his. James buried his head in her neck.

12

INVITATION TO A BALL

In the following weeks, James lived flustered, distracted, quiet. He had nightmares in which Pamela heard him calling out names—Sharon, Lawrence, Eugene, Timmy, Sally—a family of ghosts. He called and texted less during the day, arrived late to their appointments and social events. They'd grown closer since his trip east in the fall; she felt his mother's death had propelled their relationship forward. But since that book of poems arrived, he had started to withhold some of his emotional self again.

One afternoon in the kitchen while preparing for a dinner party, Pamela heard in the hall the brass flap of the mail slot clap close with a tap-tap. She entered the hall and looked down. An envelope written in the same calligraphy as the brown package of poems but addressed to her. She picked it up at the corner, smudging it with béarnaise sauce on her fingers. Her heart palpitated—an invitation to a masquerade Ball for Mardi Gras in San Simeon at Hearst Castle, not far from her father's beach house. A charitable gala with two tickets enclosed for her and James. She phoned him at work in the Mission District to question who might have sent it. "Throw them away," he said.

That evening at their dinner with friends, Pamela playfully fought with James to accept going, and all their friends took her side. It was a sought-after annual event, with an A-list of invites. Mardi

Gras costumes and masks pre-selected for chosen guests to partake in unscripted role playing. James said he was not going to dress up and pretend to be someone else, especially when his costume was predetermined by some "entertainment committee". But Pamela had already sent back the RSVP, so he had no choice. He would attend, though under protest.

In the predawn of Sunday, Pamela awakened and found James missing from bed. No light in the hall, but there was from under the door of the study. She crept in and found James asleep, head hunched down on his cherry wood desk. The lamp threw his shadow ominously onto a bay window which overlooked the Golden Gate and Alcatraz. In his grasp was a tattered letter which looked as if it had been read dozens of times. Pamela read the first line over his shoulder. *My Dearest James…* Eyes half-closed, he woke up and flattened the creamy blue letter out on the desk, the writing on it smudged from the rub of his moist palms. He slipped it in Pamela's hands and left her to return to bed. Pamela sat in a soft armchair in the study corner and read.

Feb 28, 2001
My Dearest James,

I saw you at the black and white ball in December, you looked handsomely young, sophisticated, and worldly in your tuxedo. I longed to intrude upon you, so I did quite the opposite—left with my partner.

After our release from that ordeal in Connecticut, we moved to Europe. I've thought of you over the years––waiting for you to grow up––I could not interfere knowing I might change the course of events and risk you not showing up at the appointed time. I kept my distance, and that's why I waited until now to return to the Bay Area and seek you out. I was sorry to learn of your mother's death, she was a friend who always knew how to make me laugh. It must not have been a surprise to you that I didn't show for her memorial.

I trust you not to make my existence known to anyone, least of

*all to Anne and that balding detective of hers. He's started looking
for me again, pestering my sister. I didn't want to be found. It's why
I've stayed away all these years without a trace. I swore a solemn oath
to myself when I left that other world in our town, that the confused
and insecure country club housewife I was would stay lost and buried
forever. I had a chance to reboot my life and have loved every second
of it. Sometimes when I feel my loneliest, I wonder what it would have
been like if we had stayed on the estate together. But when I think of
the children, I know I did the right thing. We'll meet soon, James—I
promise.*

Love always.

—S

*P.S. Years ago, I published a book of poems. I thought they
were out of print, but I found this copy in the City Lights Bookstore
downstairs in their used book section. I hope they don't cause you as
much trauma to read as they cost me to write.*

Risk changing the course of events? Appointed time? Who
is this woman really, and what was her relationship to James' new
business partner the Chairman who sent James to Connecticut
to help her in the first place ? The letter left more questions
unanswered. She did not yet have the whole story. From the desk
Pamela picked up the book of poems where it lay turned over on its
spine. She smoothed over its faded cloth cover, found it open to a
poem marked and underlined:

> **Reborn**
> Time is cold, dark sand I lay buried in.
> You come along and pound the ground
> searching for wild treasure.
> I keep my eyes shut, shudder
> as your spade cut close, closer,
> to my immortal body.
> You do not stop
> until you lift me out, complete. I tremble,
> having grown by your intrusion.

What did James do that she would write such deeply felt words? With such a prelude, Pamela and James left the following Friday for her father's beach side chalet in the Big Sur for Mardi Gras.

13

ALL THE WORLD'S A STAGE

Masquerade Ball, Hearst Castle, 2001

The colossal size of the Hearst Palace made the Revson Estate seem no larger than the lodgings of a humble caretaker. Pulling into the circular drive, James handed his Beamer to the valets while he and Pamela met two greeters in top hats and tails—one a Black gentleman dressed in white, the other a white woman dressed in black. One wore a smiling mask, the other frown and tears. In a torrential downpour, the two accompanied the couple up the front steps holding oversized umbrellas like upside-down teacups over their heads, thunder alive in the pines.

Pamela and James entered a red velvet and wood-paneled antechamber. An Alexandrian proverb engraved on a relucent gold plaque displayed on the wall: "The Lover Fears the Carnival."

The octagonal room was overcrowded. A short man in eighteenth-century wig and dress squeezed between guests handing out envelopes, pinning numbers on lapels.

"What are these for?" James asked, as a guest bumped into him.

"They identify what character you will play tonight," Pamela said. Somebody backed into her; she stood her ground.

He opened the envelope and read the role description, "I'm supposed to be—" A couple turned their heads to listen.

"James, shush," Pamela lowered his hand holding the letter, "you're not supposed to tell."

He read it in a softer tone, "I'm to be the French author Victor Hugo seeking out a mysterious masked princess and then fight for her in a duel." He looked at Pamela with a grim lip.

Mardi Gras bells jingled. The doors to the dressing rooms opened and the men separated from the women. The two kissed. "See you on the other side," James said.

𝕾 † 𝕾

In the dressing room, James handed his number to a wigged manservant who retrieved his costume package from a rack. He unwrapped it: dark double-breasted frock over a buff waistcoat, gray trousers with straps beneath the shoes, a tall hat and black domino; circa early nineteenth century. He gazed around at the rest of the participants, all in different period costumes; the Romantics from the early nineteen century; Italians of the Renaissance; the Lost Generation in 1920s Paris and King Arthur's court at Camelot. If she were here, this foolishness to be dressed up like a character from Dickens was worth it. Who will his rival be?

James caught the face of Pamela's friend, Harry, across the room, wearing a Parisian beret. The young man stared at James as if he were invisible. In that moment, James hated Harry as much as he had hated Lawrence. Let them meet in a made-up world and have a go at it.

A small hand tugged on James' overcoat. It belonged to a short man dressed like the hunchback of Notre Dame.

"Quasimodo?" James asked.

The man lifted his monk hood.

"Clarence! What are you doing here?"

Clarence beckoned James to lower his ear. He whispered he

was sent to take him to the Chairman who would be waiting in costume for him inside. "He's not supposed to enter my world," James muttered. Clarence shrugged, slipping his head back inside the monk hood like a turtle.

❀ † ❀

A pair of gilded and wigged sentries opened a set of ornate double doors, releasing the chosen male participants for the gala event that evening. They marched down a long corridor surrounded by applause. Masked guests stood cordoned off by velvet ropes or waved down from balconies as the men and the women participants were corralled into the circular center of a great hall. The architecture was gothic baroque; two antique chandeliers hovered luminously above. From a sashed balcony, the King of Spades and Queen of Hearts greeted the masses. James saw behind them an ominous figure in a death mask. He nudged Quasimodo.

"Look up at the king, someone in a death mask, do you see?"

Clarence looked up but the lights dimmed to darkness and he saw nothing.

A clarinet piped out the opening notes of Gershwin's "Rhapsody in Blue" with a spotlight focused on a wiry, colorfully dressed jester dancing atop the balcony's wide balustrade. Keeping in step to the music, he flung himself around a flagpole topped with bright rainbow flags, swirling and whirling his way down to the stage. Jesters in rainbow-colored leotards danced while he sang:

> *Ladies and Gentlemen, and all in between*
> *Welcome to Mardi Gras, not Halloween*
> *It's our honor and pleasure to keep you amused*
> *And in no small measure very well boozed.*
> *We offer hard spirits and Dionysian wine,*

> *At five hundred a pop the profit's all mine.*
> *Use it to help catch your nymphet or fairy,*
> *Elf, Pixie, imp, demon lover to marry.*
> *We'll celebrate love, not its dark cousin death,*
> *So that we may rise above, after we take our*
> *last breath,*
> *Your masks protect your identity,*
> *'til midnight shrouded in anonymity.*

A rope lowered from the ceiling. The jester wrapped himself around it like a Cirque de Soleil acrobat. As he was pulled upward, he sang in a hushed voice, staring at James:

> *Then the witching hour shall be over, over,*
> *And the rose turn to clover, clover, clover.*

The lights returned to their full brightness. A man with curled shoes dressed like the mayor of Munchkin Land addressed the crowd. The live entertainment for the evening he said would comprise of four ensembles spread throughout the castle with camera crews and professional actors to give cues. Their loosely scripted stories would be projected onto large screens around the hall for Gala guests to follow. At midnight, the impromptu plays would end, masks removed, and everyone re-assemble back in the grand hall for awards. The man on stage dismissed the teams to depart down tunnels which crisscrossed beneath the castle. It was a subterranean maze with low arched brick ceilings, everyone bathed in flickering shadows from dim electric torches posted along their walls.

❀ † ❀

James' group reached a hall with a long banquet table and small orchestra playing Beethoven. A bar stretched down the length of the room below Romantic period tapestries on the walls. James ordered a drink. Finishing it off, he leaned back on his elbows on the bar top to survey the rest of his ensemble's cast. He nodded with a smile as he recognized the Great Romantics of the era: Ralph Waldo Emerson with Thomas Carlisle laying the foundation for transcendentalism, Walt Whitman and William Blake discussing the influence of mysticism on nineteenth-century poetry. Coleridge and Woodsworth, the first of the romantic poets stood together, and beside them Percy Shelley with his wife Mary Shelley discussing gothic horror. John Keats was found reciting his poetry to his love Fanny Brawne and Lord Byron with Alexander Pushkin comparing their great works *Don Juan* and *Eugene Onegin*. The dark Romantics, Edgar Allan Poe and Nathaniel Hawthorne, stood to the side, drunk as hell.

"I'll have you know, Clarence," James said, "Pushkin lost his young life in a duel to protect the honor of his beautiful wife. I hope I fare better than he did tonight. Clarence?"

Gone was the hunchback of Notre Dame. In his place, a figure loomed above him, dressed in a white suit with a Panama hat and a pointed beard. Propped at his side was an ivory cane with a knob shaped like a black poodle's head. The man's character tag read Mephistopheles.

"Adolph." The tall man motioned to the bartender. "Another drink for Monsieur Hugo." Adolph poured him a glass of an effervescent green absinthe. James drank it down, shivering at its potency.

"What are you doing here?" James asked. "I thought we agreed never to be seen in public together."

"Relax." The tall man said. "I came with him." He nodded in

the direction of an older gentleman seated with the other Romantic writers. "Johann Wolfgang von Goethe, author of *Faust*. I have my part to play in this drama just like you."

"You know I never asked you to rescue me from inside there."

"I was merely protecting my investment." The Chairman lifted a shot glass with flames and drank its liquid fire.

"Just as well. I never want to feel the illusion of that place again. I'm through with my past."

"Are you?"

A trumpet blew announcing dinner. The Chairman tipped his hat to leave.

"Wait." James grabbed the arm of the Chairman who growled at him until he let go. "I need to know, is she here?"

The Chairman threw his hands up in surrender. "I had nothing to do with this." He pointed his cane to the other side of the room at a red carpeted staircase. It led to a landing where Russian Czar Alexander I stood with a young woman in a tiara on his arm. Three trumpets blew and the Chairman vanished. James eyed Adolph, who shrugged while wiping a glass dry.

14

MYSTERIOUS PRINCESS

At the top of the stairs, the Czar stood with Natalia Nicolayevna, the wife of Alexander Pushkin. She wore a diamond tiara with an emerald and gold necklace draped around her neck, accentuating her high-waisted green satin dress, evoking the image of Audrey Hepburn as Tatiana in Tolstoy's *War and Peace*. Her hair was coiffed in a bun and she waved an oriental fan in front of her masked face. Her mother, the Countess Leia, followed, resting her hand on the arm of a Russian Tartar. James tried to wriggle through to see them, but royal guards blocked him. As the entourage passed, he caught a glimpse of the princess––blonde angel hair, long piano fingers with white gloves up to her sharp elbows––Sharon? If so, she hadn't aged! Why did she choose such theatrics to frame their encounter? As Victor Hugo, James took his seat at the banquet table beside Countess Leia wearing a veil. Due to a recent outbreak of smallpox, she told him.

James hardly ate. The countess tried to carry on a conversation with him, but James' mind was elsewhere. The countess finally laid her hand over his.

"You've been quiet the whole meal, Monsieur Hugo. What is wrong?"

"Nothing," he said, finishing off his wine, never taking his gaze off the princess at the head of the table with the king. He held up his crystal goblet for a server to refill. The countess nudged him. "Don't drink so much. If you continue, you won't be in good condition for what's to come."

He looked at her. "And what's to come?"

"The climax of the evening, your duel scene with Pushkin."

James threw his napkin down. "She wants to see me fight for her again."

"That's not her intention."

"Countess," James leaned toward her ear, "I must see her alone before the duel. Can you arrange that for us?"

"Why, do you care about her?" the countess asked.

"We share a common past."

"A former lover of yours?"

"Look," James turned his chair to face the countess, "I'm with my partner tonight, a woman who I was afraid to love until I learned what it meant to lose the ones you love most. So whether we loved or—"

A herald's trumpet announced the next event. The king waved at Countess Leia and she excused herself. James grabbed her gloved hand before she walked off. The warmth of it felt familiar. "Remember you'll set up that meeting," he said. The countess nodded as she hurried off. The dark figure with the death mask and cape who James first spotted on the balcony followed her out. Lawrence! It had to be. Could anybody else see him?

15

DUEL FOR SHOW

With cameras rolling, Czar Alexander led the royal entourage to another cavernous hall. Pushkin accompanied his wife, Natalia, and Countess Leia rested her hand on the arm of the king. The crowd spread out towards the bars set up around the room. A servant handed James a message on a silver tray. Countess Lia kept her promise, the secret rendezvous was set. He was led to a partitioned room enclosed by heavy red velvet curtains. He waited alone until soft gloved hands covered his eyes. He turned around to face the princess. He took her gloved hand and kissed it, smelling a wisp of scent from the other place. A camera with a red blinking light focused upon them. James blocked the glare from his eyes.

"Princess, let's get out of here so we can talk in private."

"Run away with you, Victor Hugo?" the princess answered. "My husband Alexander Sergeyevich Pushkin is near and will suspect something."

Hugo was jerked around by a hand on his shoulder.

"How dare you scheme to abscond with my wife!" Pushkin said with a jealous scowl. The two stood before the crowd which had gathered.

"You mean nothing to her, she is just trying to make me jealous." Pushkin wiped his forehead sweating below his top hat. "Victor Hugo, you are known for your dalliances with other men's wives, but you shall not succeed with mine."

"Look who's talking," Hugo said. "You were a rake, Pushkin, always off gambling or cavorting with comrades, leaving your beautiful wife Natalia alone. You are nothing but a difficult demagogue celebrity."

"And your ego was bigger than the entire nineteenth century."

Hugo took the Princess' hand. "She's made her choice to leave with me. Now, get out of our way!"

"She's staying with me," Pushkin said. He slapped James across the face with his knotted leather glove and threw it down.

Hugo felt his bloody lip. "That was harsh for make believe."

"Who said this is make believe?" Pushkin said. "Now, choose your weapon."

A game judge held up a redwood case decorated with inlaid ivory for the cameras. He opened its gold clasp. Inside cushioned in maroon velvet were two gold barrel pistols. "These are genuine dueling arms," the judge said, "purchased by William Randolph Hearst and certified as once belonging to the Valmont Du Champ. Only one is loaded. Monsieur Hugo, you choose first."

Hugo hovered his hand above each pistol looking at the princess. He chose one and Pushkin took the other.

"Be prepared to meet death, Monsieur Hugo," Pushkin said.

"Only Death can know which of us will take leave with him tonight," Hugo said.

The crowd gave them room. Before heading ten paces in his direction, Pushkin whispered to Hugo, "Relax old sport, in the end the bell tolls for us all. The world shall never know the likes of our literary genius again." The two took their places opposite each other.

The judge raised his arm, held it in suspense, then dropped it. Both men fired. The kick of Hugo's pistol charge was so forceful, it knocked him down, yet it was Pushkin gushing fake blood from a planted prop in his chest. Neither had any control over the outcome. It was a duel whose winner was predetermined from the beginning. Hugo stood to his feet and declared himself the winner; Pushkin argued victory was his. "Let the princess decide," Hugo said. The video cameras turned their attention on her standing at the outer rim of the crowd. She wavered—then took off in a sprint. Pushkin and Hugo dashed after her, camera crews, sound engineers and guests following fast behind.

16

THE CHASE

Down the high arch ceilinged hallway, the princess ran, stopping at a heavy hellish door with grinning gargoyles carved in its frame. She pulled on its iron handle and barreled inside; it led to the bowels of the castle. James ducked in after her, bolting the door before anyone else could follow. Pushkin banged, the camera crew cursed, other guests heaved their disapproval, but James didn't care. While his heart sang adventure, his temples pulsed fear; he knew this was the last leg of a long journey about to come full circle.

The princess dodged caterers and cleaners, upended trays of pastries and leftovers, spilling buckets of soapy water and mop heads. James navigated her road hazards like a video game hero who must hop and dodge to stay alive. She zigged left down a hall, then zagged right to another. One door opened, another closed. He gained within distance when a laundry cart appeared and blocked him. Ahead, the corridor was coming to a dead end, no more adjoining halls to zigzag. If she didn't stop running, she was going to smack flat against a wall. Then, as if by magic, the wall opened and a wizard in a purple coned cap and gown stepped out. Without losing her stride, the princess whisked through his fluttering robe disappearing inside the wall before it closed. James skidded into the wizard and knocked him down. He read the wizard's character tag: MERLIN. From the floor, Merlin waved his hand and the wall opened for James to pass. He had no time to thank the aged magician; James had a rogue princess to catch.

From the end of the hidden corridor, light brightened. James felt a cold brush of outside air. He heard rumbling of engines, sonorous backup beeps of a truck. The errant princess had fled into the castle loading docks. In sparkling tiara and torn dress, she ran past laborers unloading carts of oranges and champagne. A woman driving a forklift jerked to a stop to let her pass. The princess ran up a ramp on the opposite side of the docks just as James came dashing in from the other direction. In frock coat and hat, he leapt empty boxes, sidestepped piles of packing straw. The workers cheered him on in his pursuit, cameras on tracks in the ceiling capturing the excitement of the chase. At the top of the ramp, the princess held the rail to catch her breath until she saw James. Then she ran off again. He barely made it in time to see her open a door and disappear inside. When he stepped inside the same door, he found himself at the base of a circular stone staircase leading up one of the castle towers. He heard the clattering of her heels and followed.

With adrenalin bursting in his veins, James bounded up two steps at a time, thinking the princess would slow down but she didn't. The two passed exit door after exit door on every floor, not pausing for breath as they climbed at mountain goat's paces. Slices of moon beams wrapped in rain mist slithered in through slots in the cylindrical walls to light their path. Around the next turn, Hugo tripped over her discarded high heels. Smiling, he stuffed them in his coat pockets and kept on. He didn't have much farther to go; the stairs ended at a medieval hallway where the moonlight passed through stained glass windows painting the stone floor the color of ruby, emerald, and gold. Breathing hard, he paused to consider his direction. From one end he heard a panoply of instruments; flutes, piccolos, oboes and English horns, clarinets, bassoons, trumpets, tubas and trombones, snare drums, tom-toms, triangles and cymbals, xylophone and strings and a glockenspiel. Tired, he followed the current of music, hoping at the end of the river of notes the two would be reunited at last.

❀ † ❀

James entered an empty-seated theater balcony. A camera crew was set up to film the action on a stage below. He stepped down to the rail to take in the panorama; Paris in the 1920s painted on a giant backdrop with the Sacre-Coeur, Gothic church steeples and the Eiffel Tower shadowed in pink from a setting sun. On stage, a cast dressed in red-striped naval jerseys and French berets watched a dance troupe perform around a village fountain. It was the dream sequence at the end of Gershwin's "An American in Paris."

At the fringes of the crowd below, James recognized Pamela in her striped jersey accompanied by her friend Harry. Harry looked up at James, then held Pamela in his arms and kissed her. James wanted to jump the rail to slug him. But a voice called him from above, the princess -- beckoning him with the wave of her hand to follow her back to their world to finish their story's end. He glanced at Pamela just as she slapped Harry, then returned to the hall bathed in colored lights.

At the other end of the hall the princess climbed the last set of stairs which led to the top terrace of one of the towers. When James reached it, he gazed up at a clear night sky populated with stars. Under a blossoming moon, the princess stood at the far end of the tower wrapped in damp pacific air with nowhere else to go. The rendezvous which James had dreamed of for months was about to come true.

17

UNMASKED

James walked across the cool courtyard, the slate slick from the rain; the moon tried to bounce its light off the puddles but instead died there. As he approached, the princess backed up against the stone turret.

"Stay where you are," she said. "It's not time for you to see my face."

James looked at his watch. "Ten minutes to midnight." She held her hands out for her heels and he gave them to her. "Come on, Sharon," he said. "Quit the charade."

She strapped a heel on. "I'm not who you think I am," she said.

"Take off your mask so I can see. We're alone."

"No, we're not." She strapped on the other heel. "There's a camera watching us from above the door."

He flung his hat to the ground.

"It's not yet midnight!" she cried.

He dropped his mask too.

She leaned over the turret wall, saw the long drop down. "It's against the rules to remove your mask early," she said. "We could get disqualified." She straightened her tiara on her head. He approached closer.

"Play by the rules now, do we?" James said. "I thought you were more daring than that. You're really not going to allow me to see your face before midnight." He reached for her mask and she knocked his hand away.

"Stop it," she said.

"I've waited too long for this, Sharon, whether you're ready or not." He grasped the straps of her mask and she dug her nails into his hands.

"James!"

He turned his head to see Countess Leia standing at the tower door, the figure in the death mask following behind. Lawrence. Could she see him? "Countess, careful!" he shouted.

His guard down, the princess kicked James in the groin knocking him over, stomping on him with her sharp heels. The countess ran over and pulled her off.

"Jewel! You're hurting him, stop it now!" she said.

The princess ripped off her mask, "I hate you, mother! Why did I ever go along with this! You never told me why you insisted it had to be me, why me?"

"I'm sorry, Jewel, it wasn't supposed to end this way—"

"Don't ask me for any more favors!"

"You were a good sport playing your part tonight. Now go to your father, he'll help calm you down."

Jewel removed the diamond and gold emerald necklace from around her neck and crunched it in her mother's hands. She marched off to the tower stairs. The figure in the death mask stood waiting for her.

"Countess, your daughter probably can't see him, but there's a masked devil waiting to take her with him to hell. We've got to warn her—" he tried to stand but collapsed.

"Relax," the countess said, "she's where she should be, in safe hands." The black figure cloaked the princess in his cape. Then the hood and mask lifted and the man in the costume wiped his bald head of sweat. He led the princess down the tower stairs. That left the countess and James alone.

18

TOGETHER AGAIN

James sat scuffed up on the ground against one of the turrets. Countess Leia kneeled beside him on the wet slate. Placing his head in her lap, she brushed his hair from his face. He looked up, smelled the familiar scent stronger than ever. She surveyed the cuts from the younger woman's stilettos. Pressing the knot of a handkerchief to his eye, she soaked up drops of blood and tears. He reached up to touch her face behind the veil, but she winced. With one arm pushing up on the turret sill, the other around the countess' shoulders, he stood. While one eyelid fluttered in excitement, he scrutinized her appearance with the other. Tower bells tolled throughout the castle; it was midnight.

"It's time," he said. He reached for her veil, setting his hands on each side and lifted. Wrinkled lips glossy with lipstick. He lifted further. Dotted birthmark on a mauve-brushed cheek, crows' feet ingrained at the side of the eyes, powdered forehead, silver hair. He lifted the veil off and the wind took it across the courtyard. "Beautiful as ever," he said. He leaned in to kiss her, but she shied her face away. He did not force another try.

❀ † ❀

"Why this masquerade?" he asked, dabbing his eye.

She wiped away a forming tear, smearing eyeliner with her finger. "I wanted to see how you'd react if you saw me as I was then."

"She wore your necklace. You were testing me." James felt pain where the princess had kicked him in his ribs as he breathed.

"It got out of hand," she said. "I planned this reunion in my head for years. I thought I could control it all." She fidgeted with her nails.

"My eye, my ribs," he said. "Your daughter sure paid me back for my bravado."

"She's a fighter," she said. "Takes after her father."

"That man dressed as death, who followed you and her around like a bodyguard?"

"That's my partner Charles. He insisted he stay close to protect us. He's the only father she's ever known since she was born. She's closer to him than she is to me. Truth is, we don't get along very well. But she's not his."

"If not his then—" James counted the years backwards. "Is she—his?"

She gazed down at the puddles. "No. Lawrence wasn't capable."

"Then—" James studied the darkness woven in the trees. "Oh." His heart rose and he touched his chest. "Was she conceived in this world, or the other?"

Sharon circled away. "Does it matter?"

A cold biting wind blew. She shivered. James draped his wool frock coat around her shoulders. She placed her jewelry in James' coat pockets, including the emerald and gold necklace.

"Where's Timmy?" he asked.

"Lost, at sea. As soon as he was old enough, he joined the merchant marines. I haven't heard from him since."

"Sally?"

"She has a new name and her own family and lives far from

here in France." She spotted a seagull flying lost in the night sky. "Promise me you'll never try to see her, James. It's time to put the Revson Estate behind us."

"I know I acted crazy when we parted," he said. "I'm glad you didn't listen. But being back is hard. You've had years to adjust. It's still fresh in my mind, haunting me."

"I've already lived two long lives. You'll go on."

"How does anyone go on after an experience like we had?"

"You will yourself to."

"That place will keep you and I bonded forever."

"Yes, but not together."

He cupped his eye. "Ouch this hurts."

"We need to get you to a doctor."

She took his arm and the cold wind swirled, lacing them together. And the tower around them was spinning. Sharon turned young again and they were back on the estate and the sunny green lawn was spinning. The children appeared on the town carousel and they laughed as a family spinning. Bursts of light streaked in the night while they lost themselves in their spinning. Fireworks burst in the sky around Hearst Castle and someone called his name, "James!"

Pamela stood in her Parisian beret at the tower door. James and Sharon let go of each other.

19

ONE LAST TANGLE

While Pamela approached, Sharon walked to the wall, leaving them alone. Pamela took his hand.

"The princess left crying," she said. "What did you do to her?"

"Nothing," he said. "It's what she did to me." He lowered his hand from his face, revealing an eye badly scratched and bloody.

Pamela touched his eyebrow and he winced. She spoke, with tightened lip. "James, I thought you said she was much older."

"She is." He nodded his head at Sharon, staring into the dark pines. "The princess is her daughter."

Harry appeared out of the shadows behind Pamela. She held up her hand like a stop sign without turning her back. "Harry, don't come any closer. I don't like the way you treated me on that stage tonight. You did it to get James' attention at my expense."

"You've known me all my life, Pamela," Harry said, circling away from her. "I'm just a harmless devil who likes to keep people alive on their toes against the chaos of this world. Wake them from their passionless slumber with gusto."

"You're a troublemaker, Harry, just like you were as a boy."

Sharon returned to them from the wall. Harry pushed his beret forward on his head and whistled.

"He needs a doctor," Sharon said. She and Pamela took his arm on each side and pulled him toward the door.

"Wait." He wriggled from their grip. "There's something I must say to Harry." He held Sharon's handkerchief to his eye.

The women protested, but Harry placed his arm around James' shoulders. "You two go ahead," he said, "we'll settle our differences with an old-fashioned fist fight, then make up like brothers."

"Don't worry, Pamela," James said, "I'm going to handle this."

"We'll wait," Pamela said. The two men wended toward the wall. Pamela rubbed her arms to stay warm.

"What exactly happened in Connecticut?" she asked Sharon. "James never fully explained."

"Ask him again," Sharon said. "It made its mark on us, which we'll carry for the rest of our lives."

Pamela watched her breath climb in the cold air. "Those poems, they were written by you. Many I could tell were about James, but there was another man you wrote about too. Who was he?"

"Keep your goddamn hands off my partner!"

James swung at Harry, who pinned James against the turret wall. The two women ran over to pull him off. James took a cut into Harry's nose and the larger man lifted him up and shoved him back so hard, James fell over the wall. The two women looked over the edge and screamed in horror.

20

FALLING

James fell face up, one free fall from death. He saw faces moving further away like bursts of stars, jewels flying up in blurs of colors—reds, blues, greens, golds——he felt a mossy wall, tasted pine. A voice called out his name.

James!

Here I am. And I'm going to die.

No James. You will live, but your journey is not yet over. You will soon wake in a familiar place.

It's becoming dark. I cannot see. Statue, where are we going?

AFTER THE FALL

Theater curtain opens with a spotlight focused upon the Lord standing on the top balcony of an Italian palazzo overlooking a courtyard. On a balcony below stands the Devil smoking a cigar. His puffs rise up to the Lord who waves their smoke away. He warily glares at the devil until he snuffs out his cigar. Spotlight fades leaving silhouettes of the two gazing down upon a stage. A pause lingers with no movement or dialogue. It will soon be forgotten that the two are there watching in silence.

Center stage. James wakes up on the Revson Estate. Pill container on the table, breakfast tray on the bureau, a wicker basket filled with clothes. In his boxer shorts and t-shirt, he stands up and stretches, then abruptly realizes where he is.

JAMES: Oh no. No. No-no-no.

            (He hears the revving of an engine off stage. Muslin curtains wave in the window. He runs across the room, jutting out his head, then backs up to the center again.)

JAMES: It can't be, did I learn nothing? Will I never be free of this place?

(A spotlight shines on James. He shields his eyes and looks for its source. He discovers an audience sitting before him in balconies spiraling up in nine concentric circles.

The walls to the room collapse like a disassembled stage set. The furniture slides away. James grabs his trousers and shirt off a chair before it sails out of reach. He dresses, realizing he stands alone on an empty stage.

The spotlight above widens its perimeter to reveal a woman with long flowing hair standing at its fringes. She holds a Motorola cell phone to her ear and is speaking into it. When she sees she is visible in the light, she flips it shut. She is dressed in ripped jeans, jean jacket, bangles and black dress boots. The audience gives her a standing ovation. Flower bouquets land on the stage at her feet. She slips the phone into her shoulder bag and waves, throwing kisses and bowing with a smile.)

JAMES: Statue, is that you?

(She doesn't hear, continues to wave and bow.)

JAMES: Statue!

(The woman glances at James and quiets the audience. Hugging a large bouquet, she turns toward him and curtsies with blushed cheeks smiling. Endeared to her, the audience heaves a collective, "Aaahhhh.")

JAMES: I thought you'd appear to me as an angel, not a Gen Xer.

(Soft laughter from audience).

STATUE: *(Lays flowers down, ties her hair up in a French bun).* This is how I've chosen to dress James as I accompany you back to your world in San Francisco. *(Looks down at her outfit).* Do you like it? I am returning at the same age when I left the land of the living. I shall lead my own life in the Bay Area until my last mission is fulfilled.

JAMES: *(James touches his chest with both hands).* Moi?

STATUE: *(Statue gazes at audience, smiles with raised eyebrows. Laughter from audience.)*

JAMES: *(Looks up at the concentric balconies shading his eyes from glare.)* Where is this place? Dante's Inferno, of course we are! There! I see Ugolino, Francesca and Paulo, Julius Caesar, two Popes and the rest of the damned in the circles of hell. Am I to join their ranks? What treachery have I committed that I should be placed so low in this cesspool of sinners? *(Audience boos).* I feel the grit of sulfur in my mouth, which stinks something god-awful. *(Audience hisses. Statue silences them.)*

STATUE: James, it is the dead who complain they can't taste or smell, nor can they fight with loved ones or forgive enemies. Look at them, they would give anything to trade places with you. But they have already bargained with the devil and he owes them nothing. They envy you. *Dissatisfied mumbling is heard from the audience. Then they grow silent.*

JAMES: *(Exhales a long breath).* Are you to be my Virgil, Statue, who'll lead me to purgatory? *(She shakes her head no).* Beatrice, my guide through the highest planets of heaven?

STATUE: No, James. You will wake up from this fall and live. I shall always be near, whether as a gentle breeze to inspire or a mighty wind to chastise when you lean towards the eternal emptiness of the one with whom you have chosen to be in league.

JAMES: He'll never control me. I admit I've formed a necessary partnership, but never will I give in to his insatiable appetite. I see no other way to get ahead in this world without some compromise. God is not enough. I must rely on the devil's advice too.

STATUE: Never underestimate the power of grace and love to overcome greed and hate.

JAMES: *(Faces audience).* Statue, this is why I've always felt you inhabiting my dreams, why I could not see you before. Your beauty has always been hidden within the depths of my own heart, a healing force to behold. It is frightening to imagine, what I might become without you.

            (A soft breeze truffles the woman's hair. She raises her arm and a dove lands on her finger. She glances at James with a knowing smile.)

            Theater lights shut off. Curtain drops.

            (Big Band jazz music plays.)

Dante Alighieri, from Love and the Gracious heart
(Translation by M Musa)

And then the beauty of a virtuous lady
appears, to please the eyes, and in the heart
desire for the pleasing thing is born;
and this desire may linger in the heart
until love spirit is aroused from sleep.
A man of worth has the same effect on ladies.

READING GROUP GUIDE

ABOUT THIS GUIDE

The questions, discussion topics, and other material that follow are intended to enhance your group's conversation of *American Faust*, an enigmatic tale about the power dynamics between individuals, their reckoning with immortality and death, and the inert power within us all to find healing in the midst of a chaotic world.

Between Good and Evil

1. God consents to a bet with devil, emphasizing that James is tied to his past and could use some goading. Why would he allow the devil to test his champion?

2. At the end of the novel James says "Trusting in God is not enough. I must rely on the Devil's advice too." Why does he believe this? Do you agree or disagree with this idea?

3. Who do you think won the bet between the Lord and the Devil?

The Characters

4. How are James and Lawrence alike in their natures? How are they different?

5. Within the context of her life experience, Sharon felt her only value lay in her beauty. By the end of the novel, how did her self-image change?

6. James is an entrepreneur driven by a fiercely competitive nature to overcome any challenge. What cultural, gender, or experiential factors might have contributed to this developed trait?

7. Was Lawrence capable of expressing genuine love? Why or why not?

8. What led Eugene to rethink his relationships and his later acceptance of death?

9. Timmy was wise beyond his physical age while Sally's emotional development was stunted. In the context of the story, what might their distinct stages of development signify?

Gender Dynamics

10. The novel deals with the limited roles women have had available to them in society. How do you feel this condition has changed from the 20th to the 21st century?

11. In the garden scene Memphis says to Sharon "As long as men see woman as an object to possess rather than a life to imagine they shall always belong to me." What do you think is meant by that?

12. Discuss the power dynamics of the relationships in the novel. In what situation, if any, did each feel dominant? Dominated?

13. What role did the Spirit of the Statue play in the lives of James and Lawrence? What affinities did she share with Sharon?

On Beauty

14. In classical philosophy Truth, Goodness and Beauty are held up as the three supreme values. Do you agree? Why or why not? Discuss how each of these are portrayed in American Faust.

15. In James' encounter with the Spirit of the Statue she says "It is not I who blind your sight but your own ideal of beauty. I shall always remain invisible so long as you seek my physical perfection rather than the substance of who I am. True beauty inspires reflection of the heart, not desire of the body and mind." Describe an experience in your life when this lesson became clear to you.

16. The Revson family owns Revlon, a cosmetic company which feeds consumers' needs to feel good about themselves through outward appearances. Discuss the commercialization of beauty and how it shapes our view of ourselves and others today.

17. Does inner beauty exist? If it exists, why does it exist, and if not, why not?

Trivia

18. Literary references/allusions to great works abound throughout the novel. How many (if any) were you able to identify?

19. To which character(s) would you match the following items? What might each of them signify?

    a) Cane
    b) Chestnut
    c) Sailing
    d) Rifle
    e) Toys
    f) Thunder
    g) Fire
    h) Wind

For Further Examination:

Faust, by Johann Wolfgang von Goethe, written in parts over several years (1806-1829).

Dr Faustus, a play by Christopher Marlowe (first performed 1592).

The Divine Comedy, by Dante Alighieri written over several years (1314-1320).

Great Gatsby, a novel by F. Scott Fitzgerald (pub date 1925).

"The Daemon Lover," a short story by Shirley Jackson (The Adventures of James Harris, 1949).

"The Swimmer," a short story by John Cheever (The New Yorker, 1964); film released in 1968 starring Burt Lancaster.

Film: Midnight Cowboy (1969), Cabaret (1972), The Night Porter (1974). Inspiration for Club Heaven and Hell.

For a deeper dive into the writing of *American Faust,* visit www.Ibex-Press.com

For sharing on social media: Snap a photo of someone reading American Faust, then post on Instagram with the hashtag #americanfaust.

Lyrics used by permission: